46% Better Than Dave

Alastair Puddick

RAVEN CREST

BOOKS

ISBN-13: 978-1-9997803-9-5

For Charlotte

CHAPTER 1
THE ARRIVAL

"WHAT ARE YOU up to, you sneaky old bat?"

I was stood at my living room window, half concealed by the curtain, as I watched Doris from No. 34 handing out a tray of drinks to the removal men. They took them gratefully, then smiled and nodded politely as she seemed to witter on endlessly at them. I knew what she was doing, the nosy old cow. Probing them with questions. Trying to find out what she could about the people moving into the house next door to mine. I shook my head with disapproval and cursed myself for not having beaten her to it.

It was 10 minutes since I'd heard the truck arrive. I'd been in the garden, making the most of a fresh, sunny day, when the peace was broken by the loud, growling rumble of a diesel engine.

Instantly, I knew what it was. New neighbours.

It was a few weeks since the previous owners had moved out, and the rumour mill of the street had already been spinning into overdrive as to who might replace them. They must finally be moving in.

I put down my trowel, abandoned my half-planted rose bush and walked through the back door to investigate. My planting would have to wait, and the bottle of Peroni I had chilling in the fridge would have to continue chilling for a while.

"Catherine?" I called out into the quiet recesses of the house. "I think that's a removal truck. Catherine?"

I walked through the kitchen, into the living room. "Catherine?"

Still no reply. Of course not. She'd said something about going to yoga with her annoying sister and I'd tuned out when she'd mentioned the name Karen.

"Jack? Holly?" I shouted up the stairs. Again, no reply.

I walked into the living room, picking up dirty football socks from the sofa. Bloody kids. The cat looked up at me from the armchair, squinting and meowing in annoyance at being disturbed. I know cats can't actually express anything more than a simple meow, but I'm sure she was telling me to fuck off.

The cat and I have a fairly simple relationship. I tolerate her and she hates me. We've never got along since we got her, and the first thing she did upon arriving in her new house was to take a shit in my shoe. I knew I couldn't really blame her. She was only a kitten. But there was something in her eye that suggested she knew exactly what she was doing.

Since then, she's taken every opportunity to undermine and upset me: sitting on top of the bookcase and swiping at my head when I walk past; leaping out from behind chairs and digging her claws into my bare feet; nipping the backs of my ankles; scratching chair legs and bannisters while looking me directly in the eye; and repeatedly shitting in my shoes. Nobody else's; just mine.

I swore back at the cat, kicking the armchair to make her jump. Then I moved to the large bay window, pulling the curtain to hide myself, and peered out at the enormous removal truck parked outside the house. The rumbling, coughing engine halted. Tiny electric shocks of curiosity tingled across my scalp.

Who were the new people moving in next door? The people who, like it or not, were about to become an inextricable part of my life. Would they be kind, generous people who quickly turn into life-long friends? Or irritating loudmouths who ruin my sleep and bring out my feuding tendencies? Or, like too many streets, in too many towns, neighbours that completely fail to communicate, save for the odd uncomfortable smile or nod across the lawn.

What would they be like? A sudden rush of fear prickled my skin.

Oh God, I thought, please let them be all right. No noisy louts. Or drum kits. Or late-night partiers. Or 7 a.m. bloody lawnmowers. And please don't give me another Nigel.

******

Nigel, the last-but-one owner of the house next door, had been the most insufferable bore I've ever met. In the 18 months he lived there, I never once heard him say anything of any interest whatsoever. Seriously. And I know what you're thinking: that can't be possible. Surely, even the most boring of people must have the odd off day every now and again, inadvertently saying *something* interesting. Not Nigel. I actually longed for the day the old sod would surprise me and stumble over a topic of mutually engaging conversation. But it never happened. In 18 long months.

Despite his complete inability to tell interesting stories, Nigel could drone on for hours about the most inconsequential subjects. And the saddest thing was, he had no idea how boring he was. He was completely oblivious to the glazed-over eyes and stifled yawns people threw back in his direction when he discussed potholes, temporary traffic lights, or the fat content of different types of nut.

No doubt Nigel thought of himself as loquacious. The rest of us just thought him a bore.

During one Saturday afternoon barbecue, Nigel had worked his way through nearly every resident of the street, droning on unaware of the pained expressions on his victim's faces. I eventually found 26 people crammed into the kitchen, hiding and whispering, desperate to stay away from him.

I also found Mark from No. 31 and Clare from No. 46 hiding together in the downstairs loo, but the less said about that the better. Two months later, they left their respective partners and ran away to Aberystwyth. Whether they were already having an affair, or whether it came about as a result of trying to avoid the most boring man in the street, I'll never know.

For some reason, I was his favourite. I don't know why. I just seem to attract these sad sacks. And I couldn't help taking pity on him. I mean, it wasn't his fault he was boring. Not really. But that meant I was always the one stuck talking to him. And everybody else was more than happy to let me suffer.

The fact that we lived right next door to each other made things worse. It wasn't only at parties that I had to be on the lookout for a Nigel ambush. Honestly, the number of times I'd pull into the driveway after work, and he'd be stood there waiting for me, desperate to catch me for 'a quick word'. He must have been sat by the window, waiting for me. How else could he come belting out his front door so quickly?

One time – no word of a lie – it took me a full 43 minutes and 22 seconds to make it from the car to the front door. No matter what I did, I couldn't cut him off. He just kept talking about the poor attendance at the last Neighbourhood Watch meeting and the tardiness of that week's bin collections… until I completely stopped listening. I turned around and Catherine was stood there in the window, laughing her head off with a stopwatch in her hand. She was actually timing it.

I reorganised my work calendar to avoid him. I moved appointments and meetings so I could vary when I left the office in the evening. I took different routes home from work, so I could vary which end of the close I'd enter from. I hoped it might be enough to throw him off. And every now and then, it worked. But more often than not, I'd pull into the driveway, open the door and Nigel would be there waiting, keen to discuss the events of the day. Or some other mundane crap I'd pretend to listen to.

In the end, Nigel and his wife moved away, relocating to another office for his job as a… I want to say accountant. Or maybe auditor? Or something in risk management – whatever the hell that is. I know Nigel told me plenty of times. But I never paid attention.

******

A large man with short, dark hair and a purple t-shirt stood nodding as Doris continued to interrogate him. Three other men, all wearing identical t-shirts, stood a few feet away, sipping their mugs of tea and giggling like schoolchildren at their boss's misfortune. Doris had been grilling the man for a good five minutes now, and every time he tried to walk to the rear of the van, or to collect something from the cabin, she followed him, continuing her barrage of questions.

I had to hand it to her, it was a pretty clever ruse. And she was certainly not giving up. I couldn't help but wonder what juicy nuggets of information she was uncovering about the people whose furniture they were hauling. Were they nice? Friendly? Rich? Foreign? One-eyed monsters with snakes for tongues who'd come to take over the neighbourhood?

I felt a sudden rush of guilt, standing there gawping at the goings-on. I was a Peeping Tom, sneaking a glance at unsuspecting people. It was thrilling and sickening all at the same time.

I should head outside and introduce myself, I thought. Two can play at that game, Doris. But who would I talk to? The new neighbours were yet to arrive, so I couldn't go and welcome them. The removal men certainly didn't look interested in any more conversation. And, to be perfectly honest, I didn't particularly want to talk to them. I sometimes find it hard talking to people like that. It sounds pretentious, I know. But I'm just not like them. I'm not a very handy, practical, manly sort of person, and I always feel they can tell. Like when you take your car to the garage and you know they're going to rip you off, because they can tell you don't know the first thing about cars. They'll say there's something wrong with the 'secondary flange inducer valve' and you just have to take their word for it, because, seriously, what the fuck is that?

Finally, the man in charge downed the last of his drink, handed the mug back to Doris and signalled for his men to all do the same. She walked away slowly, disappointment etched on her face, and the men walked round to the back of the truck.

The back door banged and creaked as it swung open. Three of the men climbed up and disappeared inside. The man in charge then leaned back against the truck, sighed heavily, pulled a small green pouch from his pocket and started rolling a cigarette.

I walked through to the kitchen and opened the fridge door. Gazed vacantly inside. The kids had been at it, decimating its contents. Barely anything left to eat. Again, they'd failed to put the open packets of ham and cheese into the small plastic bags to keep them fresh, so the food had gone all curly at the edges. I mean, if I've told them once, I've told them a thousand…

My mind raced to what might be happening out in the street. I rushed straight back into the living room and gazed out the window again.

As a general rule, I don't spy on neighbours. It's a nasty, intrusive way to live. And I certainly don't like the idea of people keeping tabs on me. But standing there, hidden behind my curtain, I felt an overwhelming illicit thrill. I just couldn't take my eyes off the scene.

20 minutes later, all four of the men were back out of the van, shuffling aimlessly as they smoked and glanced intermittently at their watches. The boss was nodding patiently, clearly exasperated, and trying to politely send Doris away after she arrived with a second tray of drinks. I laughed at the bold-faced cheek of it. The old girl certainly had perseverance.

I heard the distant rumble of a car engine. A brand new, jet-black BMW 7-Series turned into the close and pulled up behind the van. Seconds later, the street echoed with the even louder roar of a sparkling red Porsche that parked in next door's driveway.

"Here we go, then," I whispered to myself.

Curtains twitched all along the row of houses opposite, as eager faces sneaked furtive glances at the new arrivals. I was so curious now, I didn't even bother to hide myself. I stood right up against the window, openly staring out.

They've got a few quid, then, I thought. I've always wanted a BMW.

Or something new and expensive. Anything better than the elderly, green Ford Focus parked in my driveway.

The door of the BMW swung open and a tall man with short, dark hair stepped out. He wore blue jeans, an expensive-looking white shirt, and even more expensive shiny shoes. He looked to be in his mid-40s. A large, silver watch glistened on his wrist as the sun hit it.

The two rear doors of the car opened simultaneously as two teenagers – a boy and a girl – climbed out. They were roughly the same age as Jack and Holly. Both kids scanned the street, taking in their new surroundings, then lazily strolled up the path to the house.

The driver of the car walked over to the removal team, said something that made them stub out their cigarettes and stand to attention. Then he strode purposefully up to the house, unlocked the front door and stepped inside. The kids scurried in after him.

My eyes flicked back to the Porsche as the door opened. Out popped a long, slender leg, the foot sheathed in a shiny, stilettoed shoe. The other leg followed, and seconds later one of the most beautiful women I've ever seen stepped out of the small car.

She was stunning. Her blonde hair blew gently in the breeze, then settled around her perfectly tanned shoulders. Her legs were tight and toned, all the way up to a petite, round bottom, wrapped in impossibly tight jeans. She had a tiny waist and a very ample chest, showcased by a small white vest top. She was every bit beautiful enough to be a model.

My mouth went dry. My heart beat strangely fast. My eyes scanned right to see old Doris gazing right at me, a look of disapproval on her face, as I openly gawped at this stunning new neighbour. I jolted back in shock at being caught, catching my heel against the leather pouffe, and tumbled back onto the sofa.

Damn. I must have looked like an actual Peeping Tom. My face burned red. I knew I should retreat and stop being so nosy. But still I couldn't help it. I had to see what was going on. And I had to catch another glimpse of this woman.

I clambered back to the window, concealing myself furtively behind the curtain, and saw her flash a brilliant white smile to the removals men, who had all stopped to watch her arrival. They gushed in response, before practically tripping over each other as they clamoured to try and lift the heaviest piece of furniture. With a flick of her hair, the woman spun round and walked majestically up the drive and into the house.

I watched her enter, then looked back at the truck. The men continued ferrying items up the path and into the house. I watched for a few minutes, trying to guess what might be packed in the various nondescript brown, cardboard boxes. Then I got bored and hungry and went back through to the kitchen.

Now that the new family had arrived, I decided I should go and introduce myself. I felt a sense of responsibility to welcome them to the neighbourhood and ensure they settled in okay. When Catherine and I moved into our first home together, we were quite naïve about the ins and outs of introducing ourselves to neighbours. Knock on people's doors or wait for them to greet us? In the end, we opted for the latter.

And we lived there for a full nine months before a power cut throughout the whole street (caused by me, but that's another story) forced us into our first actual conversation. We got chatting and it soon came out that we both felt equally snubbed, as they were waiting for us to come and say hello. We laughed it off as 'one of those things'. But there was always a certain animosity between us.

Since then, I've always taken it upon myself to make the first move. It's simpler that way. And, of course, I wanted to check them out close up. Make sure they were the kind of people I was happy living next door to.

Of course, you don't want to make a bad first impression. Go over too early and you'll look too keen – the nosy neighbour who can't wait to start poking about in everybody else's business. Wait too long and you risk making your new arrivals feel unwelcome, leading to hurt feelings and subsequent years of sneers over the back garden fence.

Obviously, I couldn't go marching over there straight away. That would look utterly mental. So, I managed to find enough in the fridge to make a sandwich, then returned to my rose bush in the back garden to carry on with my work. When I heard the doors of the removal truck slam shut and the noisy diesel engine roar into life, I decided sufficient time had passed. I could nip over and introduce myself.

I would usually have waited for Catherine, but she still wasn't home. So, I changed into slightly smarter clothes and prepared to go and say hello. However, as I reached for the handle of the front door, I was interrupted by the sudden, sharp sound of knocking. It caught me so off guard that it took me a few seconds to realise it was coming from my own front door. I tentatively pulled it open to find the man with the expensive shirt stood there.

"Hi," he said, in a loud, confident voice.

"Erm, hello," I said, slightly bemused. He flashed me a quizzical smile, like he was expecting me to say something else. I realised that was probably because I had my mouth wide open, looking like I was going to say something. I promptly closed it.

"Hi," he said again, through a perfect, pearly-white smile. "You probably noticed the big van outside." I said nothing. "Anyway, looks like we're going to be neighbours, so I thought I'd pop over and say hello."

"Oh yes," I said. "Van. Neighbours. Next door."

He squinted, like he was trying to decide whether I had some kind of learning disability.

"Anyway, my name's Dave," he said, extending his hand. "Dave Brookman."

My mouth dropped open again. I stood there even more confused, my brain trying to calculate something. Like when you see something out the corner of your eye, and you know it's not right, but when you look back to check what was wrong you can't find it again.

A long pause filled the space between us. Finally, I coughed out a fake laugh. "Ha ha, good one!" I said. For some reason, I was also now pointing at him. I don't remember telling my finger to do that, it just leapt up there of its own accord.

Another long pause as I stood there grinning and my new next-door neighbour stared back at me, like I was completely deranged. "Sorry," he said, "I don't follow."

"Good joke," I said, forcing another laugh. In truth, I didn't think it was a good joke at all. It wasn't even a joke. It certainly wasn't funny. Weird at best. "Go on, who put you up to it? Scott from No. 22?" For some reason, I was still pointing at him.

"I'm not sure I understand." His expression had changed from confusion to one of genuine concern. "What joke? And I don't know Scott. Yours is the first door I've knocked on."

The smile slid from my face. My brain was starting to hurt. "I'm sorry, but I could have sworn you said your name was Dave Brookman."

"Yes, that's right. Dave Brookman. Pleased to meet you." He thrust his hand towards me again. The look on his face suggested he wasn't actually pleased to meet me at all.

"But you can't be," I said, outraged, my finger now pointing with threatening accusation. "You can't be Dave Brookman. *I'm* Dave Brookman."

CHAPTER 2
NEW DAVE

"I'M SURE THAT man thinks I'm a complete idiot."

Catherine looked at me with the pitying expression she usually saves for the times she thinks I've completely embarrassed myself. And in fairness, I usually only see it when I have, in fact, completely embarrassed myself.

The first time I ever saw it was the day she introduced me to her parents. We met at a posh restaurant and, when a well-dressed, smiling man greeted me at the door, I mistook him for a waiter. I asked him to 'give us the best table in the place, because I was trying to impress my girlfriend's stuffy old dad'. It was a mistake anyone could have made. But it made me look less the dashing sophisticate, and more like a clueless simpleton. Less Mr Bond and more Mr Bean.

Needless to say, Catherine's father was bemused and offended. And, to this day, he still makes jokes every time we go to their house. On one visit, I even went to the bathroom to find that he'd placed a sign on the toilet: *Reserved for Mr Brookman. Best seat in the house.* I had to hand it to him for that one.

The last time I saw Catherine's special disappointed look was when I tried hanging a picture in the bedroom. I banged a nail into the wall, hit a hidden wire, electrocuted myself and accidentally cut off the power to the whole street for over three hours.

"Of course, he doesn't think that," lied Catherine. "I'm sure he was as non-plussed by the coincidence as you were."

The previous day's encounter with my new neighbour had ended just as badly as it had started, with me point-blank refusing to believe the man when he said he was also called Dave Brookman. Upon his quite reasonable assertion that it really was his name, I then demanded to see his driving licence. After some cajoling, and probably just to shut me up, he finally produced it. I examined it far too closely, squinting at the little picture, and carefully reading the name printed next to it. Finally, I dismissed it as being fake and demanded to know what his game was. The rest of the encounter was something of a blur. I shuddered at the recollection.

"I'm sure he'll understand," said Catherine, "when you go over and talk it all through." She placed her hand on the front door handle, readying to open it for me.

"Do I have to?" I pleaded. "Can't we just draw a line under it and be the kind of neighbours that never speak?"

"I'm not having our new neighbours think they've moved in next door to a bunch of loonies."

"I thought you said…"

"Never mind what I said."

"But, seriously, how bad would it be if we never…"

"You're going."

"I mean, I've been thinking recently, maybe it's time to consider selling up and…"

"You're going," she said, a hint of anger creeping into her voice. "We're not moving house because you made a tit of yourself. Now, go next door and clear the air. I'm sure he'll be very understanding."

Catherine replaced her pitying look with the one she uses to let me know there's no use arguing. She opened the door and a cool breeze whistled in and shot straight up my trouser legs. I stepped out of the house and stomped down the path like a disgruntled teenager, being forced to apologise to a shopkeeper for stealing sweets. When I reached the bottom, I looked back to see Catherine still stood in the doorway, monitoring my progress. So, my plan of jumping in the car and driving off was also out of the question.

I knocked on the door. A few seconds passed. I heard mumbled speaking inside. Then the door swung open with such determination I felt like I might get sucked along with it. My new neighbour stood there with a large beaming smile on his face. It disappeared instantly when he saw me.

"Oh hello," I said, meekly. "Er… Dave, isn't it?"

"Apparently," he replied with a sneer. "Although, perhaps I should go and find some paperwork to make sure."

"Yes, about that," I said. "Look, I'm sorry about yesterday. Bit weird, wasn't it? I'm not sure why I reacted like… or, I mean… you know… And the bit with the driving licence. All very embarrassing, of course…"

He just stared at me as I mumbled along. If he didn't think I was an idiot already, he certainly did now.

"But you must admit, it's a pretty bloody weird coincidence," I laughed.

He seemed to mellow slightly, a smile creeping onto the corner of his lips.

"I'm sure Dave Brookman isn't the most uncommon name in the world. But to have another one move in next door? What are the chances? So, I'm sorry if I got a little muddled. I just wanted to apologise and try to convince you I'm not a complete nutcase." I coughed out an embarrassed laugh.

He looked at me for a short moment before chuckling back. "It is pretty bloody weird, isn't it? I wasn't sure what your problem was at first, but then when you told me you were also called Brookman, well… I must admit, it blew my mind a little bit too."

"I know, it's crazy."

"Listen, I was just about to take a quick break from unpacking. Why don't you join me for a beer?"

"Erm… well, yeah. That would be nice."

"Cool. Can I just check your driving licence, though? Don't wanna let any old stranger in." I went to pull my wallet from my pocket, but he smiled and stopped me. I could tell this was going to become a long-running joke, just like my father-in-law and his 'hilarious' seating gag.

New Dave welcomed me through to the kitchen, where he pulled two bottles of Peroni from the fridge. He might be a name thief, but at least he had decent taste in beer.

"So, where are you moving from?" I asked, taking a long swig of beer.

"Not far," he replied. "Other end of town. The old house was nice, but this is closer to the office. And we wanted something with a bit of scope."

"Scope?"

"Yeah, you know, somewhere we can do a bit of work."

"Work?" I said, suddenly concerned, but trying to remain nonchalant. I took another swig of beer.

"Yeah, nothing too major. Bit of remodelling in here. Extension on the back. We've also bought the plot of land that sits the other side of the back fence, so we'll make the garden bigger."

He already had a big garden. Much bigger than mine. And with the additional land out the back, his total property would be nearly twice the size of mine.

"Yeah, so we're gonna knock through to double the size of the living room… move the kitchen into the extension…" he said, pointing to the different areas. "That'll give us another two bedrooms upstairs… both en suite, of course."

"Of course," I agreed, hot blood rushing to my face.

"Swimming pool in the back garden… so nice to have a pool in the summer, isn't it? Practically an essential. Oh, and we might chuck in a hot tub. I'm not too keen, but the wife's desperate. You know women, eh?"

"Yes. That sounds like a lot." My heart was thumping, my head swimmy.

"But don't worry," he said, placing a hand on my shoulder, "everything's been signed off with the council in advance. And we use a great builder. Very respectful. You'll barely know they're here. Do you wanna see the plans?"

"No, that's all right. Maybe another time." I looked around at the inside of New Dave's house. I'd always considered my house to be a decent size. Certainly big enough for the four of us. Okay, it might have been nice to have a spare room. If we had the money, I might have built an extension. And who wouldn't want a swimming pool? But the house had always suited us well enough. New Dave's place was almost an exact replica of mine. But now that I tried to picture what it might look like after the renovations, suddenly my home felt very small in comparison.

"So, are you from around these parts, Dave?" said New Dave.

"Yes," I replied. "Well, no. I mean, we've been in this house for eight years now. And we've been in Stratford-upon-Avon for… oh, more than 20. My wife, Catherine, is from here. We met at university in Brighton, and I sort of followed her back. But I'm actually from down south in Crawley."

"Fuck off!"

"Sorry?" I said, taken aback.

"You're from Crawley? You grew up in Crawley?"

"Yes."

"I'm from Crawley!" he said. "I grew up there, too."

"What? Seriously?"

"Yeah, Pound Hill. Arundel Close, up near the shops."

"You're joking!" I said, totally flummoxed. "I grew up in Gossops Green. Buckswood Drive."

"Yeah, yeah, I know it well. Jesus, talk about a coincidence."

Something in my head started to pulse along with my heart. I felt like I needed to sit down.

"So, what brought you to Stratford?" I asked.

"Oh, this and that. We've moved about quite a lot in the last few years, mostly for work. London for a bit. Then a stint in Hong Kong. Worked out of the Paris office for a few years. New York for two. But once the kids were in school, we knew we had to make more of a base. So, we've been here for the last nine years."

"Wow, New York? That's amazing," I said, feeling jealous. I'd always wanted to see more of the world. Always dreamed of walking down the bustling streets of New York, hailing a big yellow taxi and eating a giant pretzel from a street food cart. But I'd never made it much further than Tenerife.

"Hey, here's a thought," said Dave, excitement sparkling in his eyes. "How old are you?"

I knew what he was thinking. I didn't want to answer. "I'm… 45. You?"

"Fuck me," he shouted. "No fucking way! I'm 45 as well."

My mouth went instantly dry. My heart beat faster. I held onto the kitchen counter to keep myself steady.

"Hang on, hang on," he said, the tension palpable. "When's your birthday?"

I hesitated. I didn't want to tell him. Surely it couldn't be.

"March 23rd," I said.

"Oh," he said, the corners of his mouth dropping. "I'm July 16th."

Silence hung between us, as he looked genuinely disappointed.

"Still, bloody crazy coincidence," he said, smiling again. "I've just moved in next door to someone with the same name as me, you're the same age and we grew up about two miles away from each other. How is that even possible?"

Again, I couldn't speak.

"Hang on," he said, suddenly suspicious, "you're not messing with me, are you? You're telling the truth?"

"No, honestly. It's all true. How would I know where you grew up? I wouldn't even know how to find that out." Then it was my turn to feel suspicious. "You're not tricking *me* again, are you? Like the driving licence thing?"

"God's honest truth," he said, reaching out his hand once again.

"Dave Brookman, 45 from Crawley. Nice to meet you."

I took his hand. He squeezed mine with one of those overbearingly hard handshakes. I squeezed back as hard as I could. "Dave Brookman," I repeated. "45 from Crawley. Nice to… er… meet you, too."

I took another long swig of beer as we stared at each other. Just long enough for it to start getting uncomfortable. Feeling a strange panic rising in my chest, I suddenly blurted out, "Barbecue!"

"Sorry?"

"Erm… barbecue," I repeated, not actually sure where I was going with it. And then, "We're having a barbecue. This afternoon. To… er… welcome you. That's it. That's the other reason I came over. To invite you."

How the hell had I managed that? I'd come over to deliver a simple apology and ended up inviting the man for dinner.

"Oh, right," he said, slightly confused.

"Yeah, we thought we might have a little impromptu barbecue to say hi. I'll see if anyone in the street is free," I continued, seemingly unable to stop myself from talking. "Then we'll fire up the barbie, have a few beers and get to know each other."

"Well, that sounds, really… erm…"

"Christ, what am I thinking?" I said, trying to dig myself out of it. "You're busy. You're still in the middle of unpacking. Don't worry, we'll do it another day. Forget I said anything."

Jesus, I thought, please let him take the bait.

"No, you know what, that sounds great," he said. "We've barely had a chance to go to the shops, save for a few essentials." He smiled, waving his beer. "Are you sure it's no trouble?"

"Of course not," I lied, "we were going to have a barbecue anyway, and I thought why not invite the new neighbours over? So, just head over any time after four."

"Great," he said, grinning.

"Great," I said, forcing my own smile.

I downed the last of my beer, then went home to break the news to Catherine that we had to host a welcoming party in about five hours' time.

CHAPTER 3
MEAT MASTER

FIVE HOURS LATER, after a mad dash to the supermarket, I was stood over the barbecue, carefully rotating sausages, burgers and chicken legs. Unsurprisingly, when I'd run around the street a few hours earlier trying to drum up attendees for my impromptu barbecue, the majority of the residents were apparently 'too busy' to come. "I mean, it is short notice, Dave," was the overriding response.

Strangely, though, when I told them they wouldn't need to bring anything with them – simply turn up and enjoy the food and drink I'd bought – nearly every one of them was suddenly able to change their plans. The freeloading bunch of sods. So, although the back garden wasn't exactly heaving, we did have a reasonable turnout and I didn't end up as embarrassed as I might have been. Instead, I got to stand there watching the greedy swine try to eat and drink me out of house and home.

"This is the last thing I need today," I'd said to Catherine, as I hastily applied barbecue sauce to some chicken wings, before people started arriving. "I should be going over the scamps and mock-ups for tomorrow's presentation."

"Yeah, well," she said, looking up from the big bowl of potato salad she was stirring, "you should have thought about that before you invited the whole street round for lunch. You think this is how I want to spend my Sunday afternoon?"

"I know; I'm sorry. But it really needs to go well tomorrow, Cath. If we land this client, they'll have to give me that promotion. More money, more responsibility…"

"Oh, God, not this again," she said. "Honestly, Dave, it's all I've heard about for the last month. And I've got better…"

She seemed to stop and think for a second. Then she put down her wooden spoon, took my face between her hands and kissed me. "You'll be brilliant," she said. "You deserve that promotion and you're going to get it. We'll have a nice afternoon welcoming the new neighbours, then you can run me through your presentation later… for the umpteenth time." She smiled, dipped her finger in my barbecue sauce and wiped a sticky, wet streak down my nose. "Now get on with it, people will be here in 20 minutes."

Half an hour later, we had a garden full of people, and my work preparation time was dwindling with every second that passed.

As is common on these occasions, the majority of the men (myself, New Dave, Chris and Mike) were huddled round the barbecue, chatting and watching the various bits of meat spit, sizzle and crackle in the heat. I'd introduced New Dave and his family to the other residents of the street as they arrived, then us men had done the manly thing of gathering to drink beer and watch food cook.

I was in charge, of course – the Alpha Male in possession of the barbecue tongs – defending my barbecuing technique from the other men, who all had their own unhelpful hints and tips. All except for New Dave, of course. He seemed strangely disinterested and barely even watched what I was doing. I wasn't sure whether to be pleased or offended.

Inevitably, it came. "It's just not barbecue, if you ask me," said Chris, going in for the attack. "With gas barbecues, you just don't get that barbecue taste. You need to cook over coal, otherwise it's just not… authentic."

"Bollocks," I said, a little too defensively. Chris was always coming out with this kind of bullshit. Usually, I'm able to let it wash over me without responding. But the past 24 hours had been tense and I couldn't help but bite. "With gas you get a far more even cook. You don't have to wait for the coals to heat up. And you don't get that acrid, burnt taste."

"Depends who's doing the cooking," he scoffed.

Everyone else laughed. I grimaced, unimpressed.

"This," I said, pointing at the barbecue with my tongs, "is the Rolls Royce of barbecues." It really was. The MeatMaster 3000 was immensely brilliant. Made out of stainless steel, it had two separate gas tanks and a grill big enough to cook a mountain of burgers, sausages, steaks, ribs, chicken breasts and anything else you could think of – at different temperatures, if you wanted. It had two different heating racks, a bun warmer (to warm buns, obviously). There was a detachable rotisserie spit, to cook whole chickens. It even had a hob on the side, so you could heat things in a pot. To be fair, I never used that bit.

It cost me an absolute fortune – about four times as much as my first car. It was a 45th birthday present to myself and I absolutely loved it, much to the annoyance of my family, who had spent the last six weeks eating barbecue food at every given opportunity (even when it was raining). Needless to say, I was somewhat defensive about it. And I wasn't going to stand for Chris spewing his 'authentic barbecue taste' bullshit.

"Rolls Royce?" laughed Chris, either not sensing the tone in my voice or reacting against it. "More like the Vauxhall Vectra of barbecues." He laughed again, waiting for everyone to join in. But to my surprise, they didn't.

Instead, New Dave said, "Sorry mate, but you don't know what you're talking about. This really is the daddy of barbecues. I had one myself and it was brilliant. And I don't buy that charcoal bullshit either. Just makes the food taste chalky and burnt, if you ask me." He flashed me a quick, supportive wink.

"Yeah," said Mike, suddenly joining in. "I have to agree."

Chris looked deflated. I brimmed with glee. New Dave Brookman to my rescue, helping me win the argument. But then, I thought, why was everyone so keen to suddenly agree with New Dave? Why was my argument not enough to settle it? I should have been grateful, but I couldn't help bristling with ignominy. I was the Alpha Male. I was holding the barbecue tongs, dammit. My word should have been final.

"Used to have?" asked Mike.

"Yeah, I had one for a year," replied Dave. "Great little thing. But I've got a 4000 on order, when it's released. I tell you what, I'll have everyone round for a barbecue at mine when it arrives."

Fuck! How did that happen? The 4000? I didn't even know they were making a 4000. That was sure to make my 3000 look like a complete pile of crap. I looked down at my prized possession which now looked a lot less shiny than it had a few minutes ago.

"Hey, Dave," said Charlie, walking over to join us. Instinctively, both New Dave and I answered at the same time.

"Oh, erm…" said Charlie, slightly embarrassed, "that's funny. I actually wanted, erm… New Dave. I suppose I'll have to call you that, won't I?"

I know it's stupid, but I couldn't help feeling betrayed. One of those ridiculous, irrational reactions, like when you were a child and you found out two of your friends went to the cinema without inviting you. How could Charlie possibly want new Dave's attention over mine? He was *my* friend. I should be the one he wants to talk to. I tried to disguise my hurt by taking a swig of beer.

"Although, thinking about it," continued Charlie, how *are* we supposed to distinguish between you? I mean, I can't keep calling you New Dave, can I? And we can't have both of you answering every time someone walks into a room."

Dave and I looked at each other, then back at Charlie.

"I mean it's not as if we can even distinguish you by your surname, for God's sake," laughed Charlie. "That's the bloody same as well."

"How about we call one of them Dave," said Chris, "and the other one David?"

"No, that would never work. They're too similar. That would just make it even more confusing. We'd soon forget which one was which."

"How about Dave 1 and Dave 2?" chipped in Mike, leaning down to grab another bottle of Peroni from the cooler on the ground. I winced as the metal cap tumbled down onto the grass.

Mike had arrived at the party carrying 10 cans of Fosters – no doubt the cheapest beer on special offer at the local supermarket. He'd headed straight out to the garden, placing them down next to the large bucket I'd filled with ice to keep all the drinks cold. He then immediately abandoned his own offering and helped himself to a bottle of the more expensive, premium lager. As brazen as that. Right in front of everyone. And he'd been helping himself to my beers ever since.

Of course, they weren't *my* beers, specifically. I was throwing the party and I'd bought them for anyone to drink. And Mike was, in fairness, the only one who'd actually brought any bloody beer with him. But whenever he took one of mine, it felt like theft.

Mike was notorious for it. Whenever there was a party in the street, he'd roll up with a box of the cheapest, weakest, piss-flavoured lager he could find. He'd dump it down, loudly, making sure everyone saw that he'd brought something. And then he'd spend the rest of the evening picking through the fridge and helping himself to the more favourable booze that other people (usually me) had provided. "Don't mind if I have one of your cold ones," he'd call out, helping himself to someone else's cans or bottles, "while those ones chill down, do ya?"

Well, yes, actually, I did mind. But what can you say? 'Fuck off, you cheapskate bastard, and drink the warm, watery dog's piss you brought with you'? Of course not. So, Mike would spend the evening getting drunk on everyone else's drink. And whichever poor sod was hosting the party would end up with loads of untouched weak beer clogging up their cupboards.

"Oh, you don't mind do you, mate?" said Mike, clearly feeling the heat of my stare. "Those ones aren't cold, and there's no room in the bucket." He pointed at his unopened box of Fosters on the grass.

"No, course not," I said, squeezing my hand into a fist in my pocket, "help yourself."

"Sweet. And feel free to help yourself to those bad boys," said Mike, "when they've cooled down a bit." He took a long swig, as I fought the urge to pick up the box of Fosters and hurl it at his head. "Anyway, what do you reckon? Dave 1 and 2?"

"I suppose we could," considered Charlie. "But who's Dave 1 and who's Dave 2?"

"Well, I would have thought that was obvious," I said, smiling. "I mean, I was here in the close first. So, I should probably be Dave 1, shouldn't I?"

If we were going down that route, I'd be securing Dave 1 for myself, before the other Dave could get in there, thank you very much. Dave 1 – the original and the best. The first one here. The one everyone knows and loves.

Far better than Dave 2. Dave the imitator. Dave the afterthought. Second on the scene and second in everyone's mind.

"I mean, that makes sense, doesn't it?" I said.

"Sounds good to me," said New Dave. "I quite like the sound of Dave 2. New and improved. Dave 2.0. The upgrade," he laughed, raising his beer and winking.

Everyone else laughed and raised their drink in salute. "The upgrade," they said in unison.

Fuck. How did I miss that? The upgrade. The newer model. Better than the old one. Shit.

"Come on, seriously, we can't call you Dave 1 and Dave 2," laughed Charlie. "It's mental."

Everyone else laughed in agreement. I breathed a sigh of relief.

"So, what do we do, then?" said Mike.

"Well, what about middle names?" said Charlie.

"Oh no," said New Dave, "you're not stitching me up with that. My middle name is so embarrassing."

"Yeah, no fucking way," I agreed. "I know what you're trying to do. I know you know what my middle name is, and I'm not having you fuckers call me Ronald every time you see me."

"Ronald?" said New Dave. "Believe me, you've got nothing to worry about. Mine's far worse than that."

"No way, it would have to be Hamburglar to beat old Ronald here," laughed Mike, taking another large swig of Peroni.

"Oh, it's worse," said New Dave.

"What is it?" asked Charlie.

"You don't want to know."

"Come off it. You can't say that and not tell us."

"Okay, fine," said New Dave, taking a long breath. "My middle name is… Ace. What can I say, my parents were kind of quirky." He looked around the group, waiting for the laughter.

"Ace isn't that bad," said Charlie, thoughtfully. "In fact, I quite like it. It's kinda… cool.

"Yeah," said Mike. "Ace is fine. It's certainly better than Ronald."

"Well, there you go then," said Charlie. "We'll call you Ace. And you," he said, turning to me, "can stay as boring old Dave."

Everyone laughed.

"Really? You think Ace is okay?" said the now newly-christened Ace. "Well, I suppose if you guys like it then, within the confines of the close, I suppose I don't mind if you all call me Ace."

"Perfect," said Mike. "I'll let everyone know. Hey, everyone…" he shouted, walking across the grass to the people assembled on the patio.

What the hell just happened? One minute I had the upper hand, securing the more popular Dave 1 option. Then I'm downgraded by Dave 2.0. And then, as if that wasn't bad enough, the smug bastard pulled a literal ace from his pocket to well and truly trump me. And I'm left as 'boring old Dave'.

Ace, for God's sake. That was a great name. A really cool name. How could he have thought that was going to be embarrassing? And then it dawned on me. It was all an act. Of course it was. *Oh, please don't call me by my embarrassing middle name.* He wasn't embarrassed by it at all.

So, now this imposter could go on using *my* name wherever he wanted. And when he was at home, he'd have everyone fawning all over him and calling him Ace. Oh, he was a clever one, all right.

I jabbed a fork hard into a sausage and took a large bite, burning my tongue.

******

"Dave was telling me all about your funny coincidence." I turned round to see New Dave's pretty wife walking into the kitchen, where I was unloading more sausages and chicken legs from the fridge. "Hi, we haven't been introduced. I'm Tamzin," she said.

After three hours slaving away over the barbecue, my guests' appetites showed no signs of diminishing. And the more they drank (of *my* booze), the more calls came in for extra food. I could almost hear them thinking to themselves, if they lingered a little longer, and guzzled down more food, they wouldn't need to go home and make any dinner. The freeloading sods.

"Oh hello," I said, slightly startled. "I didn't see you there. Erm, nice to meet you." I held out a hand to shake, awkwardly realised I was holding a pack of sausages, and immediately snatched it back. "Yes, it's, er… pretty crazy."

"You hear of actors having to change their names, don't you," she said, "because there's already another person with the same name. But this is a really bizarre coincidence. Same name, same age, grew up in the same place… and now living next door to each other. You should phone the local paper. They love stories like that."

"Oh, no," I said, dreading the thought of my face appearing in the local gazette under some twee, saccharine headline. "I don't think they'd care."

"Well, you never know," she replied. For a second, I thought she might be offended, but she quickly shrugged it off. "I had a similar thing, you know, back in my modelling days, before I met Dave. My professional name back then was Tamzin Buckingham, and there was another model on the scene at the time called Tasmine Beckworth. Not exactly the same, of course. Certainly not as close as you and Dave. But you wouldn't believe the amount of times clients mixed us up. I'd turn up for a job and they'd be expecting this other girl. Or I'd miss out on jobs because they'd stupidly booked her instead."

So, she actually was a model. I knew I was right about that.

"Oh," I said. "That must have been annoying."

"Actually, the most annoying thing about it was how nice Tasmine was. For a while, I thought she was doing it on purpose. You know, imitating me to get all my gigs. One time they booked us both on the same catwalk job, so I asked her about it. But she was just the loveliest girl. I always thought it would be easier if she was a real bitch, you know, like some of the other girls in the industry, pardon my French.

Then I could have resented her. But she was so nice we actually became really good friends."

"Right, yes," I said, wondering whether someone actually needs to be horrible before you can resent them. "So, you used to be a model? Wow, that's really cool."

"Yeah, back in the day," she said. "I had a pretty good run of it. Never quite hit the supermodel status, but I had fun and made some money. Got to work in some glamorous locations. And some real shitholes, too." She gave me a knowing wink. "It's not all luxury islands and mansions, you know."

"Really?"

"Of course not! Some of the magazine shoots I did were horrendous. Crazy photographers with crazy ideas. I once did a fashion shoot in an abattoir; I kid you not. Christ knows what they were thinking. But I was young and stupid. Definitely don't miss that part of the job."

"Oh, so you don't model anymore."

"No, those days are all behind me now," she said. There was a slightly wistful look in her eyes, and the smile dropped from her lips for just a second. "It's not a great lifestyle at the best of times: ridiculous hours; last minute casting calls; jetting off for a week at a time. Once I had the kids, I knew it was time for a more… settled lifestyle. Besides, I don't have the figure for it anymore."

"Nonsense. You have a great body." The words came tumbling out before my idiot brain had time to sense-check them.

She squinted at me slightly.

"Er… I mean… I… not that I was looking… er… I mean…"

"That's okay," she said, generously. "You're very kind."

Good one, Dave, I thought. You've known the woman for less than 24 hours and you've already embarrassed yourself in front of her. I could feel the heat burning in my cheeks.

"So, er… how are you settling in, so far?" I said, desperate to change the subject. "I mean, I know it's only been…"

"Really great," she said. "Seems like a lovely area. And everyone has been so welcoming. I can't wait to get started on the house. You know, stretch out and put our own stamp on the place."

"Yes, Dave told me about your extension plans," I said, trying to disguise the displeasure in my voice. Before long they'd be living in a giant house, with a huge garden, and making my place look tiny by

22

comparison.

An awkward silence hung between us. I went to speak, but no words came out.

"Anyway, best get back to mingling," said Tamzin, breaking the tension. "Still lots of lovely people to meet. Thanks so much for doing this. We really couldn't feel more welcome."

She walked out of the kitchen and I felt a flush of dread wash over me as I took another pack of burgers from the fridge.

******

"Well, that seemed to go pretty well," said Catherine, sneaking up behind me and squeezing my bum as I sorted empty beer cans into the recycling bin. "I reckon the new neighbours probably think you're bit less mental now."

The last few stragglers had left 10 minutes previously, and Catherine and I were sorting through the devastation only drunk people seem to find it acceptable to leave at someone else's house. I turned to face Catherine and she kissed me. Her lips tasted of red wine and burgers.

"They seemed nice, I thought," said Catherine. "Nice couple. He's very friendly and she was lovely."

"Hmmm… she seems all right, I suppose. Not sure about him. Bit flash, isn't he?"

"What a surprise, I'd never have guessed you'd say that. Well, I think he's nice. Did you talk much to Tamzin?"

"We had a brief word in the kitchen," I said, feeling strangely guilty as I remembered the exchange.

"She used to be a model, you know. I can believe it, too. She's absolutely stunning. Such a figure."

"Really?" I said, feigning ignorance. "I didn't notice."

"Yeah, right," she mocked. "Pull the other one."

"Hey, I only have eyes for you, my love," I said.

"Yeah, beer goggles, maybe."

"I barely had four beers, thank you very much. Too busy cooking for a street full of freeloaders. If anyone's got the beer goggles on, it's you."

"I may have had a couple of glasses of wine," she giggled. "Speaking of which, why don't you leave that until the morning. The kids are zonked and crashed about an hour ago. Which means I've got you all to myself for a while."

The corner of Catherine's mouth turned up slightly, as she seductively undid the top button of my shirt. She kissed me again and said, "I thought maybe we could go upstairs."

"Oh yeah?" I said, my heartbeat rising.

"Yeah," she said, kissing me again. Harder this time, as she pushed her tongue softly into my mouth. She broke away, as her fingers popped open another button on my shirt. "I thought, if we're really quiet…"

"Yeah?" I said.

"And we make sure we don't wake the kids…"

"Yeah…"

"You could run me through your presentation again." She giggled mischievously. "You know, to make sure you're ready for tomorrow."

"You bloody sneak," I said, laughing back.

"And if I find your sales patter impressive," she whispered into my ear, "who knows what you might be able to talk me into afterwards." She kissed me hard again. Then giggled and ran off up the stairs.

I dropped my empty beer cans and raced after her.

CHAPTER 4
A RUDE AWAKENING

THE BLOODY CAT was crying at the bedroom door. A desperate, high-pitched whine, like someone was trying to murder her. To hear it, you'd think she was the most ill-treated cat that ever lived. As if she'd endured terrible hardships no living thing should ever go through, and now she was reliving the memories like a traumatised war veteran. She was PTSD cat.

The reality, of course, was that the sun had come up and she was now awake. That meant we should also be awake, paying her lots of attention. And she was damn well going to get into our room to elicit that attention from us, no matter how much noise she needed to make.

It was the perfect end to a frustratingly sleepless night. After I ran through my presentation with Catherine, she had indeed been convinced by my silver tongue and we'd made love. She fell asleep seconds later, and while the exhaustion would usually see me nodding off too, the extra adrenaline kept me annoyingly awake.

Even the booze I'd drunk at the barbecue didn't help me fall into a drunken snooze. Instead, I lay there tossing and turning, running the events of that day through my mind. Mostly, I thought about New Dave.

Where had he come from? And what the hell was his game?

There I was, living a perfectly happy life, and this bloody imposter comes along, using my name and charming all my friends. Making me look bad. Trying to embarrass me.

I knew it was ridiculous to feel like that. It was just a coincidence. An incredible one, but a coincidence nonetheless. And, of course, New Dave didn't have some dastardly ulterior motive. How could he? We'd never met before. What could he possibly have against me? I knew it was paranoia. But it was keeping me awake nonetheless.

The more I thought about it, the more depressed I felt. I tried deep breathing exercises to help me fall asleep. It didn't work. I tried counting the little flowers in the pattern of the bedroom curtains, hoping the sheer tedium would help me pass out. It didn't. The more I tried to divert my mind onto any subject other than New Dave, he was all I could think about.

Don't think about pink elephants. What was the first thing you just thought about? Exactly.

No matter which way I looked at it, I was now inexplicably living next door to another version of myself. Another Dave Brookman. A richer Dave Brookman. A more successful Dave Brookman. And though I didn't like to admit it, he was clearly also a slimmer, fitter, more handsome Dave Brookman. It was as if he was better in just about every single way. And, whether it was his intention or not, he was making the old Dave Brookman look bad. Really bad.

I glanced over at the red digits of the alarm clock. 4.42 am. A little over an hour before I had to get up for work. Any chance I had of getting my usual seven hours were long gone. And with the cat doing her 'Why have you forsaken me?' act, I was never going to get any rest.

I finally relented and let the cat in, cursing my useless bloody children for not locking her in the living room like they're supposed to. Then I guiltily remembered excitedly running up the stairs last night and leaving the door wide open myself. I crashed back into bed and the cat jumped up, purring loudly, and flopped into the gap between me and Catherine. She then set about getting rid of me – pushing her paws into my back, swatting at my head and meowing loudly. I'd complained to Catherine several times about how the cat clearly had a vendetta against me, but she always laughed it off.

"Of course the cat doesn't have it in for you," she'd say. "She's just being affectionate."

"By pushing me out of bed?"

"She just likes your side of the bed. Probably because it's warm and smells like you."

Bullshit. The cat was an arsehole, plain and simple.

I climbed out of bed and stared at the cat, who twisted and squirmed her way into a more comfortable position in my vacated space. Then she looked up at me with her smug little cat face.

"This isn't over," I whispered, and left the bedroom.

I felt worn and dry, like the sole of an old shoe – a feeling I hadn't experienced since the many sleepless nights and 3am feeds when Jack was still a baby. I trudged downstairs to the kitchen and listened to my expensive coffee machine gurgle and sputter as a rich, dark stream of coffee dribbled out into the tiny espresso cup. The hot coffee was soothing on my throat and I felt an instant tingle as my brain sparked with the caffeine rush.

I loved my coffee machine. It was my second-favourite possession (after my MeatMaster) and the best part of my morning ritual, as I'd spend 10 minutes relaxing with a strong coffee before the full chaos of the house burst into life. But something was different today. I couldn't quite put my finger on it. The coffee tasted different somehow. Slightly acrid. Perhaps the machine needed descaling?

I'll bet New Dave has a far fancier coffee machine than me, I thought. I'll bet he has a super-duper deluxe model, with a special attachment for blowjobs. And I bet he only ever drinks coffee from the very finest beans, picked by naked virgins on the top of a mystical mountain guarded by ninjas and dragons.

I took another sip of coffee. It tasted like disappointment.

I carried the cup through to the living room and sat down on the sofa, but my gloomy fug only increased. I bet New Dave has a much bigger sofa, I thought. More comfortable and made from only the finest Italian leather. I looked around the room, taking in all my possessions. I bet Dave has a bigger telly, too, I thought. He probably has a fantastic home entertainment system with wireless surround sound – all voice activated, with speakers in every room, so the music follows you around the house.

The more I looked, the more comparisons there were to make. I'll bet he has lovely thick curtains and an enormous Blu Ray collection. Expensive rugs and antique furniture. I'll bet he has art on the walls (proper art, not just prints or the mass-produced paintings they sell in Next) and cabinets full of trophies and awards that he's won.

I knew it was all ridiculous. What did it matter how comfy his sofa was, or what size TV he had? Who cared what things he owned or what he paid for them? But no matter how much I tried to convince myself of that, I just couldn't.

A sickly pain throbbed in my stomach. Perhaps the coffee machine really did need cleaning? Or maybe I was just tired. I flicked the TV on and scanned through Netflix until I found a daft 80s action movie.

I guess I must have finally fallen asleep, as I was rudely awoken by a pair of football boots thudding down onto my legs.

"Ow! Jesus," I said, lurching up and clutching my aching shin.

"Sorry Dad," said Jack, "didn't see you there. Why you sleeping on the sofa?"

"Why *are* you sleeping on the sofa," I corrected him. "Speak properly please. And I'm not sleeping on the sofa, I just nodded off."

"If you nodded off, doesn't that mean you were sleeping?" he said smugly.

"Don't be a smart arse." I rubbed my shin.

"Hey, why are you sleeping on the sofa?" said Holly, rushing into the living room. "What did you do? Are you and Mum splitting up?"

"Of course we're not splitting up," I said. "And no, I didn't do anything, I just couldn't sleep so I came down here. And why do you assume it would have been me that did anything, anyway?" I exclaimed as an afterthought.

"Er, because you're a man!" she asserted.

"Good to know," I said.

"Did you get really drunk at the party last night, then Mum made you sleep on the sofa?" laughed Jack, mischievously.

"No, I didn't, you cheeky sod. Anyway, what time is it?"

"7.54," said Holly, glancing at the pink watch on her wrist.

"Shitballs!" I said, jumping up from the sofa and knocking my empty espresso cup onto the floor.

"Ha! You said shitballs!" giggled Jack.

"Damn, I'm gonna be late for work. And shouldn't you two be off to school?"

"Just about to leave," said Jack, picking up the football boots and stuffing them into his bag. "But no one's made us any lunch, so can I have a fiver to get something?"

"No, you can't. Make yourself a sandwich, there's plenty of stuff in the fridge."

Jack huffed and walked off towards the kitchen.

"And you go and make sure he makes something at least slightly healthy," I instructed Holly. "Not like that Nutella, peanut butter and M&Ms monstrosity he made himself last time."

Holly tutted loudly. I raised my eyebrow to give her my 'I'm not messing around' face, and she trudged off after her brother.

I raced upstairs to find Catherine in the shower, which meant I'd have to wait or go to work without a wash. "Honestly," I huffed to myself, "you miss your bathroom slot by more than one minute in this house, and it's like joining the queue for the bloody Vampire Ride at Chessington." I gave my armpit a cursory sniff test. A mix of mild B.O., dried booze and meat smells. I couldn't go to work like that.

Catherine finally appeared 12 minutes later, letting me in for a speedy bathroom turnaround. Living with a wife and two kids, I've managed to get the whole thing down to a fine art – multi-tasking my various bathroom activities (brushing my teeth while I pee; shaving in the shower; rinsing mouthwash while I finger product into my hair) to get in and out in under 10 minutes. I was slightly off my game this morning and made it out in a very poor 11 minutes and 12 seconds. Definitely not one for the record books.

I threw on some clothes and raced downstairs.

"You still here," said Catherine as I walked into the kitchen. "I thought you left ages ago."

"Couldn't sleep," I said, dumping two bits of bread into the toaster. "Came down here. Nodded off on the sofa."

"Oh, sorry love," she said, placing a hand gently on my cheek. "You should have told me you couldn't sleep." She leaned in close and whispered in my ear, "I could have kept you entertained. Again."

"Eurgh, gross," said Holly with a mouthful of cereal. "I heard that."

"Heard what?" said Jack.

"They're talking about sex," said Holly, scrunching her face.

"Eurgh, gross," said Jack.

Catherine giggled and gave me a big kiss.

I looked at my watch. "And now I'm seriously late."

"Oh, you'll be all right" said Catherine. "God knows you do enough hours at that place. They can't complain if you're a few minutes late every now and then." She smiled reassuringly.

"Yeah, I suppose. I've just got lots on."

"Hey, you'll be fine today," she said. "Your presentation is great. You'll smash it. That's what they say, isn't it, Jack?"

"Yeah, smash it," he shouted back.

"Oh, I hope so…" I said.

"Listen," Catherine said, "I'll be a little late back tonight. It's Jen's birthday today, so remember a few of the girls from school are going out for a drink after work."

"Jen? Drinks?"

"I told you about this weeks ago, Dave" she said, slightly miffed. "Honestly, I swear you only hear what you want to."

"Yeah, no, I remember," I lied. "Jen's birthday. Of course."

"So, can you pick up some dinner on the way home? Maybe get a bucket of KFC, or something? Bit naughty for a Monday night, but what the heck, eh?"

"KFC?" shouted Jack, punching the air. "Awesome!"

My toast popped.

"Sure," I said. "No problem."

I filled my travel mug with coffee, buttered my toast and dashed out to the car. The little clock on the dashboard told me it was 8.29. If there wasn't too much traffic, I might not be too late after all.

I sped out of the driveway, pulled out of the close onto the main road and into a long queue of traffic snaking slowly into town. Damn.

I finally made it into work at 9.17am. Technically, only 17 minutes late, but I usually like to get in by 8.15am at the latest. It gives me the chance to make a coffee in peace, scan through my inbox and get a little head start on the day before the rest of the rabble get in. Because of this, my mysterious late arrival garnered a number of 'hilarious' comments from my co-workers, ranging from: 'Half day, is it?' to, 'Glad you could make it' to, 'If I knew *you* were going to be late, I'd have had another 10 minutes in bed'.

I settled down at my desk, fired up my computer and sighed as I prepared to face the day.

"Morning mate," said Steve, handing me a cup of coffee, before sitting at the desk next to me. "Jeez, you look like you could do with that!"

"Eh?" I said, glancing at my reflection in the black computer monitor. Red face, black bags under my eyes, and slightly more of a bedhead look than I was going for. I'd have to rethink some of my bathroom multi-tasking. "Oh, yeah. Didn't get too much sleep last night."

I told Steve all about the strange events of the weekend.

"So, you're basically living next door to yourself? Only, a richer, better, more handsome you?" laughed Steve.

"No need to rub it in," I said.

"And it's all legit, is it? Not some kind of con, or something?"

"I don't think so. I mean, I can't see how. And what would be the con, anyway?"

"Dunno. Have you Googled him?"

"Erm…" I said, embarrassed that I hadn't thought to.

"Come on, man," said Steve. "You have to Google him." He quickly started typing.

"Here we go," said Steve, after several minutes scanning through the

Google results. "Dave Brookman, CEO of BrightSpark Communications. Christ, you didn't tell me he had the same job as you too – only better."

"I didn't know," I said, stunned. "We didn't really talk about work. Only that he has his own business."

"Christ," said Steve, clicking onto New Dave's LinkedIn profile, "he's got a pretty impressive CV too. Couple of years at Boggle, Bartle and Battey in New York; Creative Director at Gyrostamp; Creative Director at The Move Experience, Exec Creative Director at Wow Company... The list goes on and on. And why do marketing and advertising agencies all have such stupid bloody names? Christ, we either sound like second-rate vaudeville acts or new age hippies flogging hemp products."

I looked at the list as Steve scrolled down. It was very impressive. The kind of companies I'd love to have on my CV and the senior positions I'd never managed to get up to. And it got worse.

"Look at all the awards he's won, as well," said Steve clicking onto another search result. He was practically swooning. It was sickening. "I'm sorry mate," continued Steve, reaching over and touching me gently on the knee, then pretending to sniff back a tear, "but we might have to break up the team. I think I'm with the wrong Dave Brookman."

"Very funny," I said. "Everyone knows I'm the driving force behind this creative partnership of ours. Besides, what makes you think *he'd* have *you*, anyway?"

"Hmmm," said Steve, continuing to read. "Left LLP Creative four years ago to set up his own company. Looks like they're doing pretty well, too. Decent client list. Let's have a look at..."

I grabbed the mouse out of Steve's hand and closed the page. I couldn't look at it any longer.

"Maybe later, eh?" I said. "I'm depressed enough this morning. Don't think I can take any more negative comparisons."

"Fair enough. Must be a bit of a shocker, I guess. So, you didn't know he was in the advertising and marketing game too. I wonder how far it goes."

"How do you mean?"

"He's got your name – although, not middle name, apparently. Same age. Very similar career path – despite being way more successful, obviously." He grinned at me. I could have punched him in the teeth.

"Come on now…" I said.

Steve completely ignored my plea for leniency. "And as far as you can tell, he's done or doing better in just about every aspect of life. Better job. Same house but doing it up. Nicer car. Clearly richer. Model wife – no offence to Cath. Hey, you know I love her to bits. But I wonder how far it goes. What else is there?"

I didn't know. But Steve's line of questioning made sense. What else was there? How far did the comparison run? In exactly how many different ways was New Dave similar to me? And how else was he doing better? I suddenly had to know.

"Anyway," said Steve, "we've had enough fun this morning. Time to get your game face on."

"Eh?" I said, still somewhat distracted.

"The pitch. For KODEK. They'll be here in just under an hour. Thought we might go over it one last time. Make sure we're happy with everything and who's saying what."

"Fuck. Yes, of course. Bollocks, I could really do without that this morning."

"Well, tough titties. And you'd better be on top form. We need this account. Big money. Thomson will be a right arsehole if we don't impress. And it certainly won't help with your delusions of grandeur."

"Eh?"

"The promotion you've been going on about non-stop for the last three months. Fuck this up, and you can say goodbye to that."

"Yes, you're right. We need this one. Right, let me nip to the loo, then we'll go over everything again."

CHAPTER 5
THE SPREADSHEET

I WAS ACTUALLY feeling pretty good when we got back from the meeting. The presentation went well. The client was very positive about our ideas and I was sure we were going to win the account. Our CEO, Martin Thomson, even took me to one side to tell me how impressed he was with the work. Then he gave me a knowing wink and told me I could expect big changes if the client hired us.

So, my mood had definitely lifted.

I got back to my desk and listened to an answer phone message from Catherine:

"Hey, babe, I hope the presentation went well. I'm sure they absolutely loved your ideas. Oh my god, you wouldn't believe the amount of cake Jen brought in for her birthday today. I've already had a muffin and a slice of birthday cake, and it's only half past eleven. Fat cow, ha! I'll be working that off in the gym tomorrow. Still, it's helping the hangover a bit. Anyway, I know I only asked you this morning, but I know what you're like. So, don't forget to grab dinner on the way home. Anyway, I should be back by half seven, eightish. Love you."

Cheeky cow, I thought, assuming I'd have forgotten. In fairness, I had already forgotten. But she didn't bloody know that. My head throbbed slightly with my own hangover. Then the whole series of events from the previous day came flooding back, as I slouched down into my chair with a deep sigh.

I thought about Steve's comment. In just how many different ways was New Dave better than me? There must be at least a couple of areas where I would trump him. And, if not, just how bad was the damage? Exactly how much better than me was he in total?

I scanned through my emails to take my mind off it. No good. I opened up a new brief that had come in. A client wanted some creative ways to re-energise their flagging publishing business. Usually, I'd have been sparking with inspiration, making notes in my book, sketching out ideas for direct mail campaigns or nifty advertising stunts. But I had nothing. I just sat there, sighing and chewing the end of a biro, as a sickly wave of depression washed over me. All I could think about was

New Dave and the apparent gulf of success and status between us.

I had to find out just how big that gulf was. Then, perhaps, I'd be able to put it behind me and get on with things.

I opened up the Excel programme on my laptop and clicked to open a new document. I like Excel. I like the relative simplicity of it. The way you can lay out all the facts in one handy place. Then you can analyse things. Compare details. Assess numbers, perform calculations, draw comparisons. The numbers never lie.

Things always seem clearer somehow, when you can see all the facts in front of you. So, I decided to use it for my situation with New Dave. I could lay out all the details of our lives, achievements, various merits and negative aspects. That way, I'd be able to get a true comparison between us. I'd put both of our lives into a spreadsheet and let the numbers do the talking.

I clicked into cell B1 and typed 'Dave Brookman 1 (Me)'. I tabbed over to cell C1 and entered 'Dave Brookman 2 (Him)'. There was a certain tension in my fingers. A slight elevation in my breathing, as I typed the word 'Him'. I clicked into cell A2 and typed the word 'Salary'. In the box beneath that, I typed 'Car', and beneath that 'Car Value'. I then set about filling in the list of criteria against which I intended to compare myself with New Dave. I typed furiously, noting down everything I could think of:

Salary
Car
Car value
House size
House value
Job
Position in company
Clothes (Quality/Brands)
Attractiveness
Attractiveness of wife
Personality of wife
Cleverness of kids

By the time I was finished, there were more than 60 things in the list. I sat back to consider it. To collate a relevant mean average, I would have to score each element on a scale from 1-10. That was fairly easy for most categories like personality, friendliness and things like that. I'd just decide where I thought we fit on the scale and compare the difference.

The tricky part was things like Salary or Car value. That required more thought. In the end, I decided the easiest way was to stick to the same scale and attach an arbitrary level of how little someone of our age should reasonably be earning, or the lowest value their car should be (within reason), down at 1. Then I would assign what I dreamed I was earning (within reason, of course; there was no point putting £1 billion per month – it just wasn't realistic), or how expensive a car I would like to own, at 10. Obviously, all scores would be based on my own opinion, and therefore open to interpretation. But it was my list, so I figured I could do what I wanted.

Happy with my system, I set about rating myself and the various things in my life. For *Salary*, I gave myself a fairly respectable 6 out of 10. I was comfortable enough with what I earned – it was the going rate for a Creative Director in a marketing agency, and commensurate with my level of experience. I had enough to pay the mortgage and bills every month, with a little left over to put into savings. I wasn't wracked with debt, the kids never went without, and we had our annual two weeks in the sun. We were, by and large, quite comfortable.

Of course, I would have liked to be earning more – who wouldn't? And hopefully, my salary was set to rise. I'd spent the last year working towards a promotion at work, and I'd been told I was a shoo-in for it. Plus, there were Thomson's comments to consider. Big changes, he'd said. Hopefully, that would manifest itself into a decent pay rise. So, things were set to change. But for now, I was only a 6.

I marked myself a 7 for *House Size*. It was a good-sized house, with four bedrooms, a decent living room and dining room, one main bathroom and a downstairs loo. The garden was average, but big enough. And with the garage plus parking space, it was a good plot of land. No stately manor, perhaps, but easily a 7.

To fill in the *House Value* field, I logged on quickly to Rightmove.com and looked up the asking price on New Dave's house. Thankfully, the listing was still there, with the price marked up at £370,000. Not bad, considering we bought ours for less than half that. And it was practically identical to my house, so I figured we'd share the value as well as the layout. According to my scoring system, that gave me another solid 6, so I added that.

Next was *Car* and *Car Value*. My Ford Focus was certainly no Lamborghini. It was reliable. Comfortable. Certainly fit for purpose. And it was only nine years old, so still in good working order. But it didn't exactly scream luxury or excitement. Especially when compared with the BMW and Porsche parked next door. So, I couldn't really justify giving it more than a 5.

I carried on down the list, scoring the various elements of my life as honestly as I could. There was no point doing it if I wasn't going to be honest. I gave myself a 7 for *Job*, based on enjoyment, how good I was at it and the seniority of the position I'd reached.

I've never been the snazziest dresser or, to be honest, all that concerned with the latest fashion trends or designer labels – something the kids are always more than happy to tease me about. But I like to think I'm reasonably smart and well turned out. And people don't openly laugh at my appearance in the street (not that I've noticed, anyway). So, I awarded myself a safe 6 for *Clothes*.

I quickly got into the flow of things, awarding myself, amongst other things, 7.5 for *Intelligence*, 6 for *Fitness*, 4 for *Hairstyle* (honestly, I don't think I've ever had a haircut in my entire life that I've been happy with), 4.5 for *Singing Voice*, 3 for *Cooking Ability* (I'm great at grilling meat on the barbecue, but pretty hopeless at creating an actual meal in the kitchen), 7 for *Sense of Humour*, 6 for *Wittiness*, 6 for *Physique* and a depressingly low 3 for *Ability to Grow a Beard*.

I circled back to the harder fields that needed more thought. I clicked the cursor into the box next to the one marked Daughter's Intelligence. I paused to give this plenty of thought. Holly was a bright kid, always very inquisitive and keen to understand how things worked. She was in the A-set for all her classes and I had no doubt she would be headed to university. And then, hopefully, on to great things.

Unfortunately, she lacked application. She was happy enough scoring a B+ or A- on a test, where I always felt if she just put in a little more effort, she could get top grades every time. But she had recently discovered the presence of boys on the planet. And this had caused a detrimental effect on her levels of concentration in class and willingness to study after school. Where she might have spent time with her nose in a textbook, she apparently preferred to spend hours learning what her peers were up to on Facebook, researching make-up tips on YouTube, and documenting the daily woes of teenage life on Instagram.

I feared I was going to have to give up my dreams of her becoming a doctor and instead settle on her becoming a Human Resources Manager. I sighed heavily and typed a reasonable 7.5 into the box.

My son, Jack, was a different story altogether. We couldn't have asked for a happier, friendlier, funnier, more sociable son. But he's always been far more interested in sports than books. I've lost count of the number of different sports he plays, or the hundreds of hours I've spent driving him to practice sessions – for football, basketball, hockey, cricket, tennis… My big hope is that he gets good enough at one of them to make a career of it. Because, when it comes to academic performance, Jack has never been a shining star.

He tries. He definitely tries. And that's all I can ask for. He's not stupid, exactly. He's a C-grade student down the line. So, things could be worse. But he's never going to win a Nobel prize or discover the cure for cancer. I felt guilty as I typed it, but I couldn't honestly put down more than a 5. Again, I had to be ruthlessly honest with myself.

Then came the hardest field of all: *Wife's Attractiveness*. I took a long, deep breath as I considered how to score this one. I love my wife, of course I do. To me she is beautiful. Absolutely. I wouldn't change her for the world. But then I also had to think objectively. Would other men find her attractive? And how do her looks compare with other women? I had to be entirely honest.

My wife is attractive. It's not like she has warts or scars, or giant growths on her face. But then, she's not Charlize Theron either. And while that sort of thing shouldn't be important, everybody judges people on the way they look. To a certain extent, anyway. And if they say they don't, they're a bloody liar.

I like to think of myself as above average in the looks department. But I know I'm not in the same league as Brad Pitt or George Clooney. And there are clearly many women in the world who would find me unappealing. So, I wasn't really judging my wife. Not really. I was just taking stock. Totting things up. At least, that's what I told myself.

The first time I ever saw Catherine, I thought she was the most beautiful girl I'd ever seen. I was in the Student Union with my best mate Bonzo, drinking pints of cheap lager that I'd paid for with a cheque I sincerely hoped wouldn't bounce the next day. I looked across the room to see Catherine with a group of friends. And I genuinely had one of those cheesy, slow-motion moments you only see in films.

Everything else dropped away. The music faded out, I couldn't hear Bonzo jabbering in my ear, and the crowded room seemed to part. All I could see was Catherine.

She was perfect. I guess you'd say she was kind of homely. A little nerdy, with a quirky fringe and glasses. And, rather than dressing in typical girly clothes, she wore flared jeans and a really cool Nirvana t-shirt. It was almost like she was trying to hide the beauty underneath. But I could see it – from her dazzling eyes to the warmth of her smile, to her toned, sexy body.

It was either love at first sight, or the effects of the cheap lager (there were rumours around Uni that they hadn't cleaned the pipes in at least three years), but I felt an immediate throbbing pain in my stomach. I knew I had to be with her. So, I walked over to her table, introduced myself in as dashing a manner as I could, and proceeded to throw up all over the table.

It's important to make a good first impression – and that clearly wasn't one. And it's fair to say that the early days of my romance with Catherine were very much one-sided – with me being deeply in love with her, and Catherine thinking of me only as the drunk guy whose puke she'd spent a good hour cleaning off her Converse High Tops. But I persevered. I found out what classes she was in, and 'just happened' to be passing when they emptied out. I got a good feel for her routine – which pubs she liked, when she would be there, and I'd drag Bonzo with me so we could casually bump into her.

You might think of it as stalking. I prefer to consider it 'enthusiastic romantic strategising'.

Finally, one night at a house party, I managed to get her away from her friends and we chatted for hours, laughing and drinking alcopops into the early hours. Then we shared a kiss – a rather drunken, inelegant, slobbery affair. And since that magical moment, I've never wanted anyone else.

Catherine is still as pretty today as she ever was. But it's 27 years since we first met and time has taken its toll a little. Plus, she's had two children – so things aren't quite as tight and bouncy as they once were. But she still has a good figure. She works out regularly, with keep-fit and yoga classes. In fact, she's much fitter than I am, and her body is a far closer match to her 20-year-old self than mine is. Where I've gone a bit soft around the middle, Catherine is still quite toned.

So, she has a good figure and she's pretty. She has good fashion sense and always looks very nice – although her clothing does border more along the lines of sensible and chic than outright sexy. Her hair is always nicely styled and she wears just the right amount of make-up. Believe me, I have no complaints. But, as I say, I have to be honest and compare her attractiveness to other women and the standards the male-dominated society (for which I think I'm really only partly to blame – and a very small part at that) has placed upon women.

My hand shook a little on the mouse as I clicked into the relevant box on the screen. I breathed deeply and typed in 6.5. I know it sounds harsh, but I was trying to be honest. And I only gave myself a 5.5. Plus, she had earned a decent 9 in both *Sense of Humour* and *Personality*.

I felt wretched. I'd betrayed a sacred trust. But it was all for a good cause. And it's not like she would ever find out.

I continued working, adding more and more fields. When I was finished the list was enormous. I'd clearly got carried away. So, I went back through, assessing some of the categories. For example, I'd given myself 9 for *Ability to Use the Sky+ Planner*. Which I definitely stood by. But how was I going to determine New Dave's ability in the same field? And what relevance did it have in the grand scheme of things? I wanted this list to mean something, so I couldn't just fill it with guesswork, or nonsense that was only there to make me feel better.

After a careful bit of editing, I sat back and considered the final list. Then I started adding in scores for New Dave.

First up was *House Size*. That was an easy one as I'd already determined our houses were the same size, so I marked him down as 6 as well. But then, he had raved about the amount of work he was doing, with extensions and refurbishments. Plus, there was the plot of land he'd bought at the back. And hadn't he mentioned something about putting in a swimming pool? The work was yet to be completed, but I had no reason to think he was lying. I took it into consideration and marked him up to an 8.

Next was House Value. Similarly, the work he was doing would add a lot to his house. At least a hundred grand, I thought. So, I had to score him 8.5.

Dave's BMW 7 Series was clearly far, far nicer than my Focus. It was practically my dream car and only the fact that it wasn't a Tesla, Ferrari or Bugatti saved me from giving it full marks. So, I scored him a 9 and then an 8 for *Car Value*. New Dave was already off to a decent lead.

Next, I considered his job. He owned his own marketing agency. Practically the same job I had, but he was the boss. Not only that, he owned the bloody place. And from what he'd said, he seemed to enjoy it, too. There really was no competing on that front and I had to give him a full 10 points.

Salary was harder. I had no idea what he earned – or, more specifically, what he paid himself. Or what kind of profits his company earned him. Whatever it was, the car and house spoke volumes about how much money he had. So, I marked him what I thought was a reasonably accurate 8.

I carried on down the list, assigning scores based on what I knew or thought I knew about New Dave. I gave him 9 points for *Clothes*, based on his flash suits and abundance of designer labels. He scored 8 for *Intelligence*. His sense of humour earned him a modest 7, as I wasn't sure how funny he was. But he had laughed a lot and joined in with all the jokes at the barbecue.

New Dave had a good head of hair, always immaculately combed into one of those trendy styles that look like you haven't spent ages styling it. So, I gave him 9 points for that. And although he didn't currently have a beard, I had no doubt he could grow a very impressive specimen if he wanted. So, he massively outranked me on that front with a strong 9 to my measly 3 (I've tried growing beards in the past, but can't ever get past the wispy, patchy stage).

I paused when I got to Daughter's Intelligence. It was a fairly close-run thing, I thought, when it came to actual ability. From what I'd heard, his daughter Claire was also in all the A sets and equally as intelligent as our Holly. But she seemed to have the application that Holly lacked. So I was told, Claire always got top marks in any test. And she was always carrying a textbook. The exact kind of kid you don't want to be, or be associated with, when you're at school yourself. Kind of sickening, actually. But she was definitely more likely to become a doctor than Holly. I scored her 9.

Next was *Son's Intelligence*. This was a very different matter. New Dave's son, Michael, was a vast contrast to my own. Where my boy was happy, friendly and slightly lacking academically, Michael was like a robot. Seriously, a boy-shaped robot. He didn't play sports, he never really seemed to smile. At the barbecue, I hadn't seen him running or jumping, or acting like an annoying kid – all the things 12-year-olds are supposed to do.

He just seemed terribly serious and studious. Catherine told me he was supposed to be some kind of genius – top performer at school and talked like he'd swallowed a dictionary. If anyone was going to find the cure for cancer, I was sure he had a pretty realistic chance. I sighed heavily as I marked him a 10. I could probably even have gone to 11, if my system allowed it. But it didn't.

Of course, it wasn't long before I hit the most contentious field of all. *Wife's Attractiveness*. It was bad enough ranking my own wife's beauty. I was kind of allowed to do that, I reasoned, because we were married. And I'd been doing it for the last 25 years anyway. To actually grade the looks of my new neighbour's wife certainly felt like I was crossing a threshold. But I'd come this far.

Now, there was no disputing Tamzin's beauty. She was incredibly attractive. She used to be a model, so she was professionally beautiful.

Although she'd retired, her looks had certainly not faded. She was very pretty, with smooth skin, stunning blue eyes and big, pouty lips. Her long blonde hair was immaculately styled and seemed to bounce and sway in just the right way when she walked. She had a fantastic figure, too. There was barely an ounce of fat on her, with ample boobs and a tight, round bottom. Not that I'd looked that closely, but you can't help noticing some things.

I clicked into the box next to Catherine's score of 6.5 and a cold rush of guilt hit me as I typed in 9.5. I'd hoped to even things out a little by marking her down on personality and pleasantness. Surely a stunning, Porsche-driving, blonde ex-model would have to be a bitch, right? But, no. She was one of the warmest, friendliest people I'd ever met. She'd been the complete picture of charm at the barbecue, and she and Catherine had become firm friends as soon as they met. Again, another sickening trait which made me angry that it was so hard to dislike her.

All in all, according to my system, New Dave was clearly a very successful guy, with lots going for him. And I had bested him in only a few categories. I was already dreading seeing the final tally. But I had to know. I just had to.

I created a *Total* field at the bottom of the list, then created a mean average. Finally, I subtracted my average from New Dave's score to give us the differential.

46%.

Shit.

I slumped back into my chair as the figure sat there big and bold on the screen.

46%. New Dave was 46% more successful than me.

He was 46% *better* than me. That was the only honest conclusion I could make.

We had the same name. We were the same age. Born in the same town and grew up only a few miles from each other. We came from very similar backgrounds, so he'd started out no better off than I was. And somehow, he was 46% better than me.

I sighed loudly. Of course, I'd expected there to be a difference. I knew he would come out on top. But 46%? That was nearly 50%. And 50% was half. So New Dave was nearly a whole half better than me. How could this be? What the hell had I done with my life? Had I wasted the opportunities we apparently both shared, as New Dave took full advantage of them?

What could my life have been if I'd made different decisions along the way? Would I have my own company and a flash, expensive car? A house with a new extension and swimming pool? Would I be married to a former model, and have robotically clever children?

My life suddenly seemed like such a disappointment. As if I'd betrayed myself somehow. Squandered opportunities. Settled for second best and failed to meet my own potential. I closed the spreadsheet, slouched back into my chair and felt utterly miserable.

CHAPTER 6
ANYTHING DAVE CAN DO

"FOR GOD'S SAKE, Dave, you need to snap out of this," said Catherine, ambushing me in the bedroom before I headed out to work. I think it was her attempt at an intervention – although a far less sensitive version. "So what if the man's got more money than you? Or a nicer car? What difference does it make, really?"

"It's not just that, Catherine," I said, opening my sock drawer and rummaging around inside. "He's me, isn't he? But better. In so many ways."

I'd spent the past three weeks stewing over my spreadsheet. I'd emailed it to myself, so I could work on it at home as well as in the office. And I'd spent far too many hours revisiting it, re-evaluating my deficit to see if there was any way I could change the numbers in my favour. I added a few more fields where I thought I might be able to pip New Dave. Then I deleted some less relevant ones (was there really any point worrying that he had slightly whiter teeth than me?). But no matter what I did, New Dave always ended up 46% better than me.

I let it affect me more than I should have, moping about and feeling unhappy. Steve certainly noticed it at work. He complained that I wasn't my usual self, and informed me in no uncertain terms that it was affecting the quality of my work.

"No offence, mate," he said, one afternoon when we were trying (and failing) to think up interesting new ways to advertise the benefits of cloud computing, "but that's dog shit. Probably the worst creative you've ever come up with."

Steve can be refreshingly honest when it comes to creative feedback. Sometimes a little too honest.

But he was right. I looked down at the cringe-worthy scamp drawing of a man sitting in a cloud, giving a big thumbs up and saying, "The cloud's great!!!" I immediately tore it up and agreed that it actually was the worst idea I'd ever had.

It was that annoying fucker, New Dave. I was distracted. I couldn't focus on the projects I was working on. I was incapable of putting in my usual effort. And then I'd think about how New Dave probably never got distracted or depressed or turned in anything other than perfect work. And that just made me even more bloody depressed.

I found myself being quite terse with the kids at home. Where I was usually delighted to be asked to help with homework, I found excuses not to. And it was hard to disguise my displeasure at driving Jack to his early morning Saturday and Sunday football and rugby training sessions.

Catherine had also noticed. Apparently, I'd been 'distant and grumpy'. Foul-tempered and depressed. And when she'd tried to lure me to bed for an early night when the kids were out at friends' houses, she'd been perturbed that I'd preferred to stay downstairs and watch an episode of Mad Men on Netflix.

My relationships were suffering. My work was suffering. My marriage was under strain. I had no appetite, so I wasn't eating properly and certainly not enjoying food as much as I used to. This caused the first real concern with Catherine – eating is easily my first and favourite passion, and I never usually turn my nose up at any food. But I was even turning down the cakes people brought into work on their birthdays.

Apparently, seeing me turn down a slice of lemon meringue pie at dinner was the catalyst that led to Catherine's early morning intervention.

I was definitely depressed.

It was like I was in the most sadistic ever episode of *This is Your Life*. Like Michael Aspel had turned up at my front door with his big red book and said, "Dave Brookman, this is how your life could have been – if only you weren't such a complete bloody loser."

Ridiculous, I know. I had an amazing wife, a nice house and two great kids. And we had everything we needed in life. But it wasn't as much, or as good, or as shiny, or as expensive as everything that New Dave had. Which meant that what I had clearly wasn't as good as it could have been. Or should have been. And with that distinction in my head, it felt like what I had wasn't enough. I'd failed. Let myself down. And I couldn't forgive myself for that.

"For fuck's sake," I snapped, moving socks around in the drawer, "where are all my black socks? Why can't I find a single pair of fucking black socks?"

"I'm sure there are some in there, somewhere," said Catherine.

"No there aren't," I said. I reached in, grabbed up an armful of socks and threw them across the room. "Fucking ridiculous!" I shouted. "Is it too much to ask for a single pair of black…"

I suddenly caught myself. I looked round to see a trail of socks littering the floor and the bed. Catherine's eyebrows were raised so high I thought they might ping right off her head.

"Was there any need for that outburst?" she said. Then, as if she and the universe were conspiring against me, she reached into the now half-empty drawer and picked out a pair of black socks.

"Sorry, love," I said, bending down to clear up the mess. "I didn't mean to…" "This isn't like you," she said, concern creeping into her voice. "Throwing things. Getting angry."

"Sorry," I repeated. "I don't know why I did that."

"I'm worried about you, Dave," she said, kneeling down next to me and taking my hands in hers. "I know you've been under a lot pressure recently, what with the job and everything. But you can't let it affect you like this."

"I know. I'm sorry. I'm just not feeling myself at the moment. I'll try and cheer up."

"I don't want to seem uncaring, but I think you need to just snap out of it. It's not easy for me, you know. I'm stressed at work, too. There's this one boy in my class… Daniel… I know he has so much potential. And I know if I could just get through to him, he could do really well. But he's just distant and disruptive and God forbid he'd actually listen to a teacher's advice. And I'm usually good at helping kids like him. I've tried talking to his parents, but they don't see it… or they just don't care… I feel like I'm failing him and it's so frustrating."

"Really? You haven't mentioned it."

"No, well… it's just… the point I'm making is, there's so much going on in the world. And so many other things to worry about, rather than stressing about the people who live next door."

"I know, but…"

"No buts, Dave," she said, kissing me gently on the lips. "I'm giving you some tough love here. I love you. The kids love you. We just want our old Dave back. Not this sock-throwing numpty we've been left with." She gave a small laugh, the sort she usually gives when she's trying to hide what she's really feeling.

I promised her I'd stop acting like an idiot as I cleared up the rest of the socks. And I assured her I'd stop obsessing about our new neighbour. Then I kissed her on the cheek and headed off to work.

Of course, it was just words. A brave face. A promise designed to be broken – the words like ash in my mouth before they were spoken. Because she just didn't understand. How could she? She wasn't the one who'd been presented with a living, breathing example of everything she'd failed to achieve.

The whole drive in to work, I kept turning it over in my mind. Where had I gone wrong? What poor decision had I made? Could I have tried harder at school? Studied something different at university? Perhaps I was in the wrong career entirely. Maybe, rather than being an averagely successful creative director, I was supposed to be an exceptional teacher, a fantastic doctor or a magnificent builder. Had I followed a different path, I might have been a celebrated actor, a respected architect or the best lion tamer in the world.

Had I failed to take advantage of one seminal opportunity that might have changed the course of my whole life? Or maybe it wasn't one single thing. Had I spent the last 45 years making a series of poor choices? A collection of ill-thought decisions and missteps.

"Come on, move, you twat!" I shouted at a white-haired old biddy in the Fiat 500 in front of me. We were fourth and fifth in a queue to make it through a set of traffic lights. And if she didn't speed up, they were going to turn red before we got through.

It wasn't really like me to shout at other drivers or call old ladies 'twats'. But I'd been stuck behind for her the last 10 minutes, as she trundled along, failing to make it up to the speed limit, and stopping to let out every bloody car from every bloody side road – sometimes two or three at a time. I was already stressed enough, before I'd even made it into the office. And her dawdling was really pissing me off.

"You shouldn't be behind the wheel of a car," I shouted, as the first car in the queue went through the lights, "let alone out during rush hour and holding up people trying to get to work." I mean, where the hell was she going anyway? Most likely heading to the supermarket to bore the ears off some poor checkout assistant. No wonder she was in no hurry.

"Oh, for God's sake," I shouted as number two in the queue went through the lights. She dawdled and let the gap between her and car three grow to an unacceptable size. "The lights are gonna change and I'm gonna get…"

I looked up. The green light switched to amber. Car three sailed through. The old lady carried on at her snail's pace. "Go, go!" I urged.

If she just sped up, we could both make it through. "Put your bloody foot down."

She carried on slowly. The light changed to red. The old lady drove straight through it. I slammed on my brakes and punched my steering wheel. "Fuck's sake," I shouted. "It's not fair. It's not fucking fair."

I'm aware I was overreacting. It was just a traffic light, delaying me by no more than three or four minutes. But it felt like the whole world was ganging up on me. Stopping me. *That's your lot, Dave Brookman. This is as far as you go. All the great things further up the road are not for you.*

It felt so unjust. Why should I have to stop? Why did I have to settle for second best?

I thought of New Dave pulling up in his flash car. His fancy clothes and perfectly messy hair. The big, shiny watch glinting on his wrist and his perfect teeth glistening in his mouth. His gorgeous wife. His bulging bank balance and perfect life.

Why had one Dave Brookman, 45, from Crawley achieved so much, while another Dave Brookman, 45, from Crawley, had settled for less? We'd come from the same place. Had the same opportunities. He'd clearly made some different decisions and followed a path to greater success.

Perhaps it all came down to one single moment, decision or lucky break. Or maybe I had been lazy?

Did I just need to try harder? Apply myself? Well, if he could do it, so could I.

I was practically promised that promotion at work. When I got it, I'd have more money, with more responsibility. I could start making changes. Put my own stamp on things. I'd pretty much be running the place within a year. And then what? Who knows? Maybe do what New Dave did. Go and work in the New York or Hong Kong offices for a bit. Transfer my winning ways around the globe.

In fairness, my company didn't actually have offices in New York or Hong Kong. But I couldn't let trifling details like that derail me. I was going to be so successful I'd open up branches out there. Or find a bigger, global company that wanted me.

I could even start my own business. Yeah, take that, New Dave! A new competitor to blow you out of the water.

That was it. I just needed a new plan. A Dave-beating plan. Then we'd see which Dave was 46% better than which.

When I got to work, I barely said good morning to Steve. I just took the coffee he'd made me and fired up my laptop. I had no time for pleasantries. I wasn't even thinking about the day's work. I had another mission on my mind.

I opened my 'Dave' spreadsheet and clicked to start a new tab. In cell A1 I typed *Plan to Put New Dave in His Bloody Place*. I immediately decided that I didn't like that, so I deleted it and typed in *Plan to Become a Much Better Dave Than the Other Dave*. Hmmm, far too wordy.

I went through a list of possible titles, including: *The Best Dave Plan*, *The More-Dave-Than-You-Are Plan*, and *The FUCK YOU New Dave Plan*. Finally, I settled on *The 46% Plan*.

I could see Steve to my side, giving me strange looks as I typed furiously. I was on a roll and I had to get everything written down while it was still fresh in my head.

I started making a list of all the things I needed to do, achieve or own, in order to improve my deficit against New Dave. Of course, the chances of eradicating the full 46% were slim, let alone surpassing it. New Dave had a big head start on me. But with hard work, determination and maybe just a bit of cheating, I knew I could claw back at least 25%. Maybe even 30%.

I copied my original list of criteria from the other tab and pasted it into my new list. I then shortlisted the easiest areas to improve upon. Earning more money was definitely possible, so that made the list. At the other end of the scale, I didn't fancy my chances of increasing my ability to grow a beard, so that didn't make the cut.

Before long, rather than a list of areas in which I was inferior to New Dave, I found myself looking at a list of opportunities. A set of goals. Tangible challenges that I could work on.

Obviously, salary was the big-ticket item. The Beatles might not have cared too much for money, but I bloody well did. And no, maybe money can't buy you love, but it can buy you nice cars, and fancy clothes, and lavish holidays. And a MeatMaster 4000.

I still didn't know how much Dave earned, but it was clearly more than me. Moving up at work and bringing home a bit more bacon would do a lot for my cause. At the top of my spreadsheet I wrote *Action Points*. Next to *Salary* I typed *Secure promotion. Negotiate massive pay rise*.

Next up was fitness. I sighed as I looked down and grabbed a handful of belly fat. This was an area I'd let slip over the years. When I was younger, I was quite fit and sporty. I played in a Sunday league football team. I wasn't great, but I got a game most weeks and all the running about kept me healthy. I also used to jog once or twice a week and I could run 5k in a respectable time. Now, I could barely walk up the stairs at work without getting short of breath and a bit sweaty.

Clearly, I could make improvements. Perhaps I should join a gym? Or buy some running shoes and start jogging again? I could run around the little park near the house. I settled on that and typed *Jogging* into the spreadsheet.

As I'd done before, I made my way down the list adding action points and activities that would help me improve the different areas. But this time it was much more positive. I smiled as my fingers danced over the keyboard.

Naturally, there were a few contentious ones. For Daughter's Intelligence, I jokingly wrote: *Lock her in her bedroom until she agrees to try harder.* Under the same point for Jack, I wrote: *Private tutor? Much point? Waste of money?*

For wife's attractiveness, I put in: *Boob job? Botox? Haircut?* I didn't actually think Catherine needed any of these. Yes, she'd developed a few wrinkles on her face (who doesn't?), but I actually found them cute. They added character and experience – a face with stories to tell. And her laughter lines made her mouth so expressive. She looked like she'd enjoyed her life.

I'd always liked the size of her boobs – not too big, not too small. They weren't as pert as they had once been, but that doesn't bother me. And I actually thought she had very nice hair – certainly better than the grey/brown mess sitting atop my head. I was just on something of a roll and found myself writing down anything that came to me.

By the time I'd finished, I thought I had the makings of a pretty decent plan. I was going to start running again. I was going to up my game at work – really impress the bosses and get that promotion. I was going to look carefully at my finances to see if I could afford a newer, nicer car. I was going to look into the costs of having an extension built onto the back of the house.

Jack was going to cut down on some of his sports clubs, so he could do extra tuition. And I was going to have a serious word with Holly about bucking her ideas up. I'd explain the importance of pushing herself and securing good exam results. And I'd make sure she understood just how terrible a life she could expect if she ended up working in Human Resources.

It was all clear now. I knew what to do and how to do it. New Dave wouldn't know what hit him.

CHAPTER 7
NEIGHBESIS

EXACTLY THREE WEEKS after my new neighbesis (I'd taken to calling him a portmanteau of the words neighbour and nemesis) had moved in, I heard the low diesel hum of trucks and building machinery rumbling into the close. I slammed my espresso cup hard onto the table, put the TV on mute and dashed out the front door, still in my pyjamas and dressing gown.

It was no surprise, of course. Having already told me personally about the impending building works, New Dave had also been round the close distributing apologetic letters alerting the other residents to the builders' arrival.

The sycophantic note had begged our forgiveness for the 'forthcoming presence of diggers, cranes and other site vehicles in the close'. It assured us that he'd 'hired very quiet, respectful builders'. 'Disruption', it said, would be 'kept to a minimum' and would last 'no longer than 10 weeks'. Finally, New Dave's letter held a creeping invitation to an impromptu cheese and wine evening at his house, during which he would happily share the plans and talk people through the schedule of construction. And, of course, he would answer any questions we had, to allay our concerns. He actually used the word 'allay', the pompous tit.

Naturally, I refused to attend – despite Catherine's attempts to make me go. "He just wants to butter everyone up," I'd complained. "Then he'll trick us into agreeing with the whole scheme. Probably have us thinking it's a great idea. The man's in marketing, that's what he does!"

"So are you," argued Catherine. "Surely, you must be immune to all his snake oil trickery." She was too clever for her own good sometimes, my wife. I gave her my best 'well, you would say that' sneer.

"Seriously, he's gonna con everyone. Then, when it all kicks off and the full horror of living in a building site kicks in, we'll have lost our right to complain. Well, not me," I said, crossing my arms and pouting. "I want to be able to moan as much as I like."

"Oh, how mature. Isn't it better to have a say now, before it's too late?"

"Don't care," I said petulantly.

"Well, I want to see what they're planning. And it's nice of them to invite everyone round."

"You're all clueless sheep, going to a timeshare sales presentation in the hope of getting the 50-inch telly they've promised as a gift. Nobody ever actually gets that telly, Catherine. Nobody."

She called me a twat and stormed off to New Dave's house.

I was right about the evening, of course. Nearly the whole street went to sit through Dave's brainwashing session, lured in by a bit of cheddar and a glass of cheap plonk. And, if Catherine's view was shared by everyone else in the street, New Dave had clearly scored himself a sizeable victory.

"The plans look amaaaaazing!" said Catherine, slurring slightly as she climbed into bed next to me. I'd spent the evening half-watching House of Cards on Netflix (trying to pick up a few tricks on duplicitousness to add to my armoury of New Dave-beating weapons) and half-spying out the window to see what was happening next door. Then I'd made sure to be in bed, pretending to sleep, when Catherine got home. "They're building a really beautiful extension and moving rooms about so they get a bigger kitchen." She smelled strongly of cheap wine.

"Yes, I know," I yawned, "he told me all about it."

"They're totally redoing the garden. And with all the extra space out the back, they're putting in a swimming pool and a hot tub. And a sauna." She practically squeaked with excitement at the last word.

"Very good," I said, dismissively.

"Tamzin told me we're welcome to pop round and use the pool, if we want. Or the sauna," giggled Catherine, grabbing my buttocks suggestively and nibbling my ear lobe. "That would be fun, wouldn't it? Getting all hot and sweaty together." Her hand snaked round and slipped inside the front of my pyjama bottoms.

"Sounds terrible to me," I snapped, grabbing her wrist and pulling it away. She humphed loudly, turned over and was fast asleep and snoring within seconds.

And now the full horror of it was unveiling before me. At 8.13am on a Saturday morning.

It was the first Saturday in ages that I hadn't been up at dawn to drive Jack to one of his various sports practices. I was just enjoying my morning coffee and the chance to catch up on one of my favourite TV shows, when my relaxation was rudely shattered.

"8.13?" I muttered to myself, the wind whistling up the legs of my pyjamas as I watched a collection of scruffy workers in dirty jeans pour out of a transit van and make their way up New Dave's path. "On a Saturday bloody morning? What the hell is he playing at?"

I marched straight round there when I saw New Dave coming out to meet them.

"What the bloody hell is going on?" I said. "It's 8.13am on a Saturday morning. Bit early for all this, isn't it?"

"Sorry," said New Dave. "I know it's early. I did tell them not to come round before 9am, but you know what builders are like. They love getting an early start on a job."

"This is the first Saturday in months I've actually been able to relax," I complained, "and instead I'm disturbed by all this."

One of the workmen smirked at me as he walked back out of the house to fetch something from the van.

"Listen, I'll make sure they get the message not to be on site a minute before 9am from now on. How's that?"

Well, what was I supposed to say? It was only a minor infraction. And it was the first day of the build. So, I couldn't really go overboard on the complaints. I had to give him the benefit of the doubt. But I walked back to my house with a horrible pain gnawing away at my stomach.

I could see how disruptive it was going to be. Sweaty builders. Banging and hammering. Unsociable hours. The street constantly filled with trucks, diggers and cranes. It would be hell on earth for several months. And while the other residents of the street were more than happy to be trampled over, I wasn't going to roll over and take it.

But if I was going to complain, I'd need proof. I ran up to the study, dug out an old notebook, and set about recording everything in a journal.

Saturday, 29 April

What the bloody hell is he playing at? Builders turning up at 8.13 in the morning? It's an absolute disgrace. He clearly has no respect for anyone but himself. I told Catherine this would happen. But would she listen?

Now, we're going to be putting up with this for the next God knows how long. Sweaty builders banging and clattering about all day.

Naturally, I marched straight round there to confront him, but he's all sweetness and apologies. "Sorry," he says, pretending like he gives a shit. "I did tell them not to come round too early. But you know what builders are like." Lording it all over me again!

But he doesn't care. I could tell he was just trying to get rid of me so they could start working.

I'm the only one who understands how bad things are going to get. That's why I'm writing it all down. This journal will be my proof. Evidence of everything I know is coming. I'll make a note of every single thing. Then I can shove it down his throat – the smug git!

Tuesday, 2 May

It's only been a couple of days and it's already pissing me off. So, I get home from work tonight and there's a crane parked in my parking space. MY bloody parking space. I went to complain, of course, and Tamzin tells me it's because it's the best angle to lift stuff over into the back garden. 'It's only going to be there a week,' she says. 'Catherine said it would be fine.'

A week! A fucking week!

Turns out Catherine did give them permission to park a bloody crane on my driveway. The bloody Judas! So now I have to park halfway down the street because of all the other trucks and vehicles parked up here. Seriously, there are so many diggers, trucks, vans – just left here overnight – you'd think he was building a whole new bloody housing development. I'm so bloody angry!

Wednesday, 7 May

I got up this morning, opened the curtains, and there's this sweaty builder staring at me from the cab of the crane. He's just looking at me. I'm stood there in just my pants, and he's just looking at me. Cheeky fucker even had the audacity to give me a little wave. They're not supposed to be on site until 9am, and certainly not peering through my window like a Peeping bloody Tom. That's it, I'm going round there to complain.

Thursday, 11 May

Trying to work from home today and it's a complete bloody joke. Banging, sawing, cutting, clattering, banging, yelling, banging… all bloody day long. The whole reason I chose to work from home in the first place was to try and get a bit of peace and bloody quiet.

So, I thought I'd have a stress-free, peaceful day. And instead it's like being in a bloody war zone. Aaargh! Fuck this, I'm taking my laptop to Starbucks!

Saturday, 20 May

Oh my God, there are so many people on site today. The place is literally crawling with builders, plumbers, gardeners, landscapers, electricians, and God knows what else. Builder's bums as far as the eye can see. And they're taking it in shifts to stand at the front of the house smoking. That's it, I'm complaining again.

Wednesday, 24 May

I had to fish 12 cigarette butts out of the rose bush in the front garden this evening. I swear those bloody builders think it's an ashtray. I told New Dave about it before and he said he'd have a word with them. Bloody piss-take! They're doing it on purpose, I know they are.

Saturday, 27 May

The bloody crane's back! Tamzin popped by and asked me if they could have my driveway for another couple of days. She looked incredible. Tight black jeans and ridiculously low-cut top. And old muggins here falls right for it.

"Of course, you can use the drive, Tamzin," I heard myself saying. "Use it as long as you need." Then as soon as she's waddled back to her own house, I realise what I've done. Brilliant. I'll be parking halfway up the street again. Idiot!

That New Dave's a clever one, all right. Getting his pretty wife to fight his battles and bamboozle people with her cleavage.

Sunday, 28 May

They knocked my bloody shed down! Some knuckle-dragging, mouth-breathing oaf was lifting something into the back garden on the crane, swung it round too hard and smashed my shed to bits. Completely obliterated it! It's lucky I wasn't in there at the time, or God knows what might have happened.

Lawnmower's smashed. Plus, just about everything else I had stored in there.

New Dave came running round straight away, of course. Apologising profusely. I said, "It's a good job I wasn't in there, or God knows what might have happened." He's promised to buy me a new shed to replace it and have his guys put it up for me. And he'll replace everything else that broke, too. We'll see.

Monday, 29 May

Got home tonight and they've already built the new shed. And it's bloody incredible. It's bigger than the last one and much, much nicer. It must have cost a small fortune. At first, I couldn't believe New Dave would spend that much money. But of course, he did. He's just showing off again, isn't he? Just another opportunity to show me how much more money he has. "Oh sorry, did my builders knock down your crummy shed? Allow me to replace it with a much nicer, more expensive one."

How benevolent! How bloody arrogant!

You know, I wouldn't be surprised if the whole thing was a set-up. He probably asked them to knock down my shed on purpose, just so he could pay to replace it. The git!

Tuesday, 6 June

We're sitting here in darkness, thanks to New Dave's bloody builders. Apparently, they were digging something up earlier and cut through a power cable. Now this whole side of the street is in complete darkness with no power. And the electricity people can't fix it until tomorrow.

New Dave was highly apologetic, of course, and offered to buy pizza for everyone affected, as most of us couldn't even cook thanks to the outage. Naturally, I refused and took Catherine and the kids to Harvester instead. Which ended up costing me nearly 60 quid. But at least the smug git didn't get the satisfaction of paying for my dinner.

After running down the batteries on my laptop and both of their tablets, Jack and Holly have each taken themselves off to sleep at different friend's houses, where they'll at least be able to watch telly. Which is more than I can do. And it leaves me and Catherine sitting in a dark, silent house. She suggested making the most of the quiet and having an early night. But I'm not in the mood.

Wednesday, 14 June

The cat has shit in the bloody living room again. I swear it's those bloody builders. She's so scared to go out of the house, what with all the people and the noise, she's ended up staying in loads and had an accident. Poor girl!

Then again, knowing that cat, the miserable little beast has probably done it on purpose just to annoy me.

Saturday, 24 June

I've got a parade of sweaty builders in and out of my house today, thanks to New Dave! They've had to turn the water off next door. Something to do with new plumbing in the kitchen, or his bloody swimming pool. I forget. I was so angry at the time, having to queue up to use my own bloody bathroom. Naturally, Catherine said it would be okay for the workmen to come over and use our facilities. She's too kind-hearted, that woman! Or soft in the head.

So, they've been clogging up the bathroom all day, and hanging out in our kitchen, making cups of tea.

I even caught one of the cheeky bastards about to use my coffee machine. So, I unplugged the thing and hid it upstairs in our bedroom. Catherine told me I was being petty, but I don't care. It's one thing using the kettle to make a round of teas, but stay the hell away from my expensive coffee!

That's it. I'm going into the office for a couple of hours of peace!

Friday, 7 July

They're still here. And they're clearly not finished. Everything was supposed to be done by now, according to New Dave's 10-week schedule. But they're still here. I told Catherine they were going to overrun. Just how long do we have to live with this nightmare? That's it, he's getting a piece of my mind.

Well, he didn't like that. Of course, he's all apologies again. And he's full of excuses about why it's overrun, and how it definitely won't be more than another week. I told him: this is an absolute joke. We're all sick of the disruption and we want the builders gone. You've got one week, I told him, then I'm going to get really angry.

I mean, I didn't say it exactly like that. Not in those actual words. But he could see in my eyes that I meant business.

Friday, 14 July

They're going. Hallelujah! Thank God, the builders are finally leaving. The work is done, and the last van is packed up and about to go. Good riddance, you sweaty, noisy, bloody wankers. And don't bloody come back!

New Dave and Tamzin popped round on the last day of the build to give us the good news. Tamzin presented us with a bottle of Veuve Clicquot as an apology gift and thanked us for putting up with the disruption. Talk about ostentatious. Not just a bottle of wine, like any normal person would have brought. They come over with a bloody expensive bottle of champagne. The pair of show-offs.

"You've been such good neighbours," said Tamzin, "and we know we've made your lives difficult since we moved in."

She left the door open for us to respond with a sycophantic, 'On no, don't worry about that. These things happen'. I gave her my best 'You're not wrong there' look. But Catherine – far too kind Catherine – fell for the trick and said, "Oh no, don't worry about that. These things happen." I just about managed to hold in my sigh of disapproval.

"Seriously, though," said New Dave, "we know you guys haven't enjoyed living with all this. If only because of all the little notes Dave posted through our letter box."

He laughed. I didn't.

"But it's all done, now. Peace and quiet can return to the street. And we're ever so grateful for everything you've put up with over the last few months. From now on, we promise we'll be the best neighbours anyone ever had."

Catherine, Tamzin and New Dave all laughed together. I didn't.

"The place looks amazing, though," said Catherine. "You must be really pleased."

"We're very happy," said Tamzin. "And we're going to have everyone round in a couple of weeks, if you can make it? So you can see what all the banging has been about."

"Oh, I look forward to that," said Catherine.

"Anyway, we won't keep you," said New Dave. "We're off into town, because this one wants to pick up some new furniture and God knows what else to fill up the new rooms."

They all laughed together again. I didn't.

So, now life could get back to normal. Well, not normal. I was still living next door to New Dave. Things would never be normal again. But at least it would be quieter. And I could stop fishing cigarette butts out of my rose bush.

CHAPTER 8
MEAT MASTER 2.0

"YOU'RE COMING AND that's the end of it." Catherine had her hands on her hips and an annoyingly determined look in her eyes.

"I'm not bloody well going," I protested. "He just wants to get everyone round so he can show off how amazing his house looks… and how much money he has… and how bloody great he is. It's nothing but a big dick-measuring contest, and I'm not interested."

"Well, I certainly won't be measuring any dicks," retorted Catherine. "At least, not at Dave's house, anyway. But maybe later…" She gave me a flirty wink and a smile.

I knew she was just trying to trick me into attending with a none-too-subtle promise of sex as a reward. I wasn't biting.

"I'm not going and you can't make me." I may as well have screwed up my eyes and poked out my tongue.

I pulled the covers back over my head, cocooning myself from Catherine's next salvo. Instead, she stormed out of the bedroom and stomped down the stairs.

I was only arguing out of pure bloody-mindedness. Trying to make a point I knew nobody else cared about. And neither of us were in any doubt as to who would eventually win the argument. One way or another, I was going to a barbecue at New Dave's house.

The work had been completed two weeks previously. The trucks, diggers and cranes were now just a distant memory – the only evidence of their existence in the street the giant tyre track that had torn up a patch of communal grass at the front of my house. I'd complained to the oaf that did it, who merely shrugged and said, 'Sorry mate, but it's only council, innit?' before carrying on with his work.

Naturally, I'd written to the council, requesting immediate repair. And I'd made certain they knew which resident was responsible for it. Three weeks later, I received a response from some bureaucratic pen-pusher telling me it was 'not a high priority concern', that they had 'no immediate plans' to look into the issue and that I was welcome to 'remedy the problem myself' – with no financial assistance from the council.

So, New Dave's incredible house was complete. And he'd invited everyone in the street to come and marvel at it. I knew exactly what would happen. He'd sweet-talk everyone. Impress them with his wealth and generosity. He'd buy them all off with a few burgers, sausages and cans of lager – meagre compensation for the weeks of noise and upset to which we'd all been subjected. And they'd lap it up, the freeloading bloody simpletons. Tragic fools worshipping the king in the castle at the end of the close.

Well, I was having none of it.

******

"Dave, great to see you. Thanks for coming," said New Dave, as Catherine, the kids and I walked through into his garden. The rest of the street were already there, drinking and eating. I'd decided that, if Catherine was going to make me go the barbecue, I'd go for as little time as possible. So, I'd faked an upset tummy, changed my clothes three times and dragged my heels for as long I could. Unfortunately, Catherine had foreseen my pettiness and fed me misinformation about the start time. So, when we walked in, we were, in fact, only half an hour late. Fuck it.

"Help yourselves to beers in the kitchen," said New Dave, gripping my hand in an overcompensating tight grip. "Hey, cool t-shirt," he said, pointing to my chest, then back at his own.

I'd decided to wear the t-shirt Catherine had bought me as a novelty Christmas present two years ago. It was pale blue with the slogan: *What a Difference a Dave Makes*. I'd thought it pretty silly at the time, but then I'd worn it as a joke to a party and people had loved it, saying how funny it was and how I really was making a difference to the party. Since then, it had become a bit of a trademark.

It was going to be my secret weapon. A sly tactic to stand out at the party and remind people that I was the original Dave. The Dave they all knew and loved.

So, of course, New Dave had exactly the same t-shirt. And, of course, he was wearing his too. Except, where mine was faded and worn, his was brand new and full of colour. And where mine was hiding a pigeon chest and pot belly, his was clinging gloriously to a chunky set of abs, the sleeves practically ripping as they attempted to contain a bulging pair of biceps.

I smiled a defeated smile, my sails immediately windless.

"Hey, I thought I said not to bring anything?" said New Dave, as he spotted the box of Peroni I was carrying. The invite had strictly prohibited anyone from bringing any food or drink whatsoever. "This is supposed to be my treat, for all the banging and drilling over the last few weeks."

"Well, I couldn't turn up empty-handed," I insisted, squeezing his hand back as hard as I could.

"Well, that's damn good of you," he said, finally releasing my grip. "Let's get these in the fridge. And while they're chilling, I've got some amazing imported Belgian lagers. Really tasty and rather strong," he winked, as he went to take the beers from me.

"These are cold enough," I said, snatching them away.

Nice try, New Dave, I thought, you're not conning me with your fancy imported beers.

Catherine squeezed my arm, narrowing her eyes at me. A sure sign that I was in trouble for being rude.

"Okay, well whatever you want," smiled New Dave. "Make yourselves at home, I'll go and check on the barbecue. There's a beer fridge in the garage, so go and keep them cold in there. And I think Tamzin's in the kitchen. I know she's dying to give you the grand tour."

"Oh, I'm so excited to see all the work," swooned Catherine. Bloody traitor. "The garden looks amazing. And that pool – oh my God!"

Dave dashed off to flip his burgers and we went to the garage to offload the beers. I couldn't believe it. He had a six-foot SMEG fridge in there – his 'beer fridge'. A full-sized fridge, just for beer. The thing was immense. It was bigger than the fridge-freezer in our kitchen, which we used for our whole weekly shop. And this thing was just for beer. The opulence. The arrogance. The lucky bloody bastard.

I opened the door to find it crammed full of the most incredible array of imported beers and ciders. There were so many varieties, it was like looking through the pages of a beer encyclopaedia. There were cans and bottles of Doom Bar, Stella Artois, Birra Moretti, Asahi, Corona, Spitfire, Newcastle Brown, something called Dead Pony Club, and loads of beers I'd never even heard of.

The fridge was absolutely crammed full. There must have been at least £500 worth of beer in there. There were even 12 cans of Fosters crammed onto the bottom shelf – no prizes for guessing who'd brought those. I managed to find space on the top shelf and wedged the bottles of Peroni in. Then I opened one and took a long swig.

"Oh good," said Tamzin, appearing at our side, "you've found the beer fridge. But you shouldn't have brought anything with you, naughty. We said this was our treat."

"Is this fridge really just for beer?" I said, nonplussed.

"Yeah," replied Tamzin, shrugging. "One of Dave's toys. You know what men are like." She winked at Catherine. "Anyway, let me give you the tour."

We headed into the house to check out all the renovations. It took nearly half an hour, Tamzin droning on about what the builders had done and how much more space it gave them.

"I can't believe how light it is," said Catherine. "And who would have thought you'd get so much more space just from knocking that wall through. It's incredible. You must be so happy."

"Yes, it's not bad," said Tamzin, almost dismissively. She seemed to catch herself, then followed up with, "Don't get me wrong, we're really happy with what we've achieved, but it's not quite what the architect promised. The ceiling was supposed to be higher in the conservatory. And some of the materials he suggested – the fixtures and fittings, and some of the wood panels – they just didn't look great when they were in. So, we had to get the builder to tear bits down and start again. Obviously, the architect wasn't happy. Told us we were messing with his vision. But I said, you know, we're the ones that have to live with it. Jumped-up little berk. You know what architects can be like…" she laughed.

"Oh yes," said Catherine, trying to join in. I sneered at her. The woman had never met an architect in her life, let alone experienced any grievances about working with them.

Annoyingly, the house did look amazing. It still looked very much like ours from the front, but the inside was completely transformed. Walls had been moved, knocked down and added to create a completely new house inside. The kitchen was now in a different place, they'd doubled the size of the downstairs loo, widened the living room and created new rooms out the back. It was difficult to compare it to how it had previously been.

"Yeah, looks like a fairly decent job," I said, swigging back a large mouthful of Peroni.

"It's all down to the builders," said Tamzin. "They just really got on with things. I guess that's the benefit of paying a little extra for good people."

"So, what do you think, Dave?" said New Dave walking out of the kitchen with a giant pack of steaks in his hand.

"Yeah, it's good," I said, as neutrally as I could. "You must be pleased."

"Yep, not a bad place to hang my hat," he said.

"It gives me a few ideas, actually," I said. The words left my mouth before I realised they were coming. "We've been thinking of doing a few renovations to our place, too."

What was I saying? My mouth had taken control and my brain was struggling to keep up. Catherine flashed me a look to say, 'What the hell are you talking about?'

"Nothing quite as grand as this," I continued. "But we'd like an extension. Maybe a utility room. Knock through a few walls to add a bit more space."

"Sounds great," said New Dave. "Let me give you the number for the architect we used. He's not the cheapest, but he's good."

"So good!" agreed Tamzin.

We stood there in silence for a few moments, before New Dave finally broke the tension. "Anyway, you have to come and look at something. I think you're gonna be really impressed."

He led me out the back door and across the precision-cut lawn to a specially constructed barbecue station in the corner of the garden. The thing was incredible. Built out of brick, it must have been six feet wide and four feet high. There was a layer of decking at the base – a special platform for the barbecue chef. A small wooden roof sat atop four wooden pillars, keeping everything protected from the elements.

Not only had he greatly increased the size of his house, he'd even built a small house for his barbecue. We walked round to the front of it and my heart sank. There it was. The pièce de résistance. The MeatMaster 4000.

It was one of the most beautiful things I'd ever seen, at least a third bigger than my MeatMaster 3000. It had two separate grills, with separate lids. It had the same detachable rotisserie arm and burners at the side. It also had a bun warmer, and at the base was a pizza oven. I clenched my eyes shut, as I felt tears starting to well.

"Isn't it a beauty?" said New Dave.

I couldn't speak.

"Did you see the pizza oven at the base? I haven't actually used it yet, but I'm looking forward to trying it."

I tried to speak, but the words just wouldn't come.

"It's got three gas tanks, so you can actually cook for like 12 hours straight without needing to refuel. It even comes with a bloody drone, so when the burgers are done, you can fly them over to all the lazy people who can't be arsed to come and get them. Isn't that ridiculous?"

Heat blossomed in my cheeks as I tried to conceal my jealousy.

"Oh, and look at this. As well as the rotisserie arm, because this one has the double grill, you actually get an extended arm as well, so you can use it as a spit to do a hog roast. Isn't that crazy? You can cook a whole pig at once. We'll definitely have to get you guys over when we try that. Imagine that, a whole pig!"

He patted me on the back and it felt like every last breath went flooding out of my body. As I'd predicted, this new, improved MeatMaster made mine look like an absolute piece of crap. How could I ever cook on it again, knowing this glorious gem was just a few yards away? I could have cried.

"Anyway, how do you like your steak?" said New Dave.

*****

By 6.30pm, I was absolutely stuffed and more than a little drunk. I'd eaten so many burgers, chicken legs and steaks I'd already been through a fairly serious case of the meat sweats. And although I wouldn't have said I was drinking particularly heavily, in the few hours that I'd been there, I'd managed to get through all 12 of the Peronis I'd brought with me. I couldn't even blame Mike for helping me work through them, as he'd been far too interested in the beer emporium in the garage to even try and pinch any of mine. As soon as he'd seen the contents of New Dave's beer fridge, he'd gone on a mission to taste every one of the strong, imported beers. And I can only imagine he completed that task, as he'd been dragged home by his wife half an hour earlier, barely able to walk on his own.

The majority of the street's residents had departed at various intervals, and now only a small handful of drinkers remained, sitting around the garden table and chatting. Jack and Holly were back at our house, either playing video games or wasting their time watching overly confident idiots talking bollocks on YouTube.

Despite Catherine flashing me her 'I wouldn't if I were you' eyes, I'd cracked open a rather interesting Swedish lager called Pistonhead. And I was now waxing lyrical to anybody close enough to hear about the big new project I was working on, and how the work we were doing was so good I thought we might pick up a few industry awards.

I was feeling a little bit wobbly, but my mood had definitely improved. Rather than spending the whole day sulking in a corner, I'd decided to embrace the positives of the day. And, despite my initial reservations, I was actually having a good time. The beer had a lot to do with that.

"So, what does this event actually involve?" I heard Chris asking New Dave.

"Oh, it's nothing, really," said New Dave. "Just a bit of a run."

"Bit of a run?" chimed in Charlie. "If you're in the SAS, maybe."

"What's this?" I asked.

"Dave's signed up to do the Filthy Mutha Run in a few months," said Charlie. "It's absolutely brutal."

"Filthy Mutha Run?" I asked. "What is it?"

"Honestly, it's not that bad. It's a 10k run with a bit of an obstacle course built in. Just a few things to jump over. It'll be fine. And it's for charity, so…"

"Bit of an obstacle course?" laughed Charlie. "I've seen the website. You run through muddy ditches and swim through submerged tunnels. There's a 20-foot wall to climb, then you slide down into a giant ice bath."

"Jesus!" said Chris, wide-eyed.

"That's not all," laughed Charlie. "There's a bit where you have to carry heavy logs. There's a mine-field full of paint bombs. Electric fences to climb over. You even have to run through a tent full of tear gas… And that's all on top of running 10 bloody kilometres. It's seriously tough."

"Crikey," I said. "When are you doing this?"

"Oh, it's not for three months yet. But it's all for a good cause. Feel free to sponsor me, if you like."

"I'll do one better than that," I slurred. Again, my mouth was working without my brain's permission. "I'll sign up and do it with you." What the hell was my mouth doing? Where did that come from?

The whole table erupted with laughter. My wife was laughing the hardest. The smile dropped immediately from my face.

"What the hell are you all laughing at?" I slurred. "I'm serious."

"Yeah, course you are," said Chris.

"Yeah, I am, actually," I said. "In fact, I'm so serious, I bet you a hundred quid I finish ahead of you." I held out my hand to New Dave.

"Dave!" said Catherine, angrily. Everyone around the table laughed.

"No, come on. A hundred quid, or are you scared?"

"Okay," said New Dave, embarrassed. He tentatively shook my hand. "Nothing like a little wager to focus the training, I guess, but I mean it's all…"

"Fucking hundred quid," I slurred. "Easy money."

Catherine folded her arms across her chest, shook her head and gave me *that* look. I shrugged it off.

"No offence, mate, but when was the last time you ran further then the end of the street?" said Charlie. "Let alone 10k, jumping over electric fences."

"Screw you," I said. "I'll have you know I used to run all the time. I was pretty good. And I've run loads of 10k races in the past. This dirty mother don't sound too bad!"

"Oh, you haven't run a 10k in years though, love," said Catherine, changing tack and trying to bargain with me.

Et tu, you traitorous wife, I thought.

"No, but it's just like riding a bike, isn't it? I can quickly get back into it." My words were really slurring now. "Besides, I've been looking to get fit again. This could be exactly the motivation I need to get in shape. When did you say, three months? Piece of piss. I'll be running 10k, dodging mimes and hopping over eclectic fences before you know it! Then I'll be round for my hundred quid."

What the hell was I doing? I had the perfect way to get out of this. I could have blamed on it too much drink. I could have played it off as a big joke, without losing face. But I couldn't help it. I just dug myself deeper and deeper.

"Come on, Dave, don't be silly," said Catherine, her eyes imploring.

"Silly?" I said. "Silly? I'll show you who's silly. I *will* sign up for this race. And I'll raise loads of money for charity. And I'll probably fucking even win it, too. That'll bloody show you, won't it?"

The mood changed instantly. The gentle mocking ceased. An awkward silence hung between us. People sat uncomfortably looking at their shoes, the stars, the drinks in their hands.

"You know… you move in here," I slurred, pointing at New Dave, my head swimming and my hand wobbling, "and you're like the best bloody thing since sliced cheese. Er… bread, I mean. The best thing since cheese bread. And I'm sick of it, actually. Because you're not better than me. Not really."

The words were coming thick and fast. I'd tapped into a rich vein of resentment.

"You know… you're a man," I continued rambling. "And I'm a man. And you're a man. And… you know, other men can do equally… And it's not about how much you've got… or the size of your… barbecue… or how nice your hair is… or how many fucking beer fridges you've got… What I mean is…" And then the words just stopped, my train of thought derailing violently.

Everyone looked on curiously, wondering if I was going to continue my tirade. But my brain had crashed. My mouth was no longer receiving any signal.

Another very awkward silence.

"Well, if you're up for it, then I think that's brilliant," said New Dave, overenthusiastically. "Hey, we could even train together, if you fancy it?"

"There you go. At least someone believes in me. Thank you, David." I turned to look at Catherine. I thought I was sneering and delivering menace with my eyes. But I probably just looked drunk and squint-eyed.

"Anyway," I said, standing awkwardly onto wobbly legs, "I need a piss."

I pushed back my chair, accidentally knocking it over as I stepped away from the table. As I walked off towards the back door of the house, I suddenly felt very unstable.

It came over me like a wave. The world went wildly out of focus. I could barely keep my eyes open. My legs felt weak, like they could barely carry my weight. I swayed, my head swimming, and I wobbled this way and that. The more I tried to keep a straight line, the more my body chose to lurch violently in the opposite direction, like I was fighting a powerful magnet. It was hard enough just staying upright, let alone moving forwards.

Aware that everyone was watching me, I pigeon-stepped across the lawn, trying to stay as straight and upright as I could. I could see the swimming pool in my peripheral vision, and I tried to keep as far from it as possible. I locked in on the light from the door in front of me. All

I had to do was walk straight. But the harder I tried, the more I felt myself drifting to the left. Towards the pool.

"Careful of the pool," I heard someone shout out behind me.

"Yes, thank you," I shouted back, "I'm perfectly capable of not falling in a swimming pool, thank you."

Did I say thank you twice? I thought, as I continued to walk, stumbling closer and closer to the pool. And did I really just sign up to run a 10k obstacle course, climbing over electric fences?

I straightened myself again. I walked slowly and steadily, like a drunk driver trying to convince a police officer I was sober. One foot in front of the other. Move towards the light. Just walk in a straight line.

But the swimming pool's magnetic pull grew stronger. And the more I tried to fight it, the more it pulled me closer.

"Dave, seriously," I heard Catherine call out behind me.

I threw my hand up in the air, the middle digit extended in an act of childish rebellion. And that was all it took to completely unbalance me. I swerved violently to the left, tripping over my own feet, hopping, lurching and dancing until I tumbled over.

I went into the water sideways. Completely disoriented, my mouth and nose instantly filled with water and I sank straight to the bottom of the pool. Strangely, I don't remember panicking, flailing or splashing about. I simply went limp and descended until I landed on the bottom.

I've thought back to it several times, and I still can't quite explain the feeling. I knew I was under water. And I knew I had to get out of the water. If I didn't get out then I would die.

But submerged there, weightless and slowly sinking, I suddenly felt calm. So very calm. It was like I was in another time and place. All my stress and worries and inadequacies simply melted away. I was a baby in the womb, still unharmed by the cruelties of the world. Nothing could get me. I could feel no pain. I was totally content. And so I just lay there, making no attempt to rescue myself.

Whether this feeling would have lasted, or my natural 'fight or flight' instincts would eventually have kicked in, I'll never know. Because as I lay there, looking up at the bright white stars refracted by the water, I suddenly saw a dark figure break the surface. It came rushing down towards me, the water displaced violently, making me sway and crash against the bottom of the pool.

Strong hands gripped my t-shirt, yanking it so the material rucked up under my armpits. And then I was moving, rushing up through the water. Gliding towards the stars, suddenly awake and aware.

My head broke through the surface. I coughed out mouthfuls of water. My body reacted to the brief lack of oxygen, pulling in lungfuls of air as I coughed, then breathed, coughed and breathed.

And then I was moving again. The strong arms pulling me backwards through the water. I tried to fight them off, but I had no energy. I just floated there, coughing and spluttering as New Dave kicked and swam, pulling me to the edge of the pool.

Then we stopped. I looked up to see several people gathered around the edge, talking loud and hurriedly. Hands reached down, grabbed hold of me and pulled me up and out of the water. Then I was on the hard ground, someone pushing me onto my side and rubbing my back vigorously, as I coughed and retched.

After that, it's all a blur. I vaguely remember people helping me to my feet, shining lights in my eyes and asking if I was okay. I remember Catherine supporting my weight as she guided me home, her perfume tickling my nose and my water-logged trainers squelching loudly with each step. I remember the slap of wet clothes hitting the tiled floor as Catherine helped me undress in the bathroom, before then guiding me to bed.

And, just before I passed out, drunk and exhausted, cold and wet, I remember thinking how New Dave had got one over on me again.

CHAPTER 9
PROMOTING VIOLENCE

I SPENT THE next few weeks avoiding New Dave. I reverted back to the tactics I'd used to avoid Nigel, alternating my route home from work, leaving the office at different times and going into near-hibernation at the weekends. Anything to ensure there was no chance of bumping into him.

I know it was childish. But I was embarrassed. I couldn't look him in the eye. Even when Catherine reassured me that he wouldn't think badly of me, and that I really should go and thank him for rescuing me, I just couldn't. I could barely bring myself to sign the thank you card she bought, then delivered on my behalf.

To New Dave's credit, he didn't come around complaining about my behaviour. He didn't gloat or boast about how he'd saved my life. And I didn't hear any reports of him backbiting, joking or criticising me with the other residents of the street. I had no doubt some of the others were gleefully rubbing their hands together as they laughed about the best bit of gossip to hit street in years. But not New Dave.

He did pop round the day after it happened, to check whether I was okay. Of course, I refused to see him, partly on account of my complete shame at what I'd done – but mostly because my head was pounding so badly from the hangover, I didn't actually make it out of bed until just after 7pm.

When I'd first woken up, I had no recollection of what happened. I knew I must have been very drunk, due to the pneumatic drill going off in my head and the large bowl Catherine had set on the floor next to the bed – and which I had apparently been sick into.

Catherine was upset. She'd got up early and hadn't been back to check on me. She hadn't even brought me tea or toast, which she usually does when I have one of my bad hangovers.

The last thing I could remember was drinking a beer, eating a burger and acting in a very genial, friendly manner. When Catherine finally relented and brought me some paracetamol and Alka Seltzer – after my third time of vomiting – she sat on the bed and recounted the full horror of my actions.

As I lay there in bed, small glimpses of the day came back to me. Tiny shards of memories, gradually collecting until I could piece together a rough image of my embarrassment. Finally, I remembered drinking all those Peronis. I could picture the bored looks on faces as I slurred my way through dull stories. I remembered eating too much and sitting in a sun-lounger as the meat sweats trickled down my forehead.

I remembered being obnoxious and defensive, swearing at my wife for simply looking out for me. And, of course, I remember falling into the swimming pool.

I crawled under the covers to hide my head. I couldn't even bring myself to turn on Netflix and soothe my hangover with a movie. I just lay there, squirming and cursing myself.

And so, I spent the next few weeks avoiding everybody and trying to pretend like nothing had happened. But, most of all, I avoided New Dave. Not just because I'd let myself down, acting like a drunken fool and ruining the end of his party. I was more upset that he'd been the one to rescue me. He'd saved my life. And he'd proved, once again, that he was better than me.

I'd never saved anybody's life. The closest I ever came was rescuing birds and mice from the cat's mouth. Even then, I didn't always manage to intervene quick enough to actually save their lives – instead squeamishly wrapping their mangled, part-chewed bodies in carrier bags and concealing them at the bottom of the kitchen bin (after telling Catherine and the kids I'd given them a respectful burial in the garden).

New Dave – great, noble, powerful Dave – had saved an actual human life. And worse than that, it was *my* bloody life.

That 46% seemed more real, more justified than ever before. In fact, if I added New Dave's real-life heroism into the mix – his saving a life compared with my life having to be saved – I was sure the percentage would skew even further in his favour.

The one thing it had spurred me into, however, was preparing for the Filthy Mutha race that I'd unwittingly tricked myself into entering. I'd winced when I looked at the website and realised the full horror of what I'd subjected myself to. The 10k run I wasn't concerned about. I'd run similar distances in the past. And although it was a while since I'd done it, I knew I could get fit enough to finish the race.

It was the rest that had me panicking. There were great pits of muddy water to wade through. Long sections of barbed wire to crawl under. There was, indeed, a tent full of tear gas and a paint bomb minefield. And the electric fences had apparently been upgraded to what looked like a room full of exposed wires hanging down, and which you had to run through. There was also something called The Freezer – a giant pool of icy water. The website featured videos of people hurtling down an inflatable slide into it. Their faces as they hit the water were pictures of complete agony. Their screams and coughs, as they gasped for breath, rung loudly in my ears.

I continued scrolling through the website. There were obstacles to climb, heavy things to carry. And mud. So much mud. My heart was thudding just reading the details.

The website showed pictures of people running, absolutely exhausted but somehow still smiling widely. Surely those smiles were Photoshopped in. The whole thing was pure masochism. How could anyone possibly enjoy it? Outside of Special Forces servicemen, I couldn't believe anyone would even be allowed to take part in such an event – let alone willingly pay over £100 to subject themselves to that level of horror.

"You know, you don't actually have to go through with it," said Catherine, looking over my shoulder at the site. "You were drunk when you said it. Nobody thinks you were serious. In fact, I bet nobody even remembers."

"I can't back out now, Cath," I said. "I'm not losing face over this as well. All I need is a bit of training and I'll be fine. Besides, I could do with getting back in shape."

"No arguments from me," she'd said, giggling and jokingly pinching the soft flab of my belly. I did not laugh back.

I filled in the entry form, paid my fee and downloaded some sponsorship forms. The next day I went into town and spent £150 on special running shoes, shorts and t-shirts. I then spent another £200 on a watch that would track my runs, measure my heartbeat and give me all the stats the salesman assured me I definitely needed.

Over the next few weeks, I managed to stick to a rigid schedule of running, going out three times a week after work. It was hellish to begin with, and I ran less than a full mile the first time out. My legs ached so much I could barely walk for two days, and going up and down stairs was practically impossible. But my pig-headedness helped me power through, and after three weeks I was running two miles, with hardly any breaks to catch my breath.

Surprisingly, people at work were very generous with their sponsorship pledges. I was set to raise £343 for Cancer Research. I suspected their generosity was motivated less by philanthropy and more by a desire to see me in real physical pain. This suspicion was reinforced by the unusually large donation of £50 from Steve, and the fact he'd laughed so hard he could barely hold the pen to sign his name. So, now there was literally no getting out of it. Unless I broke an ankle.

After a few weeks, the training was going well and I actually felt pretty good. I was slightly fitter and my mood had improved. I even felt like I was losing weight, although the bathroom scales were in denial. And I was feeling better about New Dave. The embarrassment of the swimming pool incident had subsided, and I was putting my 46% plan into action.

Work was going well, too. Steve and I landed the big account we'd been trying to win for the past two months. So, I was feeling confident when Thomson called me to his office to 'discuss a few changes'.

"You deserve it mate," said Steve, patting me on the back. "And, don't forget, I'm expecting plenty of perks when you're running the place: longer lunch breaks, more holiday, better coffee in the kitchen. Ooh, and a beer fridge. No point being best mates with the boss if you can't get a little something out of it."

"I'll see what I can do," I laughed.

And I felt really good, until I walked into Thomson's office and saw Zack sitting next to him on the sofa.

I don't like Zack. Nobody does. I took an instant dislike to him on his very first day, when he walked in with an air of arrogance so great he made Liam Gallagher look humble. And he's done nothing since to dissuade me of the opinion that he's a useless, talentless moron with an over-inflated ego and a deranged sense of self-worth.

Zack was the agency's other creative director. He'd been brought in just under a year previously, and quickly proved himself completely unsuited to the job. He seemingly knew very little about the creative process. His ideas (when he actually had any) were weak and obvious. And he stole credit for other people's work whenever he could. In addition, he was a loathsome little shit, with such a big chip on his shoulder he rubbed everyone up the wrong way – even Sarah, the nicest, friendliest person in the whole agency (maybe even the world). She took me to one side after a particularly arduous meeting with Zack, during which he apparently spent an hour disinterestedly doodling pictures on his iPad and ignoring all of her ideas. She told me she thought he was a dick and point-blank refused to work with him again.

We'd all been confused about how Zack had talked himself into the job, and how the senior management team hadn't realised his ineptitude and sacked him within weeks. Then we did a little digging and found out the real reason he'd been hired. After that, we left him alone, hoping he wouldn't screw anything up too badly. In fact, it was on my list, after I got promoted, to have a serious chat with him about bucking his ideas up.

So, I was somewhat confused to see him on the sofa next to Thomson.

"Dave," said Thomson, as I poked my head round the door. "Come in. Sit down."

I walked in and sat down in the chair opposite them.

"Great work on the KODEK account. Really super creative. I think this is going to be a fantastic client to work with. We were blown away by the concepts and I know the clients were really impressed. They emailed me to say it's the best creative work they've ever seen. Seriously."

"Oh, thank you," I said, my ego inflating like a bouncy castle. "I'm really pleased. Makes all the hard work and extra hours worth it."

"Exactly. And a fantastic bit of business for the company. Really good."

"Great," I said.

"Now, of course," said Thomson, "winning a client this big means we're going to have to look at the structure of the business. We need to make sure we've got all the best people in the right places, don't we?"

"Yes," I agreed, struggling to hold in the excitement and self-congratulation, "the *best* people." I practically winked at him.

"There's a hell of a lot to do over the next 12 months. Lots of creative and plenty of project management to hit some pretty crazy deadlines," said Thomson.

Zack was being strangely conspicuous in his silence.

"So, as I say, we have to have the very best people in the right places. Which means we've had a look at the budgets and the good news is we'll be able to strengthen the creative team with a few key additions. We'll also be able to unlock more funds for freelancers."

"Great," I said, wishing he'd get to the point already.

"Of course, that's just day-to-day stuff," continued Thomson. "We also have to look at other levels." He was waffling now, almost hesitant. Skirting around the words as if he didn't want to say the next part.

"Mmm hmm," I said.

"So, we're promoting Zack to Executive Creative Director, to oversee the whole creative team."

All the air flooded out of my lungs in one quick exhale. The walls throbbed around me. A sharp pain pulsed in the centre of my brain.

"You'll report directly into Zack," continued Thomson, his words echoing, sounding far away now, like he was in another room. "He'll be there to support you, keep things on track… keep the ship steady," he laughed.

My vision blurred. I could feel the heat in my cheeks, rising up from my neck until my whole face was on fire.

"Now, I certainly don't want to come in and make big changes…" It was Zack speaking now, all tinny and distant. I stared back at them both, unable to move or speak.

I felt lost. Confused. The idiot who thinks he hears his name called out at an awards ceremony and races up to the stage to claim his prize, only to find himself looking at a sea of blank, unforgiving faces.

Heat pulsed in my face. Then everything came rushing back into focus.

"I'm sorry, what did you say?" They looked startled as I interrupted them. "I could have sworn you just said you were promoting Zack to Executive Creative Director."

"Now look," said Thomson, his tone changing. His face turned stern and cold. "I know this might not be what you were expecting, but…"

"Not what I was expecting? You're damn right it's not. I was expecting you to promote *me*."

"Look Dave, I'm not sure I…"

"You told me! You fucking well told me! You said it was in the bag. Win the business and I can expect big changes. That's what you said."

"I'm sorry if you misconstrued what I said, but…"

"Misconstrued? Why are you doing this? You promised me that promotion."

"We did consider you, Dave, but I certainly made no promises. And I'm sorry if you're disappointed, but we've made our decision. We feel Zack is the best person to take on this role."

"The best person? He's been with us less than a year. I've been here for 10. I've won millions of pounds worth of business over the years, and what's he ever done? He's never won a single pitch." I could hear the anger in my own voice. Every single word burned in my throat as I got louder and louder.

Zack was silent again, now finding his shoes incredibly interesting.

"And what do you have to say about this?" I asked. "You really think you deserve this job over me?"

"Look, I think we all have our own talents, Dave," said Zack, finally meeting my eye, "and mine are more…"

"It's not all about money, or winning projects, Dave," interjected Thomson. "As I say, it's about having the best people in the right places. Nobody's questioning your ability. We all think you're fantastic at your job. And we want that to continue. We want you to carry on leading projects, working with Steve and producing the excellent creative work we know you can. We just think Zack is better suited for the managerial responsibilities of the more senior role."

"Oh really?" I shouted. "And it has nothing to do with the fact he's married to your fucking daughter?"

"Now, Dave, be careful what you're accusing people of. This decision was based solely on ability. It has nothing to do with…"

"That's complete bullshit, you gutless spunk-bubble!" I shouted. "It's nepotism of the worst fucking kind."

I stood up, staring down at them both. Without warning, and before I knew I was going to do it, my leg jolted forwards, kicking the small coffee table between us. Cups and saucers went bouncing to the floor. A full cafetière of coffee tumbled after them, the lid bouncing off and the contents spilling out all over the rug.

"Dave, really, there's no need for that," shouted Thomson, as the two men jumped up from their seats, seemingly more concerned with keeping their expensive shoes dry than the moral repugnance of their deceitful decision.

"There's every fucking need for it," I said, darting over to Thomson's desk and petulantly pushing a stack of papers and a desk tidy full of pens onto the floor. "You can't treat people like this," I shouted as loud as I could. My anger was in full flow, I couldn't hold back. "It's not fucking fair."

I ran towards them, and they both scurried out of the way, darting round behind Thomson's desk. I bent down, grabbed the front of the sofa and flipped it up onto its back with a loud roar. It didn't do enough to quell the burning anger in my chest, so I picked up one of the discarded coffee cups and threw it down until it smashed on the hard, laminate flooring.

That was more like it. The smashing sound rang deliciously in my ears. The adrenaline coursed through me. I picked up another cup and smashed it. Then another. Then another, until I was out of cups.

Still the anger pulsed in my chest.

I suddenly became aware that I was growling. Manic and deranged. Breathing heavily and looking for more to destroy. I caught sight of the bookcase next to Thomson's desk. I dashed over to it and picked up a small porcelain elephant.

"Now, Dave," said Thomson, genuine panic in his eyes. "That's quite enough. I know you're upset, but…"

"Upset?" I shouted. "You haven't even seen upset." I threw the elephant to the ground, delighting in the loud crash as its trunk came flying off. I picked up another of the pretentious little trinkets. Rather than aiming at the floor, this time I held it high and started moving towards Thomson and Zack.

They panicked, practically falling over themselves as they darted out from behind the desk and ran out of the room, slamming the door behind them. I threw it after them and it smashed on the doorframe.

The rest of the incident has become something of a blur in my mind. I apparently spent another seven minutes in the office, working my way through every breakable object before tipping the desk over and snapping Thomson's laptop into two pieces.

Finally, Jared the security guard found me sitting on the floor, leaning against the upturned sofa and weeping quietly. He helped me to my feet, escorted me to my car and sent me home for the rest of the day.

******

I arrived home at 4.32pm to a cold, quiet, empty house. Catherine was still at work and wouldn't be back till late. Jack was at football practice, then going for pizza with the team. And I remember Holly saying something about having dinner at a friend's house. She'd been hanging around a lot recently with a new friend, Isobel, whose whole family were vegans. Naturally, Holly had spent the last few weeks telling us she also planned to go vegan – demanding we buy special foods in the weekly shop and citing various articles she'd read, which extolled the virtues of a meat-free diet and heavily criticised the conditions of British farms. Dinner at Isobel's was to be her first vegan meal. Jack and I had cruelly laughed at the prospect, and poor Holly had stormed out, desperate to prove us wrong.

It was pretty mean and also rather stupid on my part. My daughter is one of the most stubborn people I've ever met. I've no idea where she gets it from, despite Catherine saying she's exactly like me in that way. So, I had no doubt that she'd return that evening a fully-fledged vegan – whether she enjoyed the meal or not. She was more than capable of sticking with things – even when we could all tell she really didn't enjoy them and was only doing it out of sheer bloody-mindedness.

It felt surreal and uncomfortable being home so early. I felt like an intruder. I wasn't supposed to be there. I should still be at work.

I walked into the living room, sank down onto the sofa and sat there feeling utterly wretched, turning the events of the afternoon over in my mind. How dare they treat me that way? How could they? Couldn't they see what a mistake they were making?

More importantly, why had I reacted like that? I'd got so angry so quickly. Had I really flipped the table over? Smashed cups and thrown things? What was happening to me? A cold chill shuddered through me as I recalled all the details.

They were sure to fire me. How could they not? Never mind being turned down for a promotion, I'd be lucky ever to work again. God, what had I done? I sat there staring at my mobile phone, waiting for the call to tell me never to come back to the office again.

"Hi, love," said Catherine, walking in through the front door a few hours later. "Sorry, I'm so late. Parents' evening overran, as usual. Honestly, some of these people just want to chew your ears off," she said, taking off her coat and bag as she walked through the house. "They expect full presentations on how great their kids are, and what little angels they are, and how we should all be so proud of them. Never mind the queue of people stacking up behind them. And then you get the ones who want to blame *me* because *their* child is falling behind, when they clearly offer very little support or encouragement at home. And… I'm sorry, I know I shouldn't say it, but sometimes their kids are just thick. I mean, I can't work miracles. Are the kids still…"

She stopped as she walked into the living room to find me sitting in almost complete darkness, looking like the world had just ended.

"Jesus, Dave," she said. "What's happened?"

I told her the full story. She looked angry when I told her about Thomson's betrayal and giving the job to Zack. She looked stunned when I told about losing my temper and overreacting. And she looked worried when the realisation sunk in that I might now be unemployed. When I finished, she sat very calmly for a few minutes, quietly holding my hands.

"Well, stuff them," she said suddenly, anger singing in her voice. "Sod those idiots. They don't deserve you anyway. How dare they treat you like that? After all your hard work? We should sue."

"Sue?" I said.

"Thomson promised you that job. It's a verbal contract, isn't it?"

"I'm not sure it works like that, love."

"Well, it should. They can't go promising promotions, then go and…" She ran out of words, her face reddening with anger. "Well, anyway, if that's what they're like, you're better off out of it."

"But the money, Cath. How will we pay the mortgage, or the bills, or…?"

"We'll find a way," she said, cutting me off. "We've been in worse situations than this. We've always survived. And you'll bounce back. You'll get a much better job somewhere else."

I thought she'd be angry with me. But she was only angry on my behalf. She was so supportive, even when I'd massively screwed up.

"So, you're not upset with me?" I asked.

"Well, you probably shouldn't have lost your temper. Smashing up your boss's office? I mean, they'll have to sack you now, won't they? But under the circumstances, I don't blame you. It's a good job I wasn't in the room with you. I'd have broken more than a laptop and some daft little trinkets." She gave a small, reassuring laugh.

"Really?" I said.

"Yeah, screw them. I've been telling you for ages you should work somewhere that they actually appreciate you. They'll be the ones who miss you, I promise. We'll get through this."

She hugged me hard, placing her head on my chest, and we just sat there for a while, cuddling. I knew she wanted to comfort me. But I also knew she didn't want me to see the worry in her eyes.

CHAPTER 10
BACK TO IT

"DID YOU REALLY call Thomson a gutless spunk-bubble?" laughed Steve, as he placed a latte down in front of me. He'd taken me to the café down the road from the office to get the inside story.

"Honestly, mate, I don't remember," I said, shivering with embarrassment. "It's all a bit of a blur. I suppose I might have said it…"

"Man, I wish I could have seen it," said Steve, smiling like a little boy. "I'd love to smash up Thomson's office, the smug git. In fact, I can think of a few people who'd get it."

"It wasn't guts, mate," I said, shamefaced. "Pretty stupid, really. I just lost it."

Miraculously, I didn't get fired from my job. Not entirely certain what to do, I went into work as normal the next day, figuring I'd just see what happened. I was met by Jared as soon as I pulled into the car park. So, naturally, I thought the worst. He escorted me straight to the boardroom, where I was met by Thomson, Melanie from HR and, for some reason, Peter from Facilities Management. At first, I thought he was there to complain about the damage I'd done, or to present me with a bill for fixing it. But they explained that Peter was there as a moral support companion. I was pretty sure I didn't need one, but I shrugged and we smiled awkwardly at each other.

I was expecting them to sack me. After such a violent outburst, I didn't see how they could keep me on. It was gross misconduct of the highest order – about as gross as it could get.

But they didn't fire me. Rather than read me the riot act, they adopted this very calm, caring-sharing tone as they spoke. They didn't attack or accuse me; or call me a nutter. Instead, they asked how I was feeling. Was I suffering from stress? Did I need to see a doctor, or a therapist? Did I feel like the business was making me work too hard, or was it putting me under too much strain?

Stranger still, they seemed unusually concerned about how they might help me. They assured me I was a very valued member of the

AIP Communications family, and they were committed to helping me 'feel well' again.

At the end of the meeting, they handed me a book about coping with stress and sent me off for an extra week of paid leave to recharge myself. It was a suspension, of course. Both Melanie and Thomson were loath to describe it as such, but I knew they just wanted me out of the office for a while. Peter simply sat there looking confused and embarrassed.

Naturally, they went on to admonish me – in the gentlest possible way – and let me know that my behaviour was certainly not the sort of the thing they could tolerate in the future. Finally, Melanie told me they would be happy to have me back in the office on condition of me admitting I needed help. My future employment with the company was dependant on me attending a 10-week course of mindfulness training – which would help me learn techniques for tackling stress.

At the time, I was incredibly grateful they were letting me keep my job. And I went home relieved that I still had paid income.

When I told Catherine the good news, she asked me whether it was something I actually wanted. Again, she told me she'd stand by me if I wanted to walk out on them and find another job. But I could also hear the relief in her voice when I said I'd better stick it out for a while, at least until I had a more solid plan.

Of course, I should have told them to stick their job; I should have gone out and found an employer who actually valued me. But when the cold light of mortgage payments, food bills, kids' school uniforms, car insurance and the balance of next year's pre-booked holiday start to hit home, it's not so easy to be brave and principled. Besides, what company was going to hire the nutcase who threw a paddy and smashed up his boss's office?

I should have known they weren't going to sack me. Not because they were worried about being liable for inflicting stress upon me. And not because they feared I'd go to a rival agency. The fact was, they actually couldn't afford to get rid of me. Not just yet, anyway.

It was me and Steve who had won the big new contract bringing in millions of pounds. And the new client was not only expecting to work with me, they were looking forward to it. I was the one they had a good rapport with; the one whose creative work they'd bought into. Get rid of me and there was a good chance the client would rethink and cancel the job. Or at least scale it back from a few million to just a few thousand pounds. I've seen it happen before.

The company couldn't sack me if they wanted to. And what were a few smashed ornaments and a broken laptop between Thomson and his golden goose of an employee? So, he'd slapped on a fake smile and pretended he was happy to keep me – no doubt already strategising about how to sack me later on.

I spent a fairly bored, paranoid week at home, coming to terms with what I'd done, and trying to reconcile myself with the new position I'd be returning to. My job would be unchanged, but I'd now be reporting in to an underqualified, jumped-up, odious little prick who'd only beaten me to a promotion because of who he was married to. And our new working relationship had hardly got off to the best possible start – what with me screaming and swearing and throwing small porcelain animals at his head.

I was embarrassed – not only at my overreaction, but about not getting my promotion. I'd been so cocksure about it. I cringed when I thought about promising to 'see what I could do' for Steve when I became his boss.

I was also terrified of the office rumour mill, and what they'd be saying:

'Did you see what that nutter Brookman did, smashing up that office?'

'I heard he was foaming at the mouth as he broke coffee cups!'

'What a cry-baby! He didn't even deserve that promotion anyway.'

If there's one thing people in an office love, it's a good bit of gossip.

"Don't sweat it, mate," said Steve, slurping back a large mouthful of latte. "People were fascinated for a couple of hours, then it all died down when they moved on to the next bit of gossip. Speaking of which, did you know Paula from Accounts is pregnant by Tom from Marketing? She's begged him to leave his wife, but he's told her to get rid of it."

"You're joking," I said.

"Actually, yes. I made that one up to take the heat off you. Plus a few other bits of scandalous nonsense to keep people twitching. Believe me, you're not the talk of the office anymore."

"Cheers, mate," I said. "You're a good friend. And a bloody devious one, too. So, is Paula from Accounts actually pregnant?"

"No, just a bit fat, I think," laughed Steve. "But it helped convince people."

"Seriously, though, I hope none of this blows back on you. I've probably screwed my own career. I hope I haven't damaged yours."

"Fuck that," he laughed, "I'm big enough and ugly enough to take care of myself. I just wish I'd thought of doing it."

"Eh?"

"You got to put those two bell-ends in their place. You destroyed a whole office. And then they gave you a week's free holiday as a reward. Sounds pretty good to me."

"It's not quite as simple as that," I reasoned. "I have to go to these Mindfulness things too."

"Piece of piss! You sit in a room for an hour, learn a few breathing exercises... they're even letting you do it in the middle of the afternoon. So you get even more time off."

"Yeah, well, I'd rather not have to go."

"You'll be all right, mate. And listen, seriously, I'm sorry you didn't get the promotion. You deserved it. It's a fucking disgrace what they've done. But that little shit will trip up soon enough."

"Yeah, I hope so," I said. "I really hope so."

******

The rest of the day was thankfully less dramatic than I'd been expecting. I got the odd funny look from people in the kitchen. One of the receptionists, Bev, was clearly dying to ask me about what happened, but lost interest when poor Paula from Accounts walked by. Steve's little fabrication really had drawn the heat away, I thought, if one of the biggest gossips in the office wasn't interested in me.

I spent the day with my head buried firmly in the new project Steve and I were working on. I even managed to go a whole day without seeing Zack, although I was sure I could feel his presence looming around the corner several times. I figured he was just as nervous about seeing me as I was of him.

Not only would he have been worried about me blowing my lid again, he was also now my boss. I knew he'd want to 'have a chat' with me at some point. He'd probably organise some private meeting to discuss how we could best work together. No doubt lay down the law about how he saw *his* creative team operating, and my new role as his subordinate. I was relieved – and not at all surprised – that he'd been too cowardly to do it straight away. But I still had that displeasure to come.

The work was helpful. It took my mind off things. And, for about eight hours, I managed to concentrate on something else. At least until I saw it there, flashing out at me from my computer's desktop: the spreadsheet entitled *New Dave*.

I clicked it open and everything came flooding back. The jealousy. The feelings of inadequacy. The gut-wrenching sense of failure.

I scanned down the list of differences between us. Nothing had changed. He was still 46% better than me. I considered adding my most recent misfortune to the list: *Embarrassingly flies off handle and smashes up boss's office after missing out on promotion, ensuring against any future success within company.*

I wasn't sure how to quantify it into numbers. And I was feeling bad enough about myself already. I couldn't bear the thought of my deficit growing any bigger than 46%. Besides, it was possible that New Dave had experienced a similar episode in his life. Maybe he'd also lost it at a boss over a bad decision or unfair judgement.

He'd have done it much better, though. He wouldn't just have flipped a desk and thrown some ornaments, he'd probably have pulled out some slick karate moves and chopped the desk in half. Then he'd have stormed out of the company, point-blank refusing to take their bullshit, and walked into a much higher-paid job within the hour.

He certainly wouldn't have spent a paranoid week hiding at home worrying about his future. He wouldn't have gone crawling back, happy to take whatever demeaning treatment they dished out, thankful that they let him keep his job. And he wouldn't have submitted to working for a feckless, useless, under-qualified moron who'd only been promoted because of whose daughter he was shagging.

I clicked onto the second tab and reviewed my plan to improve the deficit between me and New Dave. I'd made very little progress. The first two items on the list practically screamed failure at me. I hadn't managed to secure the promotion I was so confident of receiving. After my meltdown, it felt even further away. There was no telling how long I'd be stuck in the same job now.

That first failure heavily impacted the second point on my action plan. No promotion meant no pay rise. And again, the chances of getting one now seemed out of my grasp.

Point three: 'Get fit and lose weight'. I still had a plan in place for that. I looked down at the circular lump of belly spilling heavily over the edge of my belt. I was clearly making no great strides there, either. I still had the big race coming up. With that goal in mind, it was still possible I could improve my fitness and drop a few pounds. But, truth be told, my preparation wasn't going to plan. I hadn't stuck to my own training regime. The healthy diet had gone out of the window in favour of a week of bingeing and stress-eating. And, rather than using my week off to go running, I'd spent most of it lingering gloomily in bed or in front of the telly.

The date of the race was closing in on me and I did seriously need to get training, or I wouldn't be able to do it. There was no way to back out, now that people had sponsored me. And it was one of the few ways I still had left to get one over on New Dave.

I made a mental note to get out for a run. Probably not that night after work – it was my first day back in the office, and I was pretty tired. But definitely the next day. And if not then, definitely the day after.

I scanned down the list to item four. Now, there was something I could do. It would certainly make me feel better. And it would definitely help claw back a few points in the battle of the Daves.

It was something I was planning on doing anyway, after I got my pay rise. Okay, I hadn't actually got the raise, but it was still on the 'To do' list. I deserved it. I worked hard, didn't I? Why shouldn't I treat myself every now and then?

Besides, it was more a practicality than a desire. It was something to benefit the whole family, not just me.

I logged into my online banking and checked the balance of the savings account. There was certainly enough there for what I needed. And I was pretty sure the place would still be open for at least another hour.

I packed up my laptop, grabbed my coat and practically skipped out of the office.

CHAPTER 11
NEW WHEELS

"WHAT THE HELL have you done?" said Catherine, not nearly as excited as I hoped she'd be.

"What do you mean?" I said, knowing exactly what she meant.

"Wow, this is totally cool," said Jack, opening the door of the new car and clambering onto the front passenger seat. They'd both come rushing out to see what was going on as I pulled into the drive, enthusiastically beeping the horn.

After leaving the office, I'd stopped in at the local car supermarket. I hadn't expected to buy a car right there and then; I'd just popped in to take a look. Maybe sit in a few cars and see what I could get for the budget I'd worked out. But as soon as I walked in, I saw the most beautiful Mercedes C220 sitting there. And it had a sign in the front windscreen that said, 'Take me home today'.

It was a siren song. Destiny. And I was powerless to resist.

Jet black and shiny, it was only two years old, with 31,000 miles on the clock. It was loaded with added extras, built in Wi-Fi and a very complicated central computer system. There were dials and displays everywhere, a way to connect my phone via Bluetooth, and buttons all over the steering wheel. Compared with sitting in the ageing Ford Focus I'd arrived in it was like being in a spaceship. As soon as I sat in the driver's seat, I knew I had to have it. And with the giant grin on my face, the salesmen must have been clambering over each other to get to me.

"Wow, it's got an awesome stereo system," continued Jack. "And SATNAV. And cup-holders. How fast does it go, Dad?"

"It goes pretty fast," I said, thankful that at least someone was excited. "Why don't I take you for a quick spin around the block?"

"Yeah, sweet," said Jack, reaching for the seat belt.

"No," said Catherine. "Jack has homework to do. Maybe… *maybe*, your dad will take you for a drive after dinner. Now go inside, please, and get on with it."

Jack humphed, climbed out of the car and plodded inside.

"How much did this cost, Dave?" said Catherine.

"Don't worry about the money," I said, smiling. "This is an investment for the family."

"How much?"

"It was a really good deal, and I managed to talk the guy down quite a bit, so…"

"How much did it cost, Dave?"

"It was £19,000."

"19 grand?" she shrieked. Heat bloomed in her cheeks. "19 bloody grand? Where the hell did you get that sort of money? Have you started robbing banks? Jesus, we can't afford this Dave. We can't afford this."

Catherine's face was bright red now. Her breathing faster, eyes wide with panic.

"Don't worry," I said, "it's fine. I got a great deal on the finance. I only put down four grand straight away, and then it's a little over £200 a month for five years." I didn't tell her that the 'little' was an extra £74. But that would only worry her more.

"We can't afford £200 a month," she said. "Can we?"

"It's fine. I looked at the numbers, checked our finances and we can afford it." This was, of course, a lie. We could just about afford the £200 per month, if we all ate less and only used electricity in emergency situations. The extra £74 was a slight concern, but I knew I'd figure it out somehow.

"I've put all the numbers into a spreadsheet if you want to see," I reassured her.

There was a spreadsheet, but I had no intention of letting her see it. That would only prove we couldn't afford it. I'd been through the family finances and worked out a potential deposit and monthly payments. What I hadn't anticipated was falling in love with the car as soon as I saw it. The intoxicating aroma of freshly-valeted seats and carpet; the large fancy SATNAV monitor in the central console; the bright, shiny buttons and lights twinkling in front of me; the rough roar of the engine as I pressed lightly on the accelerator; and the overwhelming feeling of newness.

And, of course, the simple difference of driving a Mercedes compared with a Ford Focus was utterly exhilarating. It was faster, more powerful, more special in every way. The way people looked at me as I passed them on my test drive – I felt important, respected, a cut above. I felt rich. I felt how New Dave must feel every time he drove his fancy BMW.

After that, the salesman hardly had to convince me. And within barely no time at all, I'd signed the papers for a car that totally blew the budget I'd prepared.

"I might need to start buying slightly cheaper beer," I assured Catherine. "But it's worth it. It's an investment for the family. And the old car was practically falling apart."

This seemed to calm her a little.

"You're sure, Dave? We can definitely afford this?"

"I told you, it was a good deal. I talked him down by three grand. Then he gave us an extra grand off for trading in the old car."

In truth, it was pretty much a 'take it or leave it' negotiation. I was so excited during the test drive, the salesman could see it dripping off me. So, I didn't manage to talk him down at all. And I only got £500 for trading in my old car.

"Well, it is a very nice car," said Catherine, smiling as she leaned in through the front passenger door. "It's very fancy inside. But I'm not sure, Dave. Perhaps you should take it back and go for something a bit more practical."

"Practical shmactical! We've always had boring cars. Volvos and Fords. I didn't want to be sensible. I wanted to be spontaneous for once. Do something nice and fun and cool. Besides, the papers are signed now, I can't take it back. And remember, you're on the insurance too, so you can drive it as well. In fact..." I held up the keys. "Let's go for a spin now."

She finally gave in and beamed from ear to ear. "Go on, then," she giggled, "but you drive, though."

Catherine climbed into the passenger seat and I ran round and hopped in next to her. She pulled on her seat belt. I started the car, pressed my foot on the accelerator and revved the engine. It was the most magnificent sound, rough and powerful. It vibrated through the whole car and Catherine actually shuddered. Then she giggled. A real innocent, excited, childish giggle. It was amazing. I hadn't seen her laugh like that in years.

I pulled on my seat belt, revved the engine again and prepared to set off.

"Hang on," said Catherine, her face suddenly serious again. "Four grand?"

"What's that?" I replied.

"You said you paid four grand up front?"

"Erm… did I? Er… yeah, that's right." Damn, had I told her that? I'd meant to keep that bit back. I must have been overexcited.

"Yeah, you said you paid four grand up front, and then it would be 200 a month for five years." Her face was stern now, the childish grin a distant memory.

"Yes. That's right. Why?"

Damn. Damn. Damn. It was all falling apart. Why did I mention the four grand? I'd practiced the speech the whole way home. I knew I could get away with the monthly payments, but there was no way she'd let the rest go.

"Well, where did you get four grand from?"

"Um… from the… er, savings account."

"The savings account? We don't have four grand in the savings account."

"Well, I… er…"

"The only place we have that kind of money is the…" Catherine's eyes widened. "Oh, Dave you didn't… The kids' university fund?"

"I needed the deposit and I…"

"How could you? You've literally stolen our children's future to buy yourself this flashy car because of some ridiculous bloody midlife crisis?"

"Well, it's not like the kids are gonna need it," I said, panicking and presenting entirely the wrong argument. "Holly's so grumpy at the moment she'll probably refuse to go to Uni just to spite us. And, I mean, can you really see Jack making it to higher education?"

She didn't like that.

"You're unbelievable! That was not your decision to make. It wasn't your money. We always said: if they didn't want it for Uni, it was theirs to help them as a start in life. And how do you know they won't make it to Uni?"

"Look, it's really not that bad," I lied. "Yes, I took money from the university fund. But I can put it straight back in three months. I've been promised a big bonus when we complete phase one of the work for the new client."

"Really?"

"Yes," I lied. "Thomson told me today." Of course, there was no bonus. Not even the hint of one.

"Well, you still shouldn't have done it," she said, climbing out of the car. "Not without talking to me first."

"Where are you going? I thought we were going for a…"

"I'm not in the mood. Come inside and eat your dinner."

Catherine disappeared up the path and into the house. I sighed, turned the engine off and climbed out. I knew she'd calm down eventually. I wasn't quite so sure about how to replace the money. I'd have to think about that later, and make sure she didn't look at the account.

As I stood there, looking at my shiny new toy, I heard the familiar rumble of New Dave's BMW driving into the street.

"Nice," he said, walking over to me. "You're moving up in the world?"

"Yeah, picked it up today," I said, like it was no big deal to spend so much money on a car.

"A Focus up to a C-Class? Very nice. They must be taking care of you at AIP. I heard you won the big KODEK account. Bonuses all round, eh?"

"Yes, we've all been thanked," I said, not technically lying but also not correcting him.

"Man, I love driving off the forecourt in a brand new car," said New Dave. "There's nothing like it, is there?"

"Well, it's not completely new," I said. "It's a couple of years old."

"No, yeah," he said, looking almost embarrassed for me, "no, I mean new, as in… like… new to you." He just about managed to save it, but those words held so much insult. *New to you.* I felt like a child being given his older brother's hand-me-downs. He might as well have patted me on the shoulder and told me 'well done for trying'.

"Lovely model, though," he continued. "One of the guys in the office has one of these. Great little car. Does yours have the parking assistance built in?"

"Erm… think so," I said. To be honest, I wasn't sure. I'd pretty much glazed over when the salesman was talking me through the features, already lost in a little dream of seeing New Dave's jealous face when I pulled into the drive.

"You'll love that. Great feature. Oh, you're making me jealous, Dave."

My eyes widened. Did he just say what I thought he did? Jealous? He was jealous of me? I couldn't keep a ridiculous, childish grin from spreading across my face. I'd done it. I'd finally beaten him in something.

"That's it," he laughed, "I'm gonna do it, too."

What was this, now?

"You know, I've been thinking of getting a new car. And you've just helped me make my mind up. I'm going to upgrade mine in a couple of months when the new model comes out. Or maybe even go for something a bit cheeky. A Tesla maybe. Or a Ferrari. I'll have to go shopping this weekend."

And just like that, he stole it all away. I'd beaten him for 10 bloody seconds. And then it was all gone.

"Yeah, well, why not?" I said, feeling utterly crestfallen.

"Anyway, best get inside. Absolutely famished," said New Dave.

He strolled up the path and into his house, leaving me looking at my shiny new car, which now seemed much less shiny. A Ferrari? A fucking Ferrari?

What was I thinking? How was I ever supposed to compete with this man? I'd raided the kids' university fund to finance a car I couldn't afford, and he'd probably buy his new car out of next month's pay. I blipped the car doors shut, taking far less pleasure in it than before, and walked into the house to microwave whatever disappointing meal was waiting for me.

******

Catherine barely spoke to me for the rest of the evening. She wasn't exactly giving me the silent treatment. But there was a definite cold atmosphere between us. And while she wasn't angry enough to exile me to the couch for the night, she went to bed early and gave me a look that said, 'You can bloody well stay up for a bit, and God help you if you wake me up when you come to bed'. She has very expressive eyes.

So, I sat there in the dark living room, watching Breaking Bad on Netflix and wondering how I'd managed to get things so wrong. It should have been a happy thing. It was supposed to be a nice surprise for the family. And it should have clawed back a few points in the competition with New Dave.

Instead, I now had an angry wife, a large debt, and I was no further ahead than I had been. I could update my spreadsheet to claw back a few percentage points, but as soon as New Dave went out and bought a ridiculous supercar, I'd be back to square one.

On TV, the main character, Walter White, was shouting at his wife and, rather than reassuring her that he was safe in his new life as a drug kingpin, he got carried away with his own ego. "I am not in danger," he said. "I *am* the danger." And like that, he changed right before her. No longer her husband, but now this new man she barely recognised.

Was I changing? Was I so caught up in myself and my secret feud that I was becoming something unrecognisable?

Catherine would calm down in time. She never stays mad at me for too long. Once she saw how fast and cool and exciting the new car was, I knew she'd see it as a good purchase. I just had to make sure she didn't look too closely at the bank accounts.

I still had the muddy run coming up. I definitely had a chance to win back a few points there. I knew I could run. I had that working in my favour. I just had to get fit again. Which reminded me, I really should get out for a training run. There were two months to go before the race. Still plenty of time to get myself up to scratch. But I'd already wasted several weeks and I couldn't afford to waste any more.

CHAPTER 12
LISTENING TO RAISINS

IN ALL 45 years of my life so far, I can honestly say I've never wondered what a raisin sounds like. So, it was something of a surprise to find myself sitting in a circle of misfits, eyes tight shut, holding a raisin close to my ear. Trying to hear it.

"What sensations are you aware of?" asked Marcus, the mindfulness instructor. He wore grey trousers, a white shirt and a loose-fitting, navy blue waistcoat. He had curly black hair and a weathered face that made him look older than I suspected he really was. He talked with the air of a born-again Christian – all worthy and caring, though you can't help but wonder what secret past they're hiding behind the soft voice, imploring eyes and loosely-clasped hands.

"And how does it make you feel?" asked Marcus.

It was my first session of mindfulness training. I was sitting on a plastic chair in a draughty council building meeting room in the centre of town, feeling uncomfortable for a number of reasons. The session had started with Marcus teaching us a series of breathing exercises, then guiding us through something called a 'body scan'. It required us to leave the discomfort of our moulded plastic chairs and decamp to an even less comfortable position lying on the cold surface of the rough, blue council carpet. Then we had to lie there, breathing deeply and thinking about the various parts of our bodies in turn, considering any sensations we might be feeling. I can only assume the whole exercise was designed to make us look and feel as stupid as possible. If so, it was working well.

Finally, we had to imagine filling our entire bodies with breath, and then 'give ourselves permission' to let our minds wander before bringing them 'back to the centre of our own experiences.' I winced every time he uttered one of these soft, hippy-like expressions.

I'd assumed mindfulness would be a relaxing experience. But, with cramp in my back and a cold draught whistling up my shirt, it was having the opposite effect. Worst of all, as I lay there trying to achieve something close to calm, my mind kept wandering to New Dave. I thought of the giant watch glistening on his wrist. I thought of an endless parade of builders ruining my flower beds. I thought of New Dave's busty, ex-model wife. I thought of his perfect kids, his vastly improved house, his swimming pool and his fucking sauna.

I turned every single statistic from my spreadsheet over in my mind. I thought about everything New Dave had and I didn't. I thought about the injustice of Zack being promoted instead of me. And I thought about how that meant I might never catch up with New Dave now.

After just a few minutes, I was feeling angrier than ever – the very thing that had landed me in this stupid position to start with.

"Now, if it's something you feel comfortable with," said Marcus, "just try really thinking about what you've got there in your hand. What does it feel like? What sensations are you aware of? And how does that make you feel?" He spoke annoyingly slowly, each syllable taking twice as long as it needed to.

I wasn't actually supposed to know what was in my hand. That seemed to be the whole idea. First, we were told to close our eyes and hold out our hands. Then Marcus went round the circle, placing something small in each of our outstretched palms. We were instructed to 'engage with it' however we felt most comfortable.

Marcus suggested rolling it in our fingers, examining the textures and 'exploring any sensations' we noticed. I couldn't be doing with that, so I just held it between finger and thumb.

I'd already guessed it was a raisin. As soon as he put it in my hand, I knew it was a raisin. It was small and raisin-shaped. And it felt like a raisin. It wasn't exactly a Mensa test.

We were invited to hold the 'mystery' object to our ears and see if we could hear anything. I tried. I didn't hear anything. Of course I didn't. It was a bloody raisin. It's not like it was supposed to have Beethoven pumping out of it.

I opened my eyes and took furtive glimpses at the other faces in the circle. They were all concentrating hard, really trying to hear it. I wondered whether they actually did hear anything. Maybe mine was just broken.

After a long minute of raisin listening, we were invited – if it was something we 'felt comfortable with' – to place the object in our mouths and explore how *that* made us feel. At that point, it seemed only sensible to re-examine my unwavering raisin conviction. Because I didn't mind putting a mystery object in my mouth if I was certain it *was* a raisin. But what if it wasn't?

It seemed quite unlikely, however, that this soft-speaking therapist would pull the old rabbit poo switcheroo joke (surely that sort of thing would be heavily frowned upon in the Mindfulness Community). After a couple of seconds of internal debate, I tossed the object into my mouth, figuring that if I did get a nasty surprise, I'd be well within my rights to jump up and punch Marcus in the face.

I examined the object with my tongue, making mental notes of the sensations, then gave myself permission to bite into it. And... yes. Raisin. Knew it!

Finally, Marcus asked us to give ourselves permission to sit and breathe deeply for a few minutes. It seemed to me there was a hell of a lot of 'giving ourselves permission' and only doing what 'felt comfortable'. As far as I was concerned, the whole experience made me feel anything but comfortable. And, if I could, I would quite happily have given myself permission to get up and go home. Unfortunately, the conditions of my continued employment relied on me getting this buffoon to sign an attendance slip.

I looked around at the other members of the group, all thinking about their recent experience with the raisin. They'd put a raisin in their mouths and ate it – what the hell was there to think about?

To my left in the circle was Sally, a middle-aged mum of four, who'd introduced herself at the start of the session as being 'a bit worn out'. She'd come to the class hoping to learn techniques for unwinding. She'd read (probably in the Daily Mail) that mindfulness was the best thing.

Next to Sally was Frank. He was at least 70 and, from the befuddled expression on his face, I wondered if he'd come along just to get out of the house. Had he actually known what he was signing up to, or did he just enrol in the first class he came across? Maybe he'd misread the sign-up forms and turned up expecting a pottery or baking class? Or something more exotic, like salsa dancing? For obvious reasons, he was given a pass from laying down on the cold floor for the body scan. And when the rest of us were doing our breathing exercises, Frank seemed to be doing his own wheezing exercises. I had to keep opening one eye to make sure he wasn't about to fall off his chair.

Directly opposite me sat Sharon, a plump woman with ruddy cheeks and lank, greasy-looking hair. She was nervous; overly smiley, and told us a recent battle with anxiety had brought her to the class. She wanted to feel more confident. I felt a strange mix of pity and shame. Who was I to feel sorry for anyone? I wasn't exactly there out of choice.

The last member of the group was Alan. He was a short, overweight businessman with a red face and an ill-fitting suit. I guessed him to be in his late 50s. He told us how he'd been finding his job stressful and was looking for a way to calm down. I could certainly sympathise. He went on to say how he feared many of his younger colleagues were itching to get rid of him. He worried how to stop that from happening. And what would happen if he couldn't? It's a younger man's world, nowadays. He couldn't afford to take early retirement and didn't think he'd find another job at his age.

After five minutes, Marcus had to step in and stop him from treating the group like his own personal therapy session. Thankfully, he did finally shut up.

Alan looked incredibly stressed. He spent the whole session shuffling in his chair, barely able to keep still. And, with his rosy complexion, and the plump belly poking out between the buttons of his tight white shirt, I hoped he would find the peace he was after. Otherwise, he probably wasn't too far away from a heart attack.

At the end of the session, Marcus went around the group handing out Mindfulness Colouring Books. Our assignment was to spend at least half an hour per day practicing our mindful breathing. Then we should spend 'as long as we felt comfortable' colouring in our new little book. Marcus even gave us a small pack of crayons each. I felt like a child in a restaurant, being given something to keep me quiet while the grown-ups read the menu.

I was dreading coming back. Not that I had any say in the matter.

Without any apparent sense of irony, Marcus bid us farewell and told us to go in peace and carry on being mindful in everything we do. The twerp. I smiled and nodded at my fellow inductees as we shuffled out of the meeting room. I wondered whether I'd see any of them again in a week's time. I had to be there, obviously. But I assumed the rest were there on a voluntary basis. If they had any sense, they'd give themselves permission to never come back again. Apart from Alan. He really needed the help.

I stepped out of the dank council building into a grey afternoon. It was drizzling and I lamented the fact that I'd forgotten to bring an umbrella. Brilliant, I thought. The perfect end to one of the most depressing, annoying and, ironically, stress-inducing hours of my life. I flicked up the collar on my jacket and I crossed the car park.

Just as I was about to set off, I caught sight of myself in the rear-view mirror. My hair was longer and shaggier than usual – I didn't remember letting it get that long. I had a good two days' worth of stubble on my face. Rather than being cool and sexy, it looked dirty, with white patches that made me look old and tired. More hip replacement than hipster.

I started the car and revelled in the gloriously loud growl of the engine. I really loved the new car. And, in the four days since I'd bought it, Catherine had started to thaw a little. When I finally got her to come for a drive, she'd tried her hardest to remain stony-faced and unimpressed. But I could see her eyes widen as I revved the engine and showed her just how fast it accelerated. She'd been surprisingly amorous that night, too. And we'd had sex for the first time in a few weeks.

I pulled out of the car park and headed home. The one real benefit of the mindfulness session was that it was held at 3.30pm. Which meant I'd had to leave work early, and there was no point going back to the office. So, without the rush-hour traffic to slow me down, I made it home in record time.

The house was strangely quiet when I walked in. Usually, Jack would have the TV blaring in the living room, or the sound of some dreadful boyband pop would be pumping down the stairs from Holly's bedroom. But there was nothing.

Great, I thought, sounds like the kids are out. Maybe I'll see if I can get Catherine out for another spin in the Mercedes. If I play my cards right, and rev the engine enough, I might get a repeat of last time.

"Hello," I called out into the quiet house.

No reply. No talking. No dishwasher whirring, no tumble-dryer tumbling. Barely any sound at all.

I walked through into the living room and practically jumped out of my skin when I found Catherine sitting on the sofa, completely silent. Her eyes were red and puffy. Mascara-streaked tears marked her cheeks. My laptop was open in front of her on the coffee table, turned towards me.

I looked at the screen. It glowed with the white and black check of an Excel spreadsheet. My New Dave spreadsheet.

"What the fuck is this, Dave?" said Catherine.

Oh, shit.

CHAPTER 13
CAUGHT OUT

"DO YOU REALLY hate your life with us this much?" asked Catherine. Her eyes were red and puffy. Long wet streaks coursed down her cheeks.

"It's not what it looks like," I said.

"Really? Because it looks like you've made a spreadsheet to rate every aspect of your life and your family. And we don't come off well, do we?"

Shit!

"Where did you find that?" I said.

"It was right here on the desktop, Dave. Don't worry, I wasn't spying on you. I only turned the computer on to Google 10k training plans. I wanted to help you with this stupid race. And then I find this thing."

"But how did you…"

"Crack your highly secure password? You have the same one for everything. And 'Dave123' is not exactly hard to guess."

Shit!

"Look, you weren't supposed to see that, okay? It was just a bit of…"

"A bit of what, Dave? A bit of fun? Is it fun to humiliate people? To make them feel bad about themselves?"

"No, it's not that… I was just feeling bad about things and I thought… I don't know what I thought."

"So, it was to make yourself feel better?" she said.

"Yes. No… I don't know."

"And is that the only way you can feel better about life, is it? Attacking and embarrassing the people closest to you?"

"No. I wasn't attacking anyone. You were never supposed to see that," I pleaded.

"Obviously not, Dave. Clearly you didn't want me to know that you only rate our home as 6 out of 10. The house we've lived in for years. Raised a family in. The place where we've built up years of great

97

memories – well, they were great for me, clearly not so much for you… How can it only score a 6?"

"It wasn't about that; it was purely based on value and market rates and… I had a system to work out…"

"And what's the rest of it? Dress sense? Handsomeness? Singing voice? I mean, what the hell is this, Dave? You're rating yourself against the next-door neighbour?"

"Yes, but it's not…"

"A new neighbour moves in and you become obsessed. Who does that? You really feel like you have to compete with someone you barely even know?"

"I've told you before, he's got the exact same…"

"Oh, and here's a fun one," she interrupted, her voice cracking. "Wife's attractiveness: 6.5 out of 10." She took a deep breath, holding back the tears. "How generous of you, Dave. Is that really what you think? 6.5?"

"No, look, it was just a…"

"I mean, that must be what you think. It's down here in black and white, isn't it? You've typed it in and saved it."

"Please, look it was just a stupid…"

"Am I not pretty enough for you? Not slim and toned enough? What exactly is it that gives me such an average mark?"

"Look, it's not like…"

"Are you in love with Tamzin from next door?"

"What? No, of course not," I said.

"Because you gave her 9.5 out of 10."

"Well, yes but…"

"I've seen you looking at her, you know. The sly glances you think I don't see. And I didn't really care. I mean, the woman used to be a model. Everyone ogles her. It's quite pathetic actually. So, is that it? You'd rather be with her, would you?"

"No, of course not. I love *you*."

"I know I'm not as young as I used to be, but 6.5? Really? You know, you're no spring chicken, Dave. I can think of better-looking men. But I would never…"

Her voice cracked as she failed to get the final words out. A single tear rolled down her left cheek and she wiped it angrily from her face.

"I'd never score you," she said, composing herself. "I'd never do anything to make you feel that bad."

"I'm sorry," I said. "Of course, I don't think that. I don't know why I wrote that. I was just…

"Just what, Dave? Jealous of the next-door neighbour? Do you know how pathetic that is? So what if he has more money? So what if he has a prettier wife? Who cares if he can grow a fucking beard better than you? I mean, really? Are you actually that petty?"

I was instantly stunned. Catherine prides herself on keeping calm in any situation. And she never swears.

"You don't understand," I said. "You've never understood. He's me, isn't he? He's me, but better. He's what I could have been. I just wrote that stupid list as way to measure up…"

"What, Dave? Measure up what? Everything you've missed out on? Everything me and the kids have been holding you back from? Do you really think you'd be that much better off without us? 46% better, perhaps?" she said, pointing to the total at the bottom of the screen.

"Look, it's just an arbitrary scoring system… It really doesn't mean…"

"At least now I understand the car. You rated our old car as…" she scanned down the spreadsheet, "…5 out of 10. Compared with Dave's, which got 9. Well, that wouldn't do, would it? So you go out and buy this ridiculously expensive car to make yourself feel better. I mean, can we actually afford it, Dave?"

I stood silent. Now wasn't the time for that particular truth.

"Is that what all that business at work was about? It's shameful they didn't give you that promotion. You were right to get angry about it. And you should have told them to stuff their job. I would have supported you no matter what. But losing your temper and smashing up your boss's office? That's not you, Dave. You're not a violent man. Where is all this coming from?"

I stared blankly at her, shame coursing through me like ice in my veins.

"And do you think you're the only one with a stressful job, or who misses out on opportunities? I should have been made Head of Year way before I was, but that useless prick Trevor gave the job to Marianne, despite the fact she was only two years out of university and had absolutely no rapport with the kids. But what did I do, Dave? I sucked it up, worked harder, proved myself and got the promotion eventually."

"I know, love. I know you've struggled and…"

"Where's the man I love?" she said, cutting me off. "The man I married? I feel like you're changing in front of me."

"I'm not... I mean... I... I..."

"Do you know the worst thing? Out of everything in this spreadsheet..." She said the word spreadsheet like it actually pained her tongue to pronounce it. "I mean, never mind how poorly you rated me, or the house..."

She went silent, waiting for me to fill in the blanks. She was clearly clinging onto some piece of information that proved just how awful I'd been. I looked on, not quite getting it. And that just made things worse. Anger flashed in her eyes, like I'd never seen before.

"The kids, Dave," she shouted, shaking her head. "You even rated the fucking kids. How could you do that? You're supposed to love them unconditionally. But instead, you reduce them to statistics. Factors that prove how bad your sorry little life is."

"No, it's not like that. I..."

"Then what is it like? Because, as far as I can see, you've rated our kids against the kids next door. And, what a surprise, they don't come off very well either, do they? Son's intelligence: 5. How could you do that?"

"Oh come on, Catherine, he's never been the brightest spark, has he? It's not like he's going to invent the cure for cancer..." I said.

Defending myself was clearly a mistake. If she was angry before, it was nothing compared with the look she gave me now.

"How dare you rate our boy's intelligence? He might not be the most academically gifted, but he has so many other qualities. It didn't occur to you to take any of those into account when you were making your little self-pity list?"

"Look, I'm trying to tell you, the list was just an arbitrary... I mean, it's not completely... And come on, you can't honestly tell me you'd give him more than 5 out of 10 for intelligence?"

"No, Dave. I would never have written a list in the first bloody place. I'd never rate our children or compare them to others. I mean, what if he was to see this? How do you think it would make him feel to see what his own father said?"

"He'd never see it. None of you were ever supposed to see it."

"You keep saying that, Dave, as if it makes things better. But I did see it, didn't I? And do you know what? I don't feel great!"

I didn't know what to say. Catherine sighed heavily, a strange calm coming over her, like all the energy was draining out of her with the breath. Then she just gazed at me with a strange look of resignation.

"Do you really think your life is that bad?" she asked. "I think that's the saddest thing. Not how poorly you've rated me. Or how cruelly you've scored the kids. But how little respect you have for the life we've built together."

"It's not as simple as…"

"I thought we had a happy life, Dave. We're not the richest. And yes, there are things I might like to have done, but never got the chance. But that's life. You don't always get everything you want. And that's fine, because it makes you appreciate what you do have. But you don't seem to appreciate any of it. You just see what you don't have. I don't know how you can think the life we have together is worth so little."

"I don't think that. I love our life together, I've just been a bit…"

"Oh, be fucking honest, Dave. Just be honest. Is this how you really feel?" she said, pointing to the spreadsheet.

"No… yes… I don't know. I've just been feeling pretty…" I wasn't sure what I wanted to say. "Since New Dave moved in, I guess I've been a bit more… critical of myself and my own life… and yes, I suppose there are things that I feel I've missed out on…"

Catherine was strangely quiet now.

"And, I mean, maybe I was a bit harsh on how I scored things. No, definitely harsh, very harsh, and I really don't think you're just a 6.5. Absolutely not. And I don't hate my life, I just wish… I mean, everybody has moments when they regret things, or wonder what if…"

"Regret?" she said, very calmly. "So you regret your life with us? You regret marrying me? Have I held you back? Do you also regret having the kids?"

"No, absolutely not. Never. I love you and the kids. I'd never change any of that. You're not getting…"

"You have a problem, Dave. I thought we were happy. But if you hate your life this much, then I don't know how to help you."

Catherine stood up from the table. It was only then that I noticed the suitcase stood up against the wall.

"What's this?" I said. "What's going on?"

"I'm leaving you, Dave."

"What? Don't be silly. There's no need for…"

"We're not going to stay where we're not wanted. I can't be in this house another minute knowing what you think of it and what you think of us. And I certainly don't want to make your life any worse than it already is."

"Well, where are you going? Is there someone else?"

"Don't be fucking ridiculous," she shouted. "And don't try and turn this into something it's not. This is your fault, Dave. We're leaving because of *you*. Because of what *you've* done. Karen said she'll put us up for a while, until I figure out what to do. She came and collected the kids earlier."

"No, look, you don't have to do this. Just stay and we'll talk about things…"

"No, Dave, I don't think so."

Catherine pulled up the handle on her suitcase and wheeled it towards the front door. I followed her through the house, begging her to change her mind.

She opened the door and turned to face me.

"At least you can delete a few lines from your spreadsheet now. I wonder how much better that will make your life."

She slammed the door behind her and walked down the path. I stood there in the hallway, silently staring at the front door as I heard her climb into her car, turn on the engine and drive out of my life.

CHAPTER 14
BEANS ON TOAST

IT'S FUNNY, HOW easy it is to take things in life for granted. Clean clothes, for example. Hot meals. Fresh towels. Food in the cupboard. The little spots of green gel in the toilet that stop it from going manky. The sound of kids laughing in their bedrooms. The sound of kids squabbling in the living room. Someone to hug you, or kiss you, or tell you everything will be all right.

Four weeks after Catherine took the kids and left me, I wasn't coping terribly well. I was sitting on the sofa in a three-day-old pair of boxer shorts and a t-shirt with several questionable stains on it, eating beans on toast for the third time that week. Even I couldn't get beans on toast wrong – although I'd had to cut several small spots of green mould out of the bread.

I'd taken to sitting around the house in my pants as an act of childish rebellion – I was on my own, so I could do what I wanted. The fact I'd already been wearing those pants for three days had less to do with rebellion, however, and more to do with the fact I still hadn't figured out how to use the damned washing machine. There were no discernible instructions on the front, just a series of nonsensical symbols that didn't relate to any of the actions I wanted it to perform. It took me three days to realise I was using the tumble dry function rather than actually washing anything. So, when I thought I was wearing freshly laundered clothes, they were, in fact, simply dry, warm, dirty clothes. If I couldn't find the instruction manual soon, I was going to have to brave the utter hell of shopping.

It occurred to me that I'd never bought underwear before. Catherine had always picked it up for me. And before that, my mother had had the honour of being chief underpants procurer. Where do you even buy pants, anyway? Are you supposed to try them on in the shop? Does somebody fit you for them, like the pervy, old white-haired gentleman who'd been a little too friendly with his tape measure when he'd fitted me for my wedding suit? And what exactly would they measure? The whole thing was a minefield. I shovelled in another mouthful of beans and tried not to think about it.

I scanned the living room. Pizza boxes were stacked seven high on the end of the sofa. The coffee table was littered with dirty mugs, glasses, plates and silver foil takeaway containers. Dirty clothes lay discarded over the floor and armchair. Several crushed beer cans covered the carpet at my feet, like miniature car wrecks in a scene from a dystopian future.

It dawned on me how little I must have done around the house when Catherine was still there. Because things that seemed to just happen before had suddenly stopped happening altogether.

There was no fresh, new food in the kitchen. Clean clothes had stopped simply appearing in my wardrobe and drawers. There were no cooked meals waiting for me when I got home from work. And there was a rather pungent, mystery smell emanating from the fridge.

Not to say that I was lazy around the house. Or completely incapable of looking after myself. I certainly wasn't the kind of husband that refuses to do 'women's work' and expects his wife to cook, clean and wait on him hand and foot. We always divided those tasks between us, and the majority of Catherine's chores just happened to be the in-house ones to do with cooking and cleaning. The things I was now greatly missing – along with my wife and kids, of course.

It was an equal, sensible division of labour, with jobs assigned to the person most capable of carrying them out. I was a pretty hopeless cook – aside from barbecuing, obviously – so Catherine made dinner every night and I drove the kids to sports practices, music lessons and friends' houses. She did the laundry and I cut the grass. Catherine did the food shopping and I put up shelves, hung pictures and did little DIY jobs. I was dab hand at emptying and filling the dishwasher, but Catherine was always the one who put in the detergent and turned it on.

It sounds kind of sexist, but it really wasn't. She did the things she was good at, and so did I. It worked for us.

With Catherine gone, the system had broken down completely. Not only did I not know how to do most of her chores, I was so depressed I'd also completely stopped doing my own jobs. The grass in the back garden was three weeks overdue a trim. The shelves I'd meant to put up in Jack's bedroom were still stacked up against the wall. The squeaky living room door – which really only needed a quick spray with WD40 – continued to taunt me with its high-pitched whine every time I opened or closed it.

The house clearly hadn't been hoovered in a long time. The bath had several dirty rings around it. The kitchen counters were peppered with crumbs, streaks of dirt and odd little circles where pools of nondescript liquids had been left to dry. The dishwasher was crammed full of dirty dishes, which had crusted over and started smelling. And whatever I hadn't managed to wedge in there sat dirty in the sink.

There literally wasn't a clean dish in the house. Which is why I'd been eating food out of the boxes and foil containers they arrived in. And why I'd taken to drinking espresso out of egg cups.

It had all sneaked up on me. One minute everything was clean, then all of a sudden it was like I was living in a crack den.

For the first two weeks after she left, Catherine completely refused to take my calls. Instead, I had to put up with the self-righteous, sneering of her sister, Karen, telling me I should be ashamed of myself, and that I was never good enough for her in the first place. And that she hoped my cock fell off.

Three weeks into the separation, Catherine thawed slightly and agreed to speak with me – albeit in monosyllables and purely to organise letting me see the kids. Of course, convincing the kids to let me see them was another matter entirely. Holly landed squarely on her mother's side of the argument. Even though Catherine hadn't divulged any details of our disagreement, Holly naturally assumed I was at fault. I think that's very much a teenage girl thing – Dad's an arsehole, Mum's blameless.

Until Catherine forgave me, neither would Holly. And so why would I possibly expect her to come and spend the day with me? Even if I was bribing her with a trip to the mall to buy clothes and eat Nando's.

Jack had a much more relaxed attitude towards things. However, despite arranging to take him to see the latest Transformers movie, he'd cried off at the last minute. Apparently, his friend, Ben, had invited him to go ice skating, and the girl he 'sort of' had a crush on was going to be there – all of which was greatly more appealing than hanging out with his boring old dad.

So, I was ceremoniously dumped and left alone. Which meant I'd spent Saturday sitting around the house in my pants with the curtains tightly drawn, feeling sorry for myself and watching film after film on Netflix.

It had been a hellish week. Naturally, most of my energy had been consumed by feeling sorry for myself, lamenting my recent abandonment, admonishing myself for letting it happen, and trying to think up a solution to win back my family. On top of that, we were ridiculously busy at work, with a new client to please and a major campaign to roll out in a very short space of time.

Steve was great. He listened to my incessant whining, melancholic rambling and self-righteous justification that Catherine couldn't understand what I'd been going through. He didn't pass judgement and said he'd help me win her back. Then he steered my mind back onto the project.

Being at work definitely helped with the breakup. It gave me something to concentrate on. Although Catherine and the kids were never completely off my mind, it stopped me stewing about it and getting more depressed. So, I'd just about made it through the week, and now that the weekend was here, I couldn't wait to get back to the office just to get away from the silence of the house.

Despite being busy with the new project, the atmosphere at work had taken a nosedive. Steve and I were lucky enough to lock ourselves away to focus on the new concepts. But, judging by their hangdog expressions and depressed demeanours, the rest of the creative department weren't taking well to their new boss.

Zack had settled into his new role very quickly. The chip on his shoulder had grown into a super-sized pack of fries. He walked around being mean, aggressive and arrogant, talking down to people and asserting his 'new boss' status. I could have written a book about his management style and called it: *How to Make Slaves and Subjugate People.*

He was clearly out of his depth. And he inspired no respect whatsoever in the people now working for him. Pretty much the whole team had assumed I'd get the job, and they were as shocked as I was when I didn't. It made it hard at first; everyone knowing I'd been snubbed. But it was great to know they were on my side – equally mortified at the injustice of it. And just as befuddled by how the board could have thought Zack was right for the job.

Zack lacked any creativity whatsoever. He didn't really seem to understand the creative process at all. During his first year in the job, his concepts had been thin, to say the least. He'd just throw out weak idea after weak idea, without really developing anything, or thinking anything through.

"I'm an ideas man," was his go-to phrase, whenever challenged.

"I'm not here for the nitty gritty. That's what the designers and writers do." All complete bollocks, of course. But it did make for quite a humorous viral email that spread round the building, in which someone photoshopped Zack's face onto an image of a crazed Donald Trump holding up an empty box, with the caption: *I have all the BEST ideas.*

That one picture showed more creativity and inspiration than any of Zack's concepts. Which is why he'd never won a pitch or sold an idea. And why Steve and I had frequently been called in to help him 'develop' (or salvage) his flawed work.

No one could figure out why Thomson kept protecting him. Then it all came out at the Christmas party, when Zack drunkenly boasted to one of the designers how he was 'protected' at work, and how he could 'get away with pretty much anything' because he was engaged to the boss's daughter. When they tied the knot three months later, the whole creative department let out a collective sigh of resignation, as we realised we'd be stuck with him for good. But I thought they'd hide him away somewhere he couldn't break anything. No one imagined they'd promote him to a senior position. It was like making the bull the manager of the china shop.

Now he was Executive Creative Director, but he was completely unable to make up his mind about anything. Designers would share creative work with him and he had no idea how to critique or develop it. Worse still, he couldn't decide which route or concept to put in front of the client. "I think they're all quite good," he'd say. "I think you should go with whatever you think is your strongest idea." What a buck-passer.

Of course, Zack's complete lack of experience or ability hadn't stopped him walking round like he owned the place. And he seemed oblivious that everybody in the building hated him.

From day one, he started making changes – 'putting his stamp on things', as he called it. He stopped us from going to the pub at lunchtime. He insisted on attending meetings he had no reason to be in. He changed the holiday rota, insisting no more than two people could be off at one time – which in a team of 20 is just stupid. He completely banned us from working from home. "I need you guys actually working," he told us, "not drinking tea and wanking off to Loose Women." The charmer.

The most annoying thing was his new seating plan, which saw everyone having to move desks. At first there seemed no rhyme or reason to it. But then, when all the desks had been moved, we realised he'd created himself an extra-large desk space in the corner, all on his own. He physically separated himself from the rest of the team, presumably to feel more important. And he angled his screens conspicuously, so no one could see what he was doing – or, more likely, not doing.

In addition to our regular work, he also gave us all stupid bloody side projects. They were all highly suspicious and ultimately pointless, but he insisted we carried them out. And as we all had heavy workloads since winning the pitch, it all had to be done by working late or at weekends.

Zack really was an odious little shit. Since he'd been promoted, the entire creative team were completely miserable. And as they all found Zack so unapproachable, they came to me for advice or help, or to sound off about how much of a prick he was. They were even asking me for holiday leave, dentist appointments and one-to-one career meetings. All the stuff Zack should have been handling, but he couldn't be bothered with.

Whether I liked it or not, I was Executive Creative Director by proxy. I was doing the fucking job, while Zack got the title and the money.

"I don't know why you let him get away with it," Steve chided me, after I'd rescued Zack from making a huge blunder with a client. "Stop covering for him. Let the fucker sink. Show the top brass what a waster he is."

"If I do that," I replied, "he could take the place down with him. You know what this business is like. Wouldn't take much to piss off one of the big clients. If we lose even one of those, it won't be long before they start making redundancies. Or worse."

"You know, we could always start looking around," he said. "I know people at BMV. I hear they're looking for a creative team."

"I dunno, mate. It's not a good time. Not with Catherine and… well, you know…"

"Hey, it's just a thought. Something worth considering. Things are only gonna get worse here." He looked at me hopefully.

"Hey, and don't worry about Catherine. She'll be back. You just need to stop moping about. Get yourself straight and show her what she's missing."

"I don't know. She was pretty upset about that list. We're still not really speaking."

"Then get down on your hands and knees. Tell her what a prick you've been and beg her to come back."

"I've already done that."

"Then do it again. And then do it again, until she remembers whatever it was she saw in you in the first place." He chuckled and patted me on the shoulder. "Then she'll come back, you'll get back to normal, and we can come up with a plan to fuck Zack over good and proper. Or, we'll run off like a couple of rats and leave the place to sink."

He was right, of course. I was in a hopeless position. And I was the only one who could fix it. Sitting there in my crusty pants, I realised I had to stop feeling sorry for myself. I had to take charge and fight for what I wanted.

But wasn't that what I'd been doing all along? The whole reason my family had abandoned me was because I'd been working to better myself. Okay, things hadn't gone quite to plan. Catherine finding the list was, obviously, not supposed to happen. But if I'd just password protected my bloody laptop, this would never have happened. My family would be at home and I'd still be working on the plan.

Catherine, Jack and Holly didn't understand what I was trying to achieve. They didn't see the end goal that I saw. Catherine couldn't see that, by beating New Dave, I would become the person I should have been all along. I'd be more successful. We'd be better off as a family. It would be good for all of us.

Where I saw an awakening in myself, Catherine just saw obsession and petty jealousy. Where I saw a path to a better life, Catherine saw a ridiculous man having a midlife crisis and reaching beyond his means. But she was wrong. The plan was sound. It was going to work.

If I stuck with it, I knew I could claw back some points against new Dave. And if I was doing better, Catherine would see what she was missing out on. She'd see me doing well, earning more money. I'd be happier and more confident. She'd see a healthier, slimmer version of me. Maybe I'd even have another go at growing a beard. Then she'd finally realise what I'd been trying to do this whole time. She'd see that she'd judged me wrong and come running back.

No, this was no time to abandon the plan. If anything, I needed to double-down and focus even more energy on it. I'd show everyone just what a Dave Brookman should and could be. They'd stop thinking of me as a second-rate version of my neighbour and see me as the man I am. I'd make them all sorry for ever doubting me in the first place.

I grabbed my laptop from the study, cleared the dirty plates from the coffee table and set it down. I turned it on, opened the spreadsheet and looked at my 'to do' list.

The promotion had slipped away from me, but that didn't mean it was completely lost. As Steve said, perhaps I needed to stop protecting Zack for a while. I could let him mess up a few jobs, show him up for what he was, then swoop in and save the day. Thomson would have to admit what a mistake he'd made. They'd fire Zack and give me the promotion that should have been mine all along. I'd probably even get a hefty bonus for saving the company.

I'd already succeeded with getting a nicer, newer car. That was a big tick in the box. Unfortunately, New Dave struck back instantly with talk of buying an even more expensive car. There was also the slight issue that I wasn't entirely certain I could afford to pay for the car I'd bought. But if I ignored those two facts, it still counted as a win.

I was still very much behind in the house stakes. There was nothing I could do about that, save for taking out a second mortgage and embarking upon a large-scale renovation project. But I was already in enough trouble with Catherine over the car. If I got us into even more debt, she'd never come back.

I scanned down the list looking for quick wins. Singing voice? I'd scored myself accurately low for that, but I didn't think I had time to embark upon a series of expensive singing lessons. And they might not help anyway.

Physique? That was all in hand. With the race coming up, I'd be exercising more. The pounds would fall off and I'd be svelte and lean in no time. But I really should get out for a run, I thought. Maybe tomorrow.

Hairstyle? There had to be something I could do there. Maybe I just needed be sterner with the barber and make sure I got exactly what I wanted. Or perhaps I'd step completely out of my comfort zone and go to an expensive, trendy 'stylist'.

I'd scored myself very low for cooking ability. It wasn't that I couldn't cook exactly. I was pretty damned good on the barbecue. But when it came to making an actual meal, I'd never really had to. My mum had always cooked for me as a kid. And Catherine was such a good cook that she'd just always done it. So, my current culinary expertise ended at microwave meals, beans on toast and calling for takeaway – as I was sorely reminded when I looked over at the various containers littering the room. But how hard could it be, really? Surely, I just needed a decent cookery book and a bit of practice.

My dress sense was also ripe for improvement. I could certainly be more adventurous with what I wore. I'd have to spend some money, but it would be worth it. And I needed to buy underpants anyway, so I might as well get a few outfits while I was there.

So, that was it. I'd head into town the next day, get a cool haircut, pick up some trendy clothes and buy myself a cookery book. By the end of the day, I'd be eating a first-rate meal, and I might even earn an extra half a point for attractiveness.

I was getting a little too excited at the prospect of it. My face was hot and I could feel my heart beating quicker. So, I got my mindfulness colouring book and my pack of crayons, and I started colouring in a bright swirling pattern in blue and red. After two minutes, that proved to be absolutely useless. So, I threw it onto the floor, got a beer from the fridge, and flicked over to the Food Channel to see if I could pick up some cooking tips.

CHAPTER 15
A DATE WITH DENSITY

IT TOOK PRECISELY seven emails, 68 texts, nine Facebook private messages, 51 failed phone calls, 27 successful (albeit monosyllabic and withdrawn) phone calls and one tweet before Catherine agreed to speak to me for longer than 30 seconds. To be honest, the tweet probably had nothing to do with it. I only have 13 followers, none of whom are Catherine, and she doesn't even use Twitter. So, there was very little chance she saw it.

Rather shamefully, I also constructed a Facebook post which featured a GIF of a heart breaking in two and the text: "I'm so sorry. I love you. My heart is broken. Call me." Needless to say, I was drunk and lonely when I wrote it. I woke up the next morning to find several messages on my timeline, varying in their degree of support.

Sorry to hear it mate. Hope you're all good, wrote my old friend, Barry.

Boo hoo! Stop whining, dickhead. You've only got yourself to blame, wrote Catherine's sister.

Gutted for you mate. Been ages since we spoke. Must get a beer some time, wrote another friend, who I hadn't seen in at least 20 years, and who I had absolutely no intention of meeting for a beer.

Want to see nude pics of me? Follow me here to see me get really crazy, wrote a complete stranger who, at best, was a bit sad and lonely, and at worst, an online scammer trying to steal my bank details. Naturally, I didn't click the link.

I heard what you did. You're such a wanker, wrote one of Catherine's friends from Pilates. She then commented on Barry's post to put him straight about exactly what I'd done. Barry replied to her message, explaining that he hadn't known the full story and, in light of the new information, was withdrawing his support for me. Thanks a bloody lot, mate.

The most cutting message of all came from Holly: *God dad your sooooooooo embarrassing!!! Stop posting depressing message's and get a life!* It was absolutely heart breaking, and not just because of the poor grammar (I mean, what the hell do they teach kids nowadays?!). Being called out on social media by your own children for acting like a child is as depressing as it gets – especially when their response gets more than 30 likes, and your original post only gets two likes and one of those little sad faces.

I deleted the post immediately.

A full eight days after that incident, Catherine finally answered the phone and agreed to 'talk properly about things'. She was very quiet at first. Listening and barely replying. Her voice fragile and timid. Still clearly very upset with me.

I apologised profusely, told her how much I loved and missed her and the kids, and admitted what a complete dick I'd been. After about 10 minutes of apologising and – I'm not ashamed to admit it, a fair bit of begging – I could feel her starting to thaw. I even managed to make her laugh a few times. So, there was still hope. And by the end of the call, I'd convinced her to meet me for dinner.

"It's not a bloody date," she was very quick to assert. "Don't go thinking you're forgiven. But there are things we need to discuss, and I'd rather do that in person. Besides, I could do with a night away from Karen."

Yes! Another thing working in my favour. She was already annoyed at being under Karen's feet, which meant she missed being at home. Did she also miss me?

We agreed to meet at the local Harvester the following evening, on the grounds that it wasn't fancy enough for anyone to construe it as a romantic situation, but you could still get a decent steak. And you're always quids-in with the free salad bar.

I arrived 20 minutes early, so I could have a quick beer to settle my nerves. The place was busy with families, happily chatting and eating. A group of men in workmans' clothes stood at the bar, drinking pints and laughing. I took a sip of cold lager, felt the bubbles burn in my throat. I couldn't believe how nervous I felt meeting my own wife – the woman I'd known for more than 25 years – for a simple dinner.

I was wearing some of the new clothes I'd bought on my trip into town. I hadn't been overly extravagant, but I'd spent more than I usually would. Of course, I used New Dave as a template – not exactly copying his outfits but trying to capture a similar style. I couldn't afford the expensive designer brands he wore, but I found comparable items in places like Next and Debenhams. Even then, they were more expensive than I'd have liked.

For this evening, I'd chosen a pair of black trousers, a pale blue

Oxford weave shirt and a black sports coat. I'd even splashed out on some shiny, new shoes. And, of course, the new pants and socks I'd gone to town for in the first place. I felt pretty good in the new clothes, and I was hoping Catherine would think the same.

My hair, naturally, was looking shit. It appeared there was literally nothing I could do about that. During my personal renovation trip, I went to one of the fancy hairdressers in the high street that charge ridiculous prices, and which I was sure New Dave must go to. If it was good enough for him, it would do for me. And it was a whole new world.

Normally, I just turn up at the barbers and sit on an uncomfortable, battered leather sofa, reading a tatty copy of The Sun until the three guys ahead of me have all been seen. This was completely different. I had to book an appointment, for starters. Luckily, they could fit me in, and I was guided to a comfortable sofa in a special reception area, where a young girl brought me a cup of tea and a little biscuit. I was then joined by my 'stylist' for a 'consultation', where she spent 10 minutes discussing various options and assessing what she had to work with.

"I think… a little off the sides and back," she said, running her fingers through my hair and lifting it up to fully inspect it. Her hands were soft and smelled like coconut.

I never got that at the barbers. I never once had a 'consultation'. I'd tell the barber how much to take off the back and sides, how short I wanted it on top, and what sort of style I was after. He'd pretend to listen, while staring blankly at me in the mirror, then proceed to give me the exact same haircut he'd given the three previous occupants of his chair, while making the exact same boring small talk about football – as if I hadn't heard him say it already. And his hands definitely didn't smell like coconut.

"So, yeah… I'll give it a trim…" continued the stylist, "and then sort of mess it up a bit. Like, make it look a bit more funky, yeah?"

"Erm, yeah… funky, yeah…" I said, not entirely certain what I was agreeing to and feeling like a pensioner who'd wandered into an arcade and got confused by all the flashing lights.

She guided me to another room, where a different girl sat me in a chair that leaned back so I was laying with my head in a sink. This new girl spent five minutes washing my hair, gently massaging my scalp and working in numerous types of shampoo, conditioner and God knows what else. When she was done, she guided me to another room and sat me down in the hairdresser's chair, where another girl brought me a fresh cup of tea. I felt a little silly in the long flowing cape and towel wrapped around my head, but it was luxury and attention I hadn't felt in years, and I was enjoying every second.

The stylist came back and spent a good 55 minutes cutting my hair. In the barbers, it usually takes a maximum of eight. The stylist took so much care and attention, it was like she was cutting each hair individually.

When she was finished, she blow-dried my hair, fingered in some kind of wax, and systematically went from front to back, pulling small clumps of hair up into stiff, messy peaks. Then she stood back and asked me what I thought.

And it looked shit. Of course, it did. My hair always looks shit.

I couldn't fault the stylist's work, or her effort. She'd done what she said she was going to, but it still looked shit. Just shit in a slightly different way.

I thought I was going to faint when she presented me the bill for £54. My usual barber never charges more than a tenner. His work is crap, but at least it's cheap crap.

And when she tried to upsell me by recommending a tiny pot of hair wax for £15, I nearly burst out laughing. Especially when she assured me it was the same brand she'd used on my hair and would be the best product to keep it looking as good as it did. I declined and took my new hair to the pub to drown my sorrows.

It was an expensive lesson – not wholly unenjoyable – but at least I now knew that I was simply destined to have shit hair, no matter how much money I threw at it.

So, I sat there in the local Harvester, with my smart new clothes and my crap new hairstyle. I'd bought some cheaper wax in Superdrug and tried to recreate the messy peaks, but it had somehow made it look even worse.

"New hair?" said Catherine, coldly, as she joined me at the table. "Is this all part of your self-improvement plan?" She might have mellowed enough to join me for dinner, but she clearly wanted me to know she still wasn't happy with me.

"Something like that," I said, sombrely. "Just thought I'd try something new. Still looks shit, though, doesn't it?" I laughed. "Just shit in a different way."

The slightest curl appeared in the corner of Catherine's mouth. A good sign.

"So, how have you been?" I asked. "How are the kids?"

"Fine," she said, "in the circumstances. It's not easy, all cooped up at Karen's. And the kids are missing their regular routines a bit."

"Sorry," I said. "Are they missing me?"

"We all miss you."

"How's Holly? Is she still a vegan?" I said, chuckling slightly.

"Oh, don't get me started on that," said Catherine. "She's so stubborn. I can tell she doesn't really like it, but she won't give in. We went to Nando's last week, and you should have seen the sneer on her face as she forced down a vegan wrap that she clearly hated. And I'm sure there were a few sausages missing from the fridge the other day. She's her father's daughter, and no mistake."

I laughed at Holly's stubbornness. "And how's Jack?"

"I'm a little worried about him, actually. I had a call from his P.E. teacher the other day. He said Jack's been a bit off. Not really interested in football. Not turning up for rugby practice. Getting lippy in class and answering back."

"That's not like him at all. Well, maybe the lippy part, but not turning up for sports practice?"

"Exactly. That's what Mr Wallis said. He wondered if Jack was ill. Of course, Jack says there's nothing wrong. Completely denies it all and just acts like his usual cheeky self. But I can tell he's… not right."

"It can't be easy, all this change," I said. "I'll have a word with him. Well, if he replies to any of my texts, of course."

She looked sad then. She breathed in deeply, looking down as she gently stroked the palm of her hand – something I've only ever seen her do when she's unhappy. She looked so vulnerable in that moment and I realised just how much I'd hurt her.

"Come home," I implored. "Please, just come home."

"Let's not, Dave. Not just yet, anyway."

"No, all right. I, erm…"

We sat there just looking at each other for a few seconds, like two anxious people on a first date, not quite sure what to say, and desperate for the other one to break the painful silence. Thankfully, our waiter appeared and eased the tension. I ordered the steak and Catherine, perhaps trying to look disinterested in proceedings, ordered a measly chicken wrap. Then, as the waiter was about to disappear, she had a sudden change of heart.

"Actually, fuck that," she said. Bring me the half-chicken and ribs combo, with a side order of onion rings. And upgrade that Diet Coke to a large white wine." She smirked with satisfaction as he changed the order.

"So, how have you been?" asked Catherine.

"Oh, you know," I said, "so, so. Got fucked over for a promotion at work. Smashed up my boss's office and got suspended. Then my wife left me and took the kids. All pretty standard," I laughed.

Catherine grimaced at me. Clearly not ready to make light of the situation.

"How are you really? I mean, you look good. A little too good, actually. New clothes as well?"

"Yeah, I went shopping. Bought some new stuff. Just trying to… I don't know… make myself look a bit better."

"That's nice for you. And how's that working?" she said, bitterness in her voice.

"Oh, come on, Cath. There's nothing wrong with wanting to dress a bit better. To look a bit better. Feel better about yourself."

"No. No, there's nothing wrong with that…"

A silence hung between us. More that she wanted to say, but she didn't want to say it yet.

"So, how's your training coming along? For the big race?"

"Yep, good," I lied. "Been out for quite a few runs now. Building up the distance each time."

"Only a few weeks until the race now, isn't it?"

"Yep. Two weeks away. Really looking forward to it." I hoped my face wasn't betraying me. "Will you and the kids come and watch? It would be great to know there's someone cheering me on."

"I don't know. We'll see."

"Please come, Cath. I really miss you all. I want to see you."

"Yes, well," she snapped. Again, she clearly wanted to say more, but held back.

The waiter arrived with our food. We turned our attention to our plates, enjoying the opportunity to focus on something else for a moment.

"Steve's worried about you," she said.

"Oh?" I replied, suspicion ringing in my voice. "You spoke to Steve?"

"He called me the other day. He said you've been turning up late for work, missing days here and there. Apparently, you're not eating properly… McDonalds for lunch? And down the pub most nights after work."

"Oh really?" I snapped, interrupting her. "He said all that, did he?" I made a mental note to ask him who the hell he thought he was, interfering in my life.

"He's just worried. He loves you and he doesn't want to see you like this. None of us do."

"Then come home, Cath. Yes, I admit I'm not at my best at the moment, but that's what happens when your wife and kids leave you. I'm lonely and I'm hurting. And I'm sorry. I'm so, so sorry I ever hurt you. Can't we put it all behind us? Can't you forgive me and just come home?"

"I want to, Dave. I really do. But what you did was so… I mean, the things you wrote… I couldn't believe you felt like that about us."

"I don't," I said. "I don't. Please believe me. It was just a moment of madness. I don't know why I did it, or what I was thinking. I was just going through a weird phase, what with New Dave moving in. I guess… maybe I got a bit overly reflective on my own life and where I was at… And then, when I didn't get that promotion at work… Well, I think I went a little bit mad."

"A little?" she said, trying to conceal a smile.

"Okay, a lot. Completely bonkers. Bat-shit crazy. But you have to believe me, I never meant a word of it. I love you and the kids. You're my whole life and I need you back."

"Well…"

"Please, Cath. Come home."

"You're still not forgiven, Dave," she snapped angrily, as if suddenly remembering a feeling – perhaps the one she felt when she first saw the spreadsheet. Then she calmed a little. "But I'm glad we could talk like this. You know, Karen was dead against me coming tonight."

Fucking Karen! That interfering, miserable bloody bitch.

"I completely understand," I lied. "She doesn't want you getting any more hurt. Neither do I."

Catherine looked down and placed an onion ring in her mouth.

"Come home, Cath."

"No," she said tersely. "Not as easy as that. I'm not saying things are over. Not completely. But I don't know who you are at the moment,

Dave. The man I married would never had said those things about me and the kids. He'd never have written it down."

"I told you, I never meant any of…"

"Worst of all," she said, cutting me off, "my Dave – the man I fell in love with – would never have been so down on himself."

I didn't know what to say then. I looked at my food and pushed a chip aimlessly around the plate.

"I don't know what's happened to you. I don't get it. A new neighbour moves in and you get this weird obsession. All of a sudden, it's like you hate your life. You hate being with us. It's like you blame me for dragging you down, or preventing you from having this better life somehow."

"No, never. I'd never blame you. Or the kids."

"But you did, Dave. You wrote it down. You were 46% worse off because of us."

"No, that's not it. That was never it. It wasn't about you guys. I mean, yes, I started feeling down about myself, but I never resented you or the kids. I just started feeling like maybe I could have been… better somehow."

"But why? I thought we were happy? I thought we had a nice life. The life we'd planned and built for ourselves."

I took a long swig of beer.

"Don't you ever wish for more?" I said. "More money? A bigger house? Nicer cars?"

"Not really. I love our house. It's our home, full of our memories. And you can always have more money, but we don't need it. Not really. We already have everything we need."

"A pool in the back garden, then? Or a sauna? I saw how impressed you were with New Dave's sauna?"

"It's nice, I suppose, but I wouldn't want one myself. It's all a bit… showy, isn't it?"

"But you were so excited when they told us we could use it," I said, confused.

"*Use it*, yes," she said, mockingly. "I thought it sounded like fun. And why wouldn't we give it a go? But I've never sat there thinking: *Oh, why can't I have my own private sauna?*"

"But… but…" Again, I didn't know what to say.

"It's all just stuff, Dave. You know me, as long as we're all healthy and we've got enough money to buy food and pay the bills, I'm happy with that."

"But I thought you wanted…"

Catherine flashed me one of her knowing looks.

"Well, I'm happy too," I said. "Or at least I will be if you and the kids come home. I just want things back to normal. The way they were. I want my life and my family back."

"Then what's all this about?" said Catherine, pointing to my new clothes and messy hair.

"Oh, I dunno. I just wanted to feel a bit…"

"Is there someone else?" she said, again cutting me off, the glint of tears forming in her eyes.

"Where's this coming from?" I said, taken aback.

"I don't know, Dave. All this… self-improvement. You wouldn't be the first. Remember Tony from my work. He started dressing differently. New shoes. New suits. Turns out he was on a different Tinder date every night for months. Women *and* men. His poor wife had no clue."

"I'm not on Tinder," I said. "You're the only woman I want. And I'm definitely not swinging both ways. Besides, who'd want this old bag of bones with crap hair," I said, pointing at my head and forcing a chuckle.

Again, Catherine didn't laugh. She took a sip of her wine.

"I do," she said. "I want my old Dave back. The one who was happy and content. The Dave who enjoyed his job, and liked cooking on his barbecue and pottering in the garden. The one who was confident and proud, and who didn't let anything get him down. I want *him* back."

"And you can have him back, Cath," I said, tears now forming in my eyes. "He's still here. You can have him back now."

Catherine smiled. Her eyes welled slightly, and she took my hands in hers.

"You can have old Dave back. But better than that. You get the new version."

"What?" she said, confusion spreading across her face.

"New and improved," I said, smiling. "Dave 4.0. The plan is working. I can see now what I need to do to be the best Dave I can be."

"What?" she said again, letting my hands drop to the table with a thud. "So, you're still doing it? You're still doing that stupid fucking plan?"

"Yes, of course."

"Have you not listened to a single word I said?"

"Of course. I get it. I know what you want. And I can see how to make us both happy again. I'm heading in the right direction, making small improvements here and there. When I do this race in a few weeks' time…"

"Jesus, Dave," snapped Catherine. "Nothing's changed has it? I thought a few weeks on your own, missing the kids, missing me… I thought that might have been enough to make you see sense. But you're still obsessed. And this *plan* of yours is just making you worse."

"Don't blame the plan, Cath. There's nothing wrong with the plan. It's starting to work. Can't you see that?"

"You're deluded," she said, sneering and taking another large swig of her wine.

"I just… don't see what's wrong with trying to improve myself. I want more money. I want a better job. I want to feel better about myself."

"And your old family don't fit with this perfect new life, eh?"

"No, that's… your twisting my words. That's not what I…"

"I saw what you wrote, Dave. How you compared us and marked us not good enough."

"I've told you, that's not what any of this was about…"

"Do you have a plan for us, too, Dave? Extra tutoring for Jack to make him smarter? Counselling for Holly, to make her less grumpy?"

"No, of course not," I lied. She obviously hadn't read that part of the spreadsheet.

Catherine's face was bright red, her eyes shiny with tears. "What about me? Do I need to go on a diet? Get a haircut? Some plastic surgery maybe? Tell me Dave, what do we all need to do to become this perfect family that fits with your perfect life?"

"Nothing. You're all perfect already."

"Not according to your spreadsheet," she said, her voice uncomfortably loud now. She took another large swig of wine.

"I've deleted that spreadsheet," I lied again. "It means nothing to me. It was all just a horrible mistake and if I could take it back, believe me I would. I never meant to hurt you. Never."

"But you've just told me you're still doing the plan. Don't you see how that makes me feel? You're not good enough. We're not good enough. And, what? You'll never be happy until you feel like you have a better life than our next-door neighbour?"

"It's not that. You don't understand."

"No, I *don't* understand. Who gives a fuck what the man's name is? It doesn't mean anything. There are thousands of people in the world with the same name. They don't all go mad and have an existential crisis. They don't get obsessed and spend money they don't have on fancy cars and new clothes, trying to make themselves feel better."

"No, but they also don't live next door to the living embodiment of everything they could have been," I said, fighting back. "They don't have the daily reminder of their own failure."

"And there we go again," she said, waving her arms. "Failure. Me, Jack and Holly… we're your failure. And how much better off you'd be without us, eh?"

Catherine stood, picked up her coat and handbag and climbed out from behind the table.

"Do you think you're the only person to ever feel like this? We all have dreams, Dave. We all have things we wanted to do, or be. Places we've never been, ambitions we've never achieved. I'm sorry to tell you, but that's just life. Do you think you're the only person who's ever felt disappointed with what they've got? Wished they had more money or nicer clothes, or a better bloody car? Everyone's looked at their life at some point and wondered what they've missed out on, or what they might have if they'd done things differently. But then they just carry on living their life."

"But that's the problem. Don't you see? You don't have to just settle for the life you've got."

"No, you don't. But it's one thing to push yourself to get fit, or get a new job, or a pay rise. It's another thing entirely to develop an obsession with your neighbour and start acting like a madman. And just for the record, I like the life I have. Or, at least, I did."

"But Cath…"

"I thought you'd changed, Dave. I hoped so, anyway. But you're still just as lost. And I don't know how to help you."

"Please don't go," I said, tears now rolling down both of my cheeks. "Please, just stay and talk."

"I won't let you make me feel like this, Dave. And I won't let you treat our kids like they've held you back from being this amazing version of you that only you can see." Catherine picked up her glass and downed the rest of her wine.

"I'm going now," she said, suddenly speaking much slower and calmer. "I really hope you figure out what you want. Before it's too late."

Then she turned and walked away.

"But it's you I want," I said quietly to myself.

I watched the restaurant door close behind Catherine as she left.

"Oh dear," said the waiter, suddenly appearing at the table. He smiled sympathetically at my tear-streaked cheeks as he started collecting up the plates. "Date didn't go too well, eh?"

"You could say that."

"Oh well, she didn't look your type anyway. But I'm sure there's somebody out there for you." He smiled sycophantically, pulled out a dessert menu and placed it down in front of me. "I'll leave this here, just in case."

CHAPTER 16
MINDFUL MOVEMENT

"JUST BREATHE IN and breathe out. And if it feels comfortable to do so, give yourself permission to lift your arms up and out to the side of your body."

Marcus, our mindfulness instructor was stood at the front of the class, breathing deeply and waving his arms like an inflatable wacky waving tube man. He looked like a knob.

He was guiding us in something called Mindful Moving – a sort of cross between Tai Chi and slow-motion rave dancing. The general idea seemed to be to move in as random a way as possible and look as ridiculous as you could. Or in my case, stretch, creak and groan, and fail to follow even the simplest instructions. I'm sure I looked even more of a knob.

I felt very uncomfortable. Over the weeks, I'd got used to lying on the rough, blue carpet with my eyes closed, drifting off inside my own head. It was safe there. I knew nobody was watching and I could actually relax. But all this arm waving made me feel like a complete berk. The fact that everyone else looked just as stupid as me did nothing to comfort me, and I felt about as relaxed as a skydiver with no parachute.

That feeling is the same reason I've always shied away from public speaking, or dancing in night clubs, or anything that puts me centre of attention – all those eyes boring in and judging, and being completely unable to run away or escape. The same reason I've always sat back and let Steve take the lead in presenting our creative work. And why I'll never become UK karaoke champion (well, that and the terrible singing voice).

It was my sixth mindfulness session, and the final one in my obligatory work-sanctioned course. I was pleased to have completed the full run. I hadn't actually had any choice in the matter, of course. My job very much depended on me getting an attendance slip signed after each visit.

But I'd turned up to every session since Catherine took the kids and left me, even when I could barely find the energy to get out of bed and put on the wrinkled clothes I hadn't been bothered to iron. I'd even somehow managed to show up to last week's class, just a few days after my disastrous date with Catherine, when she'd gone running from the restaurant and left me trying not to cry all over a dessert menu.

Bizarrely, after a stressful few days in the office, I'd actually found myself looking forward to today's session. That pretentious arsehole Zack had had the audacity to question some of mine and Steve's work, even though he had no prior knowledge of the project or the client brief – or any tangible experience in marketing and advertising. He made us work late two nights in a row, coming up with a second creative route based on his shit ideas, because he felt there was a better way to go.

When we presented the work to the client and, of course, they went with our original concept, Zack tried taking credit for that – claiming he'd pushed us to achieve a better quality of creative output. The deluded fucking tool. I was so angry, I was close to another office smashing, and Steve had to escort me very quickly to the pub down the road to prevent it from happening.

Following what Catherine had told me during dinner, I'd also spent the past few days worrying about Jack. After several text messages and phone calls, he finally agreed to meet me for a burger and chips after school.

"So, what's all this about you ditching football and rugby practice? That's not like you. You love your sports."

"Yeah, I know," he said, slightly sheepishly. "I've just, like, had other stuff to do."

"Other stuff? Like what?"

"Oh, you wouldn't get it, Dad," he said.

"I think I would, Jack. Actually, I think I understand completely," I said, tilting my head and softening my voice. "You know, just because your mum and I are having a bit of a… funny patch… that's nothing for you to worry about. We still love each other. And we still love you and Holly so, so much."

"Yeah, I know," he said, screwing up his face.

"Your mum and I are going to work things out. And things will get back to normal. But you don't need to worry about it. And don't let it get you down. You just keep doing things as normal."

"Yeah, I know," he said again, pronouncing each word with extra emphasis and looking at me like I was an idiot.

"You can't let what's happening with us affect your sports. You love that and…"

"I'm not," he said, cutting me off. "It's got nothing to do with you."

"So, why are you ditching practice?"

"I told you, I just had better things to do."

"Like what?" I said, starting to get annoyed at his effusiveness.

"I've been going to an acting class, okay?" he said, picking up his drink and sucking hard on the straw.

"An… acting class?" I said. "Why didn't you just say that? Your mum's been really worried."

"I dunno," he huffed. "I guess I was a bit embarrassed…"

"Acting, eh?"

"It's just a school thing," he said, looking up. "Like, an extra sort of class afterwards. I only started going because this girl Chloe I like goes and I was trying to impress her a bit. But… like… I started getting into it, you know?"

I didn't know what to say. I'd never seen this side of him before.

"And… like," he continued, "the teacher says I'm pretty good. He wants me to be in the school play. He reckons I could even do acting at, like, college or something, when I'm older. Could even be a career."

"Right," I said, taken aback. "I didn't realise that's something you're interested in."

"I wasn't really, but I like it now. And I think I'm pretty good. It's really cool, you know?"

"Right. And did you impress Chloe?"

"Oh, I don't like her anymore. She got off with Chris at a party and I sort of like this other girl, Sarah, now."

"Well, that's… good," I said. "I'm glad you've found a new interest. But don't give up on your other things, eh? You know, make sure you still go to football practice, at least."

He rolled his eyes and took another noisy slurp of his drink.

That was all I needed. It was bad enough when my main hopes were hanging on him becoming a professional sportsman. Now, it seemed, his key career ambitions might result in him becoming a professional out-of-work actor.

"Well, as long as you're happy," I said, not entirely meaning it, but really trying to. "That's the main thing."

With all that stress floating around in my brain, I'd actually come to appreciate the calming effects of mindfulness. I still thought it was a load of twaddle, of course. But there's something to be said about sitting quietly, breathing deeply and just being… well, mindful. It's very cathartic. And I'd genuinely got a lot out of the course. I was even considering signing up for more classes.

To my surprise, the whole group had lasted the full six weeks and seemed to be showing similar benefits. Sally told me she was finding life a bit less stressful. And though she still wanted to strangle her lazy husband when he left dirty clothes on the bedroom floor, or leave her four squabbling kids at the supermarket and just drive off into the sun, she now had the breathing techniques to calm herself down.

It turns out Frank did come to the first class by mistake – he was supposed to be taking a Seniors' Watercolour Painting course and wandered into the wrong room. However, he'd found the breathing exercises so relaxing, and enjoyed everyone's company so much, he'd just carried on coming. I worried what he might do now it was all over. I hoped he'd find something else to occupy his days, or meet a new group to keep him company.

And his name isn't actually Frank. He's really called Bill. When he mistakenly came to the first class, he quickly realised he was in the wrong place, but didn't have the heart to tell our overly-enthusiastic instructor. So, when Marcus checked the names off his register, and assumed the Bill he was looking at was the Frank on his piece of paper, Bill just went along with it. He was so embarrassed, he didn't have the heart to confess the truth. He swore me to secrecy, too.

I wondered what happened to the real Frank. Was he now going by 'Bill' one afternoon a week and becoming an expert in watercolours?

Sharon, although still a little twitchy, was definitely showing signs of improvement. Even Alan was looking calmer. The breathing techniques had helped him in stressful situations at work. Simply nipping out to his car for a short meditation when the stress levels rose had helped him get him through some tough days and avoid heated confrontations with co-workers. He was still paranoid about his colleagues planning to oust him, but mindful breathing could only do so much. And, who knows, maybe he was right. Just because you're paranoid doesn't mean they're not out to get you.

After six weeks, Alan was still treating the class as his own personal therapy session, droning on about his problems and insecurities. But we were used to his outpourings. And, in a way, I guess we all liked to think we were helping him. I really hoped he'd carry on with the mindfulness. Out of all of us, he was the one who needed it most.

Of the whole group, I was the only one whose life seemed to be getting worse, not better. When I'd come for the first session, I was still happily married. Work was shit, but my home life was solid. Over the last six weeks, I'd watched it crumble beneath my feet. I felt like Wile E Coyote, hanging in the air for a few brief seconds, knowing he's about to plummet to the ground and being completely unable to do anything about it.

I hadn't let on to anyone in the class what had happened, but I was sure my un-ironed clothes, increasingly unhealthy appearance and hangdog expression were giving me away. Marcus approached me after the previous week's class, when I must have been looking my absolute worst. He had that caring, born-again Christian, 'I'm here to help' look in his eye. I darted out the door as quickly as I could, fearing I might break down and cry in front of him. He looked like a hugger. And I wasn't sure I could ever look him in the eye again if I found myself sobbing gently, cradled in his arms.

Instead, I dashed out to the car and drove as far and fast as I could, before pulling over in a layby and crying my eyes out – much to the confusion of the owner of the burger van parked 20 yards away. And his three customers. It was not one of my high points.

After 10 minutes of ridiculous flailing, Marcus called the mindful movement to a close and we lay down on the cold, blue, council-building carpet. He then led us through a long, guided meditation. I breathed deeply, following his instructions and giving myself permission – when it felt comfortable, of course – to let my mind wander. Naturally, it wandered straight to thoughts of Catherine and the kids. I wondered what they were doing, whether they were happy, or if they missed me.

I thought of how lonely I was. How cold and quiet the house felt without them. I thought of Catherine's face, tears rolling down her cheeks as she stood up from the table and stormed out of the restaurant.

Understandably, Catherine was now completely ignoring me again. I'd called and left about a hundred messages over the last week and a half, but she was yet to answer or return any of my calls.

That night in the restaurant, Catherine was angrier than I've ever seen her. And she's been angry with me plenty of times in the past. Like the time we went away on a big family holiday to the New Forest, and I got so drunk I accidentally climbed into bed naked with her parents.

There was the time I built a small bonfire in the back garden, and accidentally left a jerry can of petrol a little too close. The resulting explosion saw the majority of the lawn scorched, three fence panels burned down, two fire engines called out, and a story on page five of the local newspaper: *Man Nearly Burns Down House with Garden Bonfire*. Bit of an over-exaggeration, if you ask me, but Catherine was too embarrassed to show her face in public for weeks.

There was also our romantic trip to Hungary before the kids were born, when I got confused and booked flights to Budapest and a hotel in Bucharest. Easy mistake to make, right? Well, she didn't think so. Especially when we spent the first two nights in bunk beds in a dodgy, dirty hostel, sleeping in our clothes and clinging to our luggage in case someone tried to steal it during the night. When we finally found a hotel to take us, it cost an extra £400, and we never got the money back from the hotel we were supposed to be in.

And, of course, there was the recent incident where I spent a large chunk of our savings on an expensive new car without consulting her first.

I've done some pretty daft things over the years. And Catherine has been pretty angry at me. But she always comes around. This time was very different. This time I'd fucked up way worse than ever before. And just when it looked like I'd clawed it all back, I fucked up again.

But that was because Catherine still didn't understand what I was trying to achieve. She only saw the Dave she'd always known. She couldn't envisage the new Dave I was trying to become.

I had to complete my mission, then maybe she'd finally realise what I was doing this all for.

"Breathe in and, as you do, imagine the breath filling your entire body, from your mouth, down your torso, into your legs and all the way to your toes," said Marcus, stopping my mind from wandering. I breathed in, filling my body with air, trying to ignore the niggling pain in my back, and the sound of Bill's snoring.

All I had to do was carry on with my plan. I'd work hard and get that promotion at work. It was only a matter of time before Zack screwed up and they'd beg me to save the day. And I'd demand a big pay rise to do it.

I already had the new car, so I was doing better in that area. I'd also spruced up my look with new clothes – I just had to figure out how to work the washing machine and get them clean (I was sure I could track down some instructions online). And, of course, I was going to prove myself at the big race. I just had to use the last few... how long was it until the day of the race, anyway?

I opened one eye to check nobody was looking, pulled my mobile from my pocket, and sneakily checked the calendar. Shit. There were only 17 days to go.

Fuck it, I thought, all the calm rushing out of my body. That wasn't very long to train.

Christ, what was I doing? How the hell was I going to manage it? My training for the run had started well, but after everything that happened, I hadn't been running in weeks. How had the race sneaked up on me so quickly?

Maybe I should cancel? I could say I was drunk and stupid, and never really meant any of it. Nobody would mind. They couldn't hold me to it, could they?

I breathed deeper, trying to restore a little calm. It wasn't working. The panic gripped me harder.

What the hell was I thinking? Perhaps I should just give up on this whole stupid plan entirely. It's not as if it had worked well so far. In fact, rather than making my life better, I'd made it immeasurably worse. Maybe Catherine was right all along?

No. Fuck that. That was the kind of thinking that had led me to settle for a life less amazing than I deserved. Taking the easy road was why I hadn't achieved as much as New Dave. Not pushing myself hard enough was why I knew I could have done better, earned more, been happier. This was no time to give up.

I deserved everything New Dave had, I just had to fight a bit harder to get it. Yes, things weren't perfect at the moment, but that was temporary. You have to go through hard times to experience the rewards they bring. No pain, no gain.

Once Catherine saw the new improved me, she'd understand I was doing this all *for* her, not because I was unhappy *with* her. She'd see a healthier, richer, happier, better-dressed Dave. A Dave 30-40% better than she'd ever seen before. And all would be forgiven. I could even buy a book on sex techniques to improve my bedroom performance. What woman wouldn't want that?

I had to go through with the run. I had to prove I could do

everything New Dave could. I'd run faster than him, jump over obstacles better. I'd beat him and show him up and walk away victorious. I could see it now – the cheering crowds, the smiling faces, the adulation.

Besides, I'd raised a fair bit of money in sponsorship. I'm sure it wouldn't make a drop in the ocean compared with the money needed to cure cancer, but every little helps. And it would be too embarrassing going around the office, returning everyone's cash.

My heart thumped with adrenaline. I drew in a long breath, trying to calm down. When I got home, I'd try calling Catherine again. I'd send her texts, WhatsApps, Facebook messages and emails. I'd do everything I could to get her and the kids to come and watch the race, so they could see my victory.

Then I'd go straight out for a run. Surely 17 days was enough time to prepare for a 10k. It's not as if I'd never run that distance before. And I wasn't starting totally from scratch. All the training I'd done before Catherine left had to count for something – a good base to build on.

"Okay," said Marcus, banging his tiny gong to signal the end of the meditation, "when it feels comfortable to do so, open your eyes and return to your present experiences."

Fuck. I was still buzzing. I needed to calm down. I drew in two more deep breaths, like a panicked student trying to answer a few last questions at the end of an exam. I clenched my eyes tightly, willing the feeling of calm to wash over me, as everyone around me sat up. But it was no good, the meditation was over.

I opened my eyes and sat up, glancing jealously at all the serene faces in the room. The bastards.

"Well done guys," said Marcus, "really good work. Now, as you know, today's the final session in our Mindfulness beginners' course. So, give yourselves a big pat on the back, you've all done so well."

Sally raised her hand and actually gave herself a pat on the back.

"Now, I hope you've all come to realise the benefits of Mindfulness," said Marcus, getting up from his chair and fishing a handful of paper from his bag. "I hope I've taught you all some really useful techniques for dealing with stressful moments. And I hope you now feel more connected with your own minds, and able to take time out to be a bit more mindful."

Marcus then went around the room handing out certificates of completion. It seemed pretty pointless. What was I supposed to do, frame it and hang it on the wall?

"Ooh, this is lovely," said Sally, smiling as she took her certificate. "I'm going to get a nice frame for this, and I know exactly which wall to hang it on."

Even Alan looked pleased with himself.

"I really hope you'll all continue with your Mindfulness breathing exercises at home," said Marcus, as I stood up from my chair and put on my coat. "You've got your CDs with the guided meditation recordings, so you can listen to those. Plus, your colouring books, and do keep writing your journals."

The whole group nodded, like children promising to do their homework over the summer holidays.

"And as you know, this was only the beginners' course. From next week, I'll also be teaching an intermediate level class. It continues on from this course, over 16 weeks, with lots more meditation sessions like this. I'll show how to reach the next level of Mindfulness. It's only £15 per session. If anyone would like to sign up, I have a few spaces left."

So, that's how it works. Get them hooked with a few cheap sessions, then sting them for the big bucks. What a scam. Unsurprisingly, the rest of the group were still in their seats, ready to take the sign-up sheet.

"How about you, Dave?" said Marcus, as I picked up my certificate and headed towards the exit. "You've made some good progress, but I think there's more we can do to help you. I'd definitely recommend the intermediate course for you."

Of course, he would.

"Yeah, sounds great," I said, rushing past him towards the door. "Let me think about it, eh?"

I didn't have time to hang around and talk about classes. I had to get home and go running. I had 17 days, and literally no time to waste.

CHAPTER 17
FILTHY MUTHA

THE SUN GLINTED over the tops of the trees, stinging my tired eyes. Small clouds of breath escaped my mouth and went flying off high into the sky. The park swarmed with people milling, shuffling, stretching and dashing about. They looked eager and excited. Far too cheerful for a cold, damp October morning. And way too keen for the hellish experience we were all about to undertake.

A cold wind slapped my bare calves and whistled up my shorts. My running shoes pinched my toes and my t-shirt clung a little too tightly to my rotund belly. The day of the Filthy Mutha Run was here. And while I might have been wearing the expensive running gear I'd bought, I was really not ready for it.

A dull ache throbbed in the centre of my brain. I felt tired, despite forcing myself into bed at 9pm the previous night to ensure I was well rested. I'd had a sensible dinner of pasta, bread and chips, loading up with as many carbs as I could cram in. I'd even resisted the temptation to drink beer, settling instead for some of Jack's orange squash.

In a bid to ensure I was fully hydrated before the race, I'd downed two pints of water and two bottles of Lucozade Sport before leaving the house. I'd also eaten four slices of toast slathered in honey, thinking an extra helping of carbs and sugar would somehow give me a much-needed boost of energy. Instead, it sat heavy in my stomach, making me hurp with indigestion. I was also now desperate to go to the toilet, and not in the best place for it.

I strolled through the park, trying to gauge what was going on and where I was supposed to be. As I got closer to the end of the path, I saw a desk with a big sign: REGISTRATION. As I got closer still, I saw a large wooden arch with people standing officiously by a machine which I took to be something to do with recording times.

A crowd of people in coats and scarves milled around a few yards from the arch, clearly non-runners, here to cheer on loved ones. They looked even more miserable than the people in shorts and t-shirts, and I wondered exactly who was supposed to be enjoying this – the idiots about to go through ritual torture in the name of sport, or the idiots watching them?

A row of 10 Portaloos lined the edge of the grass. Each had its own queue of at least six or seven people, all waiting to squeeze out their last wee before starting the race. 10 yards down from the official toilets was the unofficial toilet – about 20 men lined up, side-by-side in front of a long row of trees, too impatient or nervous to wait. With the cold wind pinching at my legs, my need to pee suddenly went into overdrive. Rather than wait in the long queues, I walked over to the treeline to join the free pee-ers. I figured propriety would soon go out the window when I was covered in mud, wading through icy pools and getting electrocuted, so there was no point worrying about proper toilet etiquette.

I walked to the tree line to see a lot of people had clearly peed here before me. The ground had turned to sludge, absolutely sodden with frothy, golden brown liquid. It squelched loudly as I walked on it and I nearly lost my footing several times as I skidded and skittered about.

The air was thick with ammonia, making me cough and cover my mouth and nose with my hand. I looked down to see my trainers – my brand new, very expensive, professional running trainers – caked in pee-soaked mud. "Bloody hell," I said under my breath, "these cost a small fortune and I've only worn them a handful of times." Then I shuddered at the realization. I genuinely had only worn them a handful of times. The new running shoes I'd bought to train and prepare for this hellish race had been on my feet less than a dozen times.

What the hell was I doing? I couldn't do this. I wasn't prepared. I was nowhere near fit enough. I didn't truthfully know whether I'd be able to manage the distance, let alone the punishing terrain and hellish obstacles.

Why the hell hadn't I stuck to my training plan? At first, it hadn't seemed that bad missing the odd training session when I was tired, or stressed, or busy with work. Or when my wife left me and my life crumbled in front of me. But the odd missed training session had turned into a week without running. Then two weeks. Then, I'd lost so much fitness and stamina I was practically back to square one, starting from scratch each time I went out.

Then came the realisation during my mindfulness class. I'd done what I could over the past 17 days, knowing I only had a short window to get race fit. But even then, it had proved difficult.

With Zack forcing late nights on us, I didn't manage to get out as often as I needed. I was too tired. Or it was too late. Or it was raining. Or I was too hungry. 17 days was never going to be enough time to prepare for a race like this – and of those 17 days, I'd actually only managed four runs.

I was more than a little scared.

'Sod this,' said a little voice in the back of my head. 'Just turn around, go home and forget all about it.'

I could say I was ill. I could fake a bout of the flu. Or a stomach bug. Could I feasibly break my own ankle to provide definitive proof of why I couldn't run? *"Oh, it's bloody annoying. I was so looking forward to doing the run, but I only went and broke my ankle the day before. Oh well, what are you gonna do?"*

Perhaps I wouldn't need to actually break it. There must be some way I could fake it convincingly. Maybe I could bribe a dodgy doctor to put my ankle in a cast. Then I'd just have to wear it for a few weeks, before staging a recovery and people would be none the wiser.

Would it even need a cast? I could buy one of those big plastic boot things on Amazon. They sell everything on Amazon. Surely, that would be convincing enough.

"Dad! Dad!"

I turned to see Jack, waving frantically at me. Holly stood next to him, her face screwed up with teenage angst. Catherine was next to her. She lifted her hand to wave at me too, then seemed to reconsider halfway through, her hand halting at her hip and dropping again.

After how things ended last time, I hadn't really expected them to come. I'd assumed Catherine would still be too angry. No doubt, word of our dinner would have got back to Holly and, quite rightly, she'd take her mother's side and be equally keen to avoid me. And, going on recent behaviour, I figured Jack would have got a better offer.

But there they were. I smiled widely as I waved back at them. I'd genuinely never been so pleased to see anyone in my life. And then another thought hit me.

Bollocks! There's no way out of it now. I was doing this stupid run whether I liked it or not.

I gestured to them to meet at the registration stand, then turned back to carry on with the business at hand.

"Come on Dave," I muttered to myself. "You can do this. You've run 10k before, so you can do it again. The rest of it can't be that bad.

It can't be real tear gas, can it? They wouldn't be allowed. And they're not going to actually electrocute people…"

"You'll be all right, mate," said an overly-enthusiastic runner who'd shuffled up next to me. He wore a battered, brown t-shirt with faded writing that said *I did your Filthy Mutha!*

I suddenly realised I'd been voicing my concerns louder than I thought.

"You're right, it's not real tear gas," he continued. "It makes your throat tickle, but it's not too bad. And it wears off pretty quick."

"Oh, good," I replied, not feeling very reassured. "You've done this before?"

"Fifth time, mate," he barked at me. He pointed at the words on his t-shirt, looking very impressed with himself, then burst out into a maniacal laugh.

"You'll be fine. The adrenaline gets you round. And the electricity's no worse than sticking your finger on an electric sheep fence. It stings and jolts, but it's fine. In fact, after a few times, I actually start to like it."

He laughed maniacally again. I realised I was probably not taking advice from the best source.

"Right…" I said, trying to smile.

He finished peeing, stretched his arms high above his head, then went into this frantic burst of on-the-spot sprinting, shuffling his feet at double-speed and peppering my legs with tiny splashes of warm, brown pee-mud.

"Of course, it's the giant fucking ice bath you have to watch out for. But I'll let you find that out for yourself eh?" He burst into another crazed laugh, slapped me hard on the shoulder, then ran off. I winced as I looked down at my muddy legs.

I managed to squeeze out a pee then walked over to the registration table. A snippy, middle-aged woman peered up at me with disdain.

"Name?" she said, sharply and without a hint of friendliness.

"Um, Dave. Dave Brookman," I said.

She sneered and looked down at a stack of envelopes in her hand. She flicked through them quickly, until she found mine.

"Confirm your address," she snapped up at me without looking.

"Um, 16 Sheppey Close," I said.

"Says 18 here. 18 Sheppey Close. You must have registered wrong. Did you fill in the application wrong online? Because, technically, if you've given us the wrong information, I shouldn't really let you run. I mean, it's not hard, filling in a number is it?"

What the hell was this woman's problem? What had happened in her life to make her such a misery?

"Actually," I said, "I filled in the form perfectly well, thank you. Can you check again?"

"I've already checked. It says 18, not 16," she said with a smug grin, clearly enjoying the feeling of putting me in my place.

"No, check the pile again."

She snorted a contemptuous laugh out of her nose, raised her eyebrows, then looked back at the pile. She couldn't wait to prove me wrong again. I could, of course, have explained exactly what had happened. But she was so rude, I wanted to put her in her place.

She sorted through the pile again, much slower this time, starting at the beginning and making a point of placing down each discarded envelope in turn. Finally, she came to my one. She held it in her hand, examining it closely. I could practically hear her eyebrows drop as the smug look fell from her face.

She held the envelope in her hand, picked up the previous one and held them side by side.

"What's going on here? Is this some kind of scam? Why have you registered twice at different addresses?"

"I haven't," I smiled, innocently. "I told you, I filled in the form correctly. That one," I said, pointing to the envelope in her left hand, "is mine. The other one is my neighbour's."

"But they have the same name."

"I know," I said, feeling more than a little smug. "We have the same name."

"What? You live next door to someone with the exact same name as you? That's stupid."

"Tell me about it."

I felt a hand on my shoulder. "That'll be mine," said New Dave, reaching over me and pointing at the grumpy woman's right hand.

After several minutes of bureaucratic to-ing and fro-ing, as the woman made us both show her identification, she finally handed over our entry packs. She clearly wanted to complain. She wanted to ban us from taking part. But what could she complain about – the fact we had the same name? For once, having New Dave as a neighbour actually paid off.

Yes, it was mean and unnecessary, treating her that way. I could have explained the situation straight away, rather than dragging it out to make her look stupid. But she started it. And the world had beaten me up so much recently, why shouldn't I get my own back where I could?

New Dave and I spent a few minutes filling in a long disclaimer form. It indemnified the organizers for any responsibility over serious injury that we might sustain during the course of the event. We signed to say we accepted the risk of electrocution, drowning and all manner of injuries. After a few paragraphs, I stopped reading, deciding ignorance was bliss.

Finally, we had to sign to say we were physically capable of undertaking such a physical test of endurance. It wasn't exactly a lie, but I'd have liked a little box to say that, although I was technically fit, I should possibly have been a bit fitter. No matter, though. The form was signed and I was doing this.

Shit! I was actually doing this.

We handed the forms back, the woman snatching them out of our hands and throwing them into a large pile.

"Good to see you, Dave," said New Dave. "You know, I wasn't sure you'd actually go through with it." He laughed heartily, slapping me hard on the shoulder.

"And why not?" I said defensively.

"Oh no, I just mean… well, we did kind of bully you into it at the barbecue. I wasn't sure if it was just… you know, bravado."

"If I say I'm going to do something, I do it. You can count on that."

"Good. Well, great. It's good to see you here, I think it should be fun."

"Yes," I snapped, a little too sharply.

"Okay, well, I need to go and speak to the wife. See you on the start line, eh?"

He ran off to where Tamzin stood talking to Catherine. They walked away and I strolled over to see Catherine and the kids.

"Hey, Dad," said Jack. "You're gonna get well muddy in this, aren't you?"

"Yeah, I'd say that's a good possibility."

"Wicked!" he laughed. "Do you think you're gonna win?"

"Erm, well I'm not sure about that. I mean, there's some pretty sporty looking people here." His eyes dropped with disappointment. "But I'd say your old dad's got as good a chance as anyone," I said, ruffling his hair.

"Cool," said Jack, giving me a high five. Catherine raised an eyebrow. Holly sighed and rolled her eyes with the *God, you're so embarrassing* look she'd perfected over the last few years.

"Thanks for coming, guys. It really means a lot. I wasn't sure you were going to make it."

"We wouldn't let you down for something like this," said Catherine. "So, you're really going through with it?"

"Yeah, course. Why wouldn't I?"

"You know you don't have to. Nobody would think any less of you, if you decided you didn't want to do it."

"What are you talking about? Of course, I'm doing it. I'm really looking forward to it," I lied.

"Yeah, course he is, Mum," said Jack. "He's gonna win."

"How has your training gone?"

"Good, good," I lied again. "Been going out two or three times a week, so I've got the distance covered. Hoping for a pretty decent time actually. Couldn't really prepare too much for the other bits, short of filling the bath with ice, or sticking my fingers in a plug socket…" I laughed.

Jack laughed loudly at my joke.

"But anyway, I'm sure it will be fine," I added. "If Next Door Dave can do it…"

Catherine didn't laugh back. She just stood there with a look somewhere between disappointment and disbelief on her face.

"Well, if you're sure…" she said, taking the race number from me and pinning it to my chest.

I sent the kids to go and find a good spot to watch the start of the race so I could have a minute alone with Catherine.

"Thanks for coming today," I said. "It really does mean a lot to me."

"Well, the kids wanted to support you."

"Both of them?" I asked.

"Holly will warm up eventually," said Catherine. "She's always been very protective of me. And she's a 14-year-old girl, full of hormones and righteous indignation. But she loves you. She'll come around."

"And how about you? Did you want to cheer me on? Or maybe just see me taking a bit of punishment."

She raised an eyebrow.

"Probably keen to see me suffer a little electric shock," I said. "Or freeze my nuts off in a giant ice bath."

She cracked. It was ever so slight, but the corner of her mouth raised into the merest hint of a smile. She fought it back quickly, but I'd seen it and she knew I'd seen it.

Catherine always found it hard to stay mad at me. Even when she thought I was the biggest arsehole in the world, I could always manage to make her smile. From there it was easy to make her laugh, just a little bit. And when you're laughing, it's hard to stay mad at someone.

I knew this wasn't going to be as easy as simply making her giggle. But her tiny smile gave me hope there was at least the possibility of a way back.

Catherine finished pinning the number to my t-shirt and touched me lightly on the shoulder. With the number in place, I bent down to attach my timing chip to my right running shoe, lifting the laces tentatively, to avoid getting the pee-mud on my fingers.

"Five-minute warning," a voice called out through loud hailer. "Newbies gather around me, please, for a pre-run briefing."

"I'd better go," I said to Catherine. "Perhaps I could take you and the kids out for dinner after this?"

"That would be nice," she said. "You know, if you can still walk."

I smiled and went to where an officious, skinny man in a high-viz jacket and camouflage-coloured cargo trousers was waving his arms to gather people.

"Okay," he said, through the loud hailer. "Who's ready to get muddy?"

People whooped and cheered either side of me, jumping around excitedly. I couldn't quite share their enthusiasm. Instead, I was trying to decide if I needed another pee.

"Okay, okay," he shouted. "Today, we're doing a 10k run, with some of the hardest, baddest, most terrifying obstacles you've ever seen. It's gonna get muddy. It's gonna get…"

"FILTHY!" shouted the excited crowd in response.

"Yeeeeah," shouted the instructor. "Now, we only have a few rules," he said, taking the tone down to sound more serious. "Rule 1: you don't have to do anything you don't want to. Which means, if you really can't face an obstacle, you don't have do it."

The crowd bristled slightly, as if this was something they didn't want to hear. A ready-made excuse to get them out of truly testing themselves. I was delighted. I had no idea that was an option. You didn't actually have to do the horrible, terrible things if you didn't want to. And nobody would judge you, he'd practically just said so. It was one of their few rules. This was brilliant.

"But if you don't do the obstacles, what does that make you?"

"A pussy!" yelled the crowd in unison, as if they'd been preparing this response for weeks.

Bollocks! I thought.

"And what are we not?"

"Pussies!" yelled the crowd.

"That's right, we're not pussies. Because, what are we?"

"Filthy muthas!" yelled the crowd.

"Yeeeeah," he shouted, jumping up and down on the spot.

The crowd reached a new level of excitement, stomping and clapping, and whipping themselves up into a literal frenzy. I felt completely deflated. They'd handed me a get out of jail free card, then whipped it back and torn it up in front of me.

"Rule 2," continued the wiry instructor, "be nice to each other. Don't hold people up. And if someone looks like they're struggling, lend them a hand."

The crowd quieted slightly, taking in the information with serious faces.

"And Rule 3," he said, holding a pregnant pause like a judge on a TV talent show, "have fun and get as filthy as possible!"

The crowd went into overdrive, shouting, clapping, stomping and slapping each other on the backs.

Was that it? Don't be a pussy, be nice to each other, have fun and get filthy – not exactly a comprehensive list of rules and regulations. What about health and safety? What if something goes wrong? I thought back to the disclaimer form I'd signed. I really should have read it more closely. I had a long list of questions I wanted to ask, but the crowd was now moving towards the starting line and dragging me with them.

We shuffled over to join the more seasoned 'filthy muthas', all hopping, stretching and readying themselves underneath the wooden arch. The guy who'd stood next to me as I tried to pee was right on the starting line, repeatedly thumping himself in the chest like a gorilla.

New Dave was a few rows ahead of me in the pack, stretching his arms and hopping slowly on the spot. I considered moving forwards to stand with him. Perhaps I should try and run along with him – a little bit of comradery to help us both make our way through the course. But then, I figured he'd set off at a pace far quicker than I could keep up with. I'd struggle to match it and he'd quickly leave me behind. I'd look stupid and probably end up injuring myself.

I'd given up on the daft illusion that I'd beat him in the race. There was no realistic hope. But if I finished, and managed somehow not to come dead last, I could still save face and hopefully impress people. So, I held my cautionary spot in the middle of the pack, where a group of other slightly overweight, less-than-peak-condition runners were also looking fearful.

"Okay, you filthy muthas," shouted a gruff voice, through a loud hailer at the front of the pack, "are you ready?"

The crowd roared back affirmative, like a braying army ready to run headlong into battle.

"Three... two... one..." he shouted. The sound of an air horn pierced the quiet calm of the Sunday morning park. Then people started running. And I started running.

So, that was it then. I was actually doing this. Definitely no way out of it now.

Shit!

CHAPTER 18
OVERCOMING OBSTACLES

"GO, GO, GO!" shouted the steward with the air horn. People whooped and cheered all around me as the crowd jolted into action and started running. I was instantly swept along with them, as we moved like an out-of-practice school of fish – hustling, bumping and very much failing to move as one.

It was hard to pace myself at first. Cheered on by the enthusiasm of the other runners, I moved along with them, matching their speed. I was running way faster than I was used to, and I was soon out of breath, feeling tired after only the first few hundred yards.

Worried that I was already struggling with such a long way to go, I told myself not to be a hero and slowed my pace right down. I felt slow, moving only just faster than if I was walking, but I knew I had to preserve energy. I'd started pretty much in the middle of the pack, but after only a few minutes I'd been overtaken by so many people I was now very much holding up the back. And if I wasn't careful, I'd end up finishing the race dead last – if I finished at all.

It was a little disheartening when a pair of chunky, middle-aged women bounded past me. But I had to concentrate on getting through it. And when I made it past the halfway mark, maybe then I could think about increasing my speed. That's what professional athletes do, I thought, as my belly wobbled and I gasped for breath. Keep a little in the tank, then get ready for the sprint finish.

New Dave was long gone, heading off at a very quick pace. I knew I had no chance of catching him. All I could do was run my own race and hope he'd fall and break an ankle or something. Nothing terrible or life-threatening – just enough to slow him down, or force him to withdraw from the race.

I ran for just over a kilometre before coming to the first obstacle – a great wooden structure, with thin sloping planks which led to the top. That didn't seem too bad, I thought. A little steep, and a bit fiddly, but I took my time, concentrated on my footing and within no time I'd traversed my way to the top. And then I saw what the obstacle really was.

High up now, I was suddenly stood on the precipice of a 15-foot drop into a large, cold, sticky pit of mud. An angry, shouty man in a steward's vest thrust a thick rope into my hand and slapped me hard on the back. With a long line of runners queued up behind me, I took heed of the instructor's rule not to hold people up. Usually, I would have procrastinated endlessly, measuring the angles, considering all the possible outcomes of any action, before even moving a foot. But I could feel the tension behind me as people urged me on. And the shouty man was shouting, "Go! Go! Go!"

I gripped hard to the rope, tumbled ungracefully off the end of the platform and swung straight down, legs flailing wildly. The obstacle was carefully measured so that you had no real chance of missing the mud pit, and I splatted down into the cold, sticky, stinking pool. Thick muddy water splashed up and covered me in one large, brown wave. A mini tsunami of shite.

Disoriented and completely blinded by the mud, I managed to get to my feet, stumbling this way and that in the thigh-high pool, with no idea which direction to go in. Then hands gripped my shoulders and someone pull me forwards to the edge of the pit. Another hand wiped the mud from my eyes, until my vision returned. I squinted to see an excited, equally muddy face smiling widely and giving me a big thumbs up.

"Keep going mate," he yelled, "you're doing well." Then he ran off.

I climbed up out of the pit, breathing heavily, my muscles throbbing and aching. The cold was intense now, the cruel wind biting at my wet skin, leaching into my bones, chilling me from the inside. I felt like I could barely keep moving.

I stumbled a few feet forwards, still unsure where to go, then slumped down to my knees and looked back at the muddy pit. As each new person crawled out, totally covered in filth, they stopped to help the next person that splatted down after them. They would then head off running again, as the next person crawled their way out, turned back and helped the person after them.

It was incredible to me, and I felt a little overwhelmed as I watched people stopping to help each other. Everyone was so nice and friendly, helping each other out, making me feel like part of the group. Part of this band of lunatic brothers who'd chosen to spend their morning torturing themselves with pain and mud. I also felt instantly ashamed that I hadn't lent a helping hand to anyone. But I'd been completely fazed, and barely made it out of the pit myself. I hoped nobody would mind.

It was incredibly heartening, watching people willing each other on and yelling encouragement. Raising thumbs into the air and smiling ridiculously big smiles. And it made me feel just a little bit warmer inside.

That was until I set off running again and realised I was now about twice as heavy and twice as frozen as I was when I'd started the race. My clothes were totally sodden and weighing me down. Nearly every inch of my skin caked in thick, sticky mud. My face and hands were completely numb. It was harder to lift my feet. Harder to balance and stay in a straight line. Harder to find the will to keep going. And I'd only done one bloody obstacle.

"Go on, son!" yelled another runner, enthusiastically patting me on the back as he went past. Somehow, I managed to smile and raise a thumbs-up back to him. He ran off and I continued trudging along slowly, wondering what the hell I was doing.

I ran for roughly another kilometre, my body temperature gradually raising again to the point that I was almost sweating. My tensed-up fingers started to thaw, the pain easing. And while my legs still ached, it was now more of a warm throb.

I still had sight of a few runners ahead of me and, though more people had passed me, I was sure there were still a fair few behind me. I crossed a field, ran through a small woods and out into a clearing. Then I saw the second obstacle.

A handful of people were bunched up into a queue at the entrance to a long white tent. A sign above the door read 'The Chokey'. Two stewards stood at the entrance, holding closed two large tent flaps, and ushering people into the tent at staggered intervals. In addition to their camouflage-coloured outfits and high-viz vests, these stewards also wore large gas masks over their faces. I guess this is the tear gas, I thought, as I jogged up and joined the back of the queue.

Whether the gas masks were actually for protection, or just to add an extra element of theatre to proceedings, I'm not sure. But they were certainly effective in scaring the people jostling and shaking ahead of me in the queue. Their knees wobbled and I could hear someone at the front of the crowd worriedly asking the steward: "It's not real tear gas, is it?"

The steward looked back at her, laughed and yelled, "Go, go, go!"

Then he lifted the flap on the tent, placed a firm hand on her back and thrust her into the thick white fog. I guessed she'd get her answer soon enough.

I was getting cold again as I waited. My legs stiffened slightly. And though I really didn't relish the thought of what was inside the tent, I wanted to get going again, if only to warm myself up. So, I was strangely thankful that the stewards managed to keep the queue moving, and before I knew it, a firm hand was pushing me into the tent.

It was dark inside, thin beams of light piercing through the thick, acrid fog. I closed my eyes to thin slits, trying to protect them from the smoke. Instantly, they started burning and itching, and I had an overwhelming desire to rub them. But I knew that would only make things worse, so I held my arms out in front of me, feeling my way through the tent, trying not to bump into other people.

The mud was slick beneath my feet and I had to move slowly, concentrating hard not to lose my footing. This made the process longer, and I was very aware that I wasn't even halfway through the tent before the deep breath I'd taken started to run out. All the running, wheezing and hyperventilating before entering the tent meant I'd only really managed half a breath, and now I was desperate for another one.

My lungs felt like lead. My throat was tight. My head started swimming. I held out as long as I could, moving quicker, my heart thudding as anxiety threatened to overwhelm me. I bumped into a woman scrabbling around on the floor in front of me. I had to fight back the urge to simply push her out of the way. Instead, I helped her to her feet and pointed her to the light shining at the other end.

She moved off ahead of me and I made to follow, but I could fight it no longer. My whole body convulsed, a hot pain burning in my chest, as I suddenly exploded and a burst of breath flooded out through my nose and mouth. Then, totally empty, I had to take another breath back in.

The thick smoke surged in through my mouth, burning my throat and inflating my lungs with its toxic, corrosive heat. No sooner had I breathed in than I felt the desperate need to expel it again. I coughed hard and loud, the horrible smoke somehow burning twice as much on the way out as it had on the way in.

It was an army of angry bees stinging everything in their way. A hundred razor blades slicing and slashing the soft, pink skin of my throat. It was stinging nettles, barbed wire and boiling water all at the same time.

I coughed and wheezed, forcing out the foul fog, then breathed it back in again. Cough, wheeze, choke, pain. Cough, wheeze, choke, pain.

My eyes widened in shock and they started burning too. Tears ran down my face in long streaks. I had to get out of this tent. Now.

I gave up on my careful footing, running as fast as I could towards the thin beam of light at the end of the tunnel. I bounced off the woman again, this time not stopping to help or apologize. I coughed and wheezed, my chest and throat on fire. I had to get out.

I thumped through the thick mud, losing my footing as I neared the end of the tent. I went tumbling through into the light, landing face down in the mud, sucking in great breaths of cold, clean air.

I felt like a new-born baby bursting out into the world. I felt like crying. I felt like curling up into the foetal position and just rocking there for the next few hours.

Instead, I again felt hands on my shoulders, picking me up and lifting me to my feet.

"You're all right," I heard a voice say. "Take a few deep breaths and it'll pass."

I tentatively opened my eyes to see the woman I'd at first helped, then pushed aside to save myself.

"Thanks for pointing me in the right direction," she said. "It's easy to get lost in there, isn't it?" She beamed a big smile, gave me a thumbs up and then ran off.

I wiped tears from my eyes, took several deep breaths. To my great relief, the burning pain in my chest quickly subsided. So, it wasn't real tear gas. But it was horrible enough.

I stood at the side of the tent for a minute, watching as people came bursting out. Some came running through, seemingly unaffected by the smoke, and just carried on running. Others emerged coughing and tear-streaked. Only one other person came flying out of the tent, as I had, landing face first in the mud. I ran over and helped him up. I offered the same reassurances I'd received, then surprised myself as I slapped him on the shoulder and ran off to the re-join the race.

Again, it was only a few minutes before my thighs were burning, my feet lead-like and my breathing short and ragged. At least I was warmer now – still sodden and heavy, but the running was heating my insides.

After roughly another kilometre, I came upon the third obstacle – another long mud pit, covered over with barbed wire. I was already covered in mud, so I no longer cared about getting dirty, as I dropped onto my stomach and started crawling through the filth.

Again, the cold hit me instantly, as if the mud was sucking out all the warmth I'd built up. My muscles ached with it. My arms and legs twitched and tensed with every effort. But I dug in and moved forward. In my head, I moved like a stealthy soldier in a well-practiced front crawl. In reality, I probably looked more like a garden worm having a stroke.

Thankfully, on closer inspection, the barbed wire was not terribly barbed. No sharp jagged bits poking down, ready to slice my delicate skin – it was really more of a wire mesh. Which was welcome news, as I seemed completely incapable of avoiding it. Every time I shunted forwards in the mud, I slammed up against it, making it rattle and shudder. If it had been real barbed wire, my back would have been a bloody pulp after only a few feet.

I was slow through the pit, again holding people up, making it out after a few minutes. A jolly man with a completely mud-soaked beard grabbed my hand and pulled me to my feet. I smiled and offered a thumbs up, then he said words that – to him – must have seemed encouraging, but which struck dread deep into my heart: "Come on mate, it's the electricity one next!" He ran off, smiling wildly. I trudged off slowly, feeling more deflated than ever.

After another kilometre of running, I was slightly warmer again but feeling really fatigued. My legs were throbbing and burning. Sharp jolts of pain shot through my ankles each time a foot hit the ground. My shoulders were tense. My back ached. My chest burned with each harsh breath. And the wet material of my t-shirt felt like sandpaper rubbing against my nipples. Despite that, I was feeling pretty positive. I'd come this far, and I still felt like I had more energy in the tank.

The fact that the obstacles were spaced out every kilometre was actually a good thing. It meant I got a short respite every seven or eight minutes to catch my breath and regroup. They also acted as pretty good markers of progress. I was onto my fourth obstacle, which meant I'd done four kilometres so far. That was nearly halfway, which meant I was doing pretty well. I tried not to think of the six kilometres and six obstacles left to go. All I could do was take one part at a time.

I had no idea how far ahead of me New Dave was. But I was

making my way round the course. I just had to keep going and I knew I could do this.

And then I came upon The Shocker. I heard it before I could see it – a strange, high-pitched electrical whine floating in the air, peppered with the odd yelp or scream. I cornered a small thicket of trees and saw it a few hundred yards away.

It was a large, wooden structure, around 10 metres long and 10 metres wide. Hundreds of strands of plastic wiring hung from the roof to the floor, like jellyfish tentacles. And just like a jellyfish, they were clearly very painful to touch.

I ran over and joined the queue of people waiting to enter. The screams were much louder now, as people tentatively waded their way through the mass of wires. Not every wire was charged, but it was easy to tell when someone found a live one, as they'd scream, shudder and drop to their knees in the mud. It would have been funny, if I wasn't waiting to wade through it myself.

If ever there was an obstacle I'd want to avoid, it was this one. But I thought back to the steward at the start, and the crowd's disdain at the thought of skipping challenges. I hadn't seen anyone else chickening out, and I certainly didn't want to be the only one. So, I gritted my teeth, moved forward and took a deep breath.

The steward lined up four of us to go in at once. I looked to my four compatriots. A young woman to my left looked genuinely terrified, as though she might start hyperventilating at any second. A slightly older woman next to her was much calmer, looking intently at the dangling wires, as though trying to memorise the live ones and plot a safe route. A young man to my right wore a Borat-style mankini, which was barely visible under the mud caking his otherwise naked body. He jumped up and down on the spot, slapping himself in the face and psyching himself up.

The steward waited until the last people cleared the obstacle, then smiled as he paused a few seconds longer to drag out the anticipation.

"GO!" shouted the steward, and the mankini nutcase bolted full pelt into the electrical field, screaming like a maniac. He made it exactly one step before a live wire caught him and sent him tumbling to his knees, shrieking and shaking. His momentum kept him moving forward into the next live wire, which delivered another sting. He shrieked again, his body juddering, and this just seemed to make him lurch forwards again.

Somewhere in his scream, I swear I even heard him laughing. And he just carried on wading through on his knees, making his way painfully to the other end. Scream, lurch, shriek, shudder, laugh. Scream, lurch, shriek, shudder, laugh. The man was clearly insane.

By the time he was nearly two-thirds of the way through, the remaining three of us were still at the start. The woman to the left of me looked even more terrified than she had before she'd witnessed Mankini Man go down. I tried to give her a reassuring smile, but every time the man shrieked, my face twitched. So, I was probably just adding to her paranoia.

The woman to my far left took a deep breath then ventured forward, carefully, methodically, as if she could see a safe route through the wires the rest of us couldn't. She took one step forward, a live wire caught her elbow and she dropped to the floor, screaming and twitching. She lurched back, breathing heavily and rubbing her elbow vigorously, reassessing her plan, confused as to what had gone wrong.

The scared woman to my left reached forward tentatively, making to part the wires like a giant bead curtain. Just as she was about to make contact with a wire, she snapped her hands back tight to her body, her face grimacing with uncertainty.

I quickly weighed up my options. I could walk through slowly and risk getting caught several times, but I could potentially reassess as I went. Or I could follow Mankini Man's tactic and just belt through. I'd almost certainly get caught a few times, but like ripping off a plaster, the pain would be over sooner. It was like running through the rain. You probably got just as wet running as you did walking, but at least you got through it and back into the dry quicker.

There was no point thinking any longer, I just needed to do it. So, I took a deep breath and ran. I made it one full step before the first live wire found me, slapping my chest with a searing jolt of pain. It was like being hit with a tennis ball. A thousand small injections administered to the exact same spot at the same time.

I yelped loudly, emitting a high-pitched, whining shriek I didn't know my body was capable of producing. But somehow, I managed to stay upright, charging on, the momentum keeping me moving. I took another large stride and was hit again, a thousand angry bees jabbing at my left thigh. Another two steps and a painful shock to my back sent me tumbling to my knees. Still, I managed to keep going, wailing and shuddering, and shuffling forwards.

At the end of the obstacle, I could see Mankini Man through to the safe zone, shouting back at me, willing me on. I managed to lift my foot, dig it hard into the mud and propel myself up and forwards again. Another jolt stung my right arm. I'm not sure if it was less powerful, or if somehow my body was getting used to being electrocuted, but it hurt slightly less. And with only a few feet left, it gave me enough forward momentum to launch myself forward, leaping like a rugby player going for a tackle.

Several more wires caught me as I flew through the air, and I shrieked as live wires bit my arms, legs and buttocks. Then I landed hard, face down in the mud, shuddering and juddering, but clear of the wires.

I felt hands on me once more, as Mankini Man lifted me to my feet.

"Yeah," he shouted, "that's how you fucking do it!"

I managed another smile and another thumbs up as I stood there still twitching. Then Mankini Man ran off towards to the next obstacle.

I looked back through the wires to see my other two comrades. The scared woman now looked twice as terrified, having seen my performance, and stood there writhing on the spot, like a child trying to hold in a wee. The methodical lady was still trying to plan a safe route through. She'd be there a long time before she found one.

I wanted to help them, but I knew I couldn't. So, I gave them a big smile and a thumbs up, turned away and started running again.

Like the tear gas before, the effects of electrocution didn't last very long, and I was soon back to normal, jogging slowly. I actually had a pretty decent sweat going on as I rounded another thicket of trees and came up to the next obstacle.

This was obstacle number five, at the end of kilometre number five. The halfway mark. I smiled at the thought of it. I'd made it halfway and I was still going. I still had to do the same again, but it felt possible now. A warm buzz of happiness came over me. It lasted for a full two seconds. Then I saw what the obstacle was.

An ascending walkway led to a platform around 15 feet in the air. I couldn't see what was on the other side of it, but I could guess. A large sign at the top read: *The Freezer*. It had to be the giant ice bath I'd been warned about.

A group of runners queued at the foot of it. I jogged over and took my place at the back. If they'd looked scared waiting for the tear gas or electricity, that was nothing compared with this. People looked genuinely terrified.

Slowly, the queue moved until it was my turn. I edged carefully up the walkway. Muscles in my legs, back and arms that I'd never felt before, screamed and throbbed with pain. It took me longer to reach the summit than I had on the first obstacle – part tiredness and part fear. But I made it up and suddenly found myself at the edge of a giant slide leading to a large pool of water.

A long rail lined the top of the obstacle. I instinctively gripped hold of it.

"Wait here," said a steward. He gazed down to the pool of water beneath us, watching as a woman dragged herself out, shivering and gasping for breath. When the pool was clear, another steward at the bottom raised a hand high in the air.

"Okay, go, go, go!" shouted the steward next to me.

Oh shit!

Suddenly I couldn't move. My hands gripped the rail tight. My legs locked in position. I stared at the pool of freezing water beneath me, barely breathing.

"Go, go, go!" shouted the steward again.

But still I remained motionless. My brain was telling me to go, but my feet weren't in agreement.

"Come on mate, you fucking going or what? You're holding up the queue." The crowd bristled behind me, tutting and sighing.

"I… er," I managed to say.

"If you don't wanna do it, you'll have to go back down," said the surly steward. "Sorry, folks, can you move to one side, this guy's coming back…"

"No, I'm going," I said, interrupting him. I couldn't back down now. I'd come too far to give in. I was sure I could complete the race, but it wouldn't count if I didn't do all the obstacles. New Dave wouldn't have chickened out. He'd have jumped straight down the slide. I couldn't let him beat me here. I had to prove I was as good as him, and that meant I had to complete every part of the race.

The steward sighed loudly. "Well, go on then," he said.

I pulled myself forward on the guard rail, bending my legs and jumping into a seated position. I thudded onto the slide, immediately hurtling down, down, down.

Everything went into slow motion – that grey, blurry feeling you get in the few seconds before you crash your car. The world slowed around me, colours streaming and blending into one. I was rushing down the slide at a hundred miles an hour, but it felt so much slower, as I thought about Catherine. How proud she would be when I completed this gruelling feat. She and the kids would come running home, unable to bear being apart from me for another second.

I thought of New Dave. He'd finally see that he'd met his match. And so would everyone else. Nobody would think me any lesser. Anything New Dave could do, so I could I. I'd make them choke on their words.

Suddenly, the world came back into focus, as the water rushed up to meet me. I hit the surface with a loud slap, freezing, arctic liquid grabbing hold of me and pulling me in. Intense pain hit my legs first, as the cruel cold smacked my skin. The shock drove all the air out of my lungs in one giant outward breath, then I disappeared under the water.

My whole body tensed immediately – a giant man-shaped icicle. I was completely unable to move. I couldn't flap my arms or kick my legs, I just sunk to the bottom of the pool. Then I lay there like a stone, my body stiff and unmoving, staring up to the surface.

People talk about seeing their past lives flash before them when they think they're about to die. I had something else. I saw my life yet to come – images of things I hadn't done, events I'd never even thought of, and would now never have the opportunity to experience.

I saw myself sitting in the stand of a premiership football club, beaming with pride and cheering as I watched Jack on the pitch, celebrating a goal he'd just scored. I saw myself picking up the keys to a new, bigger house, and the smile on Catherine's face as we prepared to move in. I watched myself holding back tears and trying to keep a straight line as I walked Holly down the aisle.

I saw myself winning awards at work and coming up with hundreds of brilliant ideas for marketing concepts. I saw myself grinning contentedly at a retirement party, before Catherine and I set off on a trip around the world.

In an instant, I saw hundreds of amazing things yet to happen. But now they never would, because I was lying at the bottom of a freezing pool, about to drown.

Again, my lungs burned. A deep, searing pain in my chest as I longed for a cool, refreshing breath. My brain was screaming at me to move. Desperate to fight my way back to the top. But my prostrate body was completely immovable – my legs frozen and arms powerless.

Every part of me ached, the cold water gripping, stabbing, and searing my skin. I could hear people shouting, panicking far away, as I focused on an image of Catherine's smile. My eyes closed slowly, the light disappearing and plunging me into darkness.

Then, I felt arms grabbing me, pulling me up through the water. And I burst up through the surface, my mouth jolting open as I gasped in a long, life-saving breath.

Wheezing and coughing, I snapped my eyes open to see the second steward in the water up to his waist. His hand gripped hard on the back of my t-shirt, and he lifted me like a naughty kitten.

"You're all right, mate. I've got you," he said, rather dismissively. "Don't worry, you're not the first one I've fished out today."

The steward dragged me over to the side of the pool. He placed one hand beneath my legs and one on my back, then unceremoniously tipped me up and out of the water.

I landed with a squelch and lay there in the mud, still completely incapable of moving.

"Okay," I heard the steward shout. "He's all right. Send the next one down."

Then the world returned to darkness.

CHAPTER 19
FIRE IT UP

I WOKE TO the smell of warm plastic and antiseptic. A bright light burning my eyes. Fingers roughly forcing my eyelids open.

I was lying on a stretcher, shivering with the cold, soaking wet clothes tightly gripping my skin. A thin, blue blanket was doing little to warm me up. A middle-aged woman with short, curly hair and glasses shone a tiny torch in my eyes, making me wince. Her other hand held my wrist tightly.

"Well, hello there," she said, as I jolted back to life, confused and looking all around me. "It's all right, you're in the back of an ambulance. We're taking care of you." She spoke slowly and loudly, like a British holidaymaker trying to order food in a Spanish restaurant.

"What… how…? What's going on?" I said. The last thing I remembered was hurtling down a slide. Then freezing cold. Then I'd woken up here. "What happened?"

"Bit of a close one, I believe," she said. "As I understand it, you went into the ice bath thing and totally froze up. Just lay there at the bottom, not moving. They had to fish you out, then you passed out on the floor."

Memories flooded back. The freezing water. Laying at the bottom of the pool. A hand grabbing the back of my collar.

"But how did I get here?" I said.

"On a stretcher. Lucky for you, the course goes round in a kind of double loop, so the ice bath is actually only a short walk from the finish line. A couple of stewards carried you back. You've been here for about 20 minutes."

"Fuck! What happened to me?" I said, through chattering teeth. "Is it bad? Was it a stroke? Heart attack? Or something… worse?"

The paramedic looked down at me, confused. Then a ripple of laughter sang in her throat.

"Stroke?" she giggled. "No, nothing like that. You're just a bit tired. Or as my old mum used to say, you've done yourself in."

"What? Tired?" I said, incredulous. "You mean it's nothing serious?"

"No, you just need to warm up, catch your breath and get your energy back. Nothing a hot bath, a bottle of Lucozade and a good old rest won't cure."

Hot bath? Lucozade? I couldn't believe what she was saying. It sounded like the kind of advice you'd give a pensioner after they had a funny turn.

"But I nearly drowned," I implored. "I couldn't move. My arms and legs completely stopped working."

"What do you expect, jumping into a giant ice bath?" scoffed the paramedic. "These races aren't for everyone, you know. You need so much stamina to do all that running, never mind all the crazy obstacles. A man of your age needs to think twice before entering daft competitions like this."

A man of my age? How bloody old did she think I was? New Dave was my age, and he was fit enough to do it. Cheeky bloody bitch. Then again, New Dave probably wasn't shivering in the back of an ambulance. No doubt he was crossing the finishing line, people cheering and whooping, as a sexy blonde placed a winner's medal around his neck.

I opened my mouth to protest, but no words came out.

A steward in a luminous, high-viz jacket appeared at the back door of the ambulance, holding a bottle of orange Lucozade and a Mars bar.

"Oh, you're awake. Good," he said.

"Erm, yeah. I erm…" I really didn't know what else to say.

"Here, get these down you," he said, handing me the drink and chocolate bar. "Bit of glucose will get your blood sugar back. Have you feeling right as rain in no time."

"Thanks," I said, sitting up on the stretcher. I unscrewed the lid from the drink and took a long swig. It was horribly sweet with a thick, syrupy texture. But I gulped down half the bottle in one go.

"Well, you've done me a favour, anyway," he chuckled. "Got me off ice bath duty for a while."

I looked more closely and saw that his clothes were soaking too. Then I realised he must have been the one who dragged me out of the water. My saviour. The man who literally saved my life.

"Oh, no problem," I said. Not exactly the gratitude I owed him. But I was embarrassed and feeling completely wretched. Not to mention exhausted.

"Anyway, looks like you're getting a little colour back in your cheeks," continued the man. "You looked so pale, laying there on the ground. Like a ghost, wasn't he?"

The paramedic laughed. "Thought you were actually a goner for a second," she agreed. Then she grabbed my wrist roughly and checked my pulse again.

"Right," said the steward, "I'm gonna go and warm up. Get out of these wet clothes. Hope you feel better mate."

He slapped me hard on the shoulder and left.

I went to call out after him. I wanted to thank him for saving my life. But something stopped me. Shame? Denial? If I didn't acknowledge the fact that I'd made such a huge fool of myself, then perhaps it never really happened.

With shivering fingers, I open the Mars Bar and took a large bite. It was so sweet – thick and cloying as it stuck to my teeth and the roof of my mouth. But it tasted good, and again I could feel the sugar doing its work. I washed it down with more of the orange drink, the synapses in my brain sparking back into life as the sugar rush took hold.

"Oh my God," said Catherine, suddenly appearing at the back door of the ambulance. "Oh Jesus, you look terrible." Her face was pale and creased with worry. Short bursts of steam escaped her pink lips, as she panted slightly, out of breath from running.

Holly appeared behind her, looking more worried than I would have expected. Then Jack came into view on the other side.

Wrapped in the itchy blanket, with a bottle of Lucozade in one hand and a half-eaten Mars bar in the other, I looked up at my son and felt more wretched than ever. His face was a picture of disappointment, somewhere between shocked and heartbroken. And I felt that feeling I suppose all fathers go through at some point, when you realise your son has lost that all-consuming admiration for you.

I remember the day I discovered that my Dad wasn't a superhero. I was 11 years old, and I'd received an Airfix model plane for Christmas. It looked a bit tricky, so I asked Dad if we could build it together. Surely, my Dad can help, I thought. Dads can do anything, and mine's the best in the world. Or so I believed.

We carefully took all the pieces out of the box, lining them up methodically. After only a cursory glance at the instructions, he started gluing parts together, telling me how simple it was. Then he realised he'd glued two integral pieces together incorrectly. I saw the panic come over his face as he realised his mistake. One that couldn't be undone because the glue was already hard set.

I could see the mistake, and he knew I could. Neither of us said anything. He just placed the model on the ground, told me he had some important work to do, and that I should call him if I needed further help. Then with his head bowed like I'd never seen before, he rushed out of the room.

I felt like crying as I packed all the pieces back into the box and stashed it under my bed. Not because the model was ruined, but because of that look on my Dad's face. I felt crushed as the man I'd looked up to all my life, and who could do literally anything, suddenly turned into a mere mortal before me. He looked so small in that moment, like he'd shrunk by a full two feet. And I felt cheated. Ashamed that I'd fallen for the lie all those years.

That was exactly what I saw in Jack's eyes when he looked down at me.

I knew he'd get over it, just as I did. At some point everyone realises their father isn't the unbreakable, all-knowing superbeing they thought, but just an ordinary, fallible man muddling his way through life. But when you're Jack's age, it's hard to take.

"What happened, Dave?" said Catherine, climbing up into the ambulance and taking my hand. "Are you all right?"

"He's fine," said the paramedic, "just a bit worn out."

I wished the interfering old bat wasn't there, so I could embellish the story a little. I could have pretended I'd taken a nasty tumble or had an allergic reaction to the tear gas. I could certainly have made up something less embarrassing than a bit bloody worn out.

"I think I just… overdid it a little," I said, shamefully. "I hit the ice bath and kind of froze with the shock of the cold water. But I'm feeling much better now."

"Nearly drowned, didn't you?" said the paramedic, dismissively. "Had to be fished out and stretchered here."

"Oh Jesus," said Catherine.

Thanks a fucking lot, I thought, staring daggers as the paramedic, but she turned away from me, fussing with a box of medical supplies. I tried to stand, but my knees wobbled and my head spun, and I tumbled back down onto the stretcher with a thud.

"Just you stay there a bit longer," said the paramedic. "You're done in and your blood sugar is probably still a bit low. Finish your drink and choccy bar and you'll be fine in a few minutes."

"I don't suppose New Dave's in an ambulance next door, is he?" I laughed.

Catherine pursed her lips, screwed up her eyes and only just managed to keep from laughing. I took another swig of Lucozade.

******

After 20 minutes of sitting, shivering and sipping my sugary drink, the paramedic deemed me fit enough to leave. Catherine, the kids and I made our way slowly up to the finish line to watch and clap as runners completed the race. Every single part of me ached and throbbed, and although my clothes were still sodden and heavy, I was feeling warmer and somewhat recovered. I could have gone to bed and slept for a full week, but at least my knees had stopped wobbling and my vision was back to normal.

Catherine let me rest my arm on her shoulder as we walked. She was still a little standoffish, but it was almost a cuddle – something I was much in need of and she was begrudgingly giving me. Holly and Jack were both quiet. Once she'd realised I wasn't actually dying, Holly slipped straight back into her usual disinterest, making it abundantly clear that she wanted to be anywhere but there. Jack had his head down, still smarting from the disappointment.

As the kids walked on to the finish line, Catherine and I stumbled along slowly behind. Admittedly, I was laying it on a bit thick and resting on her more than I really needed to. But it was the first time we'd touched in weeks and I wasn't ready for it to end.

"Are you all right, Dave?" she said.

"Yeah, I'm feeling much better now," I replied. "Just overdid it. The sugary drink really helped…"

"No," she said. "Are you all right? Are you taking care of yourself? No offence, but you look like shit."

"Well, I did just run 5k, breath in tear gas, get electrocuted and nearly drown in a freezing cold pool of water."

"You know what I mean. You look tired. Are you eating okay? Looking after yourself?"

This was great. She was concerned about me. And not because I'd nearly just died.

"It's been hard without you, Cath. Doesn't seem much point cooking for one, not that I'm any good at it, anyway," I laughed. "I miss you. I want you to come home."

"Yes, well…" she said, clearly wanting to say more, but stopping herself. "And how's the cat?"

Fuck. The cat. It suddenly dawned on me that I hadn't seen the bloody thing in a few days. Had I remembered to put food out for her?

"Yeah, she's fine," I lied, making a mental note that I'd need to search for her when I got home.

"I just… worry about you, Dave. I want you to…" She cut herself off and I felt her body stiffen beneath my arm.

"Come home, Cath."

"Let's not, Dave. Not right now," she said, making it clear the conversation was over.

We reached the finish line and cheered as several runners trudged across. I recognised some of the faces – people I'd seen throughout the race. The girl who was too terrified to enter the electricity field; the man who'd wiped mud from my face; the lady I'd barged out of the way in the tear gas tent. And, of course, Mankini man, who was now so heavily covered in mud you couldn't even see his tiny outfit. He just looked like a naked, mud-covered nutter.

They were all destroyed and so happy to be at the end. But they also shared something else. Despite looking like they'd escaped a warzone, every single one of them finished the race with a beaming smile.

I envied them that satisfaction. That feeling of triumph. And I felt even more disappointed in myself. I think Catherine sensed it, as she squeezed my hand and said, "Hey, you did well. These things aren't easy and you made it halfway. That's still pretty good."

It was little solace. Especially as New Dave came running across the line, looking like he'd barely even been out for a morning stroll. He was soaking wet and covered in mud. But he was barely out of breath. And somehow, despite being wet and muddy, his hair still looked great. It was dishevelled and dirty, but it was as if that was the look he was going for.

New Dave's family greeted him with a towel and a tracksuit top. Then they spotted us and all four came over.

"Wow, you finished before me?" said New Dave, smiling widely. "Well done, man. That was a hard race, wasn't it?"

"Erm, I…" I stumbled.

"Dad didn't finish," said Jack from behind me, in a low, disappointed voice.

I went to speak, the words of defeat tasting acrid in my mouth, but Catherine beat me to it.

"Dave had to withdraw halfway through," she said. "He picked up an injury and had to stop running." She turned to me with a reassuring, protective smile.

"Oh, bad luck," said Dave. "Well, it was a tough course. I nearly took a few tumbles myself. Hope you're not too badly hurt."

"No, I'll be fine," I said, adjusting my stance and leaning more heavily on Catherine, trying to make myself look injured. "Just need to rest up."

"Well, half way's still a good effort. Loads of people don't even make it that far."

I winced slightly, plastering my best fake smile across my face.

"And hey," continued New Dave, "that whole bet thing. It was just a joke, wasn't it? I mean, neither of us actually meant it. Just drunken banter, eh?"

I paused for a second, weighing up the options. I knew he was being magnanimous. And we both knew he was letting me off. I was desperate to fight back, to tell him I'm a man of my word and he'd be getting the full amount of money. But I was already defeated and there was no point in making things worse. Besides, I was suddenly aware of Catherine's fingernails digging deep into my side, instructing me telepathically to accept New Dave's kindness.

"Yeah, sure," I said. "Just drunk nonsense, eh?"

"Well, it's great to see you two back together," said Tamzin.

"Oh, we're not… you know…" said Catherine. "The kids wanted to come and cheer their Dad on, so…"

"Oh," said Tamzin, her eyes darting away. We all looked at each other uncomfortably.

The tension was finally broken when an overexcited steward with a pale face and greasy black hair came walking over, carrying a clipboard.

"Hey guys," he said, "well done. Congratulations on completing the course. Just to let you know, though, if you've still got any energy and fancy another challenge, we're doing a fire walk on the other side of the field. You guys up for it?"

"A fire walk?" asked New Dave.

"Yeah, you know, walking over hot coals. Take your shoes and socks off and see if you can take the heat!" he laughed.

"D'you know, I've always fancied having a go at that. Will it take long?"

"Long? No way, man. The coals are red hot and we're ready to go. Just join the queue."

"How much?" said New Dave, reaching for his wallet.

"No charge, man. It's an extra Halloween thing, for anyone still buzzing from the race. Plus, it'll warm you up after all that freezing water."

"Go on, then, I'm in," said New Dave.

"Cool," said the steward, "I just need your name for the old clipboard."

"Sure, it's Dave... Brookman..."

"Cool, cool," said the steward writing it down. "And what about you, my man?" he said, turning to me. His enthusiasm was annoying.

"Oh, no," he's injured, said New Dave, on my behalf.

Cheeky bastard, I thought. Who does he think he is, making excuses for me?

"Actually, yes, count me in, too," I said.

Everyone apart from the steward turned to look at me with complete disbelief.

"What are you talking about?" said Catherine.

"Yeah, are you sure, mate?" said New Dave. "I mean, you don't want to aggravate your injury."

"I'm fine," I said, defiantly. "Actually, I'm feeling much better already. And it's just a little fire walk."

But it was more than that. Way more. This was my chance to save face. I'd failed miserably in the race, and New Dave had come out victorious over me again. This was a chance to save at least something from the day – show I wasn't a complete failure, and that I could do something to match New Dave. I could possibly even do it faster. Or slower. Whichever was better. I wasn't sure exactly how fire walks worked.

"Cool, cool," said the steward. "What's your name?"

"It's Dave... Dave Brookman..."

He wrote the name down on his clipboard and stared at it for a few seconds. Then bewilderment flashed in his eyes. "Wait... hang on... that's, like, the same name as him..."

"Yep, tell me about it," I sighed.

"Woah, cool, man. Well, awesome, yeah? Make your way over to the fire walk and I'll see you there in a few." Then he walked off in search of other volunteers.

"You sure about this?" said New Dave. "Nobody would think less of you if you…"

"Absolutely," I said, cutting him off. "I'm fine. And it's something I've always fancied having a go at as well."

"Right, well, I guess I'll see you over there."

New Dave and his family walked off towards the other side of the field.

"Right, well, now that's over, let's get you back to your car and get home," said Catherine, sternly.

"What do you mean? I'm going to do the fire walk."

"Yeah, Mum," said Jack, "Dad's gonna do the fire walk." Excitement flashed in his eyes. Maybe his old dad wasn't such a failure after all.

"No, he's not," said Catherine. "Dave, you've just spent the last half an hour in the back of an ambulance. You collapsed during an endurance race, which you weren't even fit enough to enter in the first place, and you nearly bloody died. What the hell are you thinking of, doing a fire walk?"

Her words stung. I knew she was right, of course. Deep down, I knew I shouldn't be thinking of doing anything other than going home and going straight to bed. Every muscle in my body sang with pain. I was so tired I could barely keep my eyes open, and I was worried I'd even be able to walk as far as the car. But a strange new determination overruled every sensible thought in my head. All I could see was the chance to win back points against my next-door name thief.

"Honestly, I'll be fine. Now I've warmed up, I'm feeling really good," I lied. "And if New Dave can do it, so can I."

"Oh my God, this feud with Dave. This jealousy. It has to stop."

"You don't understand. You've never understood."

"What is there to understand? You're the same person you've always been. Regardless of who's moved in next door."

"But it's not enough, is it?"

"Oh, not this again!"

"I have to do this, Cath," I said, my knees wobbling slightly. I hushed my voice to a whisper. "I need to do this for Jack. He was so disappointed I didn't finish the race. He needs to see that I can actually do something."

"How dare you?" said Catherine, angrily. "Using your own son as an excuse? Do you think I'm stupid? I know you're just trying to win points against Dave. Honestly, I thought what happened earlier might have knocked some sense into you. But you're worse than ever."

"I'm not. I promise. It's all in the past and I'm ready for you and the kids to come home. I just want things to get back to the way they were."

Catherine looked at me the way she does when she's trying to read my mind or see if she can catch me out.

"I just need to do this. I can't explain why, but I need to."

"If it means so much to you, Dave, go and do it," said Catherine, the merest glint of a tear sparkling in the corner of her eye. "But we're going home. I've got better things to do than stand around watching you do this to yourself."

"No, come on, come and watch. It'll only take a few minutes. It'll probably be a laugh. Look, there's a snack van there," I said, fishing a tenner out of my wallet and handing it to her. "Go and get yourselves a cup of tea. I'll go over and get ready, then you can come and cheer me on. I might even fall over and burn my arse," I laughed. "Now, I know you don't want to miss that. Then afterwards, I'll take everyone out for lunch."

I didn't give her time to argue. I thrust the money into her hand, turned and walked off as fast as I could towards the far end of the field. My legs were so stiff, it was hard to walk in a straight line. I must have looked like a zombie, shuffling along awkwardly. Or like I was about to shit myself.

It was just after 1pm and black clouds filled the October sky, making it dark like dusk. I could see the fire walk a few minutes before I reached it, glowing ominously against its grey surroundings.

A long, thin, rectangle, the fire pit was about 10 metres long. Red, orange and grey coals sparked and sizzled loudly. Angry flames licked up here and there, breaking up between gaps in the coals. Tiny sparks fizzed and jumped, sailing off into the air. It was essentially a giant barbecue on the ground, ready to literally cook the naked feet of anyone stupid enough to step onto it.

A small crowd of about 30 people stood at one end, with six brave, barefoot contestants lined up at the other. The crowd was shouting and cheering, whooping as a tall man wobbled quickly across the coals – not exactly running, but not hanging around either. He made it to the other end, jumping into the cool mud and hopping about wildly as the crowd applauded and screamed even louder.

I reached the fire pit, took off my trainers and socks, and stashed them safely with the other participants' shoes. Then I took up position behind new Dave, as the clipboard-holding steward gave him a few pointers.

"There's nothing to it," said the steward. "Just walk as quickly as you can. Have fun. And remember to keep going. Trust me, you don't wanna stop in the middle for a rest."

"How many of these have you done?" I asked.

"Oh, I've never done it," he said. "Fuck that, it looks well hot." He laughed, slapped me on the shoulder and walked off.

A short, dumpy woman at the front of the queue took off, dashing, wobbling and hobbling over the coals. The crowd cheered again, whooping and yelling, and clapping loudly as she made it to the other side. The next person went, and then the next. Everyone made it safely to the other end.

The heat from the coals was intense, waves of hot air blowing against me. It had the pleasing effect of warming my cold, wet clothes, and relieving some of the stiffness in my legs. But it also made me realise just how hot those coals were. The coals that I was about to place my bare feet directly onto. I shivered with adrenaline, my heartbeat quickening.

"Bit bigger than the old MeatMaster, eh?" said New Dave, turning back to me. "Bet you could cook a fair few steaks on that bad boy?"

"Yeah, or a few feet," I said.

Dave gritted his teeth as he realised it was his turn. "Wish me luck," he said, and stepped out onto the burning coals, darting forwards. He wobbled this way and that, moving at a steady pace, waving his arms wildly at his sides to keep his balance. The crowd cheered and whooped with encouragement, as New Dave picked up speed. Then rippled with applause as he jumped the last few feet and landed in the cold, wet mud at the end.

And then it was my turn. Fuck!

I suddenly realised I hadn't really thought it through. Once again, jealousy, anxiety and adrenaline had led me to a really stupid idea. I looked down at the hot, angry coals in front of me. The heat was intense and scary. I watched devilish little flames spark and shimmy in front of me. What the fuck was I doing?

I started panicking. What if my legs seized up halfway across and I ended up just standing there, cooking like a big lump of meat? What if I lost my footing and went tumbling face first into the coals, bursting into flames like a wicker statue? I looked around. I couldn't see anyone on hand with a fire extinguisher. Shouldn't there be fire extinguishers? Or a fully manned fire engine, ready to put me out if I accidentally caught on fire?

People waiting behind me began to grumble. Then the crowd at the other end started a slow hand clap of encouragement.

Clap. Clap. Clap. Clap. Clap.

Fuck. I had to go through with it. No way out now. Not with my family watching. I couldn't fail them twice in the same day.

Clap. Clap. Clap. Clap. Clap.

I took a deep breath and stepped out onto the coals. The heat was incredible. My other foot stepped out a large stride in front of me. Then that foot was burning too. I stepped again. No time to waste. Don't hang around.

My thighs ached with each movement, but I kept on going. One foot after the other. Left. Right. Left. Right.

Stepping quickly. Practically running now. Left. Right. Left. Right.

The crowd clapped and cheered. I kept moving. Getting faster. My heart thumping hard. Left. Right. Left. Right.

Then I was nearly there. Moving fast. Left. Right. Jump.

I leapt the last metre, landing with a splat in the cold, wet mud at the end. It was instant relief. Cold and soothing. I swear I even heard my feet sizzle and steam, like pouring cold water into a hot frying pan.

The crowd yelped and screamed, loud applause echoing around the park.

I breathed deeply, holding my hands on my hips to catch my breath. A large smile spread across my lips. The satisfaction was overwhelming and I could easily have burst into tears.

I scanned the crowd, searching for Catherine, Jack and Holly. I was desperate to hug them and share my triumph. But I couldn't see them anywhere.

I searched harder, looking at every individual face. I saw New Dave and his family, all smiling and clapping for me. I saw the people who'd crossed the fire pit before me, standing with their partners and children. I recognised a few people from the race earlier. There were several stewards in high-viz vests. But my family were nowhere to be seen.

They hadn't come to watch me. Catherine had taken the kids and gone home. They'd abandoned me.

In that moment, I realised I'd lost them for good.

CHAPTER 20
ET TU, STEVE?

"NO OFFENCE, MATE, but you look like shit."

"Nice to see you, too," I said. I'd answered the door on the fifth insistent ring of the doorbell to find Steve stood there with a worried look on his face.

"Well, are you gonna invite me in for a cuppa, or what?" he said, pushing past me into the house.

I sighed as I closed the door behind him, then followed him through.

"Christ on a bike," he said, as he opened the door to the living room. The pile of old pizza boxes had grown to a ridiculous height and was threatening to tumble over. The silver foil takeaway cartons lining the coffee table were humming with the remnants of congealed food. Small spots of green and white mould had started spreading on the surface. Dirty cups, plates and glasses lined the floor and the tops of cabinets. Trousers, t-shirts, jumpers, pants and socks lay on the floor, armchair, sideboard and anywhere else they'd been flung. There was even a dirty sock draped over the corner of the TV. It had been there for a day and half because I simply couldn't be bothered to walk the eight feet required to move it, and it was only covering up part of the picture anyway.

"Bloody hell, it smells a bit funky in here. And you're a tad ripe yourself, mate," he said, jokingly leaning in and sniffing me.

I suddenly became aware of a sickly sweet, stale odour in the room. I hadn't opened the curtains, let alone any windows for four days now, so the air was thick and pungent.

"I figured you were a bit down in the dumps, mate," said Steve. "I didn't realise you'd turned into Stig of the bloody dump."

That was a good one. If I hadn't been so depressed, I'd definitely have laughed.

"I haven't been feeling too good," I said, sheepishly. "I guess I've let the housework build up a little."

"A little!" laughed Steve. "You've been off work for three days,

167

mate. This is a good few weeks' worth of…" he looked around, searching for the right word, "…degradation. Total fucking degradation."

I hadn't been doing too well since the race. No, that's not true. I hadn't been doing too well since Catherine first left and took the kids with her. Since making a complete mess of everything on the day of the race, it's more accurate to say that I'd been a complete and utter shambles.

I pulled the navy blue sleeping bag from the sofa and invited Steve to sit down. I'd spent the last four nights, and most of the last few days, sleeping on the sofa. I'd elected to sleep there the night after the race, primarily because my legs ached so much I couldn't actually make it all the way upstairs to the bedroom. It had taken me a full six minutes to make it even halfway up. And like a mountaineer who realised their own safety demanded giving up the dream of reaching the peak, I'd had to abandon my ascent and settle for the settee.

I was also happy not to sleep in mine and Catherine's bed. It felt so big and empty without her, and after the events of the race, I was sure it would feel even more expansive. So, I chose to squeeze myself onto the sofa, where the constant ache in my back was preferable to the constant reminder of my aching heart.

The Sunday after the race, I barely moved from the sofa – partly because I was so depressed I didn't want to move, and partly because I literally couldn't move. The effects of the extreme exercise had really kicked in. My body was creaking and humming with lactic acid – every single muscle aching, throbbing and singing with pain. Lifting my head sent sharp electric shocks from my scalp to my throbbing back. Reaching for the TV remote felt like a Herculean task. Staggering to the kitchen to get a glass of water took five whole minutes and nearly broke me.

Naturally, I couldn't face work on Monday. I didn't fancy my chances of making it to the car, let alone all the way into the office. But mostly, I didn't want to see anyone. I knew people would have heard what happened. And I was sure they were all waiting to take the piss – funny looks as I passed them in the corridor, barely-heard whispers from people huddled in the kitchen. And some of them would have been far less subtle.

I remember a few years back, when one of the designers, Mark, was off for a few days following a car crash. He came back to work to find his desk, chair, computer monitors and even his keyboard wrapped in bandages. They covered his desk in warning notices, first aid kits and empty packets of paracetamol. The guys from the creative studio went all out, creating fake letters from a company called *Claims for Blames*, offering him compensation. Someone even found a wheelchair and some crutches left over from a video shoot to leave next to his desk. That's advertising creatives for you.

If they'd gone to that much effort over someone who'd accidentally crashed their car, what would they do for the guy who nearly drowned during an obstacle course.

So, I phoned in sick and stayed on the sofa. I still couldn't face the humiliation on the Tuesday, so I phoned in sick again. And as I'd already been off for two days, I thought I may as well make it a hat trick, so I bunked off again on the Wednesday.

Steve dragged the curtains open, blinding light bursting in and stinging my eyes. He thrust open a window and a cool breeze whooshed into the room. Then he walked over to the sofa and moved a selection of pizza boxes, a dirty t-shirt and a pair of socks to make himself a space to sit on. I cleared an armchair of empty beer cans and sat across from him.

"We've missed you at work the last three days, mate," said Steve. "We've been pretty busy, trying to get all this work out for KODEK, and there's another pitch we need to get cracking with. I could have done with your help. I had to get one of the junior art editors to help, which didn't go unnoticed by Zack."

"Sorry," I said. "I wasn't up to coming in."

"No," he sighed. "I heard what happened during that stupid bloody race. What the hell were you thinking?"

"Oh," I said. "You heard?"

"Catherine called me. She's…"

"Oh yes," I interrupted. "I've heard about your cosy little chats." I sneered at him, as menacingly as I could. "Calling each other up in private. Talking about me and God knows what else."

"Oh, give it a rest, you tit," snapped Steve. "It's nothing like that, and you know it. She's worried about you. And for some reason, she thought I might be able to talk some sense into you."

"Go on, then," I said, crossing my arms, "talk some sense into me."

"Seriously?" he said. "Let's not get all precious. You know you've been acting like a dick recently. And the fact you haven't been into work for three days leads me to suspect it's finally dawning on you exactly what a mess you've made. Am I right?"

I didn't answer, I just crossed my arms tighter, then crossed my feet as well.

"Look at this place. Filthy dishes all over the floor. The leaning tower of pizza boxes there. Dirty clothes everywhere. And..." he noticed something out of the corner of his eye. "Christ, man, is that a fucking mushroom growing out of the carpet?" he said, pointing to the corner of the room.

I looked to where he was pointing. "Eh? Oh... yeah, I spilled some beer there. Forgot to clean it up. I guess nature took its course."

"Fuck's sake, Dave. You're not supposed to have fucking mushrooms growing out of your carpet. I say this with all the love and respect in the world, but you really need to sort yourself out."

I huffed like a petulant child.

"This place is worse than a teenager's bedroom. Have you never heard of a hoover? Or a J Cloth? Or the simple concept of putting rubbish in the bin?"

"What's the point?" I snapped. "Without Catherine, what's the point of any of it?"

"Well, you're never going to get her back with the house looking like this," said Steve. "And believe me," he pointed at the t-shirt I'd been wearing for the last four days, "this grungy new look of yours isn't helping either. Sort yourself out. Have a bloody shower. Put on some clean clothes. And what the hell is going on with your hair? I didn't think it was possible, but it looks even worse than usual."

He laughed, trying to encourage me to smile along with him. I didn't.

"I mean, do you even want Cath back? Because from here, it doesn't look like it," said Steve.

"She's not coming back," I said, widening my eyes to try and keep tears from rolling out. "I've messed it all up. She's gone for good."

"Don't be daft. She loves you. I've never known any two people love each other more. So, it's not over. But you need to sort things out. Pack it in with all this nonsense – all this shit with spreadsheets and plans. Try and realise that you have an amazing wife and two great kids... and a pretty sweet life. Get back to being the old you. That's all Catherine wants. As soon as she sees it, she'll realise what she's missing and she'll come back."

I shrugged, one of the tears breaking free and sliding down my cheek.

"I mean, you'll have to do a lot of apologising," Steve laughed. "I'm talking flowers, dinners out… maybe even a bit of jewellery…"

"I don't know, mate. You didn't see the look on her face. I don't think I can win her back. Not this time."

"Well, not if you don't bloody well try," said Steve, suddenly angry.

"You really think so?" I said.

"I know so. She damn near told me herself. She was practically ready to move back in on Sunday after the race, seeing you all forlorn and pathetic in that ambulance."

"Seriously?"

"Yeah. And then you go and fuck it up by insisting on walking across a giant fucking barbecue. What the fuck's all that about? You twat."

Shit, I thought, hanging my head. I'd been so close and screwed it all up again. Another tear broke free and slinked down my face.

"Look, there's another reason I came round," said Steve, hesitancy creeping into his voice. "I need to talk to you about work."

"Really? What's up? How's Zack been?"

"Same as usual. Jumped up little prick, too big for his boots. And he's definitely up to something. I don't know what exactly, but I'm sure he's scheming. That's why you need to get back. Too long out of the office, and he'll be thinking he's actually running the place. If that happens, he might start thinking he doesn't need you anymore."

"Oh, fuck him. And fuck that place, too."

"I'm serious, Dave. You know what he's like. You're already on the shit list with Thomson after your little… meltdown."

"There's no need to bring that up," I said.

"Hey, I was all for it. I wish I could have seen it. And I wish I could have seen the look on that old prick's face. But it hasn't been forgotten. And worse than that, your work's been suffering…"

"Jesus! Kick a man when he's down, Steve?"

"Tough love, mate. I'm sorry, but you need to hear it."

He was right, of course. I wanted to defend myself, but there was no point. My work had been pretty crap. I hadn't had a decent idea in weeks, and certainly hadn't produced anything even close to my usual standard. Steve had been carrying me – doing the lion's share of conceptual work, writing all the copy, taking the lead in client meetings as I sat there looking distant and uninterested. I hadn't wanted to admit it, but it was all too clear now.

"You've been missing days here and there and, when you have been in, you've been so distracted and moody that… well, I'm sorry, but you've not exactly been a joy to work with," said Steve.

"That's a bit below the belt. I know I've not been up to my usual standard, but…"

"I'm sorry, but I'm telling you this for your own good. These last few days haven't done you any favours, either. People are asking questions. How well off are you gonna be if you lose your job as well as your family?"

"Oh, that's not gonna happen. That little shit Zack hasn't got the balls to sack me."

"Hasn't he? I wouldn't be so sure, mate. He's a snake and he's completely unpredictable. We've always felt safe because we knew they valued our work, and they knew they'd be lost without us. But Zack is a fucking idiot. He doesn't know the business or the industry, and he's got such an inflated ego he thinks he can do whatever he likes. I wouldn't put it past him to sack the best creative team they've ever had, and he won't realise what a mistake he's made until he loses half the company's clients."

"He's not gonna sack us," I insisted. "Zack might not have a clue, but Thomson still values us, even after everything that's happened."

"Well, that's what I wanted to talk to you about. It wouldn't be a case of sacking *us*."

"I don't follow," I said. "What are you getting at?"

"I'm handing in my notice," said Steve, looking at the floor.

It took a full five seconds to register and when it did it was like a full-force punch to the gut.

"What are you saying?" I said. "You're breaking up the team?"

"I just need a… change," he said, sheepishly.

"But you can't," I pleaded. "We're a team. We've been working together for nearly 20 years."

"Look, it's not you, it's…"

"Oh, here we go. You're not seriously going to give me the whole 'It's not you, it's me' speech, are you?"

"Actually, no, Dave, I'm not. What I was going to say is, it's not you, it's the company. It's the work. It's the clients. I'm bored. I need a new challenge. And I'm not getting any younger. AIP isn't half the place it was when we first started working there. The clients are all boring and they never let us do anything interesting. We're not gonna win awards churning out the same old dull, uninteresting stuff we are now. And now they've started putting fucktards like Zack in charge. I'm sorry, but the writing's on the wall for that place."

"Hey, it pays the bills, Steve. It's good solid work," I countered.

"Good solid work? That's not why we got into this business. We both said we only ever want to have fun and do work that excites us. When was the last time you were actually excited about a project?"

"We were young when we said that. Without families and mortgages and responsibilities. There's a lot to be said for being able to pay the bills, you know."

"Oh, come on, Dave. We're wasted at that place, and you know it. I want to do exciting work again, for exciting clients who actually appreciate what we can do. I want to look forward to going to work. And I want to win awards again. I have to do this now, before it's too late."

"So, you're abandoning me to go off in search of excitement?"

"Yes," he said, smiling. "And no. I'm not abandoning you. I told you, we should be doing this together. I told you I was considering this and that you should come with me. And you still can."

"Come on, Steve, look at me. It's not a good time to be changing jobs. Not with Cath and the kids, and…"

"No," he said, raising his voice, "it's the perfect time. Christ, you've spent the last however long working on this ridiculous mission to improve yourself. Do something that will actually count. Take a leap and start a new adventure."

"I can't quit my job now, it's just too… too…"

"Exactly. That's the problem. You're too comfortable. Or, you've forgotten what you really want. So, it's never going to be a good time for you. And I can't wait in the hope that you might change your mind. I'm sorry, but I have to move on without you."

A long silence hung between us as we sat looking at each other. I breathed deeply and widened my eyes, desperate not to cry any more in front of him.

"So, where will you go? What will you do?"

"Not entirely sure yet. I reached out to my contacts at BMV. They want people, but ideally they're looking for a team. They said they might consider taking me and seeing if there's someone to pair me up with. Otherwise, I've got a few interviews lined up, and a bit of freelance work to keep me going."

"Shouldn't you wait until you've got something definite?" I implored. "Give it a few months. They're gonna realise what a mistake it was promoting Zack. Then they'll come begging for me to replace him. Once that happens, we'll be in a far better position to look for new clients with more interesting work."

"I'm sorry, mate," sighed Steve, "but that's never gonna happen."

"Okay, but wait a while. At least let me try. If it doesn't work out, I might be in a position to come…"

"No," said Steve. "I've made my mind up. If I don't do it now, I'll end up stuck at AIP for another 10 years. And then it'll definitely be too late."

Another long silence hung between us.

"So, that's it then," I said, petulantly. "You're leaving me too. Right when I need you most, you're abandoning me, just like everyone else."

"It's not like that," pleaded Steve.

"Bloody well feels like it."

"We're not gonna stop being friends. I'm just gonna be…"

"Just go," I said.

"What?"

"Get out of my house. You've delivered your bad news. And now you can go."

"Don't be like that, Dave," he said. "I just…"

"I don't want to hear it," I said. I stood up, walked out of the room and opened the front door. Steve followed me, stepped out of the house and turned to look at me.

"Dave," he said, sombrely, "please get yourself sorted. Cath and the kids will come back. Things will get better. And there's still time to come with me, if you change your mind. The guys at BMV will hire us tomorrow. It would be a great new start."

I stood there, simply staring at him.

"Okay, well, at the very least you need to get back to work. Don't give Zack any more ammunition, eh? I'm handing in my notice tomorrow, I wanted you to know before I did anything. I'll still be in the office for a few weeks, so I'll see you tomorrow, yeah?"

I didn't say anything. I simply closed the door on him. Then I walked back into the living room, slumped down on the sofa and let the tears start pouring out.

CHAPTER 21
A CONFESSION

I'M NOT SURE how long I was sitting there feeling sorry for myself. At some point I became aware that everything had grown quieter and darkness had crept in around me.

I looked at my watch – the Rolex Catherine had bought me for my 40th birthday. She'd sneakily saved up for two whole years to buy it, and spent vastly more on it than she really should have. She knew I'd always wanted a Rolex, and she'd often seen me gazing at them in shop windows if we ever went into town. So, she'd bought me it because she wanted to give me something really special, and because she knew I'd never justify spending that much money on myself. And she was right. Every now and then, I'd get a tinge of guilt when I thought of all the other things that money could have been used for – like college payments for the kids, or a holiday for the family, or so many things Catherine had gone without over the years.

It wasn't a patch on the shiny behemoth New Dave wore on his wrist, but it was easily the best and most precious thing I owned. Not because of how expensive it was, or because it was something I'd long dreamed of owning, or because Rolex watches famously hold their value (and in many cases actually appreciate). It was the thought and sacrifice behind it. Looking at it now, sparkling in the moonlight that gleamed in through the window, I felt utterly wretched. The watch felt very heavy on my wrist. It screamed of betrayal and made me think of the hurt in Catherine's eyes when she discovered that ridiculous spreadsheet. I felt like crying, but I'd spent the last few hours doing that, and I don't think I had a single tear left in my body.

The hands of my reliable, guilt-ridden watch told me it was 6.42pm. I turned on the small lamp on the table next to me, the light spreading out in a circular shape and illuminating half the room. My eyes were tired and my vision blurry. As they slowly adjusted to the new brightness in the room, I looked at the TV to see the sad, lonely image of a man crumpled on a sofa. He wore grubby tracksuit trousers, no socks and an un-ironed t-shirt with several stains of varying size and colour. His face carried a dirty swathe of stubble and his messy greying hair stood up in erratic peaks.

The man's eyes were bloodshot, with dark bags hanging below them. He looked like he'd been crying and barely slept in days. I felt an immediate dislike of this pathetic character before me. I wanted the sight of him taken away, so I picked up the remote control to change the channel. But as I pressed the button, I realised the TV was off and the cold, dark screen was simply reflecting a picture of me.

But it was a figure I couldn't recognise, refused to recognise as being myself. I was a professional, happy, competent human being, with a wife and a family. I had a good job and a good salary. I had friends and colleagues. The man staring back at me had none of these things. He was the man I used to see on dreadful daytime TV shows, and who I'd derided for collecting benefits, for refusing to work, for fathering numerous children with numerous mothers and being a general blight on society.

The man in the TV was the homeless guy I never gave my spare change to. The Big Issue seller I crossed the road to avoid. He was the loser signing the form to get his Jobseeker's Allowance and lying about how many vacancies he'd applied for that week.

He was the fool who'd thrown everything away because he couldn't get over a ridiculous obsession – the man who had everything he ever wanted, but somehow got jealous when someone else had more than him. He was the man who'd taken his own life and shattered it into a thousand pieces.

How had I fallen so far?

I stared at the image, trying to figure out what had gone wrong. When had it started? What was the one moment that led to the series of events that turned me into this shambling wreck I saw before me?

New Dave. It had all started the day he moved in next door.

I'd been happy, hadn't I? Up until that point, I don't think I'd ever really questioned anything about my life. Not to say things were perfect – nothing ever really is. But my life was good. More than good. I was genuinely happy. I had everything I needed and I don't remember ever questioning that fact. So, why had I suddenly felt so hard done by? How had I created this image of failure in my mind? An image so vivid, so overwhelming it had completely consumed me. And I'd lost everything trying to overcome it.

So, now I *wasn't* a professional, happy, competent human being, with a wife, family, good job and friends. I'd thrown them all away. And I *was* that wreck on the sofa in desperate need of a shower and a change of clothes.

Feeling worse than I've ever felt before, I turned on the TV, hoping to at least distract myself for a short while. Of course, there was nothing on. The BBC was showing the tail end of the local news, which was far too depressing to watch. And as I scanned through the myriad of channels, I found nothing but a dire selection of quiz shows, food programmes, dating shows, dating shows where they cook food, teen soap operas, dreadful American sitcoms, dreadful American crime shows, dreadful American reality shows, some pointless thing where they buy old crap then sell it for a loss at an auction, and repeats of Only Fools and Horses. I couldn't bear any of it, so I turned the TV off, deciding instead to simply retreat under the safety of my sleeping bag.

I was just about to curl up into a little ball, when I heard the unwelcome sound of the doorbell. No doubt some bloody Jehovah's Witness or pollster from the local council, so I simply ignored it. A minute later, the doorbell rang again. "Go away!" I shouted into the cold darkness of the house.

The doorbell rang again. Then again, twice in succession. A knock on the door followed, then another two rings. Whoever this joker was, they clearly weren't giving up.

I marched to the door and yanked it open. But it wasn't a Jehovah's Witness. It was New Dave.

Great, just what I needed, another glimpse into the life of perfect Dave, here to show me how much better he was than me.

"Yes?" I said, abrupt and not even trying to hide my annoyance.

"Hello mate," he said, in an overly chummy way.

I didn't reply, I just shrugged and gave him my best 'what do you want?' stare.

"How are you doing?" he said.

Again, I didn't reply, I just stared back, trying to convey the message: 'Get on with it, I'm a busy man'. I was, however, aware of how red and puffy my eyes were, and suspected they may not have been conveying any message beyond: 'I'm a shambling wreck of a man who's been crying for the last two hours, and I'm barely even able to work the washing machine, let alone carry out the normal duties of a grown man – I'm in desperate need of help!'

"We haven't seen you since the race," continued New Dave. "Tamzin says she's sure you haven't left the house in the last few days, not that she's spying on you or anything..." He gave an embarrassed laugh. Then he paused for a second, waiting for me to fill the silence. Again, I simply stared.

"Well, we were just a little worried, really. That was a tough race. I could barely walk by Sunday evening. We wanted to check you weren't... you know, suffering, or anything. What with you being in the house on your own now..."

"What do you really want?" I finally snapped. "Come to rub it in, eh? Didn't get enough out of seeing me embarrass myself on Sunday, so you've come to see if I'm suffering? Want me to see that you're doing so much better than me? Again."

"I don't follow," he said, looking genuinely confused.

"Let's drop the pretence, shall we?" I said. "I know what you're doing. What you've been doing since you moved in. You win, okay? You win. I know I can't compete. I'll never be as good as the great Dave Brookman from No. 18. I was stupid to try. I've learnt my lesson and I give up. So, what do you want, eh? You want me to change my name as well? Fine. You can have it. I'll be better off without it. It's brought me nothing but bad luck recently. So, you have it. You're now the only Dave Brookman in the street."

New Dave looked at me for a few seconds, concern turning to compete befuddlement. "What the fuck are you talking about?" he said.

"You. The competition. You win, okay. You're the best Dave. You're 46% better than me – well, actually it'll be more than that now. Way more, what with everything that's happened and everything I've lost."

"Seriously, Dave," he said, "what are you on about? 46% of what?"

"The spreadsheet," I said, incredulous, as if he should have known exactly what I was talking about. "The spreadsheet of us. The one that compares our lives and everything in them, and shows how you're 46% better than me."

"Okay, now I'm really lost..." he said, taking a deep breath and squinting.

"I made a spreadsheet to compare us," I said. "I entered as many things as I could think of to compare us on – car, house, job, salary, clothes, hair, singing voice... Then I assigned us scores, compared the difference and worked out an average. And guess what? You came out

46% better than me."

New Dave looked back at me with his mouth half open, as if I'd just told him I was a cross-dressing alien from Mars who'd come here to steal his kidneys. "What the fuck?" he finally said.

At this point, I think it finally hit me how ridiculous the whole thing was. As if saying it out loud had allowed me to see how crazy a thing it was to do, and I was literally the only person in the world that couldn't see it. Like the time at University, when I drunkenly believed I could do a backflip off the stage in the student union bar. It took a broken ankle and a fairly serious concussion to make me realise how stupid I'd been that time. This time I'd lost my family, nearly drowned – twice – and destroyed practically my whole life.

"You made a spreadsheet comparing every aspect of our lives?"

"Erm… well… yeah," I said, starting to feel ridiculous. It had seemed like such a sensible thing to do at the time – completely justified and normal. Now that I'd told New Dave about it, it was sounding more than a little bit mental.

"Well, how did you score it? I mean, how you could possibly know that much about me? You certainly never asked."

"Erm… well, some of it was obvious, like the hair," I said pointing to the perfectly-quiffed mat on his head. "Some of it was educated guessing. Some of it was just my opinion." I felt like a naughty pupil having to explain to their teacher why they'd thought it was a good idea to write 'boobs' on the blackboard when nobody was looking.

"All right," said Dave, "the hair I get. Obviously. But singing voice? Have you ever heard me sing?"

"No, but…" My argument was falling apart much quicker than I could have expected.

"How could you possibly know how much I earn?"

"Well, I don't, but I figured…"

"And what else was in this list?" he said, interrupting me. "How many things have you *guessed* about?"

At this point, it seemed fruitless trying to explain the spreadsheet or my methodology any further. And I certainly didn't want to tell him I'd been assessing the attractiveness of his wife, or comparing the various merits and failings of our children.

"Look, it doesn't matter anymore. None of it matters now. I've already told you: you win. It's over. I concede defeat. I'll never be the man you are."

"No offence, Dave," he said, "but you're really starting to piss me off now. I object to the fact you think we're in some kind of a competition – I'm certainly not. I never have been. And I don't accept the fact that I've somehow won it, based on a scoring system I don't understand, don't agree with, and which was based on guesswork. All I've done is move into a new home and try to live as peacefully as possible. I'm not out to get you, if that's what you think."

"I never said you were out to get me. That's not what this is about."

"Then what the hell *is* it about?"

"Dave Brookman," I said. "We're both called Dave Brookman."

"Yes, I'm well aware of that," he said.

"Well, don't you think that's weird? Of all the people who could have moved in next door to me, I get someone with the exact same name. Not only that, you're the same age. We even do the same bloody job. Does it not make you question everything about your life?"

"No," he laughed. "Why would it? It's a coincidence, that's all."

"A bloody big one, though," I argued.

"But so what?"

"What do you mean *so what*? You move in next door, and it's like the world put up a mirror to me. And I didn't like what I saw. It's like: 'Look at this, Dave. Look how amazing and rich, and successful this Dave Brookman is. Look at his nice clothes and house. Look at how much better he's done than you. This is what a Dave Brookman is supposed to be. How come you haven't done as well as him? What's wrong with you?'"

"Have you been drinking?" said New Dave.

"Actually, no, not today. I ran out of beer two days ago, and I couldn't face going to the shops. But that's not the point. This has been going on for months."

"Just because we have the same name?"

"Yes. No. I mean, yeah… it's like, all of a sudden, every day I have to look at this living image of what I could have, or should have become – except somehow, I fucked up along the way. And so every day I can't help but feel like a failure."

"But that's not my fault. I never put any of that on you…"

"No, I know. But that's just how I felt."

"So, that's why you entered the race? Trying to win back points against me?"

I shrugged, not quite wanting to admit to the lunacy of it.

"You know, I think this is all pretty unfair," said New Dave. "I don't think of myself as better than anyone, certainly no better than you. You have an amazing wife and two brilliant kids. You have a lovely house. I've no idea whether I earn more money than you, and frankly I don't care. It doesn't mean anything. And when it comes to work, my job's no better than yours. I'm just self-employed and you work for someone else. And you do great work. Really great."

"You've seen my work?"

"Of course. You don't move in next door to someone with the exact same name as you and not bloody Google them, do you?"

"You've Googled me?" I said incredulous.

"Yeah, and I'm sure you did the same when I moved in."

"I might have," I said under my breath.

"Well, you might have done a better job of it. For someone who's apparently been obsessed with me for the last however many months, you don't seem to know much about me. If you knew the real me, rather than this perfect image you've dreamed up, you'd realise I'm not any better off than anyone else."

"Oh, come off it," I laughed. "I'm not stupid. How much have you spent on the house since you've been here? The fancy cars you drive, the expensive clothes, all the nice things you have. The MeatMaster 4000. Don't try and pretend you're not well off."

"That's the trouble, isn't it Dave?" said New Dave, sighing. "You see what you want to see and you've instantly made your mind up. You know, I grew up without a great deal of anything. We weren't poor exactly, but definitely not well off. We lived in a small house, my parents shared a crappy old car, and my first foreign holiday was at the age of 18, on a week's piss-up in Ibiza with mates. First time I was ever on a plane, and it took me six months of overtime stacking shelves in a supermarket to pay for it."

I shrugged, urging him to get to the point.

"I remember one Christmas when I was 12, I was desperate for a replica Spurs football kit. All the lads had their teams' kit, and we were allowed to wear them for football practice after school. If you didn't have the latest kit, everyone laughed at you. And you know what kids are like…

"Anyway, I'd begged my parents for a kit, but even in those days they were stupidly expensive. So, Christmas morning, I open my only present and it's a football kit – but it's not the one I wanted. Not even a proper team. Just some blue and white-striped generic thing from Debenhams. I couldn't believe Mum and Dad had bought me the wrong thing – and a cheap, crappy version at that. I was a real little shit about it, storming off to my bedroom to sulk. And, of course, I couldn't wear it – I knew the piss-taking would be horrendous, so it went completely unused."

"That's all so sad," I scoffed, "but what's your point?"

"My point is," said New Dave, angrily, "that you never really know the whole story. I found out years later that my parents had real financial problems that year. My Dad had been laid off from his job but my parents never told me and my sister, because they didn't want us to worry. My Dad just pretended to go to work every day as usual, and instead he went to the job centre. Eventually, he found work, but not until they'd missed several mortgage payments and came close to losing the house. And, even though they were dangerously overdrawn, and maxed-out on credit cards, they couldn't bear to see us kids go without a Christmas present. So, they spent money they didn't have on a cheap doll for my sister and a football kit for me."

I didn't know what to say. I just stood there, stroking the matt of stubble on my chin and feeling like a complete arse.

"Now that I'm older, and I have a bit of money," said New Dave, "I like spending it on nice things. I deserve to. And if that makes someone else feel inadequate, well... I'm sorry, but that's really all on them. I don't flaunt what I've got, and believe me, I don't have as much as you clearly think I have.

"I'm not pleading poverty, but you don't know the full story. Yes, we've spent lots on the house recently, but that's all thanks to a second mortgage. Christ alone knows how I'm gonna pay it off. And, believe me, I lay awake some nights stressing about how over-stretched we are. But Tamzin wanted it, and I wanted her to have it.

"Yes, I have a nice car, but it's only a rental and it's paid for by the business. Tamzin paid for her own car years ago, with money from her modelling. But it's a heap. It spends more time with the mechanic than it does on the road. Damn thing costs me a bloody fortune."

I was finding it difficult to look him in the eye now.

"Yes, I have some nice clothes, but most of it comes from this website where everything's at least 40% off. Remind me to ping you a link."

He said the last words with real vitriol.

"And, if you must know," said New Dave, "the barbecue was a gift. I know the owner of the company and I did some pro bono consultancy work for them, helping with their marketing strategy. He gave me the barbecue as a thank you."

I became very aware that I was staring at my feet now, too embarrassed to meet his eye.

"So, my point, Dave, is how could you possibly consider yourself to be… what was it? 46% worse than me? How can you think that, when you clearly don't know me at all?"

I felt utterly ashamed.

"I, er… I guess I just assumed…" I said, sheepishly.

"Yes, you bloody well did, didn't you?"

"But come on," I said, "you can't deny you're more successful than me. The business. The awards. Working all around the world. You've achieved so much, and I've just, well…"

"God, you're not listening, are you? Yes, I've done all right," said New Dave, "but again, you're only looking at the surface. I've worked all around the world, but it was no picnic. I never intended to do it, I just got moved, and barely ever had any choice in the matter. They'd tell me the New York office needed help, so I'd have to go. Then the Hong Kong office needed someone, so muggins here gets sent. It's all right to start with, but after a while it's a real pain, believe me. Especially with a wife who has her own career, and you end up practically separated with thousands of miles between you."

"I never really thought about it like that," I said quietly.

"Yes, I've won some awards, but so have you. Remember, I Googled you, too. Some of your work over the years has been amazing – much better than the stuff you've done recently, no offence. But then, that's because you're working at AIP and you have the safest, most boring list of clients who clearly don't let you do anything interesting. Again, no offence, but that place is quickly becoming a bloody laughing stock. I met your new Executive Creative Director at an industry thing the other week. What's his name? Zack? My God, what a tool. Completely clueless. And so far up his own arse. You're too good for that place, and you're never gonna win clients who let you do exciting work with useless management that don't know good advertising from their own arseholes. You'd do so much better somewhere else."

My head was heavy. I felt faint. I could hear blood pumping in my ears. I was desperate to close the front door, go back to the sofa and crawl under my sleeping bag.

"Yes, I started my own business," continued Dave, "but things have been far from smooth sailing. It took us a long time to win any significant business. We're a boutique agency so we struggle to attract the big clients and most of our projects are pretty small – not like the big budgets you're working with. Things are on the up, but we're only just starting to turn a profit."

"I didn't know," I said. "I assumed you were…"

"Exactly. Assuming again, Dave. There's an old saying: When you assume, you make an ASS of U and ME. I've always hated that fucking saying. Partly because it's trite and overly American. And partly because I used to have a secretary who said it all the time, in the most patronising, whiny voice that just made you want to throttle her. But mostly because it doesn't really make sense. Although, in this case, I think that saying is pretty fucking apt."

"Hey!" I said, wounded. But I knew he was right. I had made a complete arse of myself.

"You've made all these assumptions about me, without knowing any of the facts. I wonder how different we'd actually look on your spreadsheet if you filled it in with all the right information. Hardly any different at all, I bet."

"Maybe not," I sighed. "But it all means nothing now, does it? However I was when you first moved in… well, I've fucked that all up now, haven't I?"

"You certainly have," he said, bluntly.

"Jesus, don't hold back," I said.

"No offence, but you look fucking terrible," said New Dave. "And you don't smell too good, either."

"That's not the first time I've heard that today."

"But do you know what isn't going to help? Sitting around feeling sorry for yourself."

I couldn't disagree. I wanted to. I wanted to complain that the world isn't fair, and none of it was my fault, and nobody understood how hard I had it. But it was all nonsense. I could see that now. I was the master of my own destruction, and New Dave was right – I was the only person that could fix the mess I'd made.

"What is it you actually want, Dave? Do you want your wife back? Do you want a better job? Do you want a bigger house and more money, and nicer clothes – all the things you seem to think separate us?"

"Yes," I said. "I want all those things, but look at me. I've ruined my chance of…"

"Don't be stupid," said New Dave, cutting me off. "It's never too late. If you want something, you have to make it happen. You have to fight for it. If you want your wife back, have a shower, tidy the place up and show her what she's missing."

I went to speak, but New Dave held his hand up to stop me.

"You want more money? Go and tell your bosses. I know for a fact your place would be lost without you. So, tell them you want a pay rise and a promotion, and if you don't get it, you're walking. Don't take no for an answer."

"They've already turned me down for a promotion," I sighed. "They promoted Zack instead of me."

"What? That tit? You're joking. Well, if you ask me, you're better off out of it. You and your partner, you could have your pick of agencies. Christ, I'd hire you myself, if I thought we could afford you. And if you weren't being so fucking weird. But I know people, if you want me to have a word. I'm sure BMV are looking for a team."

"Yes, I've heard," I said. "Actually, Steve has already resigned. Or he's going to tomorrow. He came round earlier to tell me."

"Shit," said New Dave. "And you're not going with him?"

"It's not a great time to be looking for work," I said, "what with everything that's happened."

Dave shrugged, shook his head and breathed heavily out of his nose. "You're still not listening, are you? Stop being so defeated. Start fucking fighting for yourself. I've just told you, you're a talented guy. I'd hire you if I could. And I know you'd walk into another job. But you're still doubting yourself."

Again, I couldn't look him in the eye. I felt like a small child who'd lost his balloon, just standing there watching it float off into the sky. Tears were welling in my eyes again.

"If those dicks at AIP Communications really think they can get away with promoting that idiot ahead of you, they don't deserve you. If it was me, I'd tell them to stick their job. But if you really don't want to move, make sure they know what they've got."

"You don't know them. It's not as easy as…"

"Do you think I've had it easy?" said New Dave, cutting me off.

"I've worked really fucking hard for everything I've ever had. Do you think it was easy to give up a good salary and start my own business? No, but I did it because I believed in myself. Start believing in *yourself*. Start fighting. March into work and let them know what they'd be missing if you left. Demand a promotion. Demand a pay rise. And don't fucking take no for an answer."

"It's really not that…"

"Yes, it is, Dave. It's exactly that easy. You just have to do it."

I looked him in the eye and, for the first time, I didn't see competition. I didn't see the villain who'd invaded my life and turned everything upside down. He was not the neighbesis who had everything I wanted. He wasn't 46% better than me.

He was just Dave – the bloke from next door who, actually, was a decent guy.

"And do me a favour, will you?" laughed Dave. "Stop obsessing about me. I know I'm totally awesome and incredibly handsome, with the singing voice of an angel." He gave a cheeky wink. "But I'm sure you've got better things to think about. And stop worrying about who's called what. It's just a bloody name. It really doesn't make any difference to who you are, or the kind of life you have. Do you want to know something funny? Dave Brookman's not even my real name?"

"What?" I said, completely non-plussed.

"My real name is Bernard Butterworth. I changed it because… well, who wants to be called Bernard? And Butterworth? Sounds like a crap brand name for biscuits. I picked Dave Brookman out of the phonebook because I thought it sounded cool."

"What?" I said. "Is that true?"

Had all of this been for nothing? Had this other Dave Brookman – who I'd been obsessing about, comparing myself with and feeling so inadequate to – never actually been Dave Brookman at all?

"Of course not, you tit," laughed New Dave. "But it made you think, didn't it? What if I really was Bernard Butterworth? Wouldn't all your obsessing over the last few months seem completely ridiculous? We're just two blokes who live next door to each other. Only, I've got considerably better hair. Nothing else really matters, does it?"

He smiled, patted me on the shoulder, and walked across the grass to his own house. I closed the door behind him, walked back into the living room and assessed the full horror that I'd created.

CHAPTER 22
DELETE AND START AGAIN

ADVICE IS A funny thing. Everyone thinks they're good at giving it. But not many of us are good at receiving it – especially when it comes unsolicited. It's even harder to take when it comes unsolicited from someone you've been in an obsessive competition with for the past six months. And you've just lost – in a big way.

A few weeks previously, I'd have been cursing New Dave's name, wondering who the hell he thought he was, coming over here and telling me how to live my life. I'd have called him every rude name I could think of, swearing and shouting, and cursing him for not minding his own business. Most importantly, I'd have told him to stick his advice up his arse.

But as I surveyed the horrific mess in the living room, I knew everything he'd told me was true.

I'd been crazy and obsessive, blinded by jealousy, when I really had no reason to be jealous at all. I should have been focusing on myself, and all the good things I'd accomplished. I should have been happy with the life I'd built with Catherine, revelling in everything we had together. Not looking over the garden fence (quite literally) and coveting all the things I didn't have.

I pulled the sleeping bag from the sofa, sat down and fired up my laptop. I opened my Dave spreadsheet and the black and white grid lit up brightly before me. Scanning down the list of categories, scores and percentages, I wondered what the hell I'd been thinking. It was all so clear now, like I'd been walking around with filthy glasses and now they were clean. Who cared if someone else had more money than me? What did it matter if their house was bigger, or they had a nicer car, or fancier clothes?

Better hair? How the hell was I ever supposed to compete with that one? Even homeless people have better hair than me. Dogs who've spent all day writhing about in muddy puddles look more stylish than I do. And, seriously, what did it matter, anyway? I clicked on that line of the spreadsheet and pressed delete. The totals at the bottom

187

recalculated. I felt a cool tingle spark across my scalp.

House size? Who cared? The house was big enough for me and my family – actually, far too big now that I was wallowing there all alone. Catherine and I had spent many happy years in this house. It was a safe, loving environment in which we'd brought up our kids. That was all that mattered. I clicked on the line and deleted it. Another deliciously cool tingle hit me, surging down the back of my neck.

The next line compared our salaries. Possibly the most meaningless of all. How could it possibly affect my life? It's not as if him earning more meant that I earned less. It was pure ego. Jealousy. And if I wanted to earn more money, then it was down to me to do something about it, not just sit there crying.

I deleted the line and my shoulders sparked with ice cold pins and needles.

My eyes landed on the most heinous of all the categories – *Wife's Attractiveness*. What the hell had I been thinking? Catherine was literally the best thing that had ever happened to me. She was beautiful and funny and loving, and the most amazing woman I'd ever known. I knew I could never love anyone as much as I loved her. And I felt deeply ashamed that I'd ever thought to criticise or diminish her in any way.

My heart ached with the betrayal – an actual pain throbbing deep in my chest.

I clicked and deleted the line. A jolt of energy surged down my spine.

I deleted all the categories to do with the kids. I deleted anything to do with cars and appearance. I deleted *Singing Voice* – I mean, seriously, what the fuck was I thinking? With each line gone, my brain flashed with another jolt of energy.

I highlighted the whole spreadsheet and deleted everything. The whole thing – months of obsession, self-doubt and stupidity all gone with a single click. Then I moved over to the second tab, which contained my 46% plan. And I deleted that too.

My whole body tingled with positive, life-affirming energy. It felt amazing – like the heaviest of weights lifted off my shoulders.

I've always thought that one of the more ridiculous idioms – that you'd actually feel physically lighter by dealing with your problems. In fact, at the start of our careers, Steve and I conceived an advert for a stress-relieving medication in which we sent up that very idea. It featured a man carrying a giant backpack which contained small boxes that represented every one of his fears, anxieties and stresses. With every new problem, he added a new box to the bag, until it grew so big he could barely carry it. But when he took the medication, his bag shrunk down to the size of a wallet, which he put in his back pocket. Then he strapped on a pair of roller blades and whizzed around town. Hey, it was the late 90s – it was practically illegal *not* to feature roller blades in your ad.

It was a silly idea but, sitting there staring at my now blank spreadsheet, I felt like that man from the ad. I wasn't quite ready to go rollerblading (I had enough problems without adding a broken hip to the list) but I did feel a great deal lighter and much more positive.

And then another thought hit me. All this time, I'd been obsessing about how much worse my life was than New Dave's. It was as if everything I thought about myself, either positive or negative, came from a time since I'd known this new Dave Brookman. Nothing I'd done before had mattered to me. He was the biggest dominating figure in my life. But that was complete nonsense. The most dominating, most important character of my life was, and had always been, Catherine.

Ever since I first saw her that night in the Student Union Bar, Catherine had been everything to me, and the person who'd helped define my life. She'd believed in me when no one else had. She'd loved me when others rejected me. She'd helped me find strength I didn't know I had. She'd pushed me, tested me, sometimes annoyed me, but always been there for me. She'd made great things seem better, and potentially awful things bearable. She'd made me laugh more than anyone I'd ever known, forgiven me when I didn't deserve it, and helped me do things I'd never thought possible.

I thought back to what I was like before Catherine – a nerdy, shy, awkward boy with so little confidence he had to get drunk just to talk to women, and ended up so drunk he'd accidentally puke on them. Since we'd been together, she'd helped me become a far better person than I could ever have been without her.

The first time we made love was truly a defining moment in my life. It wasn't the first time for either of us; we'd each had a few partners before. But it was the first time it had ever felt truly magical. So perfect and just meant to be. I remember thinking immediately afterwards that I never wanted to have sex with anyone else. And I just knew I had to have her in my life forever. Catherine was the best person I had ever met and would ever meet.

I tried to imagine what my life might have been like if I'd never met Catherine. Would I have found the confidence she somehow helped me to achieve? Without her encouragement, would I have ditched my boring History degree and switched to the Advertising course that launched my career? Would I have ended up a dusty old academic, a frustrated secondary school teacher, or flipping burgers at McDonalds?

Without Catherine's honest criticism of my early work, would I have pushed myself to produce the kind of campaigns that won me awards?

I certainly wouldn't have been blessed with two of the most frustrating, hilarious, grumpy, annoying and genuinely brilliant kids.

Into the empty spreadsheet before me, I typed two column headings: WITH CATHERINE and WITHOUT CATHERINE. Then in the first column, I started adding a list of new criteria. But I didn't care this time about fanciful, unimportant things. Wealth and salary were meaningless now. Car and house size were completely irrelevant. Instead, I focused on things that had a real bearing on my life: happiness, success, love, being loved, laughter, joy, satisfaction…

I typed fast, my fingers dancing over the keys, as I hurried to get down all the thoughts rushing through my mind.

With my new list in place, I tried to imagine a life without Catherine. I saw myself as an unhappy husband, working late to avoid going home to the wife I resented and never really loved. Then I saw another version of myself – a tragic, middle-aged singleton, who'd never found love and spent every weekend trawling seedy bars and clubs, trying to find someone to provide at least a fleeting moment of human contact. I saw a man bereft of love, and who'd never known real happiness.

I looked harder at this alternate version of myself and saw someone who bitterly resented anyone with a family, desperate to cover up the hollowness he felt at never having had children himself. I saw a man who'd spent his life working in a job he hated, trapped in a career he'd fallen into by mistake, but no one had ever helped him find the courage he needed to make a change. A man who trudged from one day to the next, taking little joy in anything, and never knowing the pride of doing something he loved.

This man had never known the feeling of truly great sex – and how with someone you really love, it can be the single greatest feeling in the world (even better than the joy of ordering six Chicken McNuggets and getting seven by mistake). Instead, he'd bounced from one lacklustre partner to another, never really feeling anything other than momentary distraction.

As I pictured this other version of my life, I went down the list, assigning myself scores out of 10 for the different categories. In the column WITH CATHERINE, my scores were all high. Under *Love* I scored myself 10, as I couldn't imagine possibly ever loving anyone more than I loved her. I gave myself another 10 for *Being Loved*, for *Sex Life* and for *Happiness*. I scored solid 9s and 9.5s for *Laughter*, *Joy*, *Success* and *Happiness*. I raced my way through, scoring highly in each category.

Then I repeated the process, for WITHOUT CATHERINE, scoring this other me as honestly as I could – again comparing one Dave Brookman with another. Unsurprisingly, I didn't award myself more than 4.5 out of 10 for any field, opting mostly for 2 or 3.

Finally, I typed in the same equation as I had for my original spreadsheet and clicked to calculate the difference. Then I slumped back in the sofa, my hand clamped tight over my mouth. The results were in. My life would have been 85% worse without my wife.

Tears welled in my eyes as I simultaneously burst out laughing and crying. It was so tragic and funny all at the same time. For the first time in a long time I could see just how important this woman was to me. And, through my petty jealousy and obsession, I'd probably lost her for good.

They say you don't know what you've got until it's gone. They should rephrase that to: *What the fuck were you thinking, you arse-brained, fucking idiot? Of course, she was the best thing you ever had, and you're a complete cretin for not realising it.*

I clicked over to the next tab and changed the title from *46% Plan* to *Catherine Plan*. Into the first empty cell at the top, I typed one single sentence: *Whether she wants me in her life or not, I will do everything in my power to bring Catherine as much happiness, joy, laughter, satisfaction and fun as I possibly can.*

I opened a web browser, clicked into my email and started writing a new message:

My Darling Catherine,
I'm so sorry. I've been so completely wrong and I can't believe I hurt you so badly. I love you. I hope someday you can forgive me. This is how I really feel (attached).

Love Dave

P.S. I've deleted that stupid spreadsheet which caused you so much pain. I can promise you that part of my life is done with. I mean, seriously, what the fuck was I thinking?

I attached the new spreadsheet, pressed send, then slumped back into the sofa, blowing out a long breath.

With the email sent, I opened a new tab and started scanning through my online portfolio of work. I have a fairly basic website, which I use to showcase some of the best work Steve and I have done over the years. I smiled at the naivety of our earliest campaigns. It was good work, but flawed, and I could easily see our youthful inexperience. I cringed at some of the hackneyed copywriting and the outlandish art direction. I wished I could go back in time and give it a little more polish.

I thought about how Steve and I were back then. So keen and creative. Hungry to make our mark, prove ourselves and turn the advertising world on its head with our fresh approach. The arrogance of youth.

I clicked on the page *Award-winning Work*. I remember the excitement of being called up on stage to collect our first award – looking down to see Catherine smiling up at me from the crowd, so proud and happy. She was always so supportive, even when focusing on my career meant putting her own teaching career on hold so she could focus on raising the kids. Even through all the late nights and weekend work, when she'd barely see me. The times she was left at home looking after two small children, and I was jetting off to some tropical location to oversee photoshoots of bikini-clad women posing with fizzy drinks on a beach (like I say, it was the 90s). A pain throbbed in my stomach as I thought of everything she'd sacrificed for me.

I scrolled on to some of our more recent campaigns. Good solid work. Strong ideas and executions. It was easy to see the maturity in the work now. More importantly, I knew how each campaign had performed and how pleased the clients were with the work. I knew how much each had cost to create, how much we'd billed for it and how much profit the company had made.

I thought about the money Steve and I had generated for that place over the years. I thought about all the late nights, extra hours and weekend work – all without extra pay, credit or even much thanks. I thought of just how fucking valuable we were to them.

And they promoted Zack over me? They really thought that know-nothing, pathetic shitweasel would do a better job?

Fuck no! Absolutely not. How fucking dare they?! My face flushed hot. Blood whooshed in my ears.

As I carried on scrolling through the pages, I thought back to what Steve and New Dave had said. I was a talented man. I produced good, profitable, award-winning work. Surely other companies out there would recognise that. They'd reward me for it, not hide me away and treat me like shit.

How had I grown to doubt myself so much? Why had I let them beat me down?

I thought of that meeting in Thomson's office. The smug, self-satisfied look on his face as he delivered the bad news and expected me to sit there and take it. Zack's shit-eating grin, delighting in seeing me crushed as he took what should have been mine.

New Dave was right. What the hell was I thinking, letting them treat me that way? Who the fuck did they think they were? And did they really think they'd get away with it? No fucking way.

I wasn't going to roll over and take it anymore. It was time to teach them a lesson. Show them they can't just push people around and get away with it. Show them exactly who they'd been fucking with. They had to learn that there are always consequences. Eventually, the little man will bite back.

I thought of the panic in Thomson and Zack's eyes when I jumped up and kicked over the table. Their mad scramble to escape the room when I started smashing and throwing things. That delicious fear – I could almost taste it in the air – when my rage came bubbling over and I lost control.

They'd know that fear again. Smashing up Thomson's office was nothing compared with what I was going to give them next. They weren't going to know what hit them. I could see now, there was only one way to make everything right and take away all the pain and suffering of the past few weeks.

I went up into the loft and started searching through old boxes. I opened one and pulled out a long length of rope. I gripped it firmly, wrapping it tightly around my knuckles, watching my fingers bulb and redden, as I yanked it tight to test its strength.

I placed the rope down next to me and dug deeper, pulling out object after object, until I found what I was looking for.

"There you are," I said, looking down at it. "Exactly what I need."

I smiled as I held it tight in my grip, anticipating the looks on their faces. But there was work to be done yet. Lots of preparation. I ran back downstairs, made a strong cup of coffee and sat back down at the laptop.

CHAPTER 23
SHOWDOWN

THE OFFICE WAS eerily quiet as I stepped out of the lift and walked to my desk. Thankfully, nobody looked up to see me – they all sat there like zombies, tapping away studiously at their keyboards. Zack had recently instigated a 'no music in the office' policy, and it had drained away what little atmosphere the department had left. There wasn't a single smile in the whole room. No one walking about and chatting. No people huddled in the kitchen or flopped out on the sofas. No buzz of creative spirit. No flair or enthusiasm. Just silence peppered with the depressing symphony of keys tapping.

My heart was beating fast, sweat beading on my temples. I was anxious about facing people for the first time after my epic failure at the weekend. The news would have reached the office by Monday, and with me being absent for three days, the rumour mill would have been spinning out of control. I dreaded to think what people had been saying about me. I couldn't bear the thought of all the questions, insincere pats on the back and judging glances.

More than that, I was terrified of what I was about to do. There was no backing down now. I'd made my decision. It had to happen. But it was still bloody scary.

I'd planned it carefully. I knew exactly the best place to confront them – the weekly management meeting. I could corner them all together in one place, and they'd be completely powerless to escape.

"What time do you call this?" said Steve quietly, smiling as I approached his desk. "Good of you to join us."

"What?" I said, surprised. My shoulders ached with tension. A small, ice cold bead of sweat trickled slowly down my neck.

I'd opted to come into the office late, so I could arrive and just gate-crash the meeting at 11am. I didn't want to be sitting around for two hours beforehand. I didn't want the opportunity to talk myself out of what I knew I had to do.

Several heads bobbed up to look in my direction. A couple of people smiled and waved, then everyone quickly returned to their work.

"What's all this?" I said. "I know Zack banned music in the office, but what's happened to everyone? It's gone full fucking automaton in here."

"Another new policy since Monday," said Steve, keeping his voice low. "Zack's gone properly power mad and issued a new 'silent workspace' rule. Apparently, it's to 'help us concentrate'. He made small quote marks with his fingers. "He read about it in some Japanese book, I think. Load of bollocks, if you ask me. He just wants to stop us talking, in case we leave him out of any decisions. The guy's fucking tonto, mate."

"But what about collaboration? How are we supposed to discuss projects, or make decisions, or ask anyone's opinion on anything?"

"Email," said Steve, raising an eyebrow. "With King Zack cc'd on everything."

"Everything? How's that supposed to work?"

"I'm telling you, mate, he's lost it. And he's ruining this department day by day. Another reason I'm doing this," he said, holding up an envelope. His resignation letter. "I'm out of here, as soon as possible."

"This can't go on," I said. "I won't let it."

"You've decided to sack this place off and come with me?" said Steve hopefully.

"Better than that," I said, "holding up my briefcase and patting it gently. I've got quite a surprise for them in there." I pointed at the board members assembled in the glass-walled room at the far end of the office. "I'm gonna crash that meeting and show them what a mistake they've made. I'll show them they can't treat people like this. And then…" I smiled wildly, "I'm gonna make them pay. Dearly."

"What are you talking about?" said Steve, worry flashing in his eyes. "Why are you all sweaty? What are you gonna do?"

"Don't worry, I've got it all planned out. Believe me, when I'm finished, they'll wish they'd taken me seriously. They've had this coming for a long, long time."

"Seriously, mate," said Steve, fidgeting in his chair, "you're worrying me now. You don't look well. Are you okay?"

"Trust me, I'm better than I've ever been. Or, at least, I will be in a few minutes. What you said last night, you're absolutely right. I've messed everything up. With Cath and the kids leaving, and this job turning to shit… I've got nothing now. I've lost everything. So, I've got nothing to lose…"

My words were coming out fast and slightly garbled, the adrenaline kicking in. I could feel myself shaking slightly with the tension.

"And those fuckers in there... they don't care about us. As long as they get their money... and they keep us all subdued... you know, they take and they take, and they take... well, not anymore. It's time they learned their lesson..."

"Look, whatever you're thinking of doing, mate, there's another way," said Steve, panic ringing in his voice.

"No, don't you see, there is no other way. I've been up all night thinking about it, and I have to do this. Don't worry, it'll all be over before you know it."

I gripped the handle of my briefcase so tight my fingers turned red. I smiled at Steve, then headed off towards the board room.

"Mate, what are you doing?" said Steve, loudly. "You're worrying me."

As I walked through the office, people stood from their desks, looking at Steve, then looking at me. My heart throbbed as I reached the boardroom. I gripped the door handle tightly, took a deep breath and walked into the room.

"I'm sorry to just come barging in here like this," I said, frantically. My breathing was ragged, my voice high-pitched. "But I have something to say. Something you all need to hear. And I'm not leaving until I've said it."

I turned back to the door and locked us all in the boardroom. At the time, I thought this would be seen as a power move – me asserting myself and reinforcing my determination. However, I now see how it could have been misinterpreted.

I looked down at the assembled faces who stared back incredulously. My briefcase rattled slightly in my shaking hand. A single bead of sweat rolled agonisingly down the back of my neck. I took a deep breath and stepped to the head of the table.

"I've worked here for 10 years, now," I said. My knees started shaking as my heart climbed into my throat. "And during those 10 years, I'd like to think I've proven my..."

"Look, this really isn't the time and place for this, Dave," interrupted Thomson, waving a dismissive hand. "Why don't you schedule a meeting with my secretary and I'll be happy to discuss anything that's bothering you at a..."

"No, Thomson!" I shouted. "No!"

Everyone sat back in shock. Marcia from Account Management visibly shook at the deep timbre of my voice. Philip from New Business Planning suddenly found the tip of his pen incredibly interesting and stared intently at it. Melanie from HR sat bolt upright in her chair, outrage written on her face. Tina from Finance sucked in a huge gasp and looked as though she might leap under the desk. And Zack, sitting next to Thomson at the far end of the room, simply smirked with delight.

In truth, I surprised myself with the ferocity of my outburst. But I'd spent all night preparing for this. I had everything worked out and I wasn't going to let them stop me doing what I needed to.

"This is exactly the right time," I continued. "I've tried talking to you, and you just brush me aside. You don't want to hear the hard truth. Well, not this time. No excuses. You're going to sit there and fucking well listen to me!"

Shit. I hadn't actually meant to swear. I wanted to remain professional, but it just popped out. I knew my argument would be undermined if I didn't stay calm. I took another composing breath.

"Now," I said, speaking coolly and trying to keep the squeak out of my voice, "you all know me. You know the quality of my work. And you know how hard I work. I'm good at my job. I'm always one of the first in, and I never complain about working late or taking work home with me…"

"Nobody's questioning your work ethic," cut in Thomson, "or your dedication to…"

"Let me fucking finish!" I shouted.

Thomson jolted back with shock. His eyes went wide and his mouth dropped open in disbelief.

Damn. Bollocks. I was swearing again. And shouting. I didn't want this. "Please, just let me say my piece," I said, as calmly and softly as I could. Then, for good measure, I flashed a big fake smile. It wasn't fooling anyone.

Marcia bristled, as if she wanted to say something, but thought better of it. Philip was still concentrating on his pen. Zack stared at me with complete contempt.

"As I was saying," I continued, "I've worked here for nearly 10 years. I've always worked hard and done a good job. I've made a lot of money for this company. And I feel like I should have been rewarded. So, when you…"

"Look, if this is about a pay rise…" said Thomson, cutting me off for a third time, "I can only tell you what I've told everyone else, and that's that we're…"

"It's not about a fucking pay rise, Thomson, you obstinate fucking dickhead," I shouted.

Fuck. That was it. I'd definitely crossed the line now. It was one thing to get heated. Another to start swearing. But the moment I personally insulted someone, I'd completely blown my argument. I knew it and so did everyone else in the room. There was no way they would listen to me now. Why didn't they just let me talk?

"I mean, it is," I continued. "Of course, it's about money. But it's…"

Tina from Finance smirked and shook her head, as if to say, *just another greedy sod looking for a handout.*

"…more than that. It's about respect. It's about integrity. It's about keeping your fucking word." There was no point trying to contain the anger now. I let the bubbling rage overflow, as my knees trembled and my face burned a bright shade of scarlet.

"Look, I know what this is about. Dave was being considered for a promotion," Thomson explained to the rest of the room. "And while we thought very carefully about it, when it came down to it, we just didn't think you were the right fit. So, we offered the role to somebody else."

Zack raised his hand to cover a self-satisfied smirk.

"Considered?" I laughed. "Considered for a promotion? How about fucking promised it? How about told that I would definitely be getting promoted if I met all my goals for the year and we won the big KODEK account?"

"Well, now, I'm not sure we made any promise like that," said Thomson, starting to look flustered. The rest of the room bristled slightly but stayed quiet.

"Yes, you fucking did. You said those exact words. And then, lo and behold, you go and give the job to your son-in-law, Zack, who's been here barely five minutes, hasn't secured one new project since he has been here, and has less creative talent in his whole body than I have in my little finger."

"Whatever you might think I told you," said Thomson, looking around the room dismissively, as if I was making it up, "the fact is, when we looked at filling the senior position, we felt Zack had more… gravitas."

"Gravitas?" I shouted. "You're all fucking deluded. Look at what he's done to the team," I said, pointing to the desks on the other side of the glass window. For the first time, I realised the whole creative team had stopped working and were now intently watching my rant. "In just a few months, he's turned a buzzing, passionate, fun team into a group of zombies, staring at their screens and afraid to communicate. No music? Silent work environment?" I said, looking directly at Zack. "That just shows you have no idea about creative people. How do you expect them to produce great work, if you don't let them breathe and express themselves? Gravitas my arse!"

My face was burning. My eyes were starting to water. My heart was thudding and I felt dizzy, like I needed to sit down. This wasn't going how I'd planned. Not at all. They weren't listening to me, and I knew I was probably inches from throwing away everything I'd worked so hard to achieve.

I should stop now. Apologise profusely. Blame it all on stress and hope I still had a job to cling to.

But no. I'd come this far. I couldn't back down now. I'd been backing down all my life. Letting people take advantage.

That was the real reason I'd been unhappy all these months. It wasn't because someone else had more than I did. It wasn't about the size of my house compared with someone else's. It wasn't about fancy cars, or clever kids; ex-model wives, expensive clothes or good hair. The reason I was feeling so down was because I'd been letting people put me down. And I'd done nothing to fight back. I'd laid there and taken it. Then along comes this other version of me, who wouldn't put up with any of this shit. And that's why he has all these things – because he believes in himself.

Well, no longer. I wasn't going to let people push me around anymore.

"Best man for the job?" I said. "He wouldn't be the best man if the job was fishing cigarette butts out of a urinal. It's fucking nepotism, pure and simple. You know, this is exactly what I'm talking about. Corporate bullshit. It doesn't matter what you know, or what you do, or how good you are at your job, the only way to get on in this company is by who you know. Or whose arse you kiss. Well, that's not good enough. It's just not fair."

"Listen Dave," said Zack, his smarmy voice like treacle in my ears, "we all get it, yeah? You're upset you didn't get the job. But get over it, man. Coming in here, throwing round accusations… Crying because life's not fair?" He raised his hands to his face, mimicking rubbing tears from his eyes. "Grow up, will you?"

"Zip it, you arrogant, jumped-up little turd," I said. Christ, that felt good. Every bit as good as I'd imagined it would. "I don't want to hear from you. I don't want to hear from any of you anymore. It's too late for that now."

I lifted my arm high, showing my briefcase to the room. Their eyes widened as they all focused on it.

"I'm gonna show you about being fair. I'll show you what happens when you don't stick to your word, and when you take advantage of good people."

"What's in the briefcase, Dave?" said Thomson, his eyes growing wide. He sat up straighter in his chair, gripping the arm rests tightly.

"What's in here," I said, patting the case, "is a lesson. It's a lesson about doing the right thing. A lesson in meeting your obligations and treating people fairly. And it's a lesson you all need to learn."

Everyone around the table looked intently at the case. They fidgeted in their seats; panic etched on their faces.

Good, I thought, I've finally got their attention.

"Now, Dave," said Melanie from HR, at the far end of the table, "I don't know what you're planning here." She stood up slowly, raising her arms, as if trying to draw my attention. She tried to sound calm, but the slightest crackle in her voice betrayed her.

"Melanie, no!" said Marcia, panic contorting her face.

"It's okay, I've been trained in situations like this," said Melanie, keeping her arms still and her voice soft.

Situations like this? I thought. Situations like what?

"It's all right, Dave," said Melanie. "Now, let's not do anything… hasty."

"Hasty?" I said. "Hasty?"

"Look, technically you haven't done anything wrong yet," she said, reaching her hands out towards me and slowing her voice, like she was trying to calm me down. She looked at everyone else, as if pleading with them to follow her lead.

"Nothing that can't be forgiven, anyway." She spread her arms further towards me in a placatory manner. "So, let's not do anything stupid, eh?"

"Stupid? You're the only ones that have been stupid. Now, sit the fuck down," I shouted, shaking the briefcase at them.

Melanie lurched back in shock, tripping over her high heels and bouncing down into her chair. Philip jolted back at the sound of it, finally looking up from his pen.

Rivulets of sweat were now running down my bright red face. My breathing was sharp and ragged, blood pumping loudly in my ears. "You're all going to sit there and learn your fucking lesson!" I shouted.

I placed the briefcase down very purposefully on the table, spinning it round to face me. I flicked the catches with my thumbs and a loud metallic snap echoed around the boardroom. Melanie shrieked slightly as I opened the case and reached inside.

I looked at Marcia, who now had her eyes closed and seemed to be silently mouthing something. Philip had turned completely white, his eyes wide and staring. Thomson was edging back from the table ever so slightly, looking out the glass boardroom wall.

I lifted my out my laptop remote control and held it up to show them.

And then bang.

A loud, crashing noise as the meeting room door flew open. A large, boot-clad foot followed into the room milliseconds later, as chunks of splintered door frame flew across the room.

Everything went into slow motion. I spun round to see Jared, the security guard, hurtling towards me. He jumped, his arms stretched wide and his mouth gaping, as he shouted something I couldn't make out. I tried to move, but my feet were glued to the floor.

Then the world rushed back to normal speed as his 18-stone frame barrelled hard into me. His shoulder crashed into my side. My ribs cracked loudly. All the air in my lungs went rushing out in one deep gasp. His hands wrapped around me. Pinning my arms to my side as I stumbled backwards with the force. Then my feet lost contact with the ground. And for the shortest of moments, it felt like we were flying, soaring through the air, before gravity took over and we thumped into the hard ground.

My body twisted and my bones cracked as I hit the floor. Jared's bulky frame punched down into me. Pinned there, all I could do was wheeze and whine, and watch the world swirl around me.

Then I was aware of another figure coming towards me. Zack, up on the desk. Racing in my direction. "Hold him, get him," he shouted, as he slid over the polished surface of the boardroom table.

He jumped down in front of me, screaming loudly. The same incomprehensible word Jared had been screaming as he barged into the room.

"Bomb," shouted Zack. "He's got a bomb."

Wait, what? What did they think I had?

Zack stamped down violently onto my hand, sending my remote control flying across the room. He took a step back, steadying himself. Squared his body up against mine. Then he threw his foot forward, kicking me hard in the side of the head.

The world exploded with light and sound. The whole room turned red, then yellow. Hot pain screamed in my face. My neck muscles strained and stretched near to breaking. Then I went totally limp as my head flopped onto the ground again.

I heard panic behind me. Voices muttering and feet stamping. I heard Jared shouting for people to get back. Lights flickered in the window. The whole room glowed blue then red. I saw people gathered round my open briefcase. Looking intently at the contents. A voice said, "What the fuck?"

Then the world turned to black.

CHAPTER 24
FALL DOWN

I CAME ROUND to see a collection of startled faces looking down at me. My vision was blurry and I couldn't make out who the people were. I was lying on the floor at the head of the boardroom table. Someone had rolled me onto my back and placed Jared's rolled-up security guard's jacket under my head for support. It smelled of body odour and Lynx Africa and made me feel slightly nauseous. The room was spinning and there was a high-pitched whine ringing in my ears.

The first pain I noticed was the burning ache in my jaw. It quickly spread out through my cheeks, nose, chin and forehead, until my whole face was one angry, pulsing throb. Next, I felt the sharp stabbing in my ribs, which grew more intense with every breath. I tried to lift my head, but a sharp spike of pain exploded in my neck. My legs and arms were useless, limp bits of rope.

I tried to talk but all that came out was a whispery moan.

"What the fuck is this?" I heard Thomson saying somewhere in the background. "It's just a laptop and a few printouts."

"What?" shrieked Marcia. "Where's the bomb? I thought there was a bomb. Where's the bomb?"

"There's no fucking bomb," said Thomson. I heard him rustling papers. "Just a... presentation about... how good Dave is... how profitable his work is... and a spreadsheet showing how much money he's made the company. What the hell is this, Dave?"

I tried to answer, but the world was spinning and buzzing. My whole head throbbed with the effort and I could only gurgle in response.

"Are you saying there's no bomb?" asked Melanie from HR, sounding panicked.

"There's no fucking bomb," shouted Thomson.

"What about a gun? Is there a gun?" asked Melanie.

"There's no gun, no bomb, no nothing."

"But he had a detonator," said Zack, cocky and boastful. "I saw it in his hand. That's why I took him down."

"No," said Philip, bending down and picking up my remote control from where it had skittered to. "This isn't a detonator. It's just a remote control for Powerpoint presentations."

"What?" shouted Zack, suddenly angry.

"Oh, this is not good. What's this all about, Dave?" asked Melanie.

I gurgled.

"So, you're saying he wasn't trying to blow us up, or kidnap us, or kill us," Melanie said, sounding more panicked by the second. "He just wanted to give us a… presentation?"

"Looks like it," barked Thomson.

I tried to nod, but I still couldn't lift my head.

"Oh, this is not good. Not good at all," said Melanie.

"Fucking hell," said Thomson.

"Jesus," said Philip.

"Shit," said Zack.

The world turned hazy again. My head swimming and dizzy. Darkness enveloped me and the world went silent.

The next thing I was aware of was loud footsteps. Fast, angry, urgent. Then four men burst into the room, dressed all in black. They had helmets and body armour and were carrying what looked like machine guns.

"Armed police," shouted one of the men. "Everybody down."

"It's okay, false alarm," said Thomson, waving them off and stupidly trying to take control of the situation.

The man grabbed him by the back of the neck and roughly forced him into a kneeling position. All three men started shouting then. "Get down, get down, get down."

The room erupted into panic, as people screamed and dropped to the floor.

A dark figure shadowed over me, like a cloud drifting in front of the sun. I looked up to see the barrel of a machine gun pointed directly at my head.

Again, the world turned to black.

******

Bright sunlight was beaming down on me. I could feel the heat on my closed eyelids. The sound of waves lapping in the distance. My arms and legs limp and totally motionless. I was floating, tranquil, relaxed.

Then I felt fingers on my eyes, forcing them open as the bright blaze of a pen torch shone into my eye. It darted left and right, leaving scorched trails hanging in the air.

"Mr Brookman? Can you hear me?" said the doctor, her face just inches from mine. "You're in the hospital Mr Brookman. You've suffered a head injury, but we're looking after you. Can you tell me your date of birth?"

Pain throbbed in my jaw, but I just about managed to whisper back my details.

"Good," replied the doctor, "we just need to run a few tests, but you're going to be okay."

The next few hours were a blur, as nurses and doctors came in and fussed over me, pulling on different limbs, injecting me with this and that. I was loosely aware of being wheeled somewhere, sitting for a while in a different room, then being wheeled somewhere else. At some point – I guess after one of the injections – my pain seemed to have dulled, and I suddenly felt a lot lighter, almost amused. I'm sure I must have passed in and out of consciousness. I remember dreaming I was sitting on the world's largest marshmallow, then came round to the disappointment of the coarse NHS sheets rubbing against my naked buttocks.

When I finally regained consciousness, Steve was sitting next to my hospital bed. Noticing my open eyes, he jolted up from his half-asleep position.

"Hey, mate," he said, "how are you feeling?"

"Pretty fucking shit," I replied. A jolt of pain shot through my jaw as I spoke. It was agonising, but at least the drugs dulled it a bit. "I feel like a herd of elephants just trampled all over me."

"Do you need anything? More painkillers? Shall I call a nurse?"

I waved my hand to indicate I was fine.

"So, what the fuck happened?" I said in a whisper. "I remember being in the boardroom, about to do my killer presentation, and then… nothing."

"Well," said Steve, sheepishly, "I think there might have been a few crossed wires. Turns out they didn't realise you were planning to do a presentation. They thought you were trying to blow them all up."

Steve ran me through the whole series of events. The panic rising in the boardroom. People watching me through the glass wall, assuming I was in full 'Falling Down' mode. Scared as I pulled something from my briefcase. Zack jumping over the desk and clobbering me. Police bursting in, waving machine guns. Then Steve coming in the ambulance with me to the hospital.

"Why did they think I was trying to blow them up?" I said.

"Well, you were acting pretty crazy, mate," said Steve. "You know, you were all wild-eyed and shouting. You can understand why they jumped to the wrong conclusion."

"But why did the police show up?"

"Well, that's kind of my fault," said Steve. "You looked pretty worked up when you came into the office, mate. Talking about how you were gonna show them they can't treat people like they did. Saying how you were gonna make them pay dearly."

"I was talking about a pay rise," I said. "I had this big presentation which showed how much money we've made for the company and how I should have been the first choice for Executive Creative Director. I was gonna show them what a mistake they'd made. And when they came to their senses, I was gonna make them pay dearly, with a massive pay rise."

"Yeah, see that makes sense now. But at the time I thought… well, I don't know what I thought…"

"You thought I was going to blow people up."

"Or shoot them," he laughed.

I tried not to laugh back, but the ridiculousness of the situation hit me, and I couldn't help but chuckle. The movement instantly caused jagged jolts of pain to surge through my jaw, neck, ribs and back. "Ah, don't make me laugh, you prick," I said, "it fucking hurts."

"Anyway," continued Steve, laughing harder, "I thought you 'might'," he made finger quotes, "be on a murderous rampage, so I called Jared from Security. He called the police, I guess, then came belting upstairs, smashed through the door and jumped you."

"Well, thanks for that, mate," I smiled.

"Anytime mate," said Steve, squeezing my hand and contorting his face in mock earnestness. "I'm always here to keep you from massacring a room full of people."

"That means a lot," I said.

"Don't you get him all worked up," said a nurse, approaching the bed, "he needs his rest."

She placed a blood pressure cuff on my arm, pressed a few buttons on a machine and I felt the cuff inflate, squeezing my bicep. The machine beeped a few more times, then she told me I was fine.

"The doctor should be in to see you shortly," said the nurse. "You've been through the wars a bit, haven't you? And you've got a mild concussion, but you should be okay to go home tonight. Now, do you have anyone to drive you and look after you? You'll need someone at home with you, to keep an eye on you."

I was about to say that I didn't currently have anyone to look after me, on account of having driven my family away, but Steve butted in and said he'd look after me. The nurse said that would be fine, then disappeared with the promise to rustle up a cup of tea for us both.

"Am I in some kind of trouble?" I said, suddenly realising the implications of what had happened. "I mean, with the police. There were lots of police there."

"There's a detective here somewhere," said Steve. "Said he needs to talk to you when you wake up."

I sighed, worried about what might happen next.

"Christ, there you are," said Catherine, appearing at the side of the bed, looking panicked. Her hair was messy, her face flushed like she'd been running. Her eyes were bloodshot, like she'd been crying or trying not to. "Oh, you look terrible. Are you all right?"

"I'm fine," I said, trying to reassure her. "Apparently, I have a concussion, but I'm okay. A bit beaten up, but I'll live. They said I can go home tonight, and Steve's gonna come and keep an eye on me."

"So, what happened? I heard you were trying to blow the building up. I thought you'd been shot."

"Nothing that dramatic, I'm afraid. I guess I… sort of kidnapped everyone in the management meeting. I was just trying to do a presentation, not kill anyone."

"A presentation?" said Catherine, confused.

I talked Catherine through the day's events, with Steve filling in all the bits that I couldn't remember. She looked horrified to start with, scared and worried for me. She flinched at the thought of me being tackled to the ground and kicked. Worried at the mention of armed police storming the room. Finally, we laughed at the ridiculousness of it all, pain stinging my face and ribs with each chuckle.

"But why the briefcase?" she asked. "You said they panicked when you opened your briefcase. You haven't used a briefcase in years."

"I thought it might help me look professional. Thought they might take me more seriously with it. I had no idea they'd mistake me for a bloody bomber. It was also supposed to be my good luck charm."

I stopped, looking away from both of them, slightly embarrassed by the confession. "I got it down from the loft last night," I said. "It's the one you bought me years ago, to celebrate my very first job in advertising. Sounds silly now, but I wanted something of you with me in the meeting, to give me a little extra confidence."

Catherine smiled, placing a hand gently on my face. And I screamed in pain.

"Oh Jesus… shit… sorry," she said, jumping back from me.

"It's okay," I whimpered, "it's just that's the spot where I was kicked."

Anger flashed in Catherine's eyes. Fury on my behalf. Then her look changed to one of worry. "So, what happens next? Are you going to prison?"

"Oh, I don't think there's any need for that," said a man approaching the bed with a Costa Coffee cup in his hand. "DS Keane," he flashed a warrant card to confirm his identity. "Thank God I found a place selling this. The coffee you get out of those hospital vending machines is utter crap."

He looked young for a policeman, maybe mid-20s. His hair was brown and neatly combed, and he wore a navy blue suit with a white shirt and yellow tie. He was immaculate and looked more like a banker than the stereotypical image of the grizzled, alcoholic detective.

The three of us looked up at him, not speaking.

"Would you mind giving us a minute alone?" said the detective.

Steve and Catherine nodded silently, moved away from the bed nervously and left us alone.

"So, Mr Brookman," said DS Keane, "you've had quite the day, haven't you?"

I smiled and winced simultaneously, not knowing what to say.

"But don't worry," he said, taking a long sip from his coffee, "you're not under arrest. Not yet, anyway. I've taken statements from your colleagues, including the gentleman out in the hallway there, a Mr…" he consulted his notebook, "Steve Whitehouse."

Again, I still didn't know what to say.

"Now, if you don't mind," he said, sitting down in the vacant seat, "would you mind running me through everything that happened today? In your own words."

I told him the full story, or at least the bits I could remember. He sat there, umming and aahing, and scribbling notes in his small pad. Then he sat back, thinking for a moment, as he placed the pad in his lap, and took another mouthful of coffee.

"Well, it all seems like a case of mistaken intentions to me," he said. "You went into the room to do one thing… people got the wrong end of the stick and thought you were there to do them some kind of harm. There was a bit of panic, at which point we were called in. In the course of all the chaos, violence erupted, and you were injured. All very regrettable. However, it appears no crime was committed. I've seen cases like this before, where people seem guilty but there's actually an innocent, albeit rather bizarre explanation. And trust me, it's more paperwork than I can be bothered with."

It's a strange thing, the power the police have to make you feel guilty, even though you know you've done nothing wrong. As he told me no crime had been committed, I was still expecting him to turn the tables and tell me things were going to go very badly for me.

DS Keane went on to tell me how he'd spoken with everyone present at the time, and while he could understand how they'd jumped to the wrong conclusion, he'd determined that I hadn't actually done anything illegal. And in any case, Thomson was adamant that he didn't want to press any charges.

"Seemed a little too adamant, if you ask me. Like he was afraid of something. I reminded him it's not actually his decision, of course," laughed the detective. "Think he's been watching too many American crime shows. But it doesn't seem like anybody's too upset about what happened. And in the circumstances, I don't think there's any point in pursuing this further. In fact, the only real crime I can see is the assault against yourself."

"Really?" I said, dumbfounded.

"The security guard was only doing his job. He thought there was a genuine threat and he was just trying to protect people. So, I think we'll give him a pass, eh?" He nodded slowly, waiting for me to acquiesce. I nodded in agreement.

"But, by all accounts, you were already on the ground when a…" Again, he checked his notebook, "…a Mr Zack Smythe attacked you by kicking you in the head. Now, to my mind, that is excessive. And I'd say you definitely have grounds to report it as an assault."

I didn't know what to say.

"Seemed like a real arsehole to me, when I questioned him," said the detective. "Arrogant fucker. I'm not really supposed to comment, of course, but sometimes you meet someone that's just really unlikeable. And you kind of hope you can arrest them for something, just to ruin their day."

I tried my best to hide a smile, wincing at the pain.

"Anyway, you don't have to make your mind up now. You're obviously in pain, and I don't want to keep you longer than I have to." He went to take another sip of coffee and looked annoyed to find the cup empty. "I'll follow up with you in a few days and you can let me know whether you want to take things further. But rest assured, we won't be bringing any charges against yourself."

With that, he stood up, placed a business card in my hand and left. I watched him walk over to where Catherine and Steve were huddled at the edge of the ward. He said something to them, then Catherine walked back over and sat in the chair next to me.

"The detective said they're not arresting you for anything. That's good news."

"Thank God, eh?" I said. "Not sure I'd last very long in prison. The food's supposed to be terrible – even worse than *my* cooking."

Catherine smiled. I was pleased I could still get her to smile at my daft jokes.

"Where's Steve?" I said.

"I sent him home."

"But he's supposed to be driving me back and keeping an eye on me."

"Don't worry about that now," she said, looking a little solemn. She seemed to think for a few seconds, then said, "I got your email last night."

"Oh," I said. Strangely, I wasn't expecting her to bring it up, so I found myself unsure what to say.

"It was nice what you said. I liked the new spreadsheet you made. I still think it's bloody weird listing your whole life in a spreadsheet and assigning scores. I mean, who the hell does that?" She stopped herself. "But it was certainly a much more positive way to look at things. Even though you clearly got the numbers wrong."

"Oh?" I said.

"85% worse off without me in your life? Try 95%." She smiled, her eyes wide and a cheeky dimple puckered in the side of her cheek. "I remember that scrawny, nervous boy I met in college. And believe me, without my help he'd never have amounted to anything."

I smiled back. "You're not wrong Cath, I'd be completely lost without you. You just need to see the state of the house to know that," I laughed. I thought I'd try and make light of it now, before she actually saw it, and sent me straight back to hospital with another concussion. "And I know now that my life would have been so much worse without you in it. You don't even want to know what I imagined I might have become if you'd never let me into your life."

Catherine just looked at me, her eyes big and sad.

"I was so stupid to make that spreadsheet in the first place," I said. "I see that now. But the worst thing was you thinking I ever thought any less of you. I don't. I love you more than anything. You're the best thing that's ever happened to me. I know I can't ever really make it up to you, and I'm so, so sorry I ever made you feel anything other than 100% amazing, special and beautiful."

My throat was dry, my voice cracking.

"I'd like to grab that me from six months ago and beat him far worse than... well... this," I said, pointing at my bruised face, "for ever questioning the life he had. I see now that I had everything I ever wanted... everything I ever could want. And I got jealous of some guy with a fancy car and a bit of money, and I threw it all away. And I lost you..."

Tears were rolling down my cheeks now. Snot bubbling out of my nose.

"The love of my life," I continued, sniffling and croaking, "the best person I've ever met and the woman any man would be lucky to even know... I can't believe I made you stop loving me."

"I never stopped loving you, Dave," said Catherine.

"What? Really?"

"Of course, not. You don't just stop loving someone after 26 years, no matter how much of a twat they're acting. And I mean, you were acting like a really big twat. Not just a bit of twat, like normal. You were a complete twat. A mega-twat. Probably the biggest twat in the world."

"You're not wrong," I said, smiling through the tears.

"But it's all over with now, isn't it?" she said.

"Yes, absolutely. Completely over with."

"No more spreadsheets? No more jealousy? No more crazy plans?"

"I promise Cath. It's all done with. I know what a... well... twat I've been. And I've realised all I want is you and the kids. I don't need flash cars, or expensive holidays, or saunas and pools. I don't care about money or jobs or any of that shit. Without you, it's all meaningless. And I meant what I said in my email, whatever it takes to make you happy, that's what I'm going to do."

"Really?" she said, tears forming in her eyes.

"Yes. Look, I'll go and stay with Steve for a bit. I'm all smashed up, so he can hardly turn me away. You and the kids move back into the house. It must have been hard, all of you crammed in at Karen's place. So, you can get back home and get on with things."

"No, I don't think so," said Catherine.

"No?"

"Look at yourself, Dave. I leave you on your own for a few weeks and you end up in hospital looking like... well... no offence, but you look bloody terrible. And your hair is worse than ever," she smiled, a single tear escaping her eye and rolling down her cheek. "Less than a week ago, you passed out during a race and nearly drowned. Today, you accidentally hold the board of your company hostage and get beaten to a pulp. You obviously can't survive without me."

She made a good point.

"A few more weeks on your own and God knows what'll happen to you," continued Catherine. "And I can't keep coming to the hospital every week, the parking costs a fortune."

She smiled and flashed me a cheeky wink. Not only was she laughing at my jokes, she was even making her own. She took a deep breath, seeming to contemplate something, then said, "So, I'll have to come back and start looking after you, won't I?"

"Really? You'll come home?"

"Someone's got to keep you alive."

"Oh, Cath, that's brilliant. Oh, that's so brilliant."

"Yes. But you're not forgiven. Not entirely. There'll be plenty of grovelling... and romantic dates... and surprise gifts... and any other way you can think to make it up to me. I'm expecting maximum effort on your part."

"You'll get it," I said, my jaw aching as I smiled widely. "Starting right now."

I lifted the rough NHS blanket from my legs and tried to climb out of bed. I made it as far as sitting up straight before searing pain shot through my ribs and back. The agony was clearly evident on my face, as Catherine held up a hand and said, "What are you doing?"

"Making a new start," I said through gritted teeth. "I'm gonna get up and carry you out of here, and show you how much I love you."

I swung my right leg out of bed. But the world spun and I spun with it. Momentum carried the rest of my body forwards, until I was leaning over, head towards the ground, unable to stop myself from falling. "Oh shit," I said, panicking, as the floor rushed up towards me.

Catherine caught me, struggled under my weight and pushed me back into the bed. I collapsed against the pillow with a loud groan.

"You're not going anywhere, mister," she said, fighting the urge to laugh. "I doubt you'll be lifting anything for a few days. And if you really think you're gonna 'show me how much you love me'," she made finger quotes, "chance'll be a fine thing. We're not quite there yet."

"No, of course," I said, my head swimming and sweat beading on my hairline. "Perhaps I'll just lay here for a bit longer. At least until the doctor gives me the all clear, eh?"

"That sounds like a good idea. Let me go and see if I can find someone to check you out, then let's get you home."

"Thanks Cath," I said, feeling like I might start crying.

"Oh, and if you think I'm clearing up that bloody mess you've made of the house," she said, smiling, "you've got another think coming. Steve told me about the pizza boxes and pants all over the place. I don't care how much your ribs hurt, or how concussed you are, that place had better be spotless."

She walked off to find a doctor. And despite a swollen eye, an aching jaw and pain radiating throughout my entire body, I felt like the luckiest man alive.

CHAPTER 25
A RECKONING

I PULLED INTO the office car park, a thick knot of anxiety lodged in my throat. I hadn't slept much the night before, turning all the possible scenarios of this morning over in my head. Thomson screaming and shouting. Zack flashing me that smug grin. Being told I'd never work in the industry again. The police changing their mind and deciding to prosecute after all. All my colleagues booing and jeering me as I walked through the corridor, shouting 'Shame' and throwing things, like that scene with the evil queen in Game of Thrones. God, they wouldn't strip me naked too, would they?

They were going to fire me, for sure. They'd thought I was going to blow them all up. That's not the sort of thing you tend to let slide. I imagined it coming up in my end of year review: "You've had a good year, Dave. Produced some good work… sick days are low… got some strong feedback from colleagues. However, you did try and murder the senior management team, so I'm afraid we can't sign off on your annual 2% pay rise."

Catherine had assured me things would be fine. "What can they do?" she'd said. "They'll realise it was all just a big mistake. And they'll know the police aren't taking it any further. I'm sure you'll all just laugh about it and get back to normal."

I knew she was just trying to make me feel better. I could hear in her voice that she was just as worried about the impending unemployment as I was.

Catherine had driven me home from the hospital on Friday night. She actually gasped when she walked into the house and saw the mess that awaited. I felt the hands supporting me slacken a little, and I got the distinct impression she wanted to drop me right there in the hall, turn around and leave me again. But she didn't. She helped me up to bed, made me a cup of tea, then nipped round to Karen's to collect the kids.

It was great having them all back. The house felt fuller and warmer than ever before. It seemed bigger somehow. Where for the last six months I'd only looked at it with disappointment, now I could see all the wonder and personality in it. The curtains we'd bought online and spent far too much on. The carpet Catherine had chosen and I'd never really liked. The IKEA bookshelf that had taken me three times longer to construct than it really should have. The poorly patched bit of ceiling where I'd stuck my leg through one day, fumbling about in the loft. Jack and Holly's annual height marks on the kitchen doorframe. The faded lino in the bathroom, which I'd been meaning to replace for at least three years. It wasn't just a house – a building to be compared with any other. This was *our* house, filled with memories and love and hope. And with my family reinstated, it was once more a home.

Despite her protestations that I was to clean and tidy the house myself, Catherine did help me. We even roped Jack into cleaning the windows – for a fiver, of course. And Catherine actually laughed when she saw my carpet mushroom, amazed at how I'd descended so far into hopelessness that I'd managed to let it grow.

Holly sulked in her bedroom for most of the day. She was going to take longer to come around, but I knew she was happy deep down that her mother and I were reunited.

The cat was even more grumpy with me than usual. In fairness, I couldn't blame her. When we got home from the hospital, and found her curled up on the doorstep, I couldn't honestly have said when I'd last seen her. I certainly couldn't remember when I'd last put food in her bowl. Thankfully, she hadn't simply run away – she must have been sneaking food from neighbours, and now Catherine was back, she'd returned. There was definitely something in her whiny, elongated meows that made me sure she was trying to grass me up, telling Catherine just how neglected she'd been. And there was more anger in her hisses and swipes than usual, catching the backs of my ankles with her claws every time I walked past.

For her part, Catherine didn't seem to hold a grudge. We didn't slip straight back into holding hands and staring fondly into each other's eyes. And we wouldn't do for a little while. But I think she could see that I'd learned my lesson. And she, too, was happy to be home.

We sat as a family on Saturday night, eating a takeaway pizza and watching a dreadful film that Holly chose, about a strange-looking, sultry girl who falls in love with a vampire, then wonders why she has a hard life. It was really bad. *Really* bad. But it was probably the best night of my life. And I genuinely couldn't see how I'd ever wanted anything more.

"I bet New Dave isn't having such a warm, cosy, enriching evening with his family," I whispered to Catherine.

She gave me a look to suggest she might stab me in the thigh with a fork, so I quickly assured her I was only joking. Bit too soon, perhaps, I thought.

The rest of the weekend was equally as lovely, despite the searing pain that shot through my face, back, ribs and legs every time I moved or breathed. We had a big Sunday roast, we watched films and played board games, and I relaxed and just enjoyed being me – Dave Brookman – an average man spending time with his amazing family.

We ignored the ugly event that took place in the office and didn't even talk about it until Sunday evening when we went to bed. It was nice not thinking about it, but I knew I'd have to face up to what I'd done eventually. Catherine reassured me things would be okay, but I wasn't so sure. Then, before I knew it, Monday morning had arrived and I was in the car on my way to the office.

When I walked in through the main door, Melanie from HR was sitting in reception, waiting for me. She wore a stern, black business suit, with high heels so thin and pointy they looked more like weapons than shoes. She had a laptop perched on her knees, tapping away quickly at the keyboard. I guessed she'd been there for some time.

"Ah Dave," she said, catching me before I'd taken a full three steps into the building. "Morning. How are you feeling?"

She looked tired. Her hair was thrown up into a messy ponytail, far from the immaculate image she usually presented. Something in her eyes betrayed the forced smile she was beaming at me, suggesting she was nervous or dreading something she was about to do.

"Sorry to catch you before you've even made it to the lift," she said, forcing a small laugh and touching me lightly on the arm. She was really going for it with the fake platitudes. This couldn't be good. "I was hoping we could have a quick chat first thing."

"Um, okay," I said, befuddlement taking over from the apprehension I'd been feeling about returning to work.

So, this was how they were going to do it. Catch me before I even make it to my desk. Drag me off to a dark meeting room somewhere, sack me, then presumably have Jared escort me out a back door so nobody saw it happening. Throw me away like rubbish, and make sure I don't have the chance to corrupt people's opinions with my side of things. Of course, I was expecting a discussion of some kind, but not like this.

"Great," said Melanie, grinning wider. She guided me into a lift, up onto the third floor and into a large meeting room where Thomson was waiting. Melanie walked round behind the table and sat next to him, directing me to sit across from them.

"Dave," said Thomson, flatly, remaining seated and only just managing to make eye contact.

Brilliant, I thought. This is what it's come to. All those years of hard work and service, and the man can barely meet my eye.

"Thanks for coming in for this chat, Dave," said Melanie. "How are you feeling?"

Thomson stayed silent. Dark bags hung like tiny hammocks beneath his eyes. He looked tired, bored and irritated. And there was something else there that I hadn't seen in him before. I couldn't tell what it was.

"A little embarrassed," I said, sheepishly. "A bit stupid. And still in a fair amount of pain."

"Yes, of course. It must have been quite an ordeal for you. Hopefully, you had a chance to relax and recuperate over the weekend," said Melanie. Thin beams of light pierced the room, illuminating her face. She also looked tired and frazzled.

"Well, the trip to the hospital wasn't much fun. I think they gave me just about every test a person can have. At one point, I thought they were going to give me a colonoscopy, just so I had the complete set."

I chuckled softly, hoping to lighten the mood, but it had the adverse effect and they both clenched. Melanie stared at the table in front of her. Thomson breathed loudly through his nose.

"And what did the doctors say? No lasting damage, I hope," said Melanie. There was something in her voice. Some slight flutter of unease.

"No, thankfully not. A bit of concussion, a few bruised ribs and… well, as you can see," I said, pointing to the mess of purple and blue that spread up from my jaw, covering my cheek, nose and eye, "a bit of bruising. But no lasting brain damage."

"Oh good," said Melanie. "That's good."

A long silence hung between us. Thomson stared at the clock on the wall. The tick, tick, ticking louder than any clock I've ever heard.

"Well, hopefully you're feeling a bit better now, and I speak on behalf of the whole company when I say we wish you a speedy recovery," said Melanie. Again, Thomson remained impassive.

The atmosphere in the room was so still and surreal, I couldn't tell where they were going next. And why were they pretending to be so nice and caring? I'd never had anything approaching a pleasant conversation with Melanie before, and my relationship with Thomson had deteriorated so badly over the last few months, I'm surprised he hadn't joined in with Zack when all the head kicking had started. If they were going to fire me, I wished they'd just bloody well get on with it and cut out all the sycophantic concern for my wellbeing.

"Now, obviously we wanted to sit down with you and touch base on everything that happened last week," said Melanie, tilting her head to one side and clasping her hands together. She looked like she was trying to channel Jesus through her forced body language.

"Yes, of course," I said, my throat dry.

Here it comes, I thought, out on my ear after 10 years with the company. How was I going to pay the mortgage? Or buy food? Or meet the payments on that ridiculous bloody car?

"Obviously, there was a very big misunderstanding," said Melanie. "And I think, on balance, when we look back at exactly what happened... well, it's understandable how we might have drawn the wrong conclusion."

"Really? I'm not sure I agree," I said.

Fuck this, I wasn't just going to roll over and take it. If they wanted to sack me, that was one thing. But I wasn't going to make it easy for them. "Okay, I probably shouldn't have just barged into the meeting. But I wanted to get you all together at once. And interrupting a meeting is hardly a crime."

"No, it's not, but I think you'll agree that you were in quite an... agitated state," said Melanie, clasping her hands tighter. She kept her voice soft and measured, picking her words carefully, as if referring to a well-rehearsed script. "You were quite red-faced and swearing. You seemed very angry."

"Yes, I was angry." I spoke slowly, keeping my voice just as soft and measured. I wasn't going to fall into the same trap as before, letting my emotions get the better of me. "You promoted that idiot Zack ahead of me, for no good reason. I think I had a right to be disgruntled. I was promised that promotion, and you stole it away from me."

Thomson shifted in his chair. He opened his mouth to speak, but Melanie placed a hand on his arm to stop him. She'd clearly coached him on how the meeting should go, and what he could and couldn't say.

"We're not disputing your reasons for being upset, Dave," said Melanie. "But you were clearly very worked up. And in the heat of the moment, we weren't sure what you were going to…"

"You thought I was going blow you up," I said. "I heard you all talking when I was laying there on the floor. You were asking if I had a bomb or a gun in my briefcase. How could you think that?"

"Well, now… yes… things were said in the heat of the moment," said Melanie, her voice getting higher, "we were…"

"Look, Dave," said Thomson, finally finding his voice, "you came in shouting the odds. You were aggressive and swearing. And you locked us all in the bloody boardroom. What were we supposed to think?"

"Not that I was going to blow you up."

"We jumped to the wrong conclusion," said Melanie, getting flustered now.

"Wrong conclusion? I wanted to give you a presentation. I wasn't going to start murdering people."

Again, Thomson went to speak, but Melanie stopped him. "I think we can agree," she said, "that mistakes were made on both parts. Very regrettable mistakes."

"Like Zack kicking me in the head?" I was on a roll now. Not going down without a fight. "You know, the police told me I'd have grounds to report him for assault."

The two of them looked at each other, worry suddenly betraying their faces.

"Something the… incident has brought to light," said Melanie, deftly changing subject, "is how we see the company, and your department in particular, running as effectively as possible."

Here we go, I thought, my shoulders tensing and my heart rate increasing. The build up to a sacking.

"One of the things we've been looking at and, in fact, something we were considering long before Friday," said Melanie, back into her prepared script, "is whether we do, actually, have the right people, in the right places, to help us reach the future goals of the business."

Images of final demand bills flashed through my head. Bailiffs turning up at the house and taking the car. Meetings with bank managers about missed mortgage payments.

"You see, it's a case of aligning the right skills to the right business functions. Consolidating capabilities and driving success with a clearly defined focus on KPIs."

The fog of nonsensical business-speak coming from her was so thick I was practically choking on it. I've found that when people are nervous, or stalling for time, or trying to sound smarter than they are, they retreat behind a wall of big, confusing words, like 'aligning', or 'consolidating'. Or 'ideation'.

"You see, creative work is not all about ideation," continued Melanie, "we have to ensure we have the right experience and performance-oriented…"

"We've sacked Zack," said Thomson, cutting her off.

I couldn't breathe. My heart was pounding now. Hang on, what did he say?

"What Melanie's trying to say is we decided Zack wasn't the right man for the job after all…"

Zack? They'd fired Zack? They weren't letting me go after all. I sucked in a huge lungful of air.

"…so, we've let him go. We realised he didn't…"

"Know the first thing about marketing, advertising or how to lead a team?" I butted in, trying not to laugh.

"I wouldn't go quite that far," said Thomson, anger tingeing his voice. "But, on reflection, we knew he wasn't best placed to lead the team."

"Really?" I said, rather smugly. "What a surprise."

"I've never pretended I'm infallible," continued Thomson. "I read your presentation over the weekend. I was impressed. And I'm big enough to admit when I've made a mistake."

His face contorted with discomfort, like he was trying to hold in a fart. Melanie smiled sycophantically.

"Hang on, what's going on here?" I said, confused. "I thought you called me here to sack me."

"Sack you? Goodness, no," said Melanie.

"No," said Thomson, "we want to promote you to Executive Creative Director."

A fuzzy itch tingled in the centre of my brain. "Promote me?" I said.

"Yes," said Thomson. "Your presentation was very convincing. You understand the business and I can't argue with the numbers. On top of that, the clients love your work and the team respects you. Since Zack took over, he's done nothing but alienate the clients and rub the team up the wrong way. There, I admit it."

"It's KODEK, isn't it?" I said, a spark igniting in my brain. "That's what this is all about. KODEK are threatening to pull their money and go with another agency. What did Zack do?"

"It's nothing like that," said Thomson gruffly. "The accounts are all fine."

"Then what's this about? Do you think I'm gonna sue you, or something? Is that why you both look so worried?"

"Look," said Thomson, nervously. "I don't think we need to start talking about suing anyone, do we Dave? Things aren't that bad. We're sorry about what happened and…"

Melanie's hand flew to Thomson's arm, too slow to stop him speaking.

"Let's not start assigning blame," she said. "Obviously, you've been through an ordeal and, as a highly respected member of the team, we want to do whatever we can to help you recover as quickly as possible. The last thing we want is talk of legal action or anything like that."

"So, you *are* worried I'm gonna sue?" I said. This was brilliant. I'd walked in expecting to get the boot, and now I had them crawling at my feet. Truth be told, it hadn't even occurred to me that I could sue them, let alone that I'd want to.

"Now, let's not get caught up in words like 'suing'," said Melanie, forcing another fake laugh. "We just want to put the past behind us and move forwards. That's why we've put together what we think is a very generous offer."

"Bloody generous," grumped Thomson.

"Now, this has nothing to do with what happened on Friday," said Melanie, "or the injuries you sustained. As Mr Thomson says, we've been considering the leadership of the department for a while now, and the role we think you could play. We'd like to offer you the position of Executive Creative Director, with a 30% rise in salary."

She pushed a piece of paper over the desk towards me.

"This would be your new salary," she said. "You'll see we're also offering a company car, and we'll raise the allowance on your health insurance to include your whole family – free of charge. Finally, as head of department, you'll qualify for a performance-related annual bonus, equalling 10% of your salary, should you meet targets. I think you'll agree that's very generous."

I stared at the piece of paper in front of me, not quite able to believe it. Thomson ground his teeth, again refusing to meet my eye. His skin was pallid. He looked like he wanted to scream.

"This *is* generous," I agreed, "but I'm wondering what the catch is."

"No catch," said Melanie, forcing another fake smile. "Although, naturally, we'd ask you to sign something saying you don't hold us responsible for any injuries you've received, and that you won't be taking any legal action."

She paused, her eyes darting to Thomson, then looked sheepishly back at me.

"We'd also like to prevent any criminal charges against Zack."

"Christ. The truth finally comes out. You're only promoting me because of this," I said, pointing to my bruised face. "To save me from suing you and to give Zack a free pass."

"Absolutely not," said Melanie, "it's about realising objectives and ensuring we have the right results-focused, business-oriented, senior leadership," she said getting lost in another sea of buzzwords.

"Look, Dave," said Thomson, cutting her off, "yes, we do want to avoid a lawsuit. I'm not going to lie."

Melanie shot daggers at him. He was clearly off script.

"But we're not just promoting you to get ourselves out of hot water. You deserve it and, truthfully, I should have promoted you ages ago. Your presentation convinced me of that. And I realise we'd be lost without you. That's the real reason we're doing this."

"There's one more thing," said Melanie. "We know what a hard time this must have been for you and your family. And you clearly need some time to get over your… injuries." She winced slightly at the word. "So, we're giving you two weeks' additional annual leave. And we'd like to send you and your family away on holiday. All paid for by the company, of course."

Again, Thomson grimaced.

"How does Tenerife sound?" said Melanie. "Five-star hotel. All inclusive. Loads for your kids to do, and plenty of chance for you to relax."

"I… er…" I was genuinely lost for words.

"We've got everything arranged; we just need your passport numbers to complete the booking."

Still I couldn't speak. I was totally flummoxed by the generosity. And then it struck me. That's why they both looked so tired. They must have spent the whole weekend worrying about what I was going to do. They'd probably met with lawyers, assessing what potential damage a lawsuit could do. And, judging by the generosity of the offer, it must have been sizeable. They were scared. And they were bribing me. Perhaps I should go and see a lawyer myself, I thought.

"That all seems too generous," I said.

Thomson shifted in his chair, again staring at the clock on the wall.

"Not at all," said Melanie. "We want to help you recover, so you can get back here and lead the team."

I looked at the piece of paper in front of me. It was a significant pay rise. A promotion they'd happily stabbed me in the back over before. And now they wanted to send my whole family on an all-expense-paid holiday?

"What's really going on, here?" I said. "Why are you so scared? And why are you so sure I'd even have grounds to sue you, anyway?"

Melanie's eyes flickered. Just the slightest movement, but it was as telling as if she'd flopped forwards with her head in her hands.

"Come on, tell me," I said. "There's clearly something else going on. Enough to get your lawyers scared, and don't pretend you haven't spoken to them. I'm surprised they're not here with us now."

Melanie looked intently at her hands clasped in front of her. Thomson continued staring at the clock.

"You might as well tell me," I said. "I'll find out sooner or later. And I'm not signing anything until I know what's really behind all this… generosity."

Melanie and Thomson looked at each other, sighed simultaneously, then looked back at me.

"It seems… there's a video," said Melanie.

"A video?"

"Apparently, somebody filmed the incident on Friday, and they've posted a video on YouTube."

"A video? Showing everything that happened? Who filmed it?"

"We don't know," said Thomson, gruffly. "And when I find out who bloody…" Again, Melanie placed a hand on his arm to stop him.

"So, this video?" I said. "I assume it shows me getting angry… then being attacked… and then you lot realising I was only trying to give you a presentation?"

"That's the nub of it," said Melanie. She breathed strangely and wriggled in her chair.

"But there's something else, isn't there? Isn't there?"

"Fine," said, Thomson, breathing loudly out of his nose. "It shows all the panic that went on. You have to understand: it was a very tense situation. People weren't thinking straight…"

"And?" I said.

"When we realised your true intentions, I'm afraid Zack started panicking. He was scared he might get into trouble… and he came up with the stupid idea of… getting a sharp knife from the kitchen and placing it in your hand." He sighed heavily, shaking his head with disappointment. "That way people would think you posed a serious threat, and his actions would look like self-defence."

"That sneaky…" I said, angrily, carefully censoring myself before I swore.

"Obviously, we would never have let him do it," said Melanie.

"No, never," said Thomson.

"You have to believe that," said Melanie. "It was only a foolish idea – that nobody else agreed with – and which happened just before the police arrived."

"A silly boy, coming up with a ridiculous idea, and we stopped it immediately," said Thomson.

"But it's all on camera," I said, "and it makes you lot look really bad. No wonder your lawyers are so scared."

"Bloody thing's already had over 600,000 views," said Thomson, defeated.

"Show me, then," I said. "I know you've got it cued up to play."

Thomson picked up a remote control. The large TV screen on the wall came to life, and I was suddenly watching myself through a glass wall, shouting and waving my arms. I saw myself reach into my briefcase. Jared kicking the door open and jumping on me. Zack sliding over the table and launching his foot into my face. Then the camera moved closer, hovering in the doorway, catching Thomson, Melanie, Zack, Philip and Marcia in a huddle, realising their mistake. And then the killer bit of evidence.

"Wow, that really doesn't look good for you guys," I said, as Thomson turned off the TV. "I know they say there's no such thing as bad publicity but, in this case, maybe there is. I can see why your lawyer is scared."

"Look," said Thomson, "we really don't want this getting more out of hand than it is. We've made you a very generous offer, and we want to move forwards together. Let's not get lawyers involved, eh?" He looked more vulnerable than I've ever seen him.

"I don't want to get lawyers involved," I said. "I never did. All I ever wanted was for you to take me seriously, give me the job title and money I deserve, and let me get on with doing some good work."

"Great, so we can put this all behind us?" said Melanie.

"Not so quick," I said. "I wish you'd just been honest about everything. I can't help but feel like you've tried to hoodwink me."

"No, we never meant…"

"Listen," I said, cutting her off. "The job offer is great and the salary is generous. But I need time to think about whether this is still a company I want to work for."

Thomson went to speak, but I held up a hand to stop him. He looked startled at my boldness. Warm confidence pulsed in my chest.

"I think I'll take you up on your offer of this holiday," I said. "Two weeks in the sun sounds like a good opportunity to really think about what I want to do."

"Actually, the holiday would only be a week," said Melanie, "and then you can have another week at home to…"

"No, two weeks away sounds right to me. You know, to really think." I emphasised the last word, staring hard at Thomson. "It won't be hard to amend the booking. And we'll need some spending money, in case the kids want to go to a waterpark, or something. Shall we say a thousand pounds? You can call Finance and get them to organise the currency."

"A thousand pounds?" said Thomson, his face turning from pallid to bright red.

"Not enough?" I said, smiling. "Maybe not. I wonder what the papers would pay me for the story. They love paying out for this sort of thing."

"Okay," said Melanie, now digging her nails into Thomson's forearm. "Two weeks away and a thousand pounds seems fine."

"Excellent," I said. "I'll nip out so I can phone the wife to get our passport numbers and make sure the kids can get time off school. Oh, they'll probably give us a fine for taking them away in term time – you're all right picking that up, aren't you?"

Melanie nodded, forcing a smile onto her face.

"Great," I said. "Catherine will be really pleased. Two weeks away is exactly what we need. I can think about whether or not I want to sign your little disclaimer. And by the time I get back, I reckon that pay increase will have gone up to 40%." I pushed the paper back across the table towards them.

"40%?" blurted Thomson. Then a resigned look came over him, and he returned to gnashing his teeth and staring at the clock on the wall.

"Back in a sec," I said. "In the meantime, why don't you get the holiday website up on the big screen there? You can show me where I'm off to."

I walked out into the corridor, fighting to keep from laughing, then called Catherine to give her the good news.

CHAPTER 26
A CHANGE IS GONNA COME

THE AIR CONDITIONING hums gently. A cool breeze catches a small patch of sweat on the side of my neck, making the skin tingle. I'm hot, not nervous. Excited. Ready for what's coming.

"So, how was the holiday?" says Melanie, sitting down across the desk from me. "You've certainly caught a bit of colour."

She's smiling, but she seems nervous. Twitchy. Thomson is sitting next to her. His face is grey and motionless, like an Easter Island statue. He doesn't want to know how my holiday was. He's tense and aggravated and just wants to get on with it. He wants to know what I've decided.

******

The holiday was great. They certainly didn't scrimp or save on the resort. I spent two weeks laying by the pool, eating and drinking as much as I wanted, and spending time with my family. It was a much-needed recuperation from my injuries. But, more than that, it was an opportunity to reconnect with my wife and kids. And not just because of everything that had happened over the last six months. Sitting on a sun lounger, watching Catherine smooth sun cream into her long, sexy legs, I realised how work had taken over my life so much that I'd been neglecting the people and things that mattered most.

So, we hung out by the pool. We swam and walked along the beach. We had three family meals every day. I even caught Holly having a sneaky burger when she thought nobody was looking. I didn't confront her or claim any kind of victory. And the next day she was back to eating meat full time, having suddenly remembered an article she'd supposedly read which said how eating meat was actually much healthier for teenagers, and the conditions on farms had become much better in recent years.

We played cards and watched terrible cabaret singers in the evenings. We laughed and joked and just hung out. And there was so much to do in the resort that we didn't leave for the whole two weeks. So, the spending money went almost completely unspent – aside from a few trinkets in the gift shop.

I had a good, long chat with Jack, about life and sports and his new passion for acting. He'd really got into it, had indeed been offered a fairly sizeable part in the school play, and was considering taking extra classes in Performing Arts. I was still a little uneasy about what that meant for his future prospects. And I wasn't overly enthused at the thought of him struggling through life trying to pursue one of the most competitive, poorly paid career choices out there. But if there was one thing I'd learned recently, it was that happiness was more important than anything else. And he certainly seemed happy. Besides, I made him promise not to give up entirely on his sports, so there was still a chance of him becoming a millionaire footballer with more than enough money to support his old dad.

Catherine was still a bit tender for the first few days, not quite able to fully forgive me. But I fussed over her and did whatever I could to make her feel special. And on the fourth day, when she suggested the kids went to watch a magic show so we could have some 'quality time', I knew we were going to be all right. Although, I can't help but feel she got a little too much pleasure from seeing me wince and cry out in pain, as my injured back and legs throbbed, while she bounced around on top of me.

It really was a magical holiday. By the time we boarded the flight home, we were all getting on so well again it was as if none of the upset from last few months had ever happened. Even Holly was being nice to me.

We arrived home from the airport at just after 10pm to find a scruffy man in jeans and a grey anorak parked in the street outside our house. His hair was a messy mat of badly dyed blond, and his face was dirty with stubble. His passenger seat was littered with takeaway food wrappers and disposable coffee cups, and he looked like he'd been camped there for a few days. I barely made it halfway up the path to the front door before he came clambering towards me.

"Mr Brookman?" he said. "Mr Brookman. My name's Pete Stephen and I'm a reporter for the Sun. Would you like to give us your side of the story? I'm authorised to offer you six grand as payment. But hold out a bit and I reckon I can get you nine."

"Side?" I said, completely baffled. "Story? What story?"

"The video," he said. "You're the man from the video, aren't you?"

It took me a few seconds to realise what he was talking about. Strangely, I hadn't thought about that video the whole time I was away. I'd kept my phone turned off and hadn't been anywhere near the internet. In fact, I was so intent on reconnecting with my family that I'd locked all our phones in the hotel safe on the first day we got there – much to the annoyance of Holly, who was outraged she wasn't allowed to spend every second of the holiday on Instagram, Facebook, or chatting with her friends on WhatsApp. I wanted to spend quality time together, talking – not ignoring each other and staring mindlessly at little black screens. I was also keen to avoid coming home to thousands of pounds worth of roaming charges.

So, I had no idea what this journalist was talking about. Until he explained it all.

Apparently, since Thomson and Melanie had first shown me the video, it had not only gone viral, it had gone completely insane. Not quite to the levels of getting dragged off a United Airlines flight, but it had certainly piqued people's interest. The number of views had risen to 2.4 million. And they were going up daily.

Websites like Buzzfeed and LadBible had run stories on it, with headlines like *Office Worker's Meltdown Ends in Kicking* and *Boardroom Beating for Furious Employee*. None of the stories named me in person. I was just 'disgruntled employee' or 'raging office worker'. Instead, they asked their readers to leave comments identifying me if they knew who I was. Talk about lazy journalism.

Eventually, one newspaper journalist had studied the tape and figured out which company the video had been shot in. He'd then hung around outside the building, questioning people as they came and went. It wasn't long before he found out the person taking the beating was me. And he'd been parked outside my house ever since.

"Your story has captured the nation's attention," said Pete Stephen. "Don't you want to tell your side of it?"

I told him to piss off and ushered my family into the house. Then I ran to the laptop and Googled 'video of man having meltdown at work'. It didn't take long to find plenty of hits, and I spent the next few hours trawling the internet, amazed at how big it had become.

There were countless articles about it. People had made memes about it. Shortened versions were floating about on Facebook and Twitter. Someone had even created a re-edited version, repeating the moment Zack kicked me in the head over and over, accompanied by Dean Martin singing *Ain't That a Kick in the Head*. I suspected that might be the work of Donnie, one of the video editors from work.

There were tweets about it. Facebook posts. It even had its own hashtag: #officemeltdownassault.

When I saw the scale of it, I just wanted to hide away in the house and never go out in public again. I imagined myself hounded in the street. People laughing and pointing at me in the supermarket. Paranoid, maybe, but you hear about people whose lives are ruined due to a single ill-advised tweet or Facebook post. I panicked that my career was over for good. I waited for the hate mail to start pouring in.

I still hadn't turned on my mobile phone since I'd locked it in the hotel safe. I powered it up to find countless voicemails, emails and text messages from other journalists, all offering competing amounts of money to hear my side of the story. It appeared Pete Stephen wasn't the only journalist to have identified me. There was even a call from BBC Breakfast, inviting me for an interview on the big red sofa.

And then something else occurred to me. I looked back at some of the articles I'd scanned over, reading them in more detail. One thing all the videos, posts, stories and memes had in common was that they all seemed to have sympathy for me. Although I came across as a bit angry and unreasonable at the start of the video, I still looked like a downtrodden employee compared with the boardroom full of apathetic, suited managers doing their best to ignore my rant.

Then, when Zack comes flying across the table and kicks me when I'm already down, I definitely look like the victim. Reading through the various comments and responses, people were siding with me – the man of the people, beaten down by the might of the global organisation.

Maybe, this could be a good thing. If Thomson was scared when the video had reached 600,000 hits, how terrified must he be now it had reached such fever pitch, and I apparently had the backing of the people? I compiled a record of all the journalists' voicemails, emails and text messages. Then I opened up PowerPoint and put together another short presentation.

When I arrived at the office the next day, Melanie from HR was once again waiting in reception, under the pretence of welcoming me back to work. Of course, she was just keen to usher me up to a private room for another encounter with Thomson.

The tension to see whether or not I'd sign their little disclaimer must have been eating away at them for the past two weeks. I assumed they'd also been keeping an eager eye on the all-important video and the resulting press coverage. I smiled as I imagined their panicked faces, watching the view counter click up every day. Melanie probably had a special file somewhere, logging all the memes, posts and comments. She'd have analysed it in a graph, or pie chart, extrapolating the worst possible outcomes for the company. She was that kind of anal, detail-orientated worrier.

I already knew they were scared. Steve had called me the previous evening to fill me in on all the goings on. Hushed meetings with lawyers. Angry rants and screaming coming from Thomson's office. Hastily arranged lunches to schmooze and reassure key clients. Thomson was afraid all right.

******

Thomson and Melanie gaze at me across the desk. They're twitchy and nervous. Desperate to know what I've decided. It feels like a lifetime since two weeks ago, when I was sat here across from them, as they tried to buy me off with a measly promotion. A lot has happened in those two weeks.

I lift my briefcase up and place it down on the desk in front of me. Thomson and Melanie's eyes both widen at the sight of it. And when I click it open and lift the lid, I swear Thomson nearly jumps up from his chair. A bit mean, I know, but it's exactly the response I was hoping for, and I only just manage to hold in a smile.

I carefully take out bits of neatly printed and stapled paper and place them on the desk in front of me.

"Listen, I'll cut to the chase," I say, before they can speak. "I've decided not to take the promotion. The holiday has done me the world of good and given me plenty of time to reflect. And I've decided this just isn't the kind of company I want to work for anymore."

"So, you're going to stab us in the back, are you?" says Thomson, red-faced. "Sell your story to the press and watch us suffer? How will you look your team in the eye, when all our clients leave us and I have to lay people off?"

"I'm not stabbing anyone anywhere," I say. "I mean, I've had lots of offers. Journalists camped outside my door. You wouldn't believe the amounts of money they want to give me."

I push a piece of paper towards Melanie, outlining the various sums the newspapers have offered. Her eyes widen and she forces a smile onto her face. Obviously, I've inflated them a bit. Okay, a lot. Plus, I've made up a few. And added a spurious book deal, for good measure. Well, they're not going to know, and how can they check?

Thomson knows the potential press coverage will be a killer, if I sell my story. What client would ever want to hire a firm that assaults their employees just for asking for a pay rise? And it's not as if they can dispute the facts – the whole thing's caught on video. By the sour look on his face, Thomson has clearly already had a whiff that clients are thinking of leaving. His face starts turning purple as he breathes angrily through his nose, like a dragon.

"But I have no intention of selling my story," I continue. "In fact, I've already drafted a press release, explaining how the whole thing was actually a clever viral marketing stunt, carried out to draw press attention to workplace stress and mental health issues."

"What?" says Thomson.

"It goes on to say that too few companies are engaging with employees about their careers and prospects, and many are happy to take advantage of staff, exploiting them and denying them opportunities. This leads to mental health issues, as 'acted out' in the video," I say, making finger quotes. "Of course, too many companies are keen to brush it all under the carpet. You'll need to pull together some extra bits pretty quickly, of course – blog posts, news articles, a quick microsite and social stuff... I've put a content plan together." I push more papers across the desk.

"But that's... that's..." stammers Thomson.

"Pretty clever? Yeah, I thought so too. Some people might call parts of the video into question, but a little re-editing will help. And if you get stuff out today, you'll survive. You might even win a bit of new business off the back of it."

"You know, that could actually work," says Melanie.

Thomson picks up the printed presentation and starts flicking through it, breathing even more heavily. "So, what do you want?" he says, his voice a mix of relief and suspicion. "I mean, you're not just doing this out of the kindness of your heart."

"Well, no..." I say. I leave a long pause, delighting in watching them squirm as I make them wait for the answer. "I'm happy to issue the release today, and get the team started on creating the rest of the content. Then I'll clear my desk and be gone by lunchtime. And all I want in return is a severance payment in the amount of a full year's salary," I smile. "The new 40% increased salary you very generously offered me, of course."

"Are you taking the…"

"Oh, and Steve is leaving too," I say, cutting him off. "I mean, you already know that, because he resigned. What I mean is, he's leaving today, rather than having to work the rest of his notice. And he'll be needing a years' severance as well. With a 40% increase."

I haven't actually told Steve I'm adding him into my bargain, but I'm sure he won't mind.

"Oh, and I recently bought an expensive car, which I can't really afford. You did offer to get me a company car, so I assume you won't mind paying it off for me."

"Out-bloody-rageous," says Thomson. His face is now so red, I genuinely think his head might explode. Like a spot waiting to be popped. "You really expect me to…"

"I don't expect you to do anything," I say, cutting him off again. "I've made you a very generous offer. You can either take it or leave it. But I wouldn't hang around. I mean, that video has been out there for a couple of weeks now. And I've got a journalist from the Sun calling me at 4pm today."

I don't. But he doesn't know that.

"Blackmail. Fucking blackmail," shouts Thomson. He opens his mouth again, but Melanie's trusty hand flies to his arm to stop him.

"No, it's not blackmail," I say. "It's options. Option one, you get to keep your clients, and Steve and I walk out of here with compensation for the last few years of piss-taking. Option two, I tell the press what really happened, plus I release the recording of you two trying to buy me off during our last meeting," I lift a small dictaphone from my briefcase and show it to them. "Then you get to lose all your clients and your business goes bust. Actually, now that I think about it, that does sound a bit blackmail-y, doesn't it?" I smile widely. There is no recording, of course. But again, they don't know that.

"Why don't you go and grab a coffee, Dave?" says Melanie, white-faced and trying to keep her voice calm. "Let us have a quick chat and we'll catch up in 10 minutes, yeah?"

It only takes five minutes before they call me back into the meeting room. Thomson won't even look at me now. He stands on the other side of the room, hands clasped behind his back, looking out of the window. Melanie tells me that they've discussed my proposal and that they've agreed to accept it. She doesn't look happy. But there's also an air of calm in her voice. And her eyes look slightly warmer. Like she's happy just to be rid of me.

"We'll need you to brief the creative team on the work you've outlined. Get them up to speed on creating the content, issue the press release and start posting some of the social. We're also going to release the story to the trade media, so we'll need you to draft a statement that we can issue. And if they want to interview you…"

"Done and done," I say, reaching into my briefcase and pulling out a pre-written statement on how and why I supposedly came up with my very clever mental health awareness campaign, and a set of interview questions and answers.

"Very well, then," says Melanie, cold and efficient. "I'll have our lawyers draft a non-disclosure agreement for you and Steve to sign, and we'll prepare severance cheques for a full years' salary each… plus 40%. We'll have it ready by the end of the day."

"Great stuff," I say. I put out my hand to shake, but she looks at it as though touching me might give her a disease.

"I just want you to know," I say, "I've genuinely enjoyed working here. Until… well, you know." And I really mean it.

Thomson doesn't react, he just continues staring out of the window. So, I turn and leave the room.

******

Steve's face is absolutely priceless when I tell him the good news. "You're fucking joking," he says. "I get to leave today? With a year's salary? And a fucking pay rise? Christ, we should get you beaten up more often."

I laugh. It feels like old times, me and Steve joking with each other. Something I've really missed.

"To be honest, I can't believe they gave in so easily," I say.

"I can," says Steve. "I mean, it only takes one person sending anonymous video links to all of AIP's clients – plus a few other big fish they're trying to attract." He flashes a conspiratorial wink. "Next thing you know, rumours are flying all round the industry and Thomson's shitting himself that we're gonna lose every scrap of work we've got."

"Jesus," I laugh, "you sent the video to all the clients? I didn't even think of that. If you'd told me earlier, I'd have asked for two years' severance."

"Sent it? I fucking filmed it and uploaded it," he laughs.

I stand, open-mouthed.

"Christ, I thought you knew. Right, well, let's get the team briefed and get the fuck down the pub," says Steve laughing.

So, Steve and I are free. With plenty of time and money to think about our next move. And for the first time in a long time, the future seems really bright again.

******

I haven't thought too much about New Dave in the few weeks since I left AIP. I haven't thought about his big house. Or his fancy clothes. Or his swimming pool. Or his sauna. I haven't thought about his ex-model wife, or his flash car, or his unfeasibly good hair.

What he said to me the night before 'the incident' has helped me see him in a new light. He's struggled too. He's not as perfect as I'd thought. And he hasn't been sat there across the garden fence, looking down at me and my sub-par life. But more than that, I now recognise the fallacy of thinking about him as anything other than just a man who lives next door to me. And despite my previous misgivings, he's actually a nice guy. Annoyingly nice.

I've been thinking more about myself, my place in the world and what I want it to be. And I've come to realise that it doesn't matter what anyone else does, or thinks, or says. It's my life and I can only live it for myself, in my own way. It seems a staggeringly obvious statement. And I'm a little embarrassed to admit I've only just figured it out. But better late than never.

So, rather than trying to be a better Dave Brookman than any other Dave Brookman, I'm trying to figure out what kind of Dave Brookman I want to be. I haven't come to any conclusions yet. But that's okay. It's only been a few weeks. And these aren't the sorts of decisions you want to rush into.

I certainly don't want to go back into a job where I'm undervalued, feel like crap most days, and end up working for some over-privileged idiot who only got the job because of who they're shagging. I want to find something that brings me joy and makes me happy. Something that makes me leap out of bed in the morning, excited to get to work. Unfortunately, the roles of Beer Taster, Movie Critic, and Professional Crisp Eater are either very hard to come by, something for which I'm completely unqualified, or, well… imaginary. I've sent a letter to the producers of Top Gear, asking if they need someone to drive cars really fast round their track. But I'm not holding out much hope.

I've had phone calls from a few different agencies, inviting me to come in for meetings and discuss opportunities. It didn't take long before word was out that I'd left AIP. I thought I'd be lucky to ever get a Creative Director role again. But people have been calling me out of the blue and telling me they like my work. All of which is very gratifying, and something I wish I'd known six months ago. I've also had a few solid offers of freelance work. Steve's keen to keep the partnership together, and he wants me to go to some other meetings he's arranged.

I guess what New Dave said was true. Other companies actually do want me.

So, I'll have something to do, when I need it. But I'm in no rush. I feel like I've just got my life back, and I want to enjoy that before I do anything else. Besides, with a whole years' salary sitting in the bank, I can afford to take at least a few months off.

And in that spirit, I've made a new spreadsheet. A new action plan. Don't worry, it's not what you're thinking. It has two columns: *New Things to Try This Year* and *Ways to Show Catherine You Love Her.*

I'm going to start filling it in right now.

THANK YOU

Thank you very much for deciding to buy my book. In a world where there are so many books being published on a daily basis, it means a very great deal that you decided to buy my book.

This is my third novel. If you've enjoyed the first two and come back for more, then thank you so much. If this is the first book of mine that you've read, then check out the other two: *The Unexpected Vacation of George Thring* and *Killing Dylan*. Both are published by Raven Crest Books and readily available in the same place you probably found this one.

If you have enjoyed this book, please feel encouraged to leave a review or a few good words on Amazon, Goodreads, Facebook, Twitter or any social networking sites you regularly use... or even good old word of mouth.

And make sure to come and say hello at www.facebook.com/alastairpuddickauthor. It would be great to hear from you.

Alastair Puddick

ACKNOWLEDGEMENTS

I really hope you've enjoyed reading this book. And while I'd like to take all the credit for creating something that hopefully made you smile (I mean, I did write it!), there are, of course, a handful of people without whom it would never have reached your hands.

First and foremost, I have to thank my long-suffering wife, Laura. Thank you for reading early drafts, listening to my daft ideas and insecurities, encouraging me when I wasn't sure it was worth carrying on, and of course, for putting up with the long hours I spent locked away working on the book.

Thank you to my good friend Pete Stephen and my mum, Elizabeth Puddick, for reading early drafts of the book and offering invaluable advice that helped me to make it better. And of course, thanks to Helen Brennan, who read the first draft in less than a day, helped with lots of useful advice, and who has insisted on being thanked in every single book I ever write (it's a verbal contract I'm honour bound to meet).

A big thanks to my editor, Alice Smales, for all her advice and for helping me make this book as good as it could be. Thanks to László Zakariás for another fantastic cover. And lastly, a huge thanks to everyone at Raven Crest Books for believing in me and for publishing my stories.

And finally, thank you for picking up this book and reading it. I hope it brought a smile to your face. Actually, no, I hope it made you fall off your chair laughing.

ABOUT THE AUTHOR

Alastair Puddick is a writer, editor and copywriter who lives in Sussex with his wife Laura, and their cat, George. *46% Better Than Dave* is his third novel. If you enjoyed this, check out his other books:

The Unexpected Vacation of George Thring
Killing Dylan

CONTACT DETAILS

Visit Alastair's website: www.alastairpuddick.wordpress.com

Visit Alastair's Amazon author page: Author.to/APuddick

Follow Alastair on Twitter: www.twitter.com/HankShandy

Like or join Alastair on Facebook:
www.facebook.com/alastairpuddickauthor

Cover designed by: László Zakariás.

Published by: Raven Crest Books
www.ravencrestbooks.com
www.ravencrestbooks.co.uk

Like us on Facebook:
www.facebook.com/RavenCrestBooksClub

Made in the USA
Monee, IL
20 November 2020